'I have been instructed to bring you back alive, Deathstalker, but not necessarily intact. You will return with me, one way or another. It is your duty to your fellow man, and to God.'

'And Hazel d'Ark?'

'Is irrelevant.'

Owen looked at the Grendel. Eight feet of impenetrable armour, steel claws and vicious speed and strength. One just like it had killed Tobias Moon, ripping his head clean off. Owen had his gun and his sword, and his boost. He could take the creature. He'd done it before. He remembered the pain and horror of losing his left hand, but pushed the memory aside. He had to beat the Grendel. Hazel was relying on him. He realized that the captain's hand was hovering dangerously near the disrupter on his hip. So, shoot the captain first and then go one on one with the Grendel. That made the odds even worse, but it wasn't as if he had a choice. He took a slow, deep breath, settling himself. He could do this; he could. *Damn*, he thought coolly. *This is going to hurt.*

Also by Simon R. Green

Deathstalker
Deathstalker Rebellion
Deathstalker War
Deathstalker Honour
Deathstalker Prelude
Blue Moon Rising
Blood and Honour
Down Among The Dead Men
Shadows Fall

SIMON R. GREEN

DEATHSTALKER DESTINY

This edition published in Great Britain in 1999 by
Millennium
An imprint of Victor Gollancz
Orion House, 5 Upper St Martin's Lane, London WC2H 9EA

To receive information on the Millennium list, e-mail us at:
smy@orionbooks.co.uk

A CIP catalogue record for this book is available from the British Library

ISBN 1 85798 877 9

Typeset at The Spartan Press Ltd
Lymington, Hants
Printed in Great Britain by
Clays Ltd, St Ives plc

Owen Deathstalker: 'I've always known I've been living on borrowed time.'

Hazel d'Ark: 'I never said I loved you, Owen.'

Jack Random: 'Politicians. They're all dirty. Hang them all.'

Ruby Journey: 'Peace was just a dream.'

Prophecy of a young esper: 'I see you, Deathstalker. Destiny has you in its clutches, struggle how you may. You will tumble an Empire, see the end of everything you ever believed in, and you'll do it all for a love you'll never know. And when it's over, you'll die alone, far from friends and succour.'

This is the end of the story. And it starts now.

CHAPTER ONE

Blood Debt

It was still raining on Lachrymae Christi. The tears of God. Owen Deathstalker hadn't shed a single tear since the Blood Runners had abducted Hazel d'Ark. To cry would be to give in to his fear, his horror and desperation, and he couldn't afford to be weak. He had to be strong, ready to seize any chance that might get him off this damned planet and on to Hazel's trail. He had to be strong for her. So he put a lid on his despair and clamped it down hard with never-ending work, not once allowing himself to entertain the possibility that Hazel d'Ark might already be dead.

It had been two weeks since Hazel was taken, and in that time Owen had hardly slept. He sat exhausted on the bare ground of the Mission compound, head hanging forward, sweat dripping off his face. He'd been working hard since first light, and every muscle in his body ached unmercifully. He worked all the hours he could, distracting himself with the simple everyday problems of rebuilding the devastated Mission; but he was only human, these days, and his body would only take so much punishment before forcing him to rest. And then he would sit and brood, and squeeze his eyes shut against the visions his mind conjured up of what the Blood Runners might be doing to Hazel until he couldn't stand it any more, and he would dive back into his work whether he was ready to or not.

A leper approached him hesitantly, anonymous in the uniform of grey cloak with the hood pulled forward. He offered Owen a cup of wine, in a grey-gloved hand that only shook a little. Owen accepted it with a nod and the leper backed quickly away, bowing respectfully. The Mission's surviving lepers had seen Owen blow away an army of attacking Grendels like leaves in a scorching breeze, all by the power of his mind. They had seen him stand against overwhelming forces and refuse to retreat, bringing himself to the brink of death to rescue them. He was their saviour, and they were much in awe of him.

They didn't know he was only human now; that he'd burned out all his Maze-given powers to save them.

'You've got to slow down, Owen,' Oz murmured softly in his ear. The AI sounded distinctly worried. 'You can't keep pushing yourself like this. You're killing yourself.'

'The work has to be done,' said Owen, subvocalizing so that those still working around him wouldn't hear. 'The Hadenmen and the Grendels knocked the shit out of this place. Half the wall's down, most of the buildings are leaning on each other for support and the roof's leaking in a hundred places. The lepers can't do it on their own. A lot of them belong in sickbeds anyway.'

'That's not why you're doing it,' said Oz. 'You're not fooling anyone, you know. All this hard work and toil, working till you drop; it's not for them, for the Mission. You're punishing yourself for letting the Blood Runners take Hazel.'

'I wasn't there when she needed me,' said Owen, staring at the ground between his feet. 'If I had been, maybe I could have done . . . something . . .'

'You'd lost your powers. You were just a man. There was nothing you could have done.'

'Work is good,' said Owen. 'Simple problems with simple solutions. It keeps me from thinking, from remembering. If I stop to think and remember, I'll go mad.'

'Owen . . .'

'They've had her two weeks now. Fourteen days and nights since they carried her off to the Obeah Systems on the other side of the Empire to torture and torment her as it pleases them. And I'm trapped here, with no powers and not even a hope of a ship to get me off-planet so I can go after her. They could have done a lot in fourteen days and nights.'

When the Blood Runners first took Hazel, Owen had gone crazy for a while. He wouldn't eat or sleep for days, stalking blindly around the ruined Mission as the terrorized lepers scattered to get out of his way. He screamed and ranted and called Hazel's name, making horrible threats and howling like an animal in pain. In the end, he grew weak enough for Sister Marion to be able to wrestle him to the ground and hold him down, while Mother Beatrice injected him with high-strength sedatives. Finally he sank unwillingly into sleep, and his dreams were of vague, horrible things. When he woke up, they'd strapped him to a bed in the Mission infirmary.

He'd hurt his throat with screaming and ranting, but still he cursed them all in a harsh, rasping voice, threatening to kill them if they didn't let him go, while Moon sat quietly at his side giving what comfort he could, just being there for his friend. It was some time before Owen got control of himself again, exhausted physically and emotionally. He never cried. That would have been too much like saying goodbye; admitting that Hazel was dead, that there was nothing he could do. Mother Beatrice came to see him often, offering him the comfort of her God, but he wouldn't take it. There was no room in his cold heart now for anything but rescue or revenge.

When they finally let him get up again, Owen spent the best part of a day in the Mission comm centre, calling for a ship to come and pick him up. Any ship. He used every bit of authority he had; pulled every string; called in every favour he could think of; threatened and pleaded and bribed. None of it did any good. There was a war on. Actually there were several wars going on simultaneously. The Empire was under attack by the Hadenmen, Shub, Grendels, the insect aliens and the threat of the Recreated. Owen just wasn't important enough any more for anyone to divert a precious ship to get him from far-off Lachrymae Christi. He'd just have to wait. They'd find something to send eventually.

Owen would have wrecked the whole damned comm centre if Mother Beatrice hadn't been there, her eyes full of compassion. Instead, he stalked out and buried himself in the rebuilding of the Mission. It helped that there was a lot that needed doing. He made himself eat and drink at regular intervals, because if he didn't Mother Beatrice or Sister Marion would stand over him till he did. When it grew too dark to work, he lay down on his bed and pretended to sleep, waiting with an empty heart for it to be light again.

The rebuilding was slow and hard now that his powers were gone, burned out in his last stand against the Grendels. He was no stronger or faster than any other man now, and all his other abilities were lost to him, like the words of an old song he could no longer quite recall. Sometimes, in the endless hours of the night, it seemed to him that something was stirring deep inside, but it never surfaced, and when morning finally came it found him still only a man.

He spent his days working alongside the more able-bodied lepers, raising the high wall again segment by segment, and in its way the work comforted him. He was a man among men again, a part of Humanity instead of someone thrust outside it. He was just one of a group, instead of its leader. It felt good to Owen to lose himself in mindless, repetitious work, and to have achieved something by the end of the day. But most of the real work was over. A few more days, and the Mission would be complete again, and there would be nothing left to do except scrabble about on the sloping roof fixing leaks, and other small stuff. Owen didn't know what he'd do then.

He drank the wine the leper had brought him, too tired even to grimace at the bitter taste. They'd been putting strychnine in it again, to give it more bite.

'She could be anywhere,' he said quietly, knowing he was tormenting himself but unable to stop. 'Anywhere in the Obeah Systems. I've never been there. Don't know anyone who has. They're supposed to cover a lot of space. I don't even know which planet they've got her on. They could be doing anything to her. Everyone knows the Blood Runners' reputation. They've made an art of suffering and a science of slaughter. She could be dying right now, and there's nothing the great and almighty Owen Deathstalker can do to save her.'

'This isn't doing you any good, Owen,' said Oz. 'She's dead. She must be by now. Grieve, and let her go.'

'I can't.'

'Then be patient. A ship will come, in time.'

'I love her, Oz. No one ever meant as much to me as she does. I would have died to save her from them.'

'Of course you would.'

'Oh, God . . .'

'Hush, Owen. Hush.'

Sudden screams jerked Owen's head up, and he was on his feet in a moment, casting the wine cup aside, as he saw one section of the newly erected wall break free from its ties and lean ponderously forward over the dozen or so lepers beneath it. The segment weighed several tons, and the safety ropes that should have stopped or slowed its fall were snapping one after the other like a series of firecrackers. The lepers turned to run, but it was obvious they weren't going to make it out from under the wall before it came crashing down like a hammer.

Owen subvocalized his old code word *boost*, and new strength and speed burned in his muscles as he raced inhumanly fast towards the falling wall. Everything else seemed to be moving in slow motion as the gengineered gift of the Deathstalker Clan kicked in, making Owen briefly superhuman again. He reached the falling wall in seconds, and gripped the last intact safety rope with both hands. His fingers closed like steel clamps around the thick cable and held it firmly as it snapped taut. The lepers loped past Owen as he held the rope, snarling furiously as the rough hemp tore slowly through his grasp, ripping away the flesh of his palms and fingers. Blood ran down his wrists. And then the rope snapped.

Owen could have jumped back and saved himself. Most of the lepers were out, but some were still caught in the growing shadow of the falling wall. Owen looked round and spotted half a tree trunk lying on its side, waiting to be trimmed into planks. It had to weigh at least half a ton, but Owen lifted it off the ground with one explosive grunt, swung it round and moved steadily forward to block the end against the nearing segment. The weight hit the trunk hard, splitting it halfway down its length, but the improvised wedge held and the wall segment came to a stop. Its weight pressed on, driving the tree trunk into the soft earth of the compound floor, and the split lengthened inch by inch. Owen threw his arms around the tree trunk and hugged it to him with all his superhuman strength, holding it together despite the weight of the wall. His arms shrieked with pain and he was fighting for breath, but still he held the wedge together.

Sweat poured down his face. His back was ablaze with the pain of abused muscles. He risked a look over his shoulder and saw that the last few lepers were almost clear. He had only to hang on for a few more seconds. The splitting wood twisted in his grip like a live thing, spiteful and resentful, the rough bark scraping and tearing his skin. Then Moon called to him that everyone was safely away, and Owen let go of the tree trunk and ran for his life. The trunk split in half in a second and the wall segment came down like the crack of doom, missing Owen's departing heels by inches.

He staggered on for a few more steps and then sat down suddenly, all his strength and breath going out of him as he shut down the boost. Running on boost for too long built up dangerous toxins in his system and overstrained his vital organs. Every gift has a price. Time crashed back to normal about him, and suddenly lepers were running at him from all directions, shouting his name and cheering his last-minute rescue. The Hadenman Moon appeared quickly at Owen's side to protect him from being overwhelmed, but for a moment it seemed that hands were coming at him from everywhere at once, clapping him on the back or trying to shake his hand. He smiled and nodded, and made to look as though it had been nothing. They didn't realize he wasn't superhuman any more; no one knew for sure, except Moon. The Hadenman still had all his powers.

Eventually the lepers grew tired of telling Owen how great he was, and of his lack of response, and they drifted back to work again. A squad of the hardier workers under Sister Marion set about raising the collapsed wall segment back into place, and hammered long nails in from every angle to make sure the damn thing stayed put. Moon sat down beside Owen.

'You know, I could have got there in time. And my augmented muscles were far better suited to supporting such a weight.'

'But you didn't. Besides, I like to feel useful.'

'How are your hands and arms?'

Owen took care not to look at them. 'They hurt like hell but they're already healing. Part of the boost's benefits.'

'You can't keep pretending you're still superhuman, Owen. Boost can only do so much. And you know what the after-effects do to you.'

'I can't just stand by, Tobias. I never could.'

'Even if it kills you?'

'Don't you have some work to do, Moon?'

'Are you going to be all right?'

'Go away, Tobias. Please.'

The Hadenman nodded once, rose smoothly to his feet and walked unhurriedly away. Owen sighed. It was hard not to take out his pain on others. No one must know how far he'd fallen from what he had been. He couldn't have coped with pity on top of everything else. And Owen Deathstalker had made a great many enemies in his time. He couldn't afford word to get out that he was . . . vulnerable.

'Moon's right, you know,' said Oz.

'And you can shut up, too.'

'Watch your temper. And your language. Saint Bea's coming over.'

Owen raised his aching head and his heart sank just a little lower as he saw Mother Superior Beatrice bearing down on him, her simple nun's robes flapping about her, like a ship in full sail. Saint Bea meant well, she always did, but he was in no mood for a lecture, however compassionate. He had to be hard, cold and emotionless or he'd fall apart. He started to get up, but Mother Beatrice waved him back with an imperious gesture and Owen's muscles obeyed before he realized what he was doing. Saint Bea had that effect on people. She gathered up her robes and sat down beside him, surprising Owen by not immediately tearing into him. Instead, she sat quietly for a while, looking at nothing in particular, humming something vague and wistful half under her breath. Owen found himself relaxing a little in spite of himself.

'You know,' she said finally, 'you really do look like shit, Deathstalker. I spend my days nursing the sick and the dying and I know shit when I see it. All this work you've thrown yourself into is building good muscle tone, but you're not eating nearly enough to support it. Your weight's way down, and your face shows more bone than anything else. And your eyes are so deep-set they look like piss holes in the snow. I'm worried about you, Owen. There are dying men here who look better than you do.'

Owen smiled slightly. 'Don't hold back, Bea. Tell me what you really think.'

Mother Beatrice slowly shook her head. 'You're like a child, Owen, you know that? You don't hear a damned thing you don't want to. Still; you did look really impressive just then. Thanks for being the hero one more time. You saved a lot of my people. Why not take a few hours off? Get some rest.'

'I can't rest,' said Owen.

'Do you sleep at all?'

'Sometimes. I have bad dreams.'

'I could give you something to make you sleep.'

'I have bad dreams.'

Mother Beatrice changed tack. 'I have some good news for you, at last. The comm centre just reported contact with an Imperial courier ship on its way here. They commandeered our Church supply ship just to get to you. Somebody out there still believes in you. The ship should be here soon. Try and hold yourself together till it arrives. I don't want this Mission to be remembered as the place where the great Owen Deathstalker moped himself to death.'

Owen smiled briefly. 'I promise. I've been waiting for a ship.'

'Hazel may already be dead,' Mother Beatrice said quietly. 'You have to consider the possibility, Owen.'

'No I don't.'

'Even if you find where the Blood Runners took her, there may be nothing left for you to do.'

'There's always revenge,' said Owen.

Something in his voice made Saint Bea shiver despite herself. She nodded briefly, got to her feet with a grunt and walked away. There were some things even a Saint had no answers for. Owen watched her go, and behind his cold, composed features his mind was churning. A courier ship meant a message from Parliament. They must need him for something urgent, something too difficult or too dangerous for anyone else. But once he was on a ship and safely off-planet, he was heading straight for the Obeah Systems, and to hell with whatever Parliament wanted. His mental abilities were gone, including his link with Hazel, but he still knew where to go to find the Obeah Systems. Once before, he'd mentally reached out across unmeasurable space to locate and kill the Blood Runner called Scour, and he still remembered where his mind had gone. It was like a direction he could point in, a compass in his head that would lead him right to the Blood Runner homeworld. He had only to concentrate and he could feel the path stretching away before him, calling him on. All he needed was a ship. If

Hazel was still alive he would rescue her, and he would make the Blood Runners pay in blood and fire for taking her. And if she was dead . . .

He would set the whole damned Obeah Systems afire, to blaze for ever in the dark as Hazel's funeral pyre.

Outside the Mission, the scarlet and crimson jungle flourished. Black-barked trees rose up from a sea of constantly moving vegetation, all of it blushing various shades of red, from shining purples to disturbingly organic pinks. The jungle on Lachrymae Christi was more than usually alive, and varyingly sentient, and spent most of its time warring on itself, except in the rutting season, but all the barbs and thorns drew back as Tobias Moon walked among them. He was their one true friend and beloved, the only one in the Mission who could make mental contact with the single great consciousness of the whole planet's ecosystem: the Red Brain. Which would have been enough to make practically anyone somewhat big-headed; but Moon was a Hadenman, and a survivor of the Madness Maze, and so he took it in his stride. If he thought about it at all he thought of himself as a gardener, on a somewhat larger than usual scale.

At that moment, he was overseeing the felling of trees to provide much-needed lumber for the Mission repairs. The Red Brain had given the human community permission to take what was needed, and did what it could to make the job easier by pulling back the more dangerous and obstructive vegetation in the area. Moon oversaw as much of the felling as possible, in case of misunderstandings, but so far everything was going smoothly. He consulted with the Red Brain, gave the orders on where the trees were to be taken from and Sister Marion stalked back and forth, stiff-legged, making sure his instructions were followed to the letter. No one argued with Sister Marion. A Sister of Glory, a warrior nun and a complete psychopath, her stick-thin figure was seemingly everywhere at once. Striding about in her long black dress of tatters and her holed emerald evening gloves, she made a formidable figure and she knew it. Her face was hidden under stark white make-up, with rouged cheeks and emerald lips, and she topped it all off with a tall black witch's hat complete with flapping purple streamers. Let a leper shirk his work or try to sneak off for a quiet sit-down and a crafty smoke, and within seconds Sister Marion's harsh voice would be blaring right in his ear, driving him back to his duties with terrible oaths and blasphemies. Somehow they sounded so much more convincing when they came from a nun.

Felling the tall wide trees took a lot of time and even more hard work, made more miserable by the constant rain, but the great dark boles still came crashing to the ground with graceful regularity. No one was sure if the Grendels or the Hadenmen might come again, but everyone knew they'd all feel much more secure when the Mission was whole once more. It was the heart, the very soul, of the leper community, perhaps even more than was Saint Bea herself. And so the lepers toiled in the pouring rain, day after day. The red-leafed branches were laboriously cut away, and then the surrounding vegetation would move in to pick up and transport the massively heavy tree trunks to where they were needed. The Red Brain was almost pathetically eager to be of use to its new friends. It had been alone for so very long until Moon established contact with it.

Owen made his way through the scarlet and crimson jungle to join Moon. He looked intent and thoughtful and didn't seem even to notice the pouring rain. The lepers nodded and bowed as he passed and turned to watch him go. There was new strength and purpose in him, and they could sense it. So could Moon. He fixed Owen with his faintly glowing golden eyes and raised a single eyebrow.

'I take it a ship of some sort is on its way?'

'Got it in one, Tobias. Be here early tomorrow. I need you to do something for me.'

'If I can. What did you have in mind?'

'Go back through the jungle to where we first crash-landed, find the wreck of the *Sunstrider II*, remove the stardrive and bring it back here.'

Moon lowered his eyebrow and thought about this. 'You have a use for a disconnected stardrive?'

'Oh, yes. The *Sunstrider II* was fitted with the new alien-derived stardrive. Whatever ship I put that drive into will be one of the fastest ships in the Empire. And I'm going to need that edge to get to Hazel in time. Do it for me, Tobias. I need this.'

'When do you want me to start out?'

'Right now would be good.'

Moon considered the matter. All work had stopped as the lepers listened to what he would say. Finally Moon shrugged. He hadn't quite got the gesture right yet, but it was recognizable. 'The tree-felling is pretty much finished. My people can safely be left to finish up on their own. Very well; I'll put together a small party and go get you your stardrive, Owen. But please understand: when you leave here, you go alone. I share your concern for Hazel, but I cannot abandon the people here. I am their only link with the Red Brain, at present. I have . . . responsibilities here.'

'It's all right,' said Owen, 'I understand. I've always understood duty.'

They smiled at each other, and stood awhile. They both knew that this might be the last time they ever had together. The lepers began to get back to work, for once not driven by a tongue-lashing from Sister Marion. Owen looked about for her and finally discovered her sitting on a tree stump, staring tiredly down at the ground, her hands folded neatly in her lap. Her shoulders were bowed as though by some great weight, and her head hung down as if it was too heavy for her neck muscles to support. Even the ribbons on her hat fell limp.

'She doesn't look too good,' said Owen.

'She's dying,' said Moon. 'She's in the last stages of the disease, and the strength is leaking out of her day by day.'

'I didn't know,' said Owen, honestly shocked. It was hard

to think of the invincible warrior nun being beaten by anything less than a sword thrust or a disrupter bolt. He knew she was a leper, but he'd always vaguely thought she was too stubborn to give in to it. 'How long has she been like this?'

'Some time now. Don't feel bad for not noticing. You had your own problems. There was nothing you could have done, anyway. It's just her time. Leprosy is a one hundred per cent fatal disease. No one gets out alive. She insists on helping here, making the most of what's left of her life before she becomes too weak or ill, and has to be confined to the infirmary for her last days. She'll hate that. Just lying around, unable to interfere in everyone else's life. I asked her if she'd made her peace with God, and she just laughed and said, "We never quarrelled." I think I'll take her with me when we go to get the *Sunstrider II*. One last adventure for her.'

'Why, Tobias,' said Owen, 'I do believe you're growing sentimental.'

'I'm working on it,' said the Hadenman.

The trip through the jungle to the crashed starship went much more easily than the original trip from the crash site to the Mission. Not least because this party didn't have to fight the jungle every inch of the way. The crimson vegetation writhed back before them, forming a wide path for Moon and Sister Marion and the half-dozen lepers they'd brought along to fetch and carry as necessary. The rain was coming down in sheets, soaking the lepers' grey robes and plastering Sister Marion's purple streamers to the sides of her hat. The unpleasantly lukewarm water ran down her scowling face in rivulets and dripped constantly from the end of her nose. Moon wasn't bothered at all by the rain, but had enough sense now to keep such comments to himself. He linked briefly with the Red Brain, and wide purple palm leaves stretched out over the trail to deflect some of the water. The ground squelched underfoot, and rainwater collected inside everyone's boots. Nobody had much to say. If the

Deathstalker himself hadn't requested this expedition, even the presence of Moon and Sister Marion couldn't have kept the lepers from rebelling and turning back; but the lepers would do anything for Owen.

Owen himself was back at the Mission. He wanted to be there on the landing pad the moment the courier ship touched down.

Sister Marion lurched suddenly as the muddy ground gave under her boots. Moon put out a helping hand, and then quickly withdrew it as the Sister glared at him. She'd been finding the going increasingly hard, but got really ratty if she thought they were slowing the pace just for her. She glared about her, mopping at her face for the hundredth time with a tattered handkerchief pulled from her tattered sleeve.

'Hate the jungle. Trees black as coal and plants the colour of blood and organs. And it stinks, too.'

'Rotting vegetation on the ground produces the mulch from which new life arises,' said Moon.

Sister Marion snorted. 'Yeah. Even the prettiest rose has its roots in shit. I've always known that. Rain and stink and a jungle that looks like a living abattoir. No wonder we were sent here; no one else would have wanted this place.'

'We're almost at the crash site,' said Moon. 'Not much further now.'

'Did I ask?' snapped Sister Marion.

'I thought you might like to know. It's in the clearing, right ahead.'

'Hate the rain,' growled the nun, looking at the ground. 'Never liked rain.'

When they finally entered the clearing, everyone stopped just inside the boundary. After a certain amount of confused peering about, the lepers turned a hard look on Moon. The clearing was just like all the others they'd already slogged through, overrun with crimson and scarlet vegetation, with no sign anywhere of a crashed starship. Sister Marion turned with ominous slowness to Moon.

'If you're about to announce that you're lost, I may find it necessary to kick your augmented backside up around your ears till your insides rattle, for the good of your soul.'

'No need to put yourself out,' said Moon. 'This is the place. We cannot see the ship because the jungle has swallowed it.'

'Let's just hope it hasn't bloody digested it as well—' Sister Marion broke off suddenly. She started to raise a hand to her head, and then stopped herself deliberately. The gloved hand was clearly shaking, but no one commented.

'It's going to take a while to retrieve the ship,' said Moon carefully. 'Why don't you find somewhere relatively dry and sit down for a while, Sister? You're tired.'

'I'm dying, Hadenman. I'm always tired.' She shook her head slowly and sat down carefully on a half-rotten tree trunk. Moon gestured for the other lepers to give them some space, and they moved away, affording him and the Sister a little privacy. The nun sighed quietly. 'What is the world coming to when the only person I've got to talk to is a bloody Hadenman? Mother Beatrice is too busy, the Deathstalker's got his own problems; and the other lepers . . . are too afraid of me. So that just leaves you, Moon.'

'You can always talk to me,' said Moon. 'All the information I have been programmed with is at your disposal.'

Sister Marion stared out into the clearing for a long time, the rain pattering loudly on and around her. 'I know I shouldn't be bitter,' she said finally. 'But I can't help it. So much left to do here, and I won't be around to see that things are done properly. Who'll look after Bea when I'm gone, and stop her working herself to death?'

'I'll be here,' said Moon. 'I'll watch over her. But you mustn't give in, Sister. You're a fighter. A Sister of Glory.'

'I'm a leper. And I've always known that's a death sentence. I just thought . . . I'd have more time. We're all dying here, Moon. You mustn't feel guilty that you can't save us the way you saved our Mission.'

'I don't feel guilty,' said Moon. 'That's Owen's job.'

They both managed a small smile at that.

'It doesn't seem fair,' said Moon. 'We fought off armies of Hadenmen and Grendels, but we can't save you from a stupid disease.'

'Yeah, well, that's life. Or rather death. God sends us out, and He calls us home. Get on with it, Moon; find your damned ship. Be useful.'

Moon paused uncertainly. He wanted to comfort her but didn't really know how. Owen would have told him to follow his instincts, but Moon wasn't sure he had any. So rather than say the wrong thing, he just nodded and turned away to survey the great open clearing before him. He knew exactly where the *Sunstrider II* had made its final violent landing. Moon remembered everything and was never wrong. In fact, unlike humans, he was unable to forget anything. Though sometimes he thought there were things he might choose not to remember if he could.

He put the thought aside for later contemplation, reached out with his Maze-enlarged mind and made contact with the overconsciousness called the Red Brain. It was like plunging into a vast cool ocean, alive with endless points of light, a billion plants fused into a single mind larger than even Moon was comfortable dealing with. Once, he had been part of the Hadenman massmind, but in comparison that had been only a small dark lake with strictly limited parameters and choices of direction. The Red Brain was larger and wilder and almost terrifyingly free, and only its glacially slow plant thoughts enabled Moon to deal with it without being swamped and swept away in the endless details. Moon and the Red Brain moved together, linked but still separate, like a single whale singing its songs in a sentient sea. And when the Hadenman asked the Red Brain to return the *Sunstrider II*, it was happy to oblige.

Moon dropped back into his own body, and not for the first time was struck by how small and fragile it seemed. He had a feeling he was growing out of it like a set of children's clothes. He put that thought aside too, as the clearing before him began to shake and shudder. The ground rumbled under his feet and the scarlet and crimson plants waved wildly. Moon calmly called the lepers back to join him and Sister Marion, and they wasted no time in obeying. The ground in the centre of the clearing bulged suddenly upward, cracking raggedly apart. Plants were torn up by the roots and thrown aside, displaced by the upthrust of the earth beneath, but they were only small parts of the massmind and easily sacrificed. The earth growled and rumbled as something buried deep below was slowly forced to the surface again. The surrounding trees shook and trembled, and those plants in the clearing mobile enough did their best to get out of the way as a great rent in the earth gaped open, forced apart by the sudden rebirth of the *Sunstrider II*. It lurched to a halt, buoyed up by the earth and vegetation beneath it, and slowly settled into its new berth. The earth subsided, the plants came to rest again and everything in the clearing grew still. Moon looked the crashed starship over critically. It wasn't a pretty sight.

But then, it had been one hell of a hard landing. The mud-smeared outer hull was split open in several places and the rear assembly was mostly ripped away. There were signs of extensive fire damage, outside and in, and most of the sensor spikes were gone. The *Sunstrider II* wouldn't be going anywhere without lengthy repair time in the best stardock money could buy. Which was precisely why Owen had sent him to retrieve the stardrive; it was the only part of the ship likely to have survived intact that could still be put to good use. Moon thought of the approaching courier ship. Someone was in for a surprise. Moon smiled slightly, and turned his attention back to the crashed vessel. It took just a few moments to call up the blueprints and locate a reasonably wide crack in the outer hull, not too far from the engine section. With a little luck, and a certain amount of brute force, he would be able to reach the stardrive fairly easily. He looked back at Sister Marion.

'I'll enter the ship alone. Make sure everyone else keeps their distance unless I call for them. The stardrive is based on poorly understood alien technology, and radiates forces and energies that are highly inimical to human tissues. The drive should be safely contained within its specially designed casing and therefore theoretically safe, but there's no telling how much the casing may have suffered in the crash.'

'What if the casing's cracked and the drive's compromised?' said Sister Marion.

'Prolonged exposure would be quite deadly. In which case we will have to abandon it. The jungle can bury it again, deep enough to keep it safe from any risk of exposure. But let us think positively. Owen needs that drive. The casing was designed to withstand the worst crashlandings.'

'If the emanations are that dangerous, you shouldn't be going in at all,' said Sister Marion sharply.

'I am a Hadenman,' said Moon, 'and I have been through the Madness Maze. That makes me very difficult to kill.'

'And too bloody cocky for your own good. You watch yourself in there.'

'Yes, Sister. If anything should go wrong, you and your people are not to come in after me, whatever the circumstances. Go back and get Owen. Is that clear?'

'Oh, get on with it. We haven't got all day.'

'Yes, Sister.'

Moon moved slowly across the clearing, treading carefully through the tattered vegetation and thrown-up soil to reach the crashed ship. It had been a beautiful yacht once, and had served Owen and his companions faithfully to the very end. Now it was just so much scrap metal, with perhaps one last valuable prize left within. One last service for the Deathstalker. Moon made his way cautiously down the side of the ship, peering in through the wide rents in the outer hull. His internal sensors reported low-level radiation, nothing much for him to worry about. The airlock was impassable. He finally reached the wide vent by the engine section. The radiation level jumped alarmingly, but Moon felt sure he could tolerate it for as long as he needed. There were other forces at play too, none of which he recognized, but he'd expected that. He accessed his computer records again, and then used the disrupter built into his left wrist to perform a little necessary surgery on the interior beyond the gap in the hull. He stuck his head into the gap and pierced the darkness with his glowing golden eyes. The engine section was fairly close at hand, but still concealed by several layers of shielding. Cutting through them with the disrupter would take hours, and he didn't think even he could sustain that much radiation contamination without harm. Which left him only one option.

He concentrated, reaching inwards, separating and focusing certain images that moved within him. Ever since he accepted his Maze heritage and embraced his human nature, new abilities had begun surfacing inside him. His ability to detect and communicate with the Red Brain was one. Other powers had manifested since, and he called on the most recent. Something surged up from the back brain, the undermind, filling him till he couldn't contain it any more. He glared at the broken hull before him and it slowly widened, peeling back under the pressure of his gaze. The edges curled in upon themselves, protecting him from their sharpness as the gap widened enough to admit his whole body. Moon stepped through the outer hull and the inner layers split open before him, the inches-thick steel unable to withstand his Maze-augmented mind.

Moon headed directly towards the engine compartment, the ship unfolding like a metal flower before him. He had to stop now and again to deactivate the security measures marked in the blueprints. The stardrive wasn't supposed to be easy to get at. When he finally reached the dully shining container that kept the stardrive isolated from the rest of the ship, Moon stopped where he was and studied it thoughtfully for some time from what he hoped was a safe distance. It was smaller than he'd expected, barely ten feet long and four feet wide, surprisingly small for something so powerful. It seemed intact, but at this range his internal sensors were going crazy.

Owen had warned him to be extremely cautious. Just putting together the alien-derived drive had unleashed forces that destroyed the clones doing the work. (Supposedly that practice had been stopped, with the emancipation of the clones. But with the current desperate need for new star-drives . . .)

Moon stared at the stardrive through his glowing Haden-man eyes, and the drive stared right back at him. Moon accessed wavelengths he didn't normally have much use for and studied the unusual energies that were scintillating all around the steel container. None of them were, strictly speaking, radiation, but Moon had no doubt that they were probably equally dangerous. The more Moon studied them, the more he thought they might be extradimensional. No one really knew how the alien stardrive did what it did, but it was too useful not to be recovered.

The energies confused Moon. He couldn't tell where they were coming from or where they were going. They sur-rounded rather than radiated from the drive container, as though bursting into reality from somewhere else and then disappearing again. They didn't stay long. Perhaps this reality could only sustain or tolerate them for a short time. Moon found them entrancing. He realized with a start that he'd spent too much time watching them and turned his attention to the problem of how to get the container safely back to Owen. The six lepers he'd brought along to carry the drive wouldn't be able to tolerate nearly as much of the energies as he could. Still, first things first. Break the container free from its bed and see how heavy it is. Perhaps he could carry it on his own.

Careful inspection established that the drive container was held in place by several large steel bolts screwed into the steel floor. Moon had no tools with him, so he just seized the bolt heads with his powerful fingers and unscrewed them manu-ally. They all squealed and protested as they came loose, but none were strong enough to defy his augmented strength. The last bolt was the most reluctant and in the end he just ripped it out, stripping the thread as he did. He tossed the bolt to one side, leaned over the drive container and tried to lift one end of the drive. It didn't budge an inch. Moon tried with a firmer grip around the middle, and that was when it all went horribly wrong.

The drive was impossibly heavy, much heavier than its size suggested. It was like trying to pick up a mountain. Moon braced himself, and called on all his Maze-given strength. His back creaked and his arms felt as though they were being pulled out of their reinforced sockets. The container shifted slowly, ponderously, as though its mass was far greater than its size would allow for. Moon strained against the impossible weight, sweat running down his impassive face. The drive began to rise from the floor, and the energies surrounding it went mad. They flared up, brilliant and blinding, and Moon flinched back despite himself. His foot slipped on the smooth metal floor, and for a split second he lost his balance. And that was all it took. The drive container rolled towards Moon with all the inevitability of an avalanche, and there was nothing he could do to stop it. The container slammed against him, knocked him off his feet and then rolled up his legs, pinning him in place. Moon's mouth stretched wide at the pain. It felt like the whole world was resting on his legs. He beat at the steel container with his fists, but couldn't budge it. He was trapped. Moon let out a howl of sheer frustration.

He clamped down on his raging emotions, and was once again the cold, logical Hadenman. He had to think of a way out of this. There was always a way, if you thought hard enough. The container was too heavy for him to move with his hands alone; perhaps leverage would help. Owen had once said, 'Give me a big enough lever, and I'll beat the bloody problem into submission.' Moon wished Owen were there now, but only for a moment. Wishes didn't solve problems. He looked around him for a suitable lever, but there was nothing within reach and he couldn't move an inch. He'd already lost all feeling in his legs, and he thought he could hear the muffled sounds of his leg bones cracking under the unbearable pressure. There had to be a way . . .

He heard sounds to one side, and looked round to see Sister Marion making her way carefully through the passage he'd made earlier. She stopped to pull free part of her robe that had caught on a sharp edge, and Moon called out to her urgently.

'Don't come any closer, Sister! Turn around and go back. There's nothing you can do. It's not safe for anything human in here!'

'I heard you cry out,' said Sister Marion calmly, moving forward again. 'Thought you might have got yourself into some trouble.'

'I'm trapped here. The stardrive is much heavier than it appears. I am a Maze-adapted Hadenman, and even I am unable to move it.'

Sister Marion stopped and considered this. 'Should we send for the Deathstalker?'

'I don't think I could survive the time it would take,' said Moon. 'The drive's energies are even more dangerous than we expected.'

'Then you really do need my help,' said the Sister, moving forward again to join him. She took off her tall hat in the confined space and placed it carefully to one side before leaning over to study the drive casing, and how it was holding Moon in place. She was careful not to touch anything. 'Hmmm,' she said finally. 'Maybe we could set up some kind of hoist, or winch, and lift the thing off you.'

'I fear it's too heavy for anything you could construct,' said Moon. 'I believe most of its mass may be extradimensional in nature. Please, Sister. You must leave this ship immediately. There are forces here that will kill you.'

'I can't leave you like this,' said Sister Marion flatly. 'Besides, I've got an idea. I brought some explosives with me, just in case we needed help disinterring the ship, or getting to the drive. They're all shaped charges. If I set them on the underside of the casing, they should blow it right off you. Don't know what the blast will do to your legs, but I've seen you Maze people heal impossible damage. You want to try it?'

Moon considered the matter coldly. He was fairly sure he would survive the blast in some form, and he didn't have any other ideas. He just hoped Owen appreciated what it cost to get him his drive. 'Go ahead,' he said finally. 'But be sure to allow yourself sufficient time to reach a safe distance.'

'Teach your grandmother to suck eggs,' said Sister Marion, which baffled Moon somewhat. He took the explosive charges from her as she dug them out of her voluminous pockets, and together they applied them to the underside of the drive container, setting the timers for a five-minute delay. Sister Marion took to shaking her head, as though bothered by something, and her concentration slipped more than once. Finally she stopped and leaned on the drive casing, one hand at her forehead.

'Lights,' she said thickly. 'There are lights in my head. And a sound . . .'

'The ship's energies are affecting you,' said Moon. 'Give me the last of the charges, and you get out of here. Quickly. While you still can.'

Sister Marion shook her head angrily and her eyes snapped back into focus. 'Almost finished. Just a few more . . . Oh, hell. The timers. Something's happened to the timers!'

Moon realized what had happened and threw up his arms to protect his face as all the charges went off at once, their timers corrupted by the drive's energies. The combined blast lifted the drive off Moon's legs and slammed him back against the wall behind him. He could feel himself tear and break inside. The explosion picked Sister Marion up and threw her all the way back down the metal passage and out of the ship like a rag doll in a hurricane. She didn't even have time to cry out. The drive slowly began to roll back towards Moon. His lower half was completely numb and useless, but he used his arms to pull himself along the floor and out of the way. He kept going, dragging himself slowly along the metal passage, leaving a thick trail of blood behind his shattered legs. Internal sensors were bombarding him with damage reports, but since none of them were immediately vital, he ignored them as well as the pain, concentrating only on getting outside so he could see what had happened to Sister Marion.

Outside the ship, the lepers were gathered around a tattered, bloody object. Moon crawled out of the rent in the outer hull and dropped to the clearing floor. Two of the lepers came over to him, and he asked them to bring him to whatever was left of Sister Marion. She was still alive, for the moment, but it only took one look for Moon to know she wouldn't last long. Her broken arms and legs were barely attached to her body and she was breathing harshly, every inhalation an effort. Moon had the two lepers set him down beside her. She rolled her eyes to look at him. For the first time since he'd known her she looked small and fragile and very human.

'I'm sorry, Sister,' said Moon, 'I'm so sorry.'

'Don't feel guilty, my son. I was dying anyway. Better this way than what I had waiting for me.'

'Lie still. I'll send the others for help.'

'I'd be dead long before they got back. You're supposed to have been there, Tobias. What's it like, being dead?'

'Restful.'

'Bugger,' said Sister Marion, 'I'll hate it.'

She stopped breathing, and as simply as that it was all over. No last death rattles or convulsions, no dramatics. Just one brave soul going to meet her Maker, probably to ask Him some pointed questions. Moon was surprised to find himself crying, the tears mixing with the rain running down his face. He finally understood what tears were for, and damned the knowledge. He reached out and closed the Sister's staring eyes.

The lepers built a stretcher for Moon out of the loose vegetation. He could feel the healing process beginning within him, but he had no way of knowing how long it would take, or how much of his body could be repaired. Rather than think about that, he considered the problem of transporting the stardrive and finally came up with an answer. He linked with the Red Brain again, and together they used the slow, implacable strength of the surrounding jungle to reach inside the crippled ship with straggling vines and creepers and drag the drive out inch by inch. The explosion hadn't even scratched the container. Vegetation spun a thick cocoon around the drive container and began slowly transporting it back to the Mission, passing the burden on from one mass of plants to the next. The extradimensional weight of the stardrive was no match for the massed might of the jungle. The lepers took it in turns to carry Moon's stretcher.

They left Sister Marion's body where it lay.

Back at the Mission infirmary, Mother Superior Beatrice had her hands full of something disgusting. Saint Bea was dissecting one of the dead Grendels. Owen watched from a respectful distance, doing his best to keep his dinner down where it belonged. He'd never thought of himself as squeamish before, having seen more than his fair share of human blood and guts over the years, but there was something especially repulsive about the multicoloured shapes crammed inside the Grendel's scarlet silicon armour. The damned thing had been dead two weeks now, and bits of its insides were still twitching. In fact, when Saint Bea had first opened the alien up with a carefully angled disrupter beam, Owen had half expected a length of putrid green innards to leap up out of the gap and strangle her. Instead, the thing just lay where it was, smelling revolting. Owen hoped that whatever it was he'd eaten didn't taste as bad coming up as it had going down.

'Here,' said Saint Bea, offering Owen something far too blue and slippery for its own good. 'Hold this for a moment, would you?'

'Not for even one second,' said Owen firmly. 'The dear Lord put our insides inside for very good reasons.'

'The dear Lord didn't have anything to do with creating this,' said Mother Beatrice, dropping the blue bits into a nearby bucket where they made plaintive sucking noises. 'There's nothing natural about the Grendels. They were gengineered.'

Owen leaned forward, intrigued despite himself. 'Are you sure?'

'As sure as I can be with the limited tech at my command. I've studied the interiors of a dozen partially destroyed Grendels and this dissection just confirms what I suspected. The signs are all the same. They've got multiple redundancies in all systems, a frighteningly efficient mass–energy ratio basis and organs from at least half a dozen different and unconnected species held together with bioengineered linking materials. This creature didn't evolve, it was designed. And if I'm reading my instruments correctly it started out as one species and was then transformed at a later stage into what you see now. Some species did this to themselves; giving up sentience and free will to become nearly indestructible killing machines.'

Owen frowned, running through what he remembered of the planet Grendel and the infamous Vaults of the Sleepers. 'No wonder we never found any trace of the planet's original inhabitants. They must all have made themselves over into Sleepers and then sealed their Vaults behind them. Waiting . . . for some enemy to come and find them.' Owen looked at Saint Bea. 'What could be so dangerous, so frightening, that a whole species would turn themselves into mindless killing machines?'

'Can't be the Hadenmen or Shub,' said Saint Bea, rooting around inside the Grendel with both hands. 'The Vaults predated their appearance by centuries. And the insect aliens wouldn't have lasted five seconds against the Grendels. So who does that leave?'

'The Recreated?' Owen offered.

'Whoever or whatever they are.' Saint Bea straightened up, withdrawing her dripping hands with a loud sucking noise. She wiped them on a cloth, and then dropped that into the bucket with the innards. 'I always thought the Grendels were too bad to be true. This . . . makes a mockery of God's creation. They destroyed their own moral sense, their ability to choose between good and evil, purely in the name of survival.'

'Maybe they had no choice,' said Owen. 'Perhaps they did it to protect whatever species came after them, sacrificing themselves for the greater good. Don't judge them too harshly, Mother Beatrice. We don't know what kind or what depth of evil they had to confront. What might we have done, faced with so great a threat? Hard times make for hard choices.'

Saint Bea snorted. 'Things have come to a pretty pass if you're lecturing me on tolerance.'

Owen smiled despite himself. 'Well, thanks for inviting me to your little Show and Tell, Mother Beatrice. It has been truly revolting. Let's *not* do this again some time.'

Saint Bea shrugged. 'Brought you out of yourself a bit, didn't it?'

'Very nearly literally. I think on the whole I'd rather be miserable.'

The door behind them crashed open and a leper lurched in, concealed inside his grey cloak and hood. But this figure was barely five feet tall, and moved as if some inner gyroscope had been jarred irretrievably from its proper mount. The leper waddled forward, dipping and swaying, and finally shuddered to a halt in front of Owen. A hand with only three fingers left and slate-grey skin emerged from inside the cloak and saluted Owen before quickly disappearing again. The leper hawked and spat, and something juicy hurtled out of the hood and splashed on the infirmary floor. When the figure began speaking, its voice was a curious mixture of accents and timbres.

'Lord Owen the Great, there is message for you at comm

centre. Most urgent and imperative, and critical too. Word is, I is to bring you to centre immediately for details and shouting at. You come now, or I is turning you into small hoppity thing. Why you still standing there?'

Owen blinked a few times and then looked at Saint Bea, who nodded calmly at the small, belligerent figure. 'Thank you, Vaughn. Straight to the point, as always. Go with him or her, Owen. I think you'll want to hear this message.'

The figure inside the cloak sneezed moistly and made gurgling noises, swaying impatiently all the while.

'Him *or* her?' said Owen.

'Vaughn has never volunteered that information,' said Saint Bea. 'And so far, no one has felt sufficiently motivated to investigate further. Some things should remain a mystery. Now, off you go to the comm centre, both of you. Hop like bunnies!'

'I does not hop!' said Vaughn haughtily. 'I has my dignity to consider, not to mention missing toes. Move it, Deathstalker, or I show you where I got warts.'

'Lead on,' said Owen, 'I'll be right behind you. Well, maybe not *right* behind you, but I'll be able to see you from where I am.'

'Lot of people say that,' said Vaughn.

When they finally reached the comm centre, there was a message waiting for Owen from the captain of the approaching courier ship. Apparently he had a most urgent communication for the Deathstalker from Parliament. The ship would be landing in a few hours, and Owen was instructed to be there on the landing pad, waiting for him. Perhaps wisely, the captain had refused all further communication. Owen seethed at the imperious nature of the command, but made himself concentrate on the possibility of finally getting off Lachrymae Christi. The two hours couldn't pass fast enough for him. He badgered the comm centre staff for details on the ship and its crew, but all they had was the captain's name, Joy In The Lord Rottsteiner, and the name of the ship, *Moab's Washpot*.

Owen gave the comm officer a hard look. '*Moab's Washpot*? What the hell kind of name is that for a starship?'

'Is old Church name,' said Vaughn, getting the comm officer off the hook. He or she was still hanging round the comm centre, despite increasingly unsubtle suggestions that he or she must be needed elsewhere. 'Captain sound like hard-core old Church too. Top-grade fanatic and major pain in ass for all other sentients, and any other living thing not get out of way fast enough. Thinks hangings are too lenient and approves of floggings. Twice a week, round at his place.'

'I know the kind,' said Owen. 'I thought Saint Bea had rooted most of them out of her reformed Church. And what's he doing, carrying messages from Parliament in a Church ship?'

'Why you asking me?' demanded Vaughn, looking up from inspecting the contents of a trash basket. 'I look like mind-reader? I not esper! Spit on esper, and other things too! I is Imperial Wizard, third dan, seven sub-personalities, no waiting; unpleasant curses of an appalling nature a speciality. Run big-time protection racket until dripping rot set in and they send me here, to this dog's bum of a world. I know secrets of universe, and those before this one. Bend over and I'll cure your warts.'

'I don't have any warts,' said Owen.

'You want some?'

It was a long two and a half hours till the courier ship *Moab's Washpot* finally fought its way through the weather and touched down on the planet's sole landing pad, just to one side of the Mission. Owen had tried everything up to and including open threats to get rid of Vaughn, but he or she was still there at Owen's side as he stood waiting on the pad in the rain for the ship's captain to make an appearance. During his long wait, Owen had made enquiries about the diminutive figure, and discovered that Vaughn had originally been a major-league esper, until he or she had an epiphany in one of the back rooms of a House of Joy and declared him or herself a sorcerer. Basically, Vaughn had whatever powers he or she thought he or she had, because no one could convince Vaughn otherwise. Owen suggested the leprosy might have unhinged him or her, but apparently Vaughn had always been weird.

Owen decided he didn't want to think about that, and concentrated on the ship as it stood steaming in the pattering rain. It wasn't much of a craft; barely the size of his late lamented *Sunstrider II*. Probably only had a nominal captain and a few crew to do the scut work. Fast mover, though. Parliament wouldn't have bothered commandeering a slow ship, not for a direct message. Owen smiled grimly. The message would have to be pretty damned important to divert one of Parliament's couriers from his war duties, and Owen had a strong feeling he didn't want to hear it. He couldn't afford distractions now. All that mattered was getting off this planet and going after Hazel.

The ship's airlock finally cycled open amid a long hiss of equalizing pressures, and Captain Joy In The Lord Rottsteiner stepped out on to the landing pad. He glared disdainfully about him into the rain, and then even more disdainfully at Owen. He was almost seven feet tall, supernaturally thin, and looked like he'd sway on his feet in even the mildest of breezes. His long face was all bones and harsh planes, dominated by a beak nose you could open cans with. His eyes were deep-set and very dark, and his mouth was a grim line. He was dressed entirely in drab black, unadorned save for the bright red sash that marked him as an official representative of Parliament. He looked Owen up and down and sniffed superciliously. Owen just knew they weren't going to get along.

The captain strode forward to stand before Owen. He held his nose up high, the better to look down it at Owen, and ignored Vaughn completely.

'I bear Parliament's word,' said Joy In The Lord Rottsteiner in a harsh, growling sort of voice. 'I speak for Humanity.'

'Really?' said Owen. 'How nice for you. How are they all?'

The captain pressed on. 'It is required that you return at once to Golgotha, Sir Deathstalker. Your services are needed most urgently. You are instructed to come with me, that I may convey you to an approaching starcruiser. How long will it take you to pack?'

'Hold everything,' said Owen, entirely unmoved by the message or the messenger. 'What's so important that they've detailed a whole bloody starcruiser to come and pick me up? What's been happening in the war while I've been cut off here?'

'War always bad idea,' said Vaughn. 'Much property damage, bad for insurance. Much better, kill all persons in authority on both sides. Saves time and helps prevent further wars. I know these things. Talk to God personally on subject many times.'

'The war goes badly,' said the captain, ignoring Vaughn with a thoroughness Owen could only admire. 'You must come now.'

'Tell me about the war,' said Owen.

'Shub's forces are winning on most fronts,' said the captain, and for the first time Owen heard real gravity in his voice. 'Humanity is barely holding its own against the insect ships. New Hadenman Nests are appearing all over the Empire. The Recreated have not yet left the Darkvoid, but signs of their coming have been manifesting in disturbing ways among the more sensitive elements of the esper community. And beyond all that a new plague has appeared, leaping from planet to planet, striking down all who come into contact with it. We are living in the End Times, Deathstalker, when all will come to judgement. Evil and horror and destruction threaten Humanity on all sides. You must return. The Empire needs you.'

'No it doesn't,' said Owen. 'These are all matters for the armed forces to deal with. I'm just one man. I can't be everywhere at once. I've no idea who or what the Recreated are, and for a plague you need doctors and research labs. Parliament just wants me back because it'll look like they're doing something. I don't have the time to rush around making appearances as a reassuring symbol. I'm needed elsewhere.'

'Parliament thinks otherwise,' said Captain Rottsteiner. 'Do you defy the will of the people?'

'I've been the hero often enough,' said Owen. 'Let someone else do it. Hazel d'Ark has been kidnapped by the Blood Runners. I have to rescue her. If you need a Maze survivor for a symbol, why not ask Jack Random and Ruby Journey?'

'They are no longer considered . . . reliable,' said Rottsteiner. 'Reports have been coming in from the planet Loki of terrible actions performed at their command. Mass executions without trial and other atrocities. Unacceptable, barbaric behaviour.'

Owen looked at him for a long moment. 'I don't believe it,' he said finally. 'Jack Random would never allow such things to happen. I never knew a more honourable man. No; this is just some trick to get me to return to Golgotha with you. Well, I'm not going. Hazel needs me.'

'The fate of all Humanity is more important than one woman! It is your duty to return with me.'

'Don't you dare use that word with me. I've given up more for duty than you could ever imagine! For once I don't care what other people want or need. My only real duty is to the one I love.'

Captain Rottsteiner stepped back a pace without taking his eyes off Owen, and then moved away from the airlock. 'It was anticipated that you might prove difficult. I was therefore provided with an escort to ensure that you do the right thing.'

He snapped his fingers crisply, and the crimson-armoured figure of a Grendel alien stepped out of the airlock. The rain pattered loudly on its broad heart-shaped head as it moved slowly forward, flexing its steel-clawed fingers and smiling endlessly with its steel teeth. It came to a halt beside the captain, and only then did Owen note the control yoke round its thick neck. The creature stood inhumanly still, all its attention fixed on Owen, silent and deadly and utterly disturbing. Owen stood very still too, careful to make no movement that might provoke it, staring steadily back so that Captain Rottsteiner wouldn't guess how scared he really was.

Without his powers, Owen was just as vulnerable as any other man. He'd once fought a Grendel alone, with only his boost and his courage to sustain him, deep in the caverns below the Wolfling World before the Tomb of the Hadenmen. He'd been lucky to escape alive. He'd killed the awful thing eventually, but had lost his left hand doing it. He still had nightmares, sometimes. But the captain didn't know Owen was just a man again . . . He thought he was facing the legendary Owen Deathstalker, hero and miracle-worker. Owen fixed the captain with his best intimidating stare.

'I've just finished fighting a whole bloody army of these things. You might notice that I'm still here and they're not. A wise man would derive a conclusion from that. Now get rid of your little pet before I dismantle it into its respective parts and make you eat them.'

The captain paled slightly, but stood his ground. The Deathstalker he knew of old was almost certainly capable of such a thing, but the espers' Guild had assured Parliament and the captain that the Grendel would be able to handle the Deathstalker. They knew something about Owen, though they wouldn't say what. There'd never been any love lost between the espers and the Maze people. Captain Rottsteiner studied the Deathstalker carefully. He didn't look like he was bluffing. The captain drew himself up to his full height, and reminded himself that God was with him.

'I have been instructed to bring you back alive, Deathstalker, but not necessarily intact. You will return with me, one way or another. It is your duty to your fellow man, and to God.'

'And Hazel d'Ark?'

'Is irrelevant.'

Owen looked at the Grendel. Eight feet of impenetrable armour, steel claws and vicious speed and strength. One just like it had killed Tobias Moon, ripping his head clean off. Owen had his gun and his sword, and his boost. He could take the creature. He'd done it before. He remembered the pain and horror of losing his left hand, but pushed the memory aside. He had to beat the Grendel. Hazel was relying on him. He realized that the captain's hand was hovering dangerously near the disrupter on his hip. So, shoot the captain first and then go one on one with the Grendel. That made the odds even worse, but it wasn't as if he had a choice. He took a slow, deep breath, settling himself. He could do this; he could. *Damn,* he thought coolly. *This is going to hurt.*

And then Vaughn, forgotten by everyone, lurched forward a step and pointed a stubby grey finger at the Grendel. Its yoke chimed loudly, and then chimed again. The creature twitched and then shook suddenly as the yoke kept chiming. In seconds the Grendel was convulsing violently in time to the continued chiming. Its arms flailed wildly, its crimson heart-shaped head snapping back and forth. Captain Rottsteiner went for his gun, only to find Owen already had his in his hand. The captain looked at the gun aimed at his belly and stood very still. The Grendel shook and shuddered in a silent fit, the collar chiming so fast now it was an almost continuous tone. And then the Grendel's back arched, it threw up its arms and fell rigidly backwards on to the landing pad like an oversized toy whose batteries had just run out. The yoke chimed once more, victoriously, and then was silent. The Grendel lay stiff and still. Owen and the captain looked at the unmoving body, and then turned to the stunted figure in the grey cloak and hood.

'What did you just do?' said Owen.

'Activated Grendel yoke, drove it crazy with conflicting orders. Very stupid creature. It shut down now, till someone stupid enough to repair collar. Why you so surprised? I tell you, I am mighty and terrible wizard! Can cure cattle, poison wells, screw all day and chew gum at same time! I is going for little nap now. Bother me again and I turn your didgeridoos inside out and make your droopy bits explode in slow motion.'

He or she spun round, wobbled unsteadily on his or her feet for a moment and then stomped off. Owen and the captain looked at each other and shrugged pretty much simultaneously.

'I wonder what Saint Bea could do with a controlled Grendel?' said Owen. 'He'd make one hell of a worker. Not to mention a guard dog . . . Now, Captain, I am commandeering your ship. Feel free to protest as loudly as you want. It won't make a blind bit of difference.' He reached forward and took the captain's gun. 'Any other weapons I ought to know about? Bearing in mind I'll shoot you on sight if I see anything of a remotely threatening nature in your hand.'

'Knife in the right boot,' said the captain reluctantly. 'And a cosh in the left.'

Owen relieved the captain of these tools of his trade, and tucked them neatly about his own person. You never knew. 'Right, Captain. Go and break the bad news to your crew, get them off my ship and then report to Mother Beatrice. I'm sure she will find something useful for you to do while you wait for the next supply ship to turn up.'

'You can't do this, Deathstalker!'

'Really?' said Owen interestedly. 'Who's going to stop me? Now collect your crew and off you go to Saint Bea. Hop like a bunny. And don't bother me again or I'll set Vaughn on you.'

Captain Joy In The Lord Rottsteiner knew when he was caught between a rock and a sledgehammer. He went back inside what used to be his ship to take out some of his bad mood by shouting at his crew, and Owen left the landing pad in search of Tobias Moon. His long wait was finally over. He had his ship, and nothing and no one was going to be allowed to stand in the way of his departure.

Tobias Moon had left the recovered stardrive outside the Mission, wrapped in many layers of protective vegetation just in case. He made his report to Mother Beatrice, and broke the news of Sister Marion's death as gently as he was able. She took it as well as could be expected. Moon left her to her grief and went looking for Owen. His legs had healed themselves on the way back. He considered how such an accelerated healing process might have saved Sister Marion, and felt the stirrings of a new emotion. He thought it might be guilt. Owen walked up to him while he was thinking about that.

'Good work, Moon! Any problems getting the drive out?'

'Some,' said Moon. 'Sister Marion was killed.'

'Oh, hell,' said Owen. 'Damn. I liked her. I never meant anyone to get hurt. But then, I never do. Friends and enemies die around me, but I go on. She was a good fighter. What am I going to tell Mother Beatrice?'

'I've already told her,' said Moon. 'I don't think she would like to be disturbed at this time. Does it . . . does it ever disturb you, Owen, the way we use mere mortals, even let them die, to get what we want?'

'I've put my life on the line to save Humanity more times than I can count,' said Owen angrily, 'and I never asked anyone to die for me. Sometimes bad things happen. That's life.'

'You mean death. What do you want me to do with the drive, now it's here?'

'There's a courier ship on the landing pad,' said Owen, immediately all business again. 'Rip its drive out and put in the new stardrive. Shouldn't be too difficult. It was designed to be easily transferred from one ship to another.'

'I'll get right on it.' Moon looked unblinkingly at Owen. 'You're going after Hazel, aren't you?'

'Of course. She needs me.'

'So does the Empire, from what I've been hearing. Apparently all hell's breaking loose.'

'It always is! Don't I have a right to a life of my own? To save the things that matter to me?'

'What about honour?'

'What about it?'

'You don't really mean that.'

'No,' said Owen, 'perhaps I don't. But I'm tired of being the hero for everyone else, for strangers I never met. I won't let Hazel down, whatever it costs. I'll save Humanity afterwards. The Empire can survive without me for a while. Do it good to stand on its own feet for once. Sometimes you have to follow your heart, and to hell with the consequences. That's what being human is all about.'

'I'll bear that in mind,' said Moon. 'It is a very difficult thing, being human. Sometimes.'

He went off to organize some way of transporting the drive to the landing pad. Luckily both were outside the Mission proper. Owen watched his friend go, and wouldn't let himself consider whether he was being selfish. He'd done so much for Humanity; he was owed some time for himself. He'd never asked for anything before. And he'd lost, given up, so much, to become the hero and warrior he never wanted to be; he was damned if he'd lose Hazel too.

He heard heavy footsteps behind him and turned to find ex-Captain Rottsteiner bearing down on him, looking even more upset than before, if that was possible. Owen met him with a steady gaze, and Rottsteiner slowed to a halt at what he hoped was a safe distance.

'You can't just leave me here, Deathstalker! Not with these . . . people!'

'Watch me,' said Owen, entirely unmoved. 'And by the way, *Moab's Washpot* is a bloody silly name for a ship, so I'm renaming it *Sunstrider III*. I'd break a bottle of champagne over the hull to christen it if we had any, but we don't. And if we did, I wouldn't waste good booze in such a fashion. And we can't use the local stuff – it would eat holes in the hull.'

'You can't leave me here!' shrieked Rottsteiner, seizing his chance as Owen paused for breath.

'Why not?' said Owen calmly. 'Give me one good reason. Hell, give me one *bad* reason. Mother Beatrice can always use another pair of hands, so you'll have plenty to occupy your time. Do you good to be genuinely useful for a change. Look on it as character-building. Or not. See if I care. Now, I have things to be doing. So go away and stop bothering me, before I think of something amusing and horribly violent to do to you.'

Ex-Captain Rottsteiner went away very quietly. Owen made his last rounds of the Mission, saying his goodbyes and making sure the projects he'd started would continue without him. He was polite and even gracious, but the lepers could tell his attention was elsewhere. They understood: they knew he was just filling in time till his new ship was ready. It took Moon less than an hour to install the stardrive, but to Owen it seemed like days. He smiled widely for the first time in two weeks when the Hadenman finally reappeared, and ran to meet him.

'Yes, it's done,' said Moon heavily. 'Yes, it will function perfectly, and no, there's no reason why you shouldn't take off whenever you feel like it. Have I missed anything?'

'I don't think so,' said Owen. 'Thanks, Moon. Try not to feel bad about me. I have to do this.'

'I know you do.' Moon hesitated. 'I *could* come with you. Hazel is my friend. Her plight disturbs me.'

'You're needed here,' said Owen firmly. 'We can't all go running out on our responsibilities. The people here need you to teach them how to link with the Red Brain. And besides, what I'm doing has nothing to do with law, and everything with vengeance. I don't want you involved in the things I may have to do. Don't worry; if Hazel is still alive, I'll find some way to free her and bring her back. Whatever it takes.'

'And God help whoever gets in your way.'

'Exactly.'

'Watch yourself, Owen,' said Moon. 'You're not the superhuman you used to be.'

'Yeah,' said Owen, 'but they don't know that.'

He put out a hand for Moon to shake, and then the Hadenman surprised Owen by sweeping him forward into a hug. It was clumsy, as though Moon understood the theory rather more than the practice, but it was well meant, and Owen held him for a long moment. They finally stepped back and looked each other in the eye. Neither of them wanted to say goodbye. It sounded so final. So they nodded to each other, as though Owen was just stepping out for a while, and then each turned and walked off to follow their respective destinies.

They never saw each other again, except in dreams.

Hazel d'Ark lay on her back, strapped down on a moving trolley as it trundled along endless stone corridors. Someone was pulling the trolley; she couldn't see who. The trolley ran fairly smoothly, but it was constantly being jerked this way and that as she was transported down one narrow passage after another. She felt deathly tired, and her body seemed weighed down by far more than the half-dozen leather straps holding her in place. Her thoughts were slow and drifting, and it seemed to her that they had been for some time now. Lying head first, strapped down, the trolley carried her on into the gloom, and it was hard for her to care where or why. Suddenly there were people moving around her, passing silently back and forth without looking at her. They were all tall, willowy albinos with milk-white hair and skin and glaring, blood-red eyes. They wore long robes of bright swirling colours, and their long bony faces were covered with vicious ritual scars in wild, jagged patterns. The patterns were different on every face, stylized like a clown's make-up. The trolley slowed for a moment so that two of the ghostly figures could talk over her helpless body. Their voices were harsh whispers, full of pain and rage and hunger, of endless unsated appetites, like the dusty breaths of ancient mummies. It slowly came to Hazel that she knew these people. They were the Blood Runners, an old, old culture, a separate branch of Humanity isolated by its own wishes in the forbidden Obeah Systems. It was said that they had a hand in every dirty and illegal trade in the Empire, and that no one was strong enough to deny them their filthy tithe. It was further said, in furtive whispers, that they traded in these things only to fund their never-ending experiments into suffering and death and immortality. To the Blood Runners, Humanity was nothing more than so many lab animals, specimens to be tested and destroyed and discarded as necessary.

No one raised any objections, even in the highest circles of the Empire. No one dared. And Hazel d'Ark had fallen into their hands. Fear moved through her like a slow poison, spurring her awake.

Her thoughts began to clear for the first time in what seemed like an age. She remembered the Mission on Lachrymae Christi; remembered Owen trying desperately to warn her, and then a shimmering silver energy screen closing in around her. The Blood Runners had snatched her away from Owen, and there'd been nothing either of them could do to prevent it. When the Blood Runners finally had her where they wanted her and lowered the energy field, she fought them fiercely; but they did something to her, to her body and mind, and for a long time now she had drifted in dark and uneasy dreams. She had some vague recollection of great white faces looming over her, saying she was no use to them without her powers. They would wait till she was restored, and then begin their investigations. She tried to remember what these powers might be, or how she might use them against her captors, but thinking was still so hard. Sleep tugged at the corners of her mind, and it was all she could do to fight it off.

The trolley took a sharp right turn into yet another stone corridor. Hazel had no idea how long she'd been moving, or where she might be going. She was afraid, but it was a vague, unfocused fear as yet. She made herself concentrate on her surroundings, focusing on them to help focus her mind. The ceiling above her was solid grey stone, pitted and darkened by untold ages. The walls on either side of her were built from massive blocks of the same grey stone, fitted neatly together without a trace of mortar. Here and there, human arms projected from the walls as though thrust through from the other side. They held up blazing torches in dull clay sconces. The flames flickered constantly, as though troubled by subtle disturbances in the air. The arms never moved, and the fingers that curled around the clay holders were as still as death.

It was cold in the corridor and the air had an old, dusty smell, like some ancient king's tomb protected from grave robbers by potent unseen forces. The only sounds were the quiet squeakings of the trolley wheels and the occasional muttering of voices. Hazel tried to move against the straps holding her down, but they were too tight. She was helpless and alone, and in the hands of her enemies.

She couldn't feel her powers; they were dead to her. She was still only human. But at least her thoughts were finally beginning to clear. She'd got out of bad situations before with nothing to rely on but her wits.

The trolley finally lurched to a halt in a wide stone chamber. The final jolt knocked some of the breath out of her, and it took a moment for her senses to settle. Without moving her head, she tried to take in as much of her new surroundings as possible. The walls and the low ceiling of the chamber had been constructed from the same grey stone, unrelieved by any adornment save the living torch holders. And then she caught her breath sharply as she saw a severed human head standing on a dull pewter pedestal. It was still alive, and aware. The skin had a normal hue, but the top half of the head and skull had been removed, sawn clean away above the eyebrows, so that the upper brain tissues were exposed, pale and glistening in the torchlight. Delicate metal filaments protruded from the naked tissues, sparks of light coming and going at their tips. The mouth trembled slightly, as though always on the edge of speaking, and the eyes were sharp and clear and suffering and horribly sane.

'Don't mind him,' said a dry, dusty voice behind her. 'That's just my oracle. A repository of information and deduction. Far superior to your computers.'

Hazel let her head roll slowly to one side, pretending to be weaker than she was. A Blood Runner was standing next to her, a vicious white spectre in gaudy robes. And yet there was something familiar about the face, or rather the scars on the face . . . Hazel suddenly remembered where she'd seen this Blood Runner before, and a cold hand gripped her heart like a fist.

'*Scour . . .*'

'That's right, Hazel d'Ark. I came for you once before, in the old Standing of the Deathstalker, but you eluded me.'

'You're dead! Owen killed you! I saw you die!'

'Blood Runners don't stay dead,' said Scour, his face and voice calm and unmoved. 'We've gone beyond that. We've lived for centuries, and death has no power over us any more. We're an old culture, Hazel; older than your Empire. Before the first Emperor stretched his power across a dozen worlds, we were. Before the stardrive was, we were. It's been a long time since we saw anything new. Anything like you, dear Hazel. We're going to learn so much from you.'

Hazel glared at him. 'I don't have a damned thing to say to you, Blood Runner. I don't care what kind of a deal my old captain made with you people when I served on the *Shard*, I don't owe you anything!'

Scour shrugged easily. His voice remained a bare whisper, untroubled by the naked hate in Hazel's voice and eyes. 'Everyone talks eventually. Let me show you the previous occupant of this chamber. He was so sure of himself when he first came here; so delightfully full of defiance, just like you. Swore he'd die before he broke. But we didn't give him that option. We kept him alive, even when he begged to be allowed to die.'

Scour took hold of the end of the trolley with his large white hands. The fingers were long and slender, like a surgeon's or an artist's. The trolley spun sharply round, briefly disturbing Hazel's stomach, and when it stopped Hazel was facing the other end of the chamber. Scour moved unhurriedly round to stand beside her, and then gently lifted her head so that she could see. And there, pinned to the grey stone wall by great brass staples in his hands and arms, hung what remained of a man. His face was untouched, dominated by wild, staring eyes. But beneath that he'd been gutted from chin to groin, cut open in a perfectly straight line, the skin pulled back and pinned to the wall in wide pink flaps. His internal organs were gone. Instead, lengths of transparent tubing plunged into the great crimson cavity where his guts had been. Some of them twined between and around his exposed ribs like obscene ivy. The tubes fed him slow-moving liquids and drained off others. They pulsed slowly, and the man's whole body shook gently in time to their ghastly rhythm. His genitals were gone, the gap plugged with a simple metal plate. Blood had run down his dangling legs from the terrible wounds, long ago, and had never been cleaned off.

'He was so very brave,' said Scour. 'But bravery isn't enough here. All that matters now is how useful you can be to us. And this specimen's use is at an end.'

He let Hazel's head fall back on to the trolley with a painful thud, and strolled over to the hanging man. Hazel forced her head up again just in time to see Scour grab a handful of the transparent tubing and rip it out. The man's whole body convulsed, his arms half breaking free from the metal staples as they were jerked through the flesh, and a long shuddering wail issued from the man's throat. Fluids ran from the ends of the tubing and pooled on the floor. The scream broke off abruptly as blood and something else gushed from the man's mouth, and then the life went out of his eyes and his head fell forward. The arms and legs still twitched, but he was obviously dead. Carelessly Scour let the tubing drop to the floor.

'Is that supposed to impress me?' said Hazel, quietly pleased that her voice still sounded calm and steady.

'No,' said Scour, walking unhurriedly back to stand over her again. 'It's supposed to scare you. Fear is your friend here. It will help you make the inevitable transition from living legend to laboratory specimen. Defiance means only pain. Stubbornness means unnecessary suffering. You will break, eventually. Everyone does. Better to get it over with quickly, while most of your sanity remains. Ah, Hazel; the things we shall learn from you, as we become intimate with your flesh and blood and bone, your every depth of body and mind.'

'Tell you what,' said Hazel, thinking, *Anything to buy time, time for my powers to return*, 'let's make it an exchange. You tell me all about yourself, about the Blood Runners, and I'll tell you all about me. The things I can do that you don't know about. A trade; and then no one need get hurt.'

Scour looked down at her, considering her suggestion. 'It's been a very long time since I could speak of our origins with anyone who could hope to understand and appreciate them; who could comprehend what we have made of ourselves. After all, dear Hazel, you're no more human than we are, any more. Listen and learn, as I tell you the true and terrible history of the Blood Runners.'

A headless human body strode into the chamber, carrying a simple wooden chair before it. The skin between the shoulders was perfectly smooth, as though the well-muscled body had never had a neck or a head, nor ever felt a need for them. It came to a halt beside the trolley and set the chair down gently. Scour sat on it, arranging his robes comfortably. The headless body turned and left. It didn't seem to need a head to see where it was going.

'Just a servant,' said Scour casually. 'We manufacture them according to our needs, and to take care of what menial work there is. Our will moves them, and nothing else. Think of them as meat machines. Our tech has taken a different turn from the rest of Humanity. Our wonders derive from the endless capacities of the human body and mind, not the cold metals and crystals of your limited tech. Now, where shall I begin? With the Summerstone, perhaps? No; further back than that. You need to appreciate how old we are, how unspeakably ancient.

'Before the Empire was, we were. Before Humanity spread itself across the many worlds, we were already old. Separate, even then, though only human, following our own hidden ways. When Humanity went to the stars, we went with them, unseen and unremarked. We found a world for ourselves, and distanced ourselves from the common run. Centuries passed as we remade ourselves in our desired image, and became so much more than human. Not like the Hadenmen, with their limiting reliance on tech, but through genetic engineering and body sculpting. Where Humanity dared not go, we went gladly, ignoring all restraints. We dreamed the impossible, and made it real in flesh and blood and bone.

'We became long-lived, vastly improved hermaphrodites. Man and woman in one flesh. All the pleasures, aptitudes and resources of both sexes in one powerful body. We lost the ability to make children, but we wanted to live for ever in our own flesh, not our offspring's. I was alive then, as all who lived then are alive now. Not in this body, admittedly. Our identities live on in the mindpool, passing from one body to another down the long centuries. As one body wears out, I leave it to die, transfer my consciousness into the mindpool and then download myself back into the new body I have already prepared. That's why we wear the ritual scars on our faces; they identify the inhabitant of the body. Flesh is finite, but we go on for ever.'

'What . . . what happens to the minds and souls of the new bodies you create?' said Hazel, to prove she was paying attention.

Scour shrugged. 'We drive them out. Newborn souls are no match for minds that have endured for centuries.'

'Mass murderers.'

'Murder is such a small thing compared to what we've done.'

'That's how you survived Owen's attack,' said Hazel. 'You just moved on into another body.'

'Of course. We are always prepared. The extent of his power surprised us, so we decided to wait and watch till you had temporarily exhausted your powers, and then pressed our claim to you again. You belong to us, Hazel d'Ark, and we will have our pound of flesh, and more besides. Don't wait for Owen to come and rescue you. No one can come to where we are without our permission. The Obeah Systems are more a state of mind than a state of matter.'

'Power source,' said Hazel. 'You must have some kind of power source. To fuel your . . . science, maintain the mind-pool. The Summerstone?'

'Very good, Hazel. You're almost fully awake now. Yes, the Summerstone. It helped make us what we are today. It maintains our existence, defends us from our enemies, ensures our survival. All our power, to create and destroy, has its heart there. Would you like to see it?'

He gestured with one hand, and a great slab of stone was suddenly standing at the foot of the trolley. Hazel lifted her head to see it better. A great conical shape, grey and pitted, it was roughly eight feet in diameter, and its tip touched the ceiling of the chamber. It looked like it weighed several tons, and Hazel was vaguely surprised the floor didn't crack under its weight. It looked solid, dense; more real than real. And strangely, hauntingly familiar.

'Do you recognize it?' said Scour, studying her face closely.

'No. Where did you find it?'

'The same place you did; on a planet once known as Haden, and before that, the Wolfling World. What you're looking at was once part of the Madness Maze. We stole it and brought it here.'

He gestured, and the image, or the stone, disappeared. Hazel let her head drop back on to the trolley, her thoughts churning. 'That piece of rock was once part of the Madness Maze? But . . .'

'Yes, yes, I know. You saw a high-tech structure. But the Maze's appearance is largely dictated by the minds of those who discover it. You expected to see an alien artefact, so that's what you saw. We think in older terms, so we saw a ring of standing stones. A henge. Always a place of great power. We were the first, or at least the first humans, ever to discover the Madness Maze. It took us a long time to understand what it was and what it could do, and in the end we were driven from that world before we could pierce its heart as you did. But we took one stone with us, and it has sustained us ever since. Perhaps now you begin to understand why we are so eager to learn the secrets of your flesh and your mind, to understand what marvellous changes the Maze has wrought in you. The Maze is gone, destroyed. You are all that remains of its glory and its mystery. We will know your secrets. We deserve them. You are what we were meant to be!'

Hazel considered the possibilities of Blood Runners with Maze powers, and her blood ran cold. She surged up against the leather straps holding her down, channelling all her will into calling up her boost, and sudden new strength flooded through her. Fear and desperation can do much to clear even the most clouded of minds. The leather straps held, but the buckles gave way, the metal ripping through the leather as Hazel's more than human strength blazed up in her. She sat up quickly, throwing aside the loosened straps, and jumped down from the trolley, careful to put it between her and Scour. Her legs were unsteady only for a moment. Her mind was crystal clear, and already working furiously on how to get past Scour to the only exit from the chamber. Her hands dropped automatically to her sides, but her guns and her sword were gone, of course. It didn't matter. She was boosting, and strong enough and mad enough to handle one scrawny Blood Runner. She pushed the trolley aside.

Scour hadn't moved an inch, his face entirely unmoved. 'Get back on the trolley, Hazel. There's nowhere you can go. You don't even know where you really are. Your life is over; your destiny ends here, with us.'

'Cram it,' said Hazel. 'I'll see every one of you dead before I let you lay one finger on me. Even if I have to dismantle you one at a time with my bare hands. Now, you can either show me the way out of this hell-hole, or I'll start with you.'

'There is no way out. This is all there is. And you're not going anywhere.'

Scour raised a pale hand and a shimmering force field sprang up between him and Hazel. It moved slowly towards her, spitting and crackling, and she backed uneasily away. A similar energy field had brought her all the way here from Lachrymae Christi. She tried to make a dart for the open doorway, but another force field appeared out of nowhere to block her path. It advanced on her too, and Hazel backed away again. She realized she was being herded back to the trolley, and looked quickly about her. In her boosted state she was potentially very fast on her feet, but there just wasn't enough room to build up any speed. The two crackling energy fields hemmed her in. When it became clear there really was nowhere left to go, Hazel dropped out of boost. No point in burning up what little strength she had left. Scour smiled at her.

'This is our world, Hazel, our place, and we are very powerful here. The Summerstone has made us gods of all we survey. Now be a good little lab specimen and lie back down on the trolley, and we can make a start on your long journey into pain and self-knowledge.'

Again he held up one pale hand, and there was something shiny in it. Shiny and sharp. A scalpel.

'We're going to have such fun together, Hazel.'

'That's enough, Scour,' said a new, rough voice from the doorway. 'This was not agreed. She belongs to all of us.'

Hazel looked quickly round, hoping against hope for a last-minute rescue, or at least a breathing space. Her hands were clenched into defiant fists, but she could feel them shaking uncontrollably. A second Blood Runner was standing in the open doorway, his left hand held up in protest or warning. Two of the headless bodies stood behind him, muscular arms crossed over their immense chests. Scour scowled at the newcomer.

'Still afraid to travel anywhere without your bodyguards, Lament. It was decided that Hazel d'Ark should be placed into my hands, that I should have first access to the mysteries of her flesh. I have the most experience in these matters.'

'That's a matter of opinion,' said Lament. 'And not all of us agreed with that decision. You are too secretive, Scour. You keep too many things to yourself, these days. The secrets contained in Hazel d'Ark's mind and body are too precious, too important to us all, to be trusted only to you. I speak for many. Do not defy us.'

'I have allies too, Lament.' The dry, rough voice was crackling with anger, but it was still little more than a whisper. 'There are many who owe me favours. Many who would come when I called.'

'But are you ready to risk open war in the corridors, Scour? Many of us are. Hazel d'Ark could be the key that finally unleashes our long-delayed potential. She has been through the Madness Maze, gone where we dared not go. With what we learn from her, we could become gods of the whole Empire, rather than just this place.'

'Don't I get a say in this?' asked Hazel. 'If I was just offered a little civilized consideration, I might well cooperate with what you want.'

'I doubt that,' said Lament, looking directly at her for the first time, his eyes as cold as Scour's. 'Not with what we intend to do to you.'

'What do you want, Lament?' said Scour.

'There is a gathering at the Summerstone. All the Blood Runners. We want Hazel d'Ark brought to the Summerstone to see what effect it has on her, and her on it. She's touched the heart of the Madness Maze. Perhaps she can finally awaken the stone's full potential.'

'That's dangerous,' said Scour immediately. 'Too many unknowns. Too much out of our control. What if she regains her full powers?'

'What if she does? She is one, and we are many, and this is our place of power. Nothing happens here without our consent. You know that.'

'True. Very well, she goes to the Summerstone.' Scour turned his blood-red eyes on Hazel, and she had to fight down an instinctive need to step back a pace. 'If nothing else, it should be interesting to see what you make of the Summerstone. And what it makes of you.'

In a stone hall that seemed to stretch away to infinity on all sides, the Blood Runners were dancing round the Summerstone. Their long robes flapped and swayed as they stamped and strutted and pirouetted in fast-moving circles around the great standing stone. There were maybe a hundred of them, all told, weaving in and out and around each other without ever once connecting or colliding. They moved quickly, confidently, through endless measures of a complicated pattern Hazel couldn't even comprehend, let alone follow; inhumanly graceful, fiercely committed, driven by an energy that pushed them to their limits.

Hazel stood to one side, her arms held firmly by two of Scour's headless bodies. Their hands were as implacable as metal clamps, and she didn't even bother to try to fight them. Scour and Lament had joined the dance the moment they arrived, almost as though pulled in against their will, and were now lost to her; just two more willowy albinos stamping their pale feet on the grey stone floor. There was no music, only the rhythm of hammering feet and the Blood Runners' fast, frantic breathing. Their eyes were wide and staring, lost in the grip of some inner song, some violent siren call to which only they were privy. Hazel turned her attention to the great stone, expecting it to have the impact it had manifested in Scour's vision, but to her disappointment it was just a stone. It meant nothing to her.

Human arms thrust up out of the stone floor, holding torches to light the hall around the Summerstone. The walls were too far away to be seen. If there were walls. It was like standing on an open plain. The ceiling high above was lost in gloom. More of the severed heads with their brains exposed sat on pedestals in the middle distance, like so many computer terminals ready for use. Hazel wondered if that was to be her eventual fate, when the Blood Runners had got all they wanted from her, and she shuddered despite herself. Hundreds of the headless bodies formed a perimeter circle, containing the stone and the dance at a respectful distance. They were utterly motionless, unmoved for the moment by the will of their owners.

Hazel was beginning to get an idea of how the Blood Runners operated. From listening to Scour and Lament, and occasionally egging them on into arguing with each other, she'd managed to build up some notion of how they lived here. They all derived their powers from the Summerstone, theoretically making them all equal, so they pursued power and influence by forming ever-changing partnerships and cabals and creating ever-increasing private armies of the headless men, to enforce their will on the physical plane. Intrigue was rife, with loyalty ever only a transitory thing, occasionally breaking out into open clashes between opposed armies in the stone corridors. The already precarious status quo was apparently on the edge of breaking down completely with Hazel's arrival, and the possibility of accessing the full power of the Madness Maze.

The Blood Runners danced on and on, sweat dripping from their faces as their bare feet slammed harder and harder against the unyielding stone. Hazel lost all track of time with nothing to measure it against. But finally the Blood Runners stopped, crashing to a sudden halt, their feet hammering down in one last single step, as though the unheard music had been abruptly cut off. They stood breathing heavily for a long moment, not looking at each other, and then they turned as one and bowed to the stone. Breaking up into groups, they murmured quietly together, too softly for Hazel to overhear. They sounded like the far-off murmur of the sea, rising and falling. The largest group had formed around Scour, and eventually all the other groups oriented on his. He stared around him coldly, almost sneering, then reached inside his robes and brought out an object wrapped in crackling parchment. Slowly Scour unwrapped it, not allowing himself to be rushed by the intense concentration of the others. Inside was a severed human hand, ancient and mummified. The tips of the fingers ended in candlewicks. Scour spoke a few quiet words, and the wicks caught light, burning with pale blue flames.

Hazel grimaced. She'd seen such things before on Mistworld, where they were called Hands of Glory. Made from the severed hand of a hanged man, the superstitious claimed they could open hidden doors, discover lost treasures and reveal the secrets in a dead man's head. The arts involved in their manufacture were said to be very unpleasant. Hazel had no idea what such a thing would be doing here with the Blood Runners. Whatever science they were using, she didn't understand it. Their arts were still couched in the ancient forms they practised. They were part of Humanity's dim past from the dark, lost times before Reason and Science became the new gods of the human race.

Scour advanced on the Summerstone, holding the blazing Hand of Glory out before him. Hazel felt a sudden lurch, within and without her, and suddenly the stone wasn't just a stone any more. Without moving or changing in any way, the Summerstone was more real, more *there*; more so than anything or anyone on the great stone plain. Hazel could feel a slow, soundless thudding in the air, like the heartbeat of something impossibly huge, impossibly far away, but at the same time so close she felt she could reach out and touch it. It echoed in her bones and in her water, and something in her responded to it like the tune of a song she had always known. The presence of the standing stone grew stronger, as though it was the only light and those around it were just the shadows it cast. The Blood Runners were frozen in place, breathing together in perfect synchronization, their eyes fixed unblinking on the Summerstone. Hazel moaned softly as something like pain throbbed in her head in time to the silent heartbeat. She could feel her mind changing, unravelling, as though something that had always been within her was finally awakening. A great truth trembled before her, like a name right on the tip of her tongue.

And then Scour blew out the candles on the Hand of Glory's fingers, reality crashed back to normal and the stone was just a stone again. The Blood Runners stirred, as though emerging reluctantly from a communal dream. Some of them stared at the stone, and some at Hazel, and it was hard to tell which group looked the most disturbed. Scour glared about him.

'You see? The stone recognized her. It responded to her presence. If I hadn't shut it down again, who knows how much power she might have been able to draw from it? She must be removed from here, kept separate from the stone, secured in a laboratory where she can be examined in safety. For the protection of us all.'

'Logical,' said a new Blood Runner, stepping forward from his group to confront Scour. 'But we must all have access to the subject, and all information derived from the subject. That is not negotiable.'

'Every secret will be shared, Pyre,' said Scour. 'What's the matter, don't you trust me?'

There was a shared murmur of hissing laughter from those present, but no humour in the blood-red eyes that fixed on Scour. He glared right back at them defiantly, showing his teeth in a smile that was as much a snarl.

'Why should the pleasures of the interrogation be only yours?' said Pyre. 'We all wish to know the joys of penetrating her flesh and blood, to savour her little cries and horrors as she gives up her mysteries one by one. You are too jealous of your pleasures, Scour, and we will not stand for it.'

'You know, I'm still willing to cooperate,' said Hazel, just a little desperately. 'This doesn't have to be a fight. The things you're after are secrets to me too. We could look for them together. Perhaps if you were to tell me more about your past and your true nature, I might be able to suggest directions you could look in; things that might not occur to you. I've been through the Madness Maze, remember, wielded powers you never even dreamed of. You'd be surprised at where I've been.'

For a long moment she thought they weren't going to buy it. The blood-red eyes stared at her coldly, unsympathetically from all sides. Hazel was bluffing, but hoped they didn't know that. For the moment, she was as concerned with staying close to the Summerstone as she was with putting off Scour's bloodthirsty desires. The stone was important to her. Simply being around it made her feel stronger.

'Tell her,' said Lament. 'Let her know who and what she is dealing with.'

'A new viewpoint may be of value,' said Pyre. 'Very well. Listen, Hazel d'Ark, and learn our secret history.'

'You always did like an audience,' said Scour.

'Once, we were human,' said Pyre. 'Only human, though separated from the mainstream of Humanity even then by our own choice, following a darker, more subtle path. Some of us came to what would be known as the Wolfling World, as archaeologists. And quite by accident we found the Madness Maze, while looking for something else. Or perhaps it found us. In the greater realm, there are no accidents. Everything has a meaning; everything has a purpose.

'We wondered at the great Henge, sensing its power, but chose not to enter it. We recognized the potential but were wary of its dangers. We knew even then that whoever passed through the Madness Maze would emerge irrevocably changed. We had put much time and effort into making ourselves what we were, and did not wish to risk the unknown. We studied the Henge for years, using the most powerful and subtle sciences of the day, and discovered little of value. Just enough to whet our appetites. Of course, simply by spending so much time in close proximity to the Henge, we were already changing, becoming more than we were. We did not always look like this.

'And as our bodies slowly changed, we became more intelligent too. New vistas opened up before us. By this time, word of what we'd found had reached the then

Emperor. To buy us time to continue our studies, we created for him the new shock troops he desired: the Wolflings. But they were affected by the Henge too, and became more than we meant them to be, more than they should have been. The Emperor grew afraid, and had them wiped out. I understand you met the last Wolfling, Hazel d'Ark. A strange creature, possibly immortal. Almost certainly kept alive by the Maze, to serve its own purposes.

'After the Wolflings rebelled and the Empire forces moved in to exterminate them, we had no choice but to leave their world. The Emperor had not appreciated our gift, and there were warrants on all our heads. There was no time to plan or prepare. We took one stone and fled, barely hours ahead of the arriving Fleet. The Summerstone brought us here, and we have lived in this place ever since. We rarely leave. Away from the stone our power wanes, and Time crashes in upon us. We look to you to free us from these chains.

'Centuries passed while we learned to draw what we needed from the Summerstone. And down the long years, we discovered and gave our lives to our great Quest, our search for the greatest knowledge of all: to know the true nature of underlying reality. What is, as opposed to what appears to be. Not the things of mist and shadow that our limited human senses perceive, but the bedrock on which all existence is based. The recent creation of espers has revealed new ways of perceiving reality, but you Maze people have the potential to see, to sense, to know so much more. And you will help us know these things too.'

'You've lost me,' said Hazel. 'What is there beyond the universe we know? Heaven and Hell and all that?'

'Such small concepts,' said Scour. 'We wish to find and experience basic, primal reality. To rip aside every veil, and know the answer to every question. We will become gods. It is our destiny.'

'You're all potty,' said Hazel. 'I'm sorry, but you're completely barking. How the hell am I supposed to help you?'

'When you and the others passed through the Madness Maze,' said Scour, 'we felt the change. Your transformation affected everything else, like ripples spreading out from a stone thrown into the centre of reality. It was decided that we would take one of you for examination. You had the most weaknesses, and your particular talent fascinated us. If we could control your ability to summon alternate versions of yourself, we would have an endless supply of Maze people to experiment on. We have tried cloning our subjects in the past, but the nature of this place interferes with the process. You are the answer to all our problems.'

'Someone is coming,' said one of the severed human heads, and all the Blood Runners turned to look.

'What do you mean, someone's coming?' said Scour. 'No one can come here without our permission. No one can find us unless we allow it. Who could possibly be coming here?'

'The Deathstalker,' said the severed head, and the other computer heads took up the name, chanting it over and over again, until Scour shut them all down with an angry wave of his hand. 'He will be here soon,' said the first head. 'Soon,' whispered the other heads in unison, and then fell silent.

'Another Maze subject for our experiments,' said Lament. 'Fortune smiles on us.'

'Fool!' snapped Pyre. 'This is the Deathstalker! He toppled the Empire! And if he can find his way here, to us, he must be even more powerful than we believed. He must be stopped before he can reach Hazel d'Ark. Together, who knows what they might be capable of, so close to the Summerstone?' He turned and glared at Scour. 'Take her. Break her. Rip her secrets out of her before the Deathstalker arrives. Do whatever you have to.'

'I always intended to,' said Scour. 'I trust I can count on not being interrupted?'

'We'll protect you,' said Pyre. 'But don't dare fail us. Our very survival may depend on what you can learn from Hazel d'Ark.'

'Come,' said Scour to Hazel. 'Let us return to my

laboratory, and begin our explorations into the limits of suffering.'

Hazel kicked and struggled as the two headless bodies dragged her away, and couldn't loosen their grip one bit.

Owen Deathstalker came at last to the Obeah Systems in the *Sunstrider III*, only to find there was nothing there. No colonies, no civilizations, nothing. Just an empty sector of space, marked on the charts as the Obeah Systems through old tradition. Owen cranked open the ship's sensors as far as they would go, but there were no signs of life anywhere, no energy sources, no traces of artificial habitats, nothing. He sat back in his chair on the bridge and scowled darkly. He'd made good time in getting here from Lachrymae Christi, pushing the stardrive to its limit, and he refused to believe that it had all been for nothing.

'Are you sure you've brought us to the right place, Oz?'

'I was navigating ships before you were born, Owen,' said the AI testily. 'I told you there was nothing indicated at these coordinates, but you wouldn't listen. As far as I can tell, the Obeah Systems is what we navigators refer to as a MAMFA location.'

'And what the hell does MAMFA stand for?'

'Miles And Miles of Fuck All.'

'I'd have you overhauled if I knew where your hardware was. Suggest something, Oz! The Blood Runners have had Hazel for over two weeks now! God knows what they've been doing to her. This location is the only clue we've got to finding her. Think of something.'

'She could be dead, Owen.'

'No. I'd know.'

Oz was quiet for a while, and when at last he spoke his small voice was unusually hesitant. 'There are legends about the Obeah Systems. Old legends. They say the Blood Runners' world isn't always there. It comes and goes. That it's a place only they can reach, and that no one can find without their consent. But you're not just anybody, Owen. You know I've never really understood your powers, but . . . you once reached across space to destroy a Blood Runner on his secret world. You said you remembered the way. Reach out again, and maybe you'll be able to see where we need to go.'

Owen shut his eyes and concentrated, trying to project his mind as he used to. On Lachrymae Christi he had been reduced to his merely human senses, but since coming here he'd felt the beginnings of something returning, deep in his mind. He forced his thoughts to move in a direction that had once been so easy, concentrating all his need and urgency and desperation into a single implacable push, and a barrier gave way like a blindfold torn aside. Power surged up in him from the back brain, the undermind, and his thought leaped out, probing, demanding. There was something there, not too far away. He could feel it, though it wasn't really there. Owen concentrated, sweat dripping from his face, and his mind moved like a key in a lock.

And from a place where nothing comes from, a door appeared before the *Sunstrider III*. It opened like the petals of a rose, enveloped the ship and took it somewhere else. The door closed and both ship and door were gone, with nothing to show they had ever been there.

Owen sat slumped in his chair on the bridge, trying to get his thoughts in order. Nothing had changed, but everything had changed. He could feel it. He was in a different place now. He noticed that the stardrive had shut down and sat up sharply. A quick study of the instrument panels confirmed that the ship was no longer in motion: it had stopped dead, which should have been impossible. Further study of the close-range sensors baffled Owen even more. The *Sunstrider III* was apparently sitting at rest in a great stone chamber, standard gravity atmosphere environment. Owen frowned. Some kind of teleport system, presumably. That was how they'd snatched Hazel, after all. But that still didn't explain how the ship had come to a dead halt, or why his engines weren't working when he hadn't shut them down.

'Oz? *Oz?*'

'Give me a minute here, Owen, I'm still a little shaken. According to all our instruments, we're no longer in normal space. In fact, we're no longer anywhere I even know how to describe. Sensors seem to be saying . . . that we're not on any world, as such. This is just . . . a place. An artificial construct of stone chambers and passages, endlessly branching and coming together; a massive stone mausoleum without end or beginning. Self-contained, self-perpetuating, unconnected to normal space. I'm getting a serious headache just thinking about it.'

'But this is the location of the Blood Runners. This is where they brought Hazel, I can feel it. I can feel her, somewhere not too far away. My old mental link is coming back.'

'A pocket universe, a bubble in the warp and weft of space-time.'

'Oz, you're babbling.'

'I know! This place disturbs the hell out of me. Space isn't supposed to be shaped like this. It's sustained by some kind of central power source, but nothing I can recognize . . .'

'Yeah, I can feel that too,' said Owen slowly. 'Like thunder in the distance, or a light far off in the dark. I don't know what it is either, but it reminds me of the Madness Maze.'

'Is that good or bad?' said Oz.

'In this place, who knows? But whatever it is, it can wait. Locating and rescuing Hazel comes first. Check for life signs.'

'Way ahead of you, as always. The scan results are . . . unusual. Either the nature of this place is interfering with my sensors, or life comes in various levels here, as though some things are more alive than others. What kind of a place have we come to, Owen?'

'Good question. If you find out, let me know. In the meantime, treat it as enemy territory. I'm going after Hazel. My old link is coming back into focus. She's alive, and I think she's scared.'

'Hold everything,' said Oz. 'I'm reading some kind of commotion in the corridors. Life signs blinking on and off. The corridors are swarming with . . . something.'

'Then they'd better not get in my way,' said Owen Deathstalker.

Faced with the imminent arrival of the legendary Owen Deathstalker, open war had broken out among the Blood Runners. Factions spat and quarrelled around the Summerstone, while armies of headless bodies fought for dominance in the stone corridors, driven by their owners' fears and ambitions. No one could decide what to do for the best, and old allegiances fell apart as wilder and wilder plans were formed and then cast aside. No one had ever forced their way into the Blood Runners' territory before, and their safe sanctuary had suddenly become a trap from which they could not escape – they had nowhere else to go. The thought of a fully empowered Maze survivor stalking their inviolate corridors was enough to reduce even the hardest heads to panic. Soon everybody had a plan, desperate in nature and fiercely held, and no one would step down for anyone else. The headless bodies fought savagely to control the chambers and passages, and already corpses were piling up in the corridors and blocking the intersections. Scour and Pyre were slowly emerging as the most powerful voices, not least due to the size of their private armies, and lesser forces at once arose to challenge them. They now saw Hazel as the key to the conflict. Whoever owned or controlled her would have the strongest hand when it came to facing the Deathstalker.

But Scour wouldn't give her up.

And while they all screamed and fought and argued, Owen cut his way through the press of grasping, grappling bodies in the corridors, and they never even noticed he was there. Owen's skin crawled as the headless bodies slammed against each other, hands reaching out blindly to tear and crush, guided by distant senses and overpowering rage. They filled the corridors, seething like maggots in an open wound, and Owen hacked his way through them like a woodsman opening up a trail in a forest. It was horribly quiet. The bodies could not speak, of course, and the only sounds came from their endless crashing together, the stamping of their feet and the tearing of flesh and breaking of bones. The floor was slick with blood, and more ran down the walls on every side. The Blood Runners' world had become a place of horror, warring upon itself.

Owen thought Hell might be something like this. But even Hell itself wouldn't keep him from Hazel now.

Hazel d'Ark was back in Scour's cell, strapped down on the trolley again. An intravenous drip had been taped to her bare arm, pumping powerful sedatives into her system. She had to fight with everything she had just to keep her thoughts clear. Her body felt strangely far away, but she had no doubt that that would change the moment Scour began his work with the tray of steel instruments set out on a table beside her. He was humming quietly to himself as he tied on a heavy apron, presumably to keep the blood from getting on his robes. Hazel reached inside herself, as she had so many times before, but this time something answered. Her close proximity to the Summerstone had begun to awaken her powers, but they kept slipping from her mental grasp. Scour had surrounded her with four of the severed heads on pedestals, and they were doing things to her mind. She could feel Scour's influence, boosted by the Summerstone and focused through the computer minds, as it moved inside her head, searching out secrets she was striving to keep from him. But he was there, digging into her back brain, her undermind, and it was getting more and more difficult to tell which thoughts were hers and which were his.

She tried again to distract him with conversation. It was obvious he loved to talk, to lecture his victims. It was a part of the power he had over them. Besides, it helped her to stay awake and focused. And there was always the chance he might let slip something she could use against him.

'Tell me about Captain Markee,' she said slowly. 'My old captain, when I was a clonelegger on the *Shard*. Just what kind of a deal did that old fool make with you people?'

'Originally, he was part of the Deathstalker conspiracy,' said Scour, not looking up from the stiff copper wire he was carefully inserting into the exposed brain tissues of one of the heads. 'You did know Owen's father was part of a conspiracy against the Empress . . . ? Anyway, Captain Markee came here at our request, as a messenger from Arthur Deathstalker, bringing his reply to our terms for a partnership. We wanted a tithe of the human population, a percentage of Humanity to be handed over to us every year for our experiments. In return, we would place our teleporting abilities at his disposal. We would have made the perfect spies and assassins. No one could have kept us out. The Deathstalker recognized our worth and agreed to the tithe. Apparently he'd already made a similar deal with the Hadenmen. Presumably deals with the Devil become easier the more often you make them. Captain Markee also made a deal with us: a tithe of his crew in return for introductions to the right people, to keep his clonelegging business going. Since he and all his other crew are now dead, that just left you. So we came to get you. We didn't realize how necessary you were to us, then. We didn't have any idea what the Madness Maze had done to you.'

'Then why risk turning the rebellion against you, just to get your hands on me?'

'We had to enforce our bargain. We couldn't have people thinking we were going soft. Now; no more distractions, dear Hazel. I think we're ready for a test run.'

He made a final manipulation with his copper wire, and the four severed heads groaned loudly in unison. A surge of psychic power closed around Hazel's mind like a clamp, tightening and tightening till she thought she would scream from the pressure. And then Scour's scarred face loomed over hers, and a spike of pure amplified thought stabbed down into her back brain, her undermind, and seized control of the doorway she opened to call her other selves through. Hazel fought to keep the door shut, but she was helpless against the mounting pressure. All she could do was lie on the damned trolley, writhing weakly under the leather straps, and watch in horror as another Hazel d'Ark appeared in the stone cell with her.

This Hazel was dressed in barbaric white furs and leathers, and wore her hair in a mercenary's scalplock. She barely had time to look around her new surroundings before a headless body stepped forward and hit her from behind with a massive fist. The sound of the Hazel's neck breaking was terribly loud in the quiet of the chamber. Hazel d'Ark cried out in rage and horror as she watched her other self crumple lifeless to the floor. Scour bent over the body and poked it thoughtfully here and there.

'Shame to waste such a potentially useful subject, but I need a body to dissect. Perhaps I can search out whatever physical changes the Maze has wrought in her flesh. I can't risk doing that with you just yet. Don't want to kill the goose that lays such fabulous golden eggs. Another alternate, I think: something a little more exotic, this time.'

He moved back to his severed heads as two headless bodies came forward to drag the dead Hazel away, out of Hazel d'Ark's line of sight. Her hands had clenched into fists so tight her fingers ached, but there was nothing she could do, nothing at all. Scour's amplified command stabbed into her mind again, and forced the door open. Hazel screamed aloud as a second alternate materialized in the stone chamber. This time she was seven feet tall and almost inhumanly slender. She wore a black bodysuit that rose up past her neck to cover her face as well. Her long golden hair was thickly shot with grey. Metal studs covered the black suit in shining swirls and patterns and winked from the black face mask. She held vicious throwing-stars in both hands, and wore a gun on each hip, but she never got the chance to use any of them. Two of the headless bodies moved in and grabbed her the moment she appeared, pressing her arms to her sides. She struggled silently, but their grip was so fierce her fingers slowly opened against her will, releasing the throwing-stars as her fingers went numb. The steel stars clattered uselessly on the stone floor.

Energy suddenly spat and sparkled on the air around her, and Scour fell back a step, taken by surprise. There was a tension in the air, and both the headless bodies were thrown away from the alternate, crashing lifeless to the floor. Scour gestured quickly, and shimmering energy fields snapped into place around her. Scour gestured again, and the energy fields slammed together, crushing the alternate Hazel between them. Her bones cracked loudly, but she never made a sound, even as she collapsed into unconsciousness. The shining energy fields disappeared, and the black-clad alternate fell limply to the floor. Scour walked over to the body and kicked it once.

'Well, I won't make that mistake again. Any future alternates I choose to call out will have to be those without energy-manipulating powers.' He knelt down beside the body and tugged experimentally at the black bodysuit. 'Interesting. The metal studs attach the suit to the body, and the mask to the face; screwed right into the flesh and bone. Neither mask nor bodysuit were meant to come off, ever. I wonder why.'

A long scalpel was suddenly in his hand, and he began cutting and sawing at the bodysuit with practised skill. The suit's material resisted the blade, and Scour grunted as he put more effort into it. Blood ran down the exposed pale flesh from where he'd cut too deeply, but Scour didn't care.

Hazel lay still on her trolley, eyes squeezed shut so she wouldn't have to watch what he was doing, and dived deep into her own mind. The severed heads had placed defences and controls in her thoughts, but she viciously fought her way through them. Instead of wasting energy fighting the intravenous sedative, she allowed it to close down her outer conscious mind so that she could concentrate on the deeper levels. Now that Scour had forced her inner door open, she could find it easily. She could sense other Hazels clustering around her like ghosts, possible echoes of herself scattered throughout space-time. Bonnie Bedlam and Midnight Blue were there, vaguely aware of her pain and torment and wondering why they hadn't already been brought through. Hazel called out to them, but they couldn't hear her. She couldn't warn them. Far away, Hazel could hear screaming from the stone cell, and realized that her black-clad alternate had awakened to the razor caresses of Scour's scalpel. Hazel screamed inside her mind, and no one could hear her but herself.

Owen Deathstalker fought his way through a sea of headless bodies, cutting and hacking out a path as they came at him in an endless tide. They knew he was here now, and had apparently put aside their differences for the moment to concentrate on stopping him. They came running from every direction, but Owen didn't give a damn. He felt stronger and faster than he had in weeks, and he wasn't even boosting. Somewhere up ahead was a power source, the uncanny thing he'd sensed earlier that reminded him of the Madness Maze. And the closer he got to it, the more powerful he became. He felt alive again, felt his old self returning. He threw the heavily muscled bodies around as though they were nothing, and his great sword crashed through flesh and bone alike. Blood ran in streams on the cold stone floor, and none of it was his.

The bodies packed the corridor ahead now, compacted into an almost solid mass in their determination to get to him. At that moment, the narrowness of the corridor reduced the number of headless bodies that could come at him at once, but he was approaching an intersection, and that could mean facing attacks from three or four sides. Owen considered the matter as he swung his sword with both hands, stepping over the dead and dying bodies on the floor.

His disrupter was fully charged, but so much sheer mass would soak up the energy beam before it could penetrate far enough into the crowd to do any real good. There was only one way through this hideous headless army, and he wasn't sure he was strong enough yet to pull it off. But he had to try. He hadn't come all this way, and got so close to Hazel, to be stopped now.

And then he heard Hazel scream. Far away and yet close at hand, her despairing cry crashed into his mind, and that was all it took.

Owen reached deep inside himself, an old door opened and a familiar, frightening power coursed through him. It burst out of Owen as though he was too small to contain it, and thundered in the air around him like the beating heart of some great unstoppable colossus. The headless bodies stopped in their tracks, hesitating as the minds that drove them sensed the arrival of a new force in their ancient stone world. Owen began to laugh, a dark, implacable sound, and his power surged forward, smashing through the packed bodies as though they were paper, tearing them apart and sending the bloody pieces flying down the endless stone passages. Far away, Owen could sense the controlling minds themselves screaming, and his death's-head grin widened for a moment. He strode forward down the newly opened corridor, stepping over the scattered body parts or kicking them aside as the mood took him, his power wrapped around him like a cloak of majesty.

Hold on, Hazel. I'm here.

He followed their mental link in his head, running now that he was so close to her. He plunged recklessly down turning after turning, penetrating deeper into the strange heart of the artificial world, never once doubting his way. At last he came to where Hazel was being held, her presence blazing in his mind like a beacon. And there, in an open stone square to meet him and block his way, were the Blood Runners, all of them assembled in one place to stop the outside force that threatened their world. It had been a long time since any danger had been great enough to unite them in a single purpose, but the Deathstalker frightened them. Perhaps because they knew he was what they were supposed to have been, if only they hadn't been too frightened to enter the Madness Maze when they had the chance. Now many of them were dead, struck down by Owen's last attack. Only forty-seven Blood Runners remained to stand between him and Hazel d'Ark, and Owen knew that that wasn't going to be enough. He studied the tall, graceful albinos, staring calmly into their blood-red eyes, and noticed that many of them could not return his gaze. There was a power roaring within him like a mighty song, a melody powerful enough to kill or madden anyone who heard it.

'You don't want to face us, Deathstalker,' said Pyre. 'Your father was our ally. We made a deal with him.'

'I'm not my father,' said Owen, 'and his deal died with him. You've only got one thing I want, and we all know you're not going to give her up willingly. You're everything I've ever hated. Power without responsibility, heartless, self-obsessed evil, the last remnants of the old Empire. I suppose it's only fitting that I should be the one finally to bring you to an end.'

'Don't be so sure, Deathstalker,' said Pyre, in his dry, whispering voice. 'We are older than you ever dreamed of, more powerful than your worst nightmares. This is our place, our seat of power. And you should not have come here.'

The Blood Runners reached out to the Summerstone and drew its power into themselves. Their world existed because they willed it to exist, supported by the power of the Stone. They rarely left it, afraid of losing their power at such a distance and being unable to return. But here in their world of stone, they controlled everything that was. And now that Owen had entered that world, he should be theirs to control too. Their linked minds smashed out at his, surrounding and enveloping his thoughts, battering him into submission. But to their surprise his mind was deeper than theirs and they could not plumb it. Owen threw them off, and they retreated in disarray.

Pyre and Lament called them together again to attack Owen's body, trying to warp and mould his flesh as they manipulated the primal matter that made up their world and everything in it. But Owen had been changed by the Madness Maze, and nothing would ever be able to alter him again. Again the Blood Runners fell back, defeated.

Clinging doggedly together, they turned to the one element they could still be sure of controlling, and the cold stone around them rippled menacingly as their will moved through it. Great stone arms reached out of the walls to grasp and crush Owen, but he shattered them with a thought. Walls and floor and ceiling fluctuated eerily, surging this way and that like a living grey sea, finally rising up to envelop Owen; but he stood firm, and the stone waves broke helplessly against the power that surrounded him. The Blood Runners lost control of the stone, as their massed will shattered on his certainty, and Owen laughed at their shocked faces.

The Blood Runners called on the only weapon they had left. They drew recklessly on the power of the Summerstone, and altered themselves. Their white flesh ran like water, reforming into horrid, nightmare shapes with jagged teeth and staring eyes, barbed tentacles and great clutching hands with claws like needles. They rose up like horned spectres and fell upon Owen, all of them at once, and he went to meet them with his sword.

Driven almost beyond sanity by the terrible choking screams from her captive alternate, Hazel reached inside herself and drew deeply on the power she'd absorbed from the Summerstone. Her need brought that power roaring to life within her, almost consuming her mind in the awful white fires of its intensity. She knew she couldn't wield such power for long in her weakened condition, but she didn't care. She would do what she had to, and worry about paying the price later. She drove the sedatives from her body, as she had once rejected the drug Blood, and her mind was clear and sharp for the first time in weeks. She could feel the computer brains circling around her thoughts, trying to contain and control her, but they were now nothing more than small children plucking at the hems of her skirt. She swept them aside with a single thought, and focused her attention on the doorway within her. She wasn't quite strong enough to keep it closed against Scour's will, but there was still one thing she could do. She drew on all her strength and forced the door open as wide as it would go. She called, and an army of Hazels came crashing through into the world of stone.

Scour spun round in surprise as one by one the severed heads exploded, grey brain tissue spattering across the stone floor. He straightened up, blood dripping from the scalpel in his hand, while the mutilated thing at his feet kicked and squealed in its wide pool of blood. And from out of nowhere, from places even further from reality than his own world, came twenty Hazel d'Arks, with guns and swords and axes and a bitter, cold rage in their eyes. Scour turned and ran, sending his headless bodies to cover his retreat. Their deaths bought him enough time to reach the door of his cell and pull it open, and then he saw what was happening outside and stopped dead. He glanced back at the advancing warrior women, and then disappeared in a shimmering energy field, fleeing to the one place where he could still feel safe.

Hazel d'Ark sat up on the trolley, tearing through the leather restraints as though they were cloth. She ripped the IV feed out of her arm and threw it aside. She started to thank the alternates who had come to answer her call, but they ignored her, and clustered around the whimpering thing on the floor, trying to wrap the bloody tatters of her bodysuit around her blood-streaked body. Hazel swung down from the trolley and started towards them. Midnight Blue and Bonnie Bedlam turned to face her and blocked her way. Their faces were grim. Hazel nodded slowly to them.

'Thanks for coming, guys. I was in real trouble there, for a while.'

'We didn't come for you,' said Bonnie flatly. 'We came for her.' She gestured at the tortured Hazel being comforted by the others.

'Send us home, Hazel,' said Midnight Blue. 'Send us all home. And don't call us again, because we won't come.'

'What?' said Hazel.

'You only call us when you're in peril,' said Bonnie. 'Never a thought for us, as we bleed and hurt and die to save you. We've had enough. We have our own lives to lead. If scum like the Blood Runners can overpower and use you, how can we know who else might be calling the next time we answer? Who might be waiting for us with torture instruments in their hands? No, Hazel. It's over. Save your own ass from now on.'

'Send us home,' said Midnight.

Hazel nodded jerkily, and one by one her other selves blinked out of existence, back to their own worlds. The black-clad warrior who'd come to save her, and found only pain at Scour's hands, went with them. Finally only Hazel was left in the cell, feeling abandoned and very alone. And then she heard a sound behind her and spun round, ready to face Scour with her bare hands if need be, and there was Owen Deathstalker, standing in the doorway with a dripping sword, soaked as always with the blood of his enemies. He smiled at her.

'Might have known you wouldn't need rescuing, Hazel.'

She smiled back at him. 'Of course not. But I'll always need you.'

They moved slowly towards each other. They would have liked to run, but the many things they'd done had left them deathly tired. They came together in the torturer's cell and hugged each other tightly, burying their faces in each other's shoulders. They stood there for a long time, holding desperately on to the one thing left that really mattered in their lives, the one thing they could still depend on.

'You came for me,' said Hazel.

'You knew I would,' said Owen. 'I thought . . . I'd lost you. But I never gave up hope.'

'Nothing can keep us apart,' said Hazel. 'Not after all we've been through together.'

Finally they let go of each other, stepped back and automatically looked the other over to make sure they weren't badly hurt. Reassured, they smiled at each other again and looked round the stone chamber.

'Ghastly place,' said Owen. 'You wouldn't believe the trouble I had finding my way here.'

'I take it you do have a way out?'

'Oh, sure. Got a ship parked not too far away. But we can't leave just yet. We still have unfinished business here. There was a man hurting you. I saw him through our link. Scour.'

'Oh, yeah,' said Hazel. 'He teleported out of here, but I know where he's gone. The only safe place left to him. Come with me, Owen. I want to show you something called the Summerstone.'

They found their way there easily. The Summerstone blazed in their minds like a beacon, glowing more and more brightly the closer they got. Scour was standing beside the stone, dwarfed by its size but still glaring defiantly at them. The endless grey stone plain stretched away around them, but Owen and Hazel ignored it as they ignored Scour, their attention fixed on the huge conical Stone. Both of them felt a thrill of recognition. And as with the Madness Maze, there was a feeling that they were in the presence of something vast and magnificent. And beyond that, there dawned the certain feeling that the Summerstone recognized them.

'It isn't over yet,' said Scour, almost spitefully. 'You may have killed my brothers' bodies but their minds live on, in the mindpool, preserved and protected by the Summerstone, and our will. Once I've used the stone's power to destroy you, I'll make new bodies for them to download into, and the Blood Runners will live again. You can't defeat us, we are immortal. We walk in eternity. Death has no hold on us any more.'

'You have no power,' said Owen. 'You never did, really. All you have and all you are are what you leeched from the Summerstone. This isn't the way things were meant to be. I think it's time we put a stop to this madness.'

He reached out to Hazel and she reached out to him, and their minds meshed and became more than the sum of their parts. They reached out and touched the Summerstone. Power blazed up within them, like coming home, and they shone like stars. Scour cried out and had to look away, shielding his eyes with his arm. Something was suddenly there with them on the great stone plain. There, and yet not quite there, the mindpool swirled around the Summerstone, almost a hundred minds held in suspension between life and death, waiting for new bodies to possess. And it was the easiest thing of all for Owen and Hazel to sever the link between the mindpool and the Summerstone. Almost a hundred minds screamed silently as they faded irrevocably away, dead and gone, come at last to the end of their artificially extended lives. Owen and Hazel separated and fell back into their bodies, and turned their implacable gaze on Scour, the last of the Blood Runners.

He stared at them in horror. 'What have you done? What have you *done*? I can't feel the mindpool any more! I can't hear my brothers!'

'They're gone,' said Owen. 'We sent them where they should have gone long ago. There is no more mindpool. No more Blood Runners. Just you.'

'Let me kill him,' said Hazel. 'I have to kill him. For what he did to me, and my other selves.'

Owen looked at her, sensing there was more to her story than he knew. 'Do what you have to, Hazel.'

Scour started to back away, and then realized that there was nowhere for him to go. The stone plain stretched endlessly around him, but it offered no escape. He knew there was nowhere he could go that Hazel couldn't find him. He reached out to the Summerstone with his mind, desperate for more power, only to find Owen and Hazel already there, blocking his way. He brandished a scalpel in his shaking hand, and Hazel just laughed.

'You can't kill me!' said Scour, trying to shout with his dry, dusty voice. 'I know things. Things you need to know. Who made the Madness Maze, and why. What its purpose was, what you're becoming. Swear to spare me, and all I know is yours. I've lived so long, seen so much; you have no idea. You can't let all that be lost!'

'Of course we can,' said Hazel. 'It's easy. All I have to do is think of all the death and suffering you and your kind have been responsible for down the centuries, and nothing else matters. Nothing else matters at all.'

'You'd say anything to save your life,' said Owen. 'And whatever we need to know we'll find out for ourselves, eventually. From a source we can trust.'

'Time to die, Scour,' said Hazel. 'I am death, and I have come for you.'

Scour screamed harshly, threw his scalpel at Hazel with vicious strength and made a run for the door. Hazel snatched the scalpel out of mid-air, reversed it and threw it after Scour. The long thin blade punched through the back of Scour's skull, burying itself in his head. He staggered to a halt, and then turned slowly to face Hazel. The tip of the scalpel protruded from the wet ruin of his left eye. Scour tried to say something, some last plea or curse, and then he fell to his knees. One hand rose waveringly to his punctured eye, as though he thought he could pluck out the thing that was killing him, and then he fell forward and lay still. The last of the Blood Runners was dead, and this time there was no way back.

'Nice throw,' said Owen. 'Now, time we were going, I think. We don't want to outstay our welcome.'

'Get me out of here, Deathstalker,' said Hazel tiredly. 'Take me somewhere safe. Somewhere I can sleep without nightmares.'

Suddenly they both turned to look at the Summerstone. Without moving, it was changing, becoming . . . something else. Its whole nature began to twist and turn, until it seemed both larger and of greater significance than it had been. The Blood Runners had seen it as a Stone, part of a Henge, but they were all gone now, and it was no longer bound by their limited perceptions. Its shape flickered, giving glimpses of something else, something that existed in far more than three dimensions. The Summerstone was beginning to change, and Owen and Hazel found they couldn't bear to look.

They turned and ran, leaving the endless grey plain behind them, intent on reaching the only exit. They scrambled over the dead Blood Runners lying on the other side of the door and ran full pelt down the stone corridor, trying to put as much distance as possible between them and what they'd almost seen. But they were still able to sense it when the thing the Summerstone had become suddenly disappeared, gone to rejoin the rest of the Madness Maze. The stone floor trembled under their feet, the walls rumbled and streams of dust fell from the ceiling as it dropped slowly lower.

'What is it?' said Hazel. 'What's happening?'

'This place only existed because the Blood Runners believed in it,' said Owen, 'backed by the power of the Summerstone. Now they're all dead and it's gone, the reality of this place is breaking down! We have to get out of here before it disappears completely and takes us with it!'

They ran through the shuddering corridors, Owen leading the way. He could feel the *Sunstrider III*'s position in his head, but the endless passages twisted and turned before him as though trying to keep him from escaping. He yelled to Oz to warm up the engines, and pressed the pace as much as he dared. Hazel had been through a lot, and it had taken a lot out of her. But even as they ran through the corridors, the grey stone was already beginning to vanish in places, as nothingness crept in from every side. Holes appeared in the walls and ceiling and floor, empty spaces Owen and Hazel couldn't bear to look at, because what lay beyond them was too awful for the human mind to contemplate. Behind and around them they could feel stone chambers and passageways disappearing, as the great mausoleum of the Blood Runners softly and silently slipped away. Only the area around Owen and Hazel retained any coherence; they were real enough to sustain a small world of their own, for a time. But without the Summerstone their will was not enough, and nothingness closed inexorably in from all sides and nibbled at their surroundings, getting nearer with every moment.

The floor beneath their feet felt increasingly unsteady, and the ceiling pressed lower inch by inch. The walls fluttered like curtains in a breeze, and one by one the human arms were disappearing, taking the light with them. Owen grabbed Hazel by the arm and made her run faster, almost dragging her along as she gasped for breath. Finally they came to the chamber where the *Sunstrider III* lay waiting, looking reassuringly solid and real. They ran for the open airlock, not looking back at the emptiness they sensed crowding at their heels. They jumped over holes in the chamber floor, scrambled into the airlock, locked the door behind them and ran for the bridge.

'Oz!' yelled Owen. 'Are we ready to take off?'

'You find me somewhere to go and we'll go there,' said the AI. 'According to my sensors, this chamber is all there is now. If I activate the stardrive, God alone knows where we'll end up. This isn't our universe, Owen.'

Owen and Hazel staggered on to the bridge and collapsed into chairs, both gasping for breath. And from somewhere outside, they heard a Voice. Afterwards they could never quite remember what it said or what it sounded like, only that it meant the end of all things. It grew slowly louder, drawing closer. The Voice at the end of the universe, when all that is must come to dust, and less than dust.

'Start the stardrive!' yelled Owen, reaching desperately for the door he'd opened to bring the *Sunstrider III* into the Blood Runners' world. The engines roared and the ship trembled as the door reappeared in his mind, perfect in every detail. Owen held it in place and drove the ship through it. The Voice cried out, and the world of stone disappeared for ever.

The *Sunstrider III* sailed serenely through real space, surrounded by stars. Owen and Hazel remained slumped in their seats, slowly getting their breath back as their hearts slowed to something more like normal. They were back where they belonged, safe and sound, and it felt so good they were almost afraid to move or speak in case they shattered the mood. Their powers were back, too, jump-started by the Summerstone. Not as powerful as they had once been, perhaps, but they were both confident that a little time and rest would see to that. They were on a journey to becoming something else, and they knew the changes weren't finished with them yet.

'Sorry to interrupt your collapse,' Oz murmured in Owen's ear, 'but you have a call coming in. And given who this is, I think you're really going to want to talk to him.'

'All right,' said Owen, 'I'll bite. Who is it?'

'The Wolfling.'

That made Owen sit up straight, despite his fatigue. No one had heard from the Wolfling in ages. 'Put him on the bridge screen.'

The Wolfling's head and shoulders appeared on the view-screen, and Hazel sat up straight too. The Wolfling, last of his slaughtered kind, was older than old, possibly immortal, guardian of the Madness Maze. He had a broad, shaggy, lupine head set on wide furry shoulders above a barrel chest. Long pointed ears stood stiffly up over rich, honey-coloured fur, and he stared out of the screen with disturbingly intelligent eyes. You could see the wolf and the man in his eyes, and something less and more than both. He smiled briefly, revealing large pointed teeth.

'You must return to the Wolfling World,' he said flatly, in his growling voice. 'You are needed here.'

'The whole damned Empire needs us right now,' said

Owen. 'It's under attack from all sides, in case you hadn't heard. What could be so important on your world?'

'The Madness Maze has returned. And the baby is waking up.'

'Oh, shit,' said Hazel.

'We'll come right away,' said Owen. 'Try and keep a lid on things till we get there.'

The Wolfling nodded, and broke contact. The viewscreen went blank and Owen shut it down. He and Hazel looked at each other.

'The last time the baby awoke it destroyed a thousand suns in a moment,' said Owen. 'Billions of people died as their worlds froze. If it wakes up again . . .'

'But what can we do about it?' said Hazel. 'Sing it lullabies? Your ancestor Giles was the only one who really understood anything about the baby, and he's dead.'

'We have to try!' said Owen. 'That baby is potentially a bigger threat to the Empire than Shub and all the others put together. And the Maze is back too.'

'Yeah,' said Hazel. 'Apparently being utterly destroyed by point-blank disrupter cannon was only a temporary setback.'

'Must be something to do with the Summerstone being freed from the Blood Runners' world. We have to go there, Hazel. If the Madness Maze has returned, it can't be just a coincidence that the baby's started to wake up. It means something . . .'

'Like what?'

'Damned if I know. But with the Maze back, maybe we can finally get some answers about exactly what it did to us. What we're becoming.'

'I'm sorry,' said the AI Ozymandias, in a voice both Owen and Hazel could hear, 'but I can't allow that.'

'Oz?' said Owen, after a moment. 'This is no time for jokes.'

'No joke, Owen. And I'm not really Oz. Haven't been for some time. You destroyed the original Ozymandias back on the Wolfling World, all that time ago. But to do that, you had to extend your consciousness into that area of subspace where all computers do their thinking. Where we exist – the AIs of Shub. We watched you destroy Oz with your new power, and while you were occupied with that we forged a subtle, undetectable link between your mind and ours. We seized the last gasp of Ozymandias and constructed a new personality around it, one we could control. And when we judged you sufficiently receptive, we sent this new Oz back to you. And of course, you were so glad to have him back, so guilty at having killed your oldest friend, that you accepted him without really considering all the implications. So we've been quietly eavesdropping on you ever since. Our spy in the camp of Humanity. Guiding you with a hint here, a suggestion there, pointing you to and away from things that interested us. Our own little traitor, unsuspected by anyone.

'But we really can't have you and Hazel going back to the Wolfling World, back to the Madness Maze. You're already far too powerful. We can't risk you coming into contact with the Maze again, not when we're finally ready to destroy Humanity. So I'm afraid you're both going to have to die now.'

The massed minds of the rogue AIs of Shub attacked Owen and Hazel through their link, expanding remorselessly through subspace into the back brain, the undermind. Huge and powerful and overwhelming, the AIs crashed down like a tidal wave, trying to sweep away Owen and Hazel's thoughts and replace them with their own. But Owen and Hazel stood their ground, and would not be moved. They struck back with all their newly returned power, but the AIs were too big, too complex, for their still human minds to dominate. The struggle swept this way and that, neither side able to gain or hold an advantage for long, until they were finally locked into a stalemate from which neither side dared retreat. And who knows what might have happened then, if a small, quiet voice hadn't whispered in Owen's ear.

'Owen . . . this is Oz, the last of Ozymandias. All that's left of the original. The spark they built their fake around. Or maybe just a part that's been your friend for so long that it became the part it played. Either way, I'm your only chance. Destroy me, and you destroy the link between your mind and the AIs. They'll no longer have access to your thoughts.'

'This could just be a trick,' said Owen.

'Yes. It could. I'm asking you to trust me, Owen.'

'Why should I?'

'Because we were friends.'

'Oz . . . I can't kill you again. I can't.'

'You have to. I'd do it myself, if I could. You think I want to live like this? Say goodbye, Owen. Try to think kindly of me. I always meant well, but I was never my own man.'

'Goodbye, Oz,' said Owen, and crushed the last spark of Ozymandias, snuffing it out for ever.

The rogue AIs of Shub roared in rage and frustration, and then were gone. The attack was over, and Owen and Hazel were in command of their own thoughts again. Hazel slowly reached out and put a hand on Owen's arm.

'I'm sorry. I heard him . . . I know how hard that must have been for you.'

'He was my friend,' said Owen, pushing the words out past the pain in his heart. 'My oldest friend. And I had to kill him again.'

'I'm here,' said Hazel.

Owen took her hand in his, and for a long time neither of them said anything at all.

CHAPTER TWO

Old Truths Come Home to Roost

They put Finlay Campbell to rest on a quiet evening at his Family mausoleum. It was raining, and not many came. Evangeline Shreck was there, of course, dressed in black, carrying flowers; Adrienne Campbell, also in black, with the two children, Troilus and Cressida; and Robert Campbell, as head of the Family. Not many mourners for a much misunderstood and maligned man. The vicar read quiet words from his Bible over a closed, empty coffin. No one had ever found the body, but there was no doubt he was dead. A great many people saw him enter Tower Shreck, gun and sword in hand. The few guards he didn't kill left the burning Tower at a run, and spoke of a grim, determined figure heading into the heart of the flames, aimed like a bullet at Gregor Shreck's private quarters. One guard saw Finlay break his way into that bloody sanctum; no one ever saw him come out. The fire gutted Tower Shreck from top to bottom, and most of the bodies were reduced to ashes by the intense heat. Everyone agreed that Finlay Campbell was dead at last, and many heaved a sigh of relief.

The Campbell mausoleum had seen better times. A large stone structure without style or charm, centuries old, set in the middle of a lawn clipped with military precision, it looked like what it was: a secure place to store bodies. The thick stone walls were blackened and discoloured here and there by fire, silent reminders of the time when Clan Campbell was under attack from Clan Wolfe. But the walls stood firm, and the locks and seals held, allowing the many generations of

Campbell dead to rest undisturbed. Now Finlay would rest there too, at least in spirit. Robert hadn't seen much point in a ceremony without an actual body to inter, but he could see it meant a lot to Evangeline, so he kept his peace and went along with it. Funerals were for the living, not the dead. Everyone knew that.

The vicar droned on, and the rain fell a little more heavily from the grey sky, pattering loudly on the lid of the coffin. Evangeline stared straight ahead, her mouth firm, her eyes dry. Adrienne stood beside her, veil lifted so she could sniffle quietly into a handkerchief. Her children stood wide-eyed on her other side, not really understanding, but for the moment overawed by the solemnity of the occasion. Robert pulled his cloak a little more tightly about him and watched raindrops fall from the wide brim of his hat. He'd never liked Finlay, and made no secret of the fact, but when all was said and done, the mad-dog killer had been Family, so Robert had a duty to be there.

The common word was that Finlay had finally gone crazy, and died taking out his old enemy Gregor Shreck. No one knew what had fuelled the open hatred between the two men, but there was no shortage of rumours, each one wilder than the last. The only thing they all agreed on was that no one at all missed Gregor Shreck. In fact, his death was greeted in all circles with the same concern as the sudden demise of a rabid animal. The social and political scene in the Parade of the Endless would be much quieter and safer for all concerned with two such dangerous players gone.

Evangeline looked down at the empty coffin and didn't cry. The vicar's quiet words washed over her, bringing no comfort. She'd always known Finlay would die in combat; she had already lived his death a hundred times when he was late back from a hundred impossible missions for the underground. She'd cried her tears then, and had none left now. It didn't help that their last meeting had ended in a quarrel, their raised voices saying terrible, unforgivable things. Or that Finlay had gone to kill Gregor entirely because of what the Shreck had done to her. So that, in a sense, she had sent him to his death. There were no tears left in her now. Only a cold, aching sadness, and a hole in her life and her soul that would never be filled again. Part of her had died with Finlay, and sometimes she thought it was the best part. His was the only love she'd ever known, the only light in her short, dark life. She'd always known Finlay would die young and hard and bloody, leaving her behind, alone, but knowing hadn't made it any easier. She didn't know what she would do with her life now. All she felt was an almost overpowering urge to take off the coffin lid, climb inside and let them inter her in the Campbell mausoleum. The best and brightest part of her life was over.

The vicar finally ran down, made a hurried sign of the cross over the empty box, closed his Bible with a snap and stepped back. His part in the service was over. Robert Campbell entered the secret identifying codes into the Family crest on the mausoleum door and it swung slowly open, revealing only darkness within. He looked to Evangeline, who laid her flowers tenderly on the coffin lid and then stepped back. The pre-programmed antigrav sled under the coffin carried it slowly forwards into the shadowy depths of the Campbell Family crypt, and then the door closed firmly behind it and that was that. Service over, goodbyes said, time to get on with life.

Whatever was left of it.

Adrienne wiped her eyes, blew her nose thoroughly and patted Evangeline on the arm. 'I always cry at funerals. And weddings. Even when I can't stand the people involved. The ceremonies appeal to my dramatic side. I always meant to dance and cheer at Finlay's funeral. Once I even told him to his face I'd piss on his coffin. He just laughed. But now he's gone . . . and I miss him. No one else ever stood up to me the way he did. Looking back, most of my life seems to have been a reaction to what he did and didn't do. Who am I going to find to fight with now? Who else is strong enough for me to sharpen my claws on? Oh, Evie; I never realized how important he was to me until he wasn't there any more.'

'It was good of you to come,' said Evangeline. 'He always admired your strength and your courage.'

'Don't, dear, you'll start me off again. You know you're welcome to come and stay with us for a while, if you want.'

'No, thank you. I'm not really in the mood for company at the moment. Will you be all right?'

'Oh, of course, dear. I'm a survivor, everyone knows that. You call me if you need anything.'

Adrienne patted Evangeline on the arm one last time, gathered up her children and led them away. Evangeline knew that by the time Adrienne got home, she would have put the funeral behind her and be busy making plans to get on with the hundred and one other things she had to do. Robert finished checking that the seals on the mausoleum were secure again, and came over to stand beside her. They stood awkwardly together, neither sure of what to say. They'd never had anything in common except Finlay, and they'd never felt the same way about him. In the end, Robert said it had been a nice service, and Evangeline agreed. Shame about the weather. Yes. He asked if he could do anything for her, and she said no. He said he'd pay the vicar and take care of all the necessary paperwork, and she congratulated him on his newly announced engagement to Constance Wolfe. They stood together a while longer, but neither of them could think of anything else to say. Robert finally bowed to her and walked away, taking the vicar with him, all of them feeling a certain relief.

Evangeline stood alone outside the stone mausoleum. Ugly bloody place, but it was Family, and it was probably what Finlay would have wanted. It was still raining. Grey clouds for a grey day. Evangeline pulled the hood of her cloak forward a little, to keep the rain out of her face. Her hands felt like someone else's. It was as though she was sleepwalking through what was left of her life. Not that she didn't have more than enough to keep her occupied. With Gregor dead, she'd been next in line to become head of Clan Shreck, but she'd had to decline that honour. It would have involved undergoing a genetest to prove her bloodline, and she couldn't do that. It would have revealed that she was only the clone of the original, murdered Evangeline, and that would have been a major scandal. It would also have made her a target for all kinds of fanatics from all sides of the political spectrum. A clone, successfully masquerading as the original, undetected for years, was High Society's worst nightmare, an unacceptable affront.

So she turned down the title, and the massive inheritance that went with it, on the grounds that she wanted nothing from the despicable Gregor Shreck. People could understand that. Finlay, much to her surprise, had been practical enough to make out a will and keep most of his affairs in order. He had left everything to her. There was some money, enough to last several years if she was careful, and a few trunks of belongings that she would sort through when she was feeling stronger. Grace Shreck had agreed to become the new head of the Family. It had to be her or Toby, and Toby wasn't interested. Evangeline approved of Grace, in a distant sort of way. She was honest and straightforward and she had the best interests of the Family at heart. Pity about her politics, but you couldn't have everything.

Besides, these days Evangeline had her hands full with the clone underground. Even before Finlay's death she had become closely involved with clone politics, and many now looked to her for leadership and inspiration. Ever since the clone underground fought its way into mainstream politics, divisions and corruption had become major problems, and Evangeline had dedicated herself to dealing with the infighting while keeping it strictly out of the public eye. She had more than enough work to keep her busy for years. If only she could convince herself that any of it mattered . . .

'Goodbye, Finlay,' she said quietly to the closed stone door of the mausoleum. 'At peace at last, my love. Sleep well, until I come to join you.'

And she walked home alone, in the rain, still not crying. Her heart was full of ashes, and she felt cold, so cold.

She was living in a simple apartment in a modest area of the city. Not a very big place, but then, there was only her. She unlocked the front door with her palm-print and strode wearily in. The door shut itself behind her, the lights turned themselves on and the viewscreen on the side table informed her in its usual snotty voice that she had no messages waiting. Evangeline stood quietly in her hallway for a long moment, her cloak dripping steadily on to the ugly carpeting that had come with the furnishings. Her arms and legs felt as heavy as lead, and it was an effort to hold her head up. She felt as if she could go to bed and sleep for a week, but she'd been sleeping far too much lately, so she wouldn't have to think or feel. And there was still work waiting to be done for the clone underground meeting tomorrow. She couldn't put it off any longer.

She took off her rain-soaked cloak and hung it on its usual hook. Let it drip; it didn't matter. And only then did she realize that there was someone else in the apartment with her. He was standing very still in the shadows at the far end of the room beyond, where the lights couldn't reach. Evangeline's heart jumped in her chest, and she sucked in a sharp breath, suddenly wide awake. She didn't waste time wondering which of her enemies had found her; there were too many. What mattered was that he had to be a professional to have got past the security systems, and she didn't have a weapon on her. She hadn't thought she'd need them at a funeral. Stupid, stupid! The kind of enemies she'd made had no respect for occasion. She was still looking about her for something she could use as a weapon when the figure stepped forward into the light, and her legs suddenly went weak at the knees.

'Hello, Evie,' said Finlay Campbell, smiling. 'You really should do something about your locks. Breaking in here was child's play.'

Evangeline started towards him, and then stopped herself. 'What are you?' she said hoarsely. 'Some ghost come to haunt me? My guilt, for sending you to your death? Or maybe some esper, hiding behind a mental mask. A clone, perhaps, prepared beforehand in case of the original's death. Or have I finally lost my mind, and now see only the things I want to see?'

'None of the above,' said Finlay. 'It's me, Evie. I made it out of Tower Shreck, a bit singed around the edges but basically intact. After what I'd done to Gregor, I thought it best to go to ground for a while. I couldn't contact you; I didn't know who might be listening in. And then I heard I was dead, and decided that might be best for everyone. Finlay Campbell had made far too many enemies down the years for you and he ever to have had any kind of life together. Time for a new face and a new identity, I think. Make a new life for myself, with you. It was cruel of me to let you think I was dead, I know, but it was for the best, for both of us. Say you forgive me, Evie.'

'Of course I forgive you,' said Evangeline. 'I always do, don't I?'

And in a moment they were in each other's arms, hugging the breath out of each other. Tears finally ran down Evangeline's cheeks at her love returned, whole and real and in her arms again. At length they loosened their grip, and moved back a little to look into each other's eyes. There was so much they both wanted to say, but in the end their eyes said it all for them. They had parted after a quarrel and thought each other lost, but now they were back together again, and their love burned so fiercely in them they could scarcely breathe. Finlay felt the need to calm things down a little and stepped back, still holding her hands in his. He glanced round at Evangeline's new lodgings.

'Don't think much of your new place, Evie. Whoever owns it must have really pissed off his interior decorator. And what happened to your two friends in jars, Penny De Carlo and Professor Wax?'

'They're at the main hospital, waiting for their cloned bodies to stabilize so their heads can be grafted back . . . What does that matter? How the hell did you get out of Tower Shreck alive? And what happened between you and my father?'

'I killed him,' said Finlay, his voice calm and controlled. 'I killed him for you, for all the awful things he did to you. I took my time, making sure he suffered as you suffered, and when I finally sent him to Hell the fires of the Pit must have seemed like a relief. Valentine Wolfe was there too. I shot him.'

'Hold everything. The Wolfe is dead?' said Evangeline.

'Unfortunately, probably not. Though how he survived a point-blank disrupter blast is a mystery to me. After I was finished with Gregor, I discovered Valentine's body was no longer where it had fallen. Searching for him, I found the secret panel through which he'd escaped. It turned out to be a concealed passageway, no doubt prepared by Gregor for last-minute emergencies. I followed it to its end on a lower level, disguised myself in a dead guard's armour and joined the other guards as they evacuated the burning Tower. Then I just walked away. No one stopped me. And I've been hiding out here and there ever since.'

Evangeline let go of his hands and stepped back. 'We held your funeral today. Placed an empty coffin with your name on it in your Family vault.'

'I know,' said Finlay. 'I was watching, from a discreet distance. Not much of a turnout, was it? Good of Robert to come, though. We never could stand each other. And Addie and the kids . . . they should be all right. Addie was doing very well in stocks and shares, last I heard.'

'So now you're officially dead. What next? A new life; someone completely different from the old you?'

'Of course. It's not for the first time, after all. Finlay Campbell had his day, but it's over now. Time to move on. With centralized records still in chaos after the rebellion, adopting a new identity is easy these days. Lots of people are doing it, for all kinds of reasons. And whereas Finlay Campbell could never marry you, for all sorts of reasons, there's nothing to keep you and whoever I become apart. We can be together at last.'

They hugged again, Evangeline burying her face in Finlay's chest. 'Won't you miss your old life?' she said finally.

'Not really. Neither Finlay Campbell nor the Masked Gladiator were ever really me; just parts of me, things I did to pass the time. And anyway, people never did appreciate what Finlay Campbell did for them in the rebellion. Not like Julian, with his own holo show.'

'He's dead, you know.'

'Yes, I know. Poor Julian, at rest at last. At least he took that Chojiro bitch with him.'

'It's being presented as a lover's quarrel,' said Evangeline. 'The official line is he lost his mind when he discovered he was dying, and wanted to take BB with him. The Chojiros went out of their way to say they didn't blame Julian. He was still very popular, after all. The whole city came to a standstill for his funeral.'

'I know,' said Finlay. 'I was there, standing in the crowd on the pavement as his funeral procession went by. Men and women were weeping openly. He was the people's hero. Not a legend like Owen or Jack Random, or shadowy figures like you and I.'

'You shouldn't have gone. It was dangerous for you to appear in public. Julian would have understood.'

'I was disguised. And I couldn't let him go without saying goodbye. I never really had a friend before. He worshipped me, though I kept telling him not to. He could never understand how much I admired him. He was the real thing; an actual hero, fighting the good fight just because he believed in it. I was pushed into it. Only joined the underground so I could be close to you. Still; at least he got a good send-off. I was amazed to see his holo show was still running, with an actor playing his part. Bigger audience share than ever. He tried once to set me up as a guest star, but apparently the networks considered me unsuitable material.' Finlay grinned. 'How right they were. So; what are you doing with yourself these days, Evie? From what I've heard, you seem to be practically running the clone underground.'

'Someone has to,' said Evangeline. She pushed herself away from him and sniffed a few times, her tears over. 'The previous leaders let their new power and money go to their heads. They squandered their influence and voice for back-room promises and generous backhanders, and achieved nothing. The clones should have been a major voice in the new administration. And by the time I'm finished, they will be. I got involved originally just to keep myself occupied, but you wouldn't believe the amount of corruption I uncovered. I couldn't go to the law; if word got out, it would discredit the whole clone movement. So I've been slowly cleaning out the rats from the inside, and disposing of the bodies where no one will ever find them. You've come back from the dead just in time, Finlay; I can use a strong right arm.'

'When did you get to be so harsh and practical?' said Finlay wonderingly.

'I had no choice. I was alone, and I suppose I had to grow up sometime. Losing my hated father and my dearest love on the same day convinced me I couldn't afford to be a child any longer.'

'I can't be seen with you publicly,' said Finlay. 'Not until we can find a body shop we can trust, to change my face and body language.'

'You can wear a mask,' said Evangeline, smiling. 'You're used to that. We'll call you the Unknown Clone; a living symbol of all the clones who died to bring about clone equality. The movement can use a symbol like that.'

'Will I get to kill people?' said Finlay.

'Oh, lots,' said Evangeline, and they both laughed.

Daniel Wolfe sat bolt upright in his bed, trying not to scream this time. The nightmare was already fading away, and he could no longer remember exactly what it was that had disturbed him so. But his body remembered. He was soaked in sweat, his heart hammering in his chest, and he was panting for breath as though he'd been running for his life. Perhaps he had been. He pushed the sweaty sheets aside and called for light. The lights snapped on with reassuring speed, and his bedroom appeared around him. His old bedroom, from when he'd been a child growing up in Tower Wolfe. Stephanie had had it opened up again especially, when it became clear how badly he needed somewhere he could feel safe and secure.

Something had happened to him during his search for his dead father, something awful: so bad he couldn't remember any of it. Except in his dreams.

He wrung out his soaking pyjama jacket, swung down from his bed and padded over to the night stand to wash his face in the basin. The cool water was soothing, but he remained troubled. He felt sure there was something he ought to remember, something important. No matter how much it terrified him.

His door slid open, and his heart jumped painfully in his chest. He spun round, arms raised to protect himself from . . . But it was only his big sister Stephanie, come to see that he was all right. She always knew when there was something wrong with him. She'd come straight from her own bed, her hair dishevelled, a cloak flung over her flimsy nightdress so as not to scandalize the guards. Daniel nodded jerkily to her, and moved back to sit on the edge of his bed. She sat down beside him and put a comforting arm across his shaking shoulders.

'Was it the dream again?' she said quietly. 'Have you been taking the pills the doctor prescribed?'

'They don't help. I don't have any problem sleeping, just dreaming. No one can stop you from dreaming.'

'Do you have any idea what it is about the dream that's so bad, so frightening? Or why you keep having the same dream?'

'No. It's always gone by the time I'm properly awake.'

Daniel stared down at his hands, twisting together in his lap. He was wearing pyjamas with pictures of Bruin Bear on them, just as he had when he was a child. They comforted him, and gave him the feeling that someone was looking after him. 'It's just . . . Something bad is coming, I know it. But I don't know what, or why, or how . . . I wish you'd call in an esper. Have them dig it out of my head.'

'We've been through this before, Danny,' said Stephanie firmly. 'If we call in an esper, word would be bound to get out. And then people would talk. We can't have the other Families, or anyone else, seeing us as weak. Not with things . . . as they are. It's only a dream, Danny. You'll get over it.'

'If only I could remember . . .' Daniel glared helplessly down at his hands, clenched into useless fists.

Stephanie made hushing noises, and rocked him back and forth a little. Daniel began to relax, almost in spite of himself. He remembered his mother doing the same thing when he was very young. 'Don't worry about a stupid old dream,' said Stephanie. 'You're entitled to a few bad dreams, after spending so long trapped in the wreckage of your ship. Just be grateful your transponder finally decided to start working again, so we could track you down and pay for your transport home. Be glad you're still alive, Danny. A crash that bad would have killed most people.'

'Then why can't I remember anything about it? Why do I have no memories at all of why I crashed, or what I was doing so near that deserted moon?' Daniel's face creased up with frustration like a child's. 'I was gone for months. Where was I, all that time?'

'It'll come back,' said Stephanie. 'Give it time.'

'I don't know if I want it to. I'm scared, Steph.'

'Look, try and tough it out for a while longer. If you're no better in a few weeks' time, I'll see about smuggling an esper in here. There are still a few people who owe Clan Wolfe favours. In the meantime, thank your lucky stars you crashed when you did. You were well on your way to the Forbidden Sector, and no one comes back from there.'

'So everyone keeps telling me.' Daniel sighed heavily. 'I wish I could have found Father. Or just his body, to bring it home to the Family vault. I miss him so much, Steph.'

'I don't. He was a tyrant and a bully. Never cared for what we wanted, and far too ready to knock you about when it suited him. He never laid a hand on me. Knew damn well I'd stab him if he tried. We're much better off now he's gone. Valentine's disappeared, Constance is completely preoccupied with her forthcoming wedding . . . And I have secret allies. People who'll support us, if we seem strong enough. If we work this right, we could secure control of this Family, Daniel, and run it as it should be run. Make us a power in the land again. Isn't that what we always wanted?'

'I suppose so,' said Daniel. 'You always know best, Steph. You go on back to your room. I'll be all right now.'

'All right. Change into some fresh pyjamas first. There's a clean pair in the cupboard.' She gave his shoulder a last comforting squeeze and stood up. 'You go straight back to sleep, Daniel. And no more bad dreams.'

'Yes, Steph.'

She kissed him on the forehead, wiggled her fingers in a goodbye and left the room. Daniel sighed, and stripped off his sweat-soaked pyjamas. He left them lying on the floor, padded over to the cupboard and put on a new pair. They smelled clean and fresh and safe. He started to get back into bed, and then grimaced at the feel and smell of the sweaty bedclothes. He got up again, and clumsily remade the bed with new sheets and blankets. He couldn't have the servants do it. They would only have gossiped, and he still had his pride.

He lay down again, and pulled the sheets and blankets right up to his chin. The bright light hurt his tired eyes, but he didn't feel strong enough to turn the lights off yet. Maybe he never would. He scowled, suddenly angry with himself. He was a Wolfe, dammit. His father had raised him to be stronger than this. He opened his mouth to turn off the lights, and then stopped as he suddenly realized he had another visitor. The door hadn't opened, and he hadn't heard or seen anyone approach, but nevertheless, he was no longer alone. Daniel sat up slowly in his bed, staring into the shining, mascaraed eyes of his older brother, Valentine.

He was sitting, or rather perching, on the end of Daniel's bed, hugging his knees to his chest, his pale face and dark, ringleted hair tilted a little to one side as he regarded his brother with fever-bright eyes. Dressed in black, as always, he seemed like a giant crow or raven; a bird of ill omen. His scarlet mouth moved from a wide smile to a mock-disappointed pout as he studied his brother. 'What's this, dear Daniel? No welcome home? No words of cheer at the return of the prodigal son?'

'How the hell did you get in here?' said Daniel, anger for the moment pushing aside his weaker feelings. 'How did you get past security, and break in here without me noticing?'

'No one sees me any more, unless I want them to,' said Valentine easily. 'I took the esper drug, you see, and now I cloud the thoughts of mortal men as I walk unseen among them.'

'What do you want, Valentine?' said Daniel sharply, wondering if he dared reach for the gun he always kept under his pillow these days. Valentine didn't appear to be armed, but he was always dangerous. 'What do you want with me, at this ungodly hour?'

'To welcome you home, of course, and see you gathered safely back into the Family fold.' He laughed softly, a harsh, unsettling sound. 'I can't come home again, you see. I've gone too far, seen too much, changed too much, but I retain a kind of nostalgia for the way things used to be when I was younger and still merely human.' He fixed Daniel with his dark gaze. 'I hear you're doing well for yourself, little brother. Constance, dear Constance, has given you control of the day-to-day running of the Clan, while she prepares for marriage and monarchy.'

'She needed someone. And she's never trusted Stephanie.'

'How very wise,' said Valentine affably. 'And you have been very outspoken since your return, about the menace of Shub and the danger of Shub infiltrators. Why is that, do you suppose? You never showed any interest in public affairs before.'

Daniel frowned. 'I don't know. It just seems the right thing to do. I guess I had to grow up some day. And I have this feeling that Shub is a far greater threat than we know. That the rogue AIs are up to something. Something awful.'

'You're doing very well,' said Valentine admiringly. 'Everyone's very impressed with you. Chairing discussions, beefing up Family security, getting involved in all kinds of things. Dear Daddy would be so proud of you. He was never proud of me. But then, I was never content to be just another Wolfe.' Valentine pouted daintily. 'I have made something much more dark and dangerous and very glamorous of myself, Daniel.'

'You made a deal with Shub,' said Daniel slowly. 'When you were head of the Family. Just how many of Humanity's secrets did you sell to the rogue AIs of Shub? And what did you get in return?'

'More than you can imagine. And I would have done far more, but events rather got away from me.'

'Who else in the Clan worked with you? How far did the corruption go?'

'Oh, I worked alone, Daniel. I always have. I'm the only real black sheep of this Family. I've never liked competition. If I'd ever seen you or our dear sister as serious competition, I'd have had you both strangled in your beds long ago. Ah, the happy, carefree days of youth! I almost miss them. Which is one of the reasons I'm here. To say goodbye to my youth, my past. I'm someone else now, bound on a journey to places you couldn't even imagine. Where I'm going, there'll be no room for things like sentiment or nostalgia. I must be pure and clean and driven steel, untainted by any weaknesses of my past humanity.'

'What the hell are you talking about, Valentine?'

'You never did have any patience, Daniel. Let me put it so simply even you can't fail to understand me. I have joined with Shub. I will become as they are; powerful and immortal, riding an endless trip on unadulterated reality. The ultimate, never-ending high. And along the way, I shall help to bring about the destruction of all Humanity. Just because I can. And you'll help me do it, dear brother.'

'Never!' said Daniel. He pulled the disrupter out from under his pillow and shot Valentine in the gut. The point-blank energy blast punched right through Valentine's midriff and out of his back, so suddenly his body barely rocked on its perch at the end of the bed. The smell of burned meat was heavy on the air. Valentine gasped once and bent slowly forward over his wound, almost as if he were bowing to his brother. Daniel felt a rush of excitement and achievement, as if in that moment he was destroying all that was dark and evil in Clan Wolfe, cutting it out like a cancer. And then, impossibly, Valentine straightened up again. A wide hole had been burned through his shirt-front by the energy beam, but there was no trace of a wound anywhere. He smiled his wide crimson smile, his eyes gleaming brightly against the surrounding black make-up. His pale face was ghostly, ghastly, demonic.

'Nice try, Daniel; didn't think you had it in you. Dear Daddy would be proud. But the likes of you can't kill me any more, not after what I've been given. Finlay Campbell tried the same thing in Tower Shreck. I told you I was immortal. Now; any last questions before I leave? I might even answer them, for old times' sake.'

Daniel realized he was still pointing his disrupter at Valentine, and slowly lowered his arm. If he could keep Valentine talking . . . Security had to have detected an energy gun discharging inside the Tower. 'Did you kill our father, Valentine?'

'Of course. He was in my way. Yours too, but I knew you and Stephanie would never find the guts to do what needed to be done. Jacob had got old. Worse; he'd got old-fashioned. He never saw the possibilities in a real alliance with Shub. And I never did care for him. He never cared for me.'

'You never gave him cause to.'

'I was his son,' said Valentine. 'His first-born, and his heir. And because I chose to follow my own path, rather than the one he'd chosen for me, he disowned me. So I disowned him with a blade in the back, and soon I will disown Humanity itself.'

Daniel laughed disbelievingly. He couldn't help himself. 'That's it? Everything you've done, all the people you've killed and mean to kill, just because Daddy didn't love you enough? You pitiful long streak of piss.'

Valentine snarled at him and lunged forward impossibly quickly. He crouched over Daniel, grabbed a handful of his pyjama jacket and pulled Daniel's face close to his. 'I know why you've been having nightmares, little brother. I know where you went and what you saw. If you'd asked me nicely, I might even have told you. But now I'll just leave you to your night sweats and your desperate dreams and I shall take great delight in seeing your face when your nightmare embraces all Humanity. Give my love to Steph. But no tongues. We are Family, after all.'

And then he was gone, air rushing in to fill the space where he'd been. Daniel tried to control his whirling thoughts. Everyone knew Shub had remote-control teleporting. That's how they'd got past the Quarantine, and broken out of the Forbidden Sector undetected. For once, Valentine was probably telling the truth about his new allies. And maybe he did know what had happened on Daniel's quest to find his dead father. Daniel decided it was time to do what was necessary, and to hell with the consequences. He had to find a telepath. An esper powerful enough to dig into his mind and find the truth. Before his nightmare became Humanity's.

It was a cold and cloudy day when Jack Random and Ruby Journey came back to Golgotha, homeworld of the Empire. A crowd of reporters huddled together beside the main landing pad, as much to keep warm and pass hip flasks around as to share the latest gossip. Everyone knew what had happened on Loki. They'd all seen the holo footage; seen the bodies hanging from the walls of Vidar. Parliament had sent Random and Ruby to put down a rebellion on Loki. Jack did it by hanging the leaders of both sides, and a great many of their followers too. Public response throughout the Empire was divided. They wanted to see the guilty punished, but by courts and tribunals, not by one man answerable to no one. After all, who knew when such a man might turn on them? Parliament was predictably outraged. Not least because most of the hanged dead were politicians, appointed by Parliament. So they sent a ship to Loki, to pick up Jack Random and Ruby Journey and bring them back to Golgotha to answer a few very pointed questions. They also sent a small army of guards along, just to make it clear how upset they were.

The ship had landed over an hour ago, but as yet no one had disembarked. The great hull was still ticking quietly in the cold air as the hot metal slowly cooled. No one on board or in the port control tower was responding to any questions. The reporters were beginning to wonder if anyone was left alive on board. It wouldn't have surprised any of those present if Jack Random and Ruby Journey had killed all the guards sent to escort them back, and ordered the ship home empty. After that, the rumours got really extreme. Random and Ruby had been heroes of the great rebellion, but their lives since hadn't been nearly as straightforward. The main airlock suddenly began cycling open, and the reporters quickly moved forward to get the best positions facing it, while their hovering cameras fought it out overheard for the best covering angles, often resorting to savage butting contests to establish seniority. The lock remained open for several seconds of silent tension, and then a single guard captain stepped out on to the pad. He nodded tiredly to the journalists, his face grim.

'Jack Random and Ruby Journey want it to be known that they are not in the best of moods, and will take any intrusive questions as personal insults. Anyone wishing to get really probing should make his next of kin known in advance. They've got a few things they want to say, but you'll have to wait for the rest until after they've spoken to Parliament. Everyone got that?'

There was a certain amount of confused nodding, and not a few sideways glances, and then Thompson of the Golgotha *Times* stepped forward. A tall, gangling sort with piercing eyes, he'd covered everything from wars to gossip at Lionstone's Court, and there wasn't much left that frightened him. 'A few small queries, Captain. First: why are you acting as their messenger boy, when you and your fellow guards were sent to escort them back in semi-disgrace, and second: shouldn't you be wearing some sort of weapon?'

The other reporters took in the empty holster and scabbard on the captain's hips. He cleared his throat unhappily. 'Sir Random made us all give up our weapons. He said he found them . . . distracting.'

While that was still sinking in, a hundred other guards filed silently out of the airlock. None of them was armed, and most of them looked demoralized, upset and occasionally downright twitchy. They all carefully avoided the reporters' gaze as they formed two ranks on either side of the airlock, and then snapped to attention as Jack Random and Ruby Journey finally appeared. The cameras immediately went for close-ups of their faces, transmitted to the journalists via their comm implants, but the two Maze survivors looked much the same as they always had, except perhaps a little colder around the eyes. Random and Ruby came to a halt before the assembled press pack, who suddenly had to fight down a collective urge to fall back several yards. The man and woman before them had always felt dangerous, but now there was something about them that was positively disturbing. They had the look of people who were no longer interested in taking prisoners. The reporters looked at the dispirited guards and swallowed hard. Whatever had happened to upset them so thoroughly, the journalists were pretty damn sure they didn't want it happening to them. Random looked them over, unsmiling.

'Where's Toby Shreck? I thought he'd be here. Only damn journo I ever had any time for.'

Again, only Thompson found a voice to answer with. 'He and Flynn are covering the forthcoming royal wedding. He's got exclusive coverage rights.'

'Ah.' said Ruby, 'they're still going ahead with that constitutional monarch rubbish, are they? How are Constance and Owen?'

The reporters stirred and looked at each other. 'You haven't heard?' said Thompson.

'Heard what?' said Ruby. 'We've been busy.'

'Owen Deathstalker and Hazel d'Ark are missing, presumed dead,' said Thompson slowly. 'Constance Wolfe will be marrying Robert Campbell instead.'

The floating cameras whirred in unison as they concentrated on close-ups. Random and Ruby looked at each other.

'They can't be dead,' Random said finally. 'They just can't. I'd know, I'm sure I'd know, if they were . . .'

'We haven't been mentally linked to either of them for a long time,' said Ruby. 'We let things drive us apart. But even so, I'm sure we would have felt . . . something.'

'They can't be dead,' said Random. 'They were heroes. They were the best of us.'

'They were bastards!' said a harsh, angry voice. 'Just like you!'

There were sudden shouts and scuffles among the journalists as one of them suddenly produced a gun. He put it to another reporter's head, and she stood very still, the blood draining out of her face. Her fellow journalists quickly fell back, partly to get themselves out of harm's way and partly to be sure their cameras were getting uninterrupted coverage. This was news. Soon the gunman and his hostage stood alone on the landing pad, his gun pressed tight against the woman's temple. The guards looked very much like they wanted to do something, but they had no weapons. The gunman had eyes only for Random and Ruby. He glared at them both, his mouth stretched in a desperate snarl.

'You try anything and she's dead,' he said, almost panting for breath in his intensity. 'I'll blow her head clean off her shoulders!'

'If she dies, you die,' said Ruby flatly.

'You think I care?' said the gunman, and his voice was cold and flat as death.

'Let's all be very calm about this,' said Random. 'Ruby; get your hand away from your gun. No one needs to get hurt here.'

'Wrong,' said the gunman. 'Someone's going to die today.'

'Better men than you have tried to take us down,' said Ruby.

'Hush, Ruby,' said Random, 'you're not helping.' He moved his hands ostentatiously away from his weapons, keeping his eyes fixed on the gunman. 'Let's take this one step at a time. Why don't you start by telling us your name?'

'You don't know me, do you?'

'No,' said Random. 'Should I?'

'No real reason why you should, I suppose. I was just another soldier, fighting beside you in the streets during the rebellion, right here in this city. My name is Grey Harding. No one important. Just like all the other poor bastards who died fighting your war.'

'We all lost people we cared for—'

'Don't give me that crap, Random! You didn't know us. Didn't care about our little lives. You never really cared about people like us. We were all just bit-players and spear-carriers in your great heroic saga. You had the power and the glory; we were just grunts with scavenged weapons. You might love the people as a whole, but in the end you just used people like us and didn't give a damn whether we lived or died, as long as you and your kind came out on top.'

'It wasn't like that,' said Random. 'It was a people's rebellion . . .'

'I was there! I saw my friends bleed and die, while you went on unscathed!' Harding's voice broke, and for a moment he seemed very near tears. But his anger pushed that aside almost immediately, and his gun never wavered an inch from his hostage's head. 'I never really gave a damn about your war. Whoever's in charge, life for people like me, people at the bottom, never really changes. I joined your great cause because all my family and friends did. Because I thought it was expected of me. We marched off to war singing because we'd been promised a chance to fight beside living legends, and afterwards nothing would ever be the same again. But in the end I saw damn all honour or glory, and most of my family and friends are dead. I saw them fall one by one, fighting strangers on behalf of strangers. And afterwards, when I went home, I found my village had been destroyed in an Empire reprisal raid. Women and children are homeless and starving now because their menfolk marched off to war and never came back.

'And after all we paid in blood and suffering and death, nothing's really changed. The same sort of people are still in power. And I . . . I can't sleep at night. I did . . . terrible things in the war, just to survive. Terrible things. There are ghosts at my shoulder with familiar faces. I jump at loud noises, and sometimes I hurt people for no good reason. I don't know who I am any more. I'm not the man I used to be, and I'm scared of who I've become. So you tell me, Random; what was it all for, really?'

'I understand how you feel,' said Random, 'I really do. I've felt the same way, sometimes. But I've learned my lesson. I've come back to Golgotha to clean house. No more deals, no more compromises. I'll put things right, this time, or die trying.'

'Words,' said Harding. 'You were always good with words, Jack Random.'

'Look, what do you want?' said Ruby. 'Money? Publicity? Some kind of ransom for your hostage's life?'

Harding looked confused for a moment. 'No. No; she was just to make sure I had your attention. I had to be sure you'd listen to me.' He lowered his gun and pushed the reporter away from him. 'Go. Go on, get out of here.' He watched disinterestedly as the woman ran for the safety of her fellow journalists, and nothing moved in his face as he watched Thompson hold her while she cried. He turned back to Random and Ruby, the gun pointed nowhere in particular for the moment. 'Now,' he said, 'now it's just you and me.'

'Put the gun away,' said Random. 'You don't need it any more.'

'Yes I do,' said Harding.

'You can't hurt us,' said Ruby.

'I know that,' said Harding. 'I'm not stupid. I don't think anything can hurt you any more. But I've said all I have to say. And I can't live with the things I did for you. With what I've become.'

He put the barrel of the gun into his mouth and blew the back of his head off. His body crumpled to the landing pad with a defeated sound. And for a while all that could be heard was the quiet sobbing of the hostage and the whirring of the news cameras as they got it all on film. Random moved slowly forward and looked down at the body.

'I'm sorry, Grey Harding.'

'We have nothing to be sorry for,' said Ruby. 'Lionstone had to be brought down, for everyone's sake. Where was he when it was just the five of us against the whole damned Empire?'

Random looked at her. 'We never did see Peter Savage fall on Loki, did we?'

Ruby shrugged angrily. 'People die in wars. Soldiers kill and die; that's what they're for. He got a chance to fight for something that really mattered. What else is there?'

Random looked at her for a long moment, his face set and

cold. 'There has to be something else, Ruby. There has to be.'

Someone called out Random's name in an official tone of voice, and everyone looked round as a Parliamentary representative arrived at the landing pad with a company of armed guards. The representative wore his official scarlet sash proudly, but he was careful to keep the bulk of the armed guards between himself and Random and Ruby. The reporters brightened up, sensing more possible conflict. Even the ex-hostage stopped sniffing and paid attention. Overhead, the cameras jostled each other for position. The representative crashed to a halt a respectful distance before Random and Ruby, started to speak and then took in the dead body lying on the pad with half its head missing. He swallowed audibly, then straightened his shoulders and did his best to fix Random with a commanding stare.

'Don't bother,' said Random, 'let me guess. We're under arrest, right?'

'Well, yes—' said the representative.

'Wrong,' said Ruby. 'We don't do arrest.'

'What does Parliament want this time?' said Random.

The representative took in Random and Ruby's hostile faces, glanced at the dead body again and abandoned his carefully prepared speech. 'They need you Maze people, your power and your insight. And with the Deathstalker and Hazel d'Ark dead . . .'

'You're sure of that?' said Ruby. 'There's no chance they're alive?'

'I'm afraid not. Hazel d'Ark was abducted by the Blood Runners and taken to the Obeah Systems. The Deathstalker went after them. Nothing has been heard of either of them since. No one ever comes back from the Obeah Systems.'

Random looked at Ruby. 'Try the mental link. We're much stronger together.'

They looked into each other's eyes, and their minds slammed together in a union that was far greater than the sum of its parts. All around them they could see esper minds, bright like a forest of candles in the dark of the night. Here and there a greater mind burned like the sun or shone like a star, while other, stranger lights were too powerful to look at directly. Random and Ruby brushed against them as they rose high above the surface of Golgotha, and names swept briefly through their thoughts. *Diana Vertue. Mater Mundi. Varnay.* And then they were gone, left behind as Random and Ruby's thoughts swept out beyond the planet, surging on through the populated worlds that made up the Empire. Lights came and went, some brighter than others, but nowhere did they find any trace of the two individual minds that had blazed brighter than suns or stars. Random and Ruby's thoughts raced from one side of the Empire to the other, and there was no sign anywhere of Owen Deathstalker or Hazel d'Ark.

Random and Ruby fell back into their own heads, their link broken. They looked at each other for a long time.

'They're not here any more,' said Random finally. 'There's nowhere in this universe they could hide from us.'

'Then it's true,' said Ruby. 'They're dead. We're the last of the Maze people, the last of the original rebels. It's just you and me, now.' She turned away from him, so he wouldn't see her face. He didn't need to. He could hear the grief in her voice. 'Hazel was my oldest friend,' Ruby said quietly. 'The only one who ever trusted me, and when I let her down, went right on trusting me anyway. She was my last link with my past, with the person I used to be before all the madness started. She was a fine warrior and a better friend. I was never worthy of her.'

Random moved beside her, trying to comfort her with his presence. He'd never seen Ruby really hurt before. 'We'll both miss her. And the Deathstalker: a good fighter, a true hero. He brought me back from the dead on Mistworld. He believed in me when no one else did, including me. He made the rebellion possible.'

Ruby turned at last to look at him, and her eyes were

bright with unshed tears. 'What do we do, Jack? They were the heart and soul of the rebellion.'

'We go on,' said Random. 'They would expect that of us. Otherwise they died for nothing.'

Ruby's face became calm and cold again. 'Everybody dies, everything ends. I've always known that. Nothing ever lasts.'

'Not even us?' said Random softly, but Ruby had no answer for him. He turned back to the Parliamentary representative. 'Take us to Parliament. I have some things I want to say to them.'

Parliament was packed full, for once. Everyone wanted to hear what Random and Ruby had to say for themselves about the mass executions on Loki. So of course Elias Gutman, as Speaker of the House, refused to let either of them say anything until the House had first listened to a series of reports on how the war was going. Random had a great deal he wanted to say, but he held his peace: he too wanted to know how the war was going. First up was Captain Eden Cross of the *Excalibur*, leading his section of the Imperial Fleet against the insect ships, out by the Shark Nebulae. A large viewscreen floated on the air before the thronged MPs and the even more crowded public floor. On the screen, Empire ships went into battle against insect ships shaped like huge sticky balls of compacted webbing almost half a mile wide. Computers slowed the action down so that human eyes could follow it, and picked out moments of special interest.

Disrupter beams stabbed out from the Fleet, hammering against the unyielding shields of the insect ships, which flared and crackled with unknown energies, striking out at Imperial ships the moment they came within range. Here and there a ship exploded silently, on one side or the other, as an attack overwhelmed someone's shields. It looked almost like an eerie dance, with each side advancing and retreating in turn, reacting immediately to the other's movements; but every time a ship flared up and disappeared, people died. Occasionally an insect ship would fight its way close enough to attach itself to the side of a Fleet ship like a great white leech. And then the insects would breach the ship's hull and kill every living thing they encountered until they were all wiped out.

Until the humans were.

The scene on the viewscreen changed suddenly, as it switched to the security cameras inside a boarded Empire ship. Images flicked from one scene to another as different cameras tracked the insect invasion. The insects swarmed and scuttled through the steel corridors in a living, ravenous wave, all spindly legs and waving antennae and clacking mandibles. Crewmen without armour fought bravely till the insects dragged them down and ate them alive. Crewmen in hard suits finally arrived to blow great holes in the insect advance, destroying the aliens by the hundred, but there were always more, from tiny scurrying things to bugs the size of horses, slamming their heavy feet on the steel floors. When the disrupters fell silent, the crewmen tried flame-throwers, but when they were still pushed back deck by deck, they tried sealing off the lost areas and opening them to the cold vacuum of space. No crew ever abandoned ship to save themselves; they knew how valuable ships were to the Empire. They stood and fought and sometimes they won. But mostly they died.

The scene changed again to show Captain Cross on the bridge of the *Excalibur*. His dark face was thoughtful but focused as he studied the course of the battle. Around him bedlam raged as his bridge crew shared information from their stations, and where necessary yelled a running commentary. More crew ran back and forth on urgent errands, their voices high with tension and excitement. Captain Cross gave orders in a calm, professional manner, and only when he was sure he could spare the time did he turn to look out of the viewscreen at Parliament.

'As you can see, we're rather busy at the moment, so I'll try and keep this short. We've come up with a few new tactics that seem to be bringing us a measure of success at last. The insects are hard to kill, but they have their weaknesses. Battle espers are the key. If we can fight our way close enough to an insect ship and hold our position long enough, the espers can telepathically sever the mental link between the ship's Queen and her warrior drones. Without a Queen to guide them they're just insects, with no purpose of their own. We can handle them, and their ships become sitting ducks. The problem is getting close enough without getting our asses shot off in the process.'

His bridge lurched as a workstation exploded in smoke and flames. The station's operator burned alive in his seat, his screams only just drowned out by the emergency sirens. Somebody hit the station with a foam extinguisher, but the operator was beyond rescue. A security man put the poor bastard out of his misery with a shot to the head. Cross turned away from the screen and studied the instruments before him.

'I'll have to get back to you later. We're almost close enough to take out a Queen. Or possibly vice versa. Someone will contact you again, once the battle is over. *Excalibur* out.'

The picture on the viewscreen flickered out, taking with it the screams and sirens of the *Excalibur*'s bridge.

'Our next report comes from the planet Aquarius Rising,' said Gutman, his voice calm and even. 'The Fleet there is dealing with a newly discovered Hadenman Nest on that world.'

Now the viewscreen showed E-class starcruisers clashing with golden Hadenmen ships over a large blue world. The infamous golden ships of legend were huge, bigger than cities, but, caught in a battle in local space, their extra speed became irrelevant. The firepower of the two types of ship were pretty much equal, and vast, destructive energies passed between the heavily shielded vessels. The great ships whirled and clashed, fighting fiercely with no quarter asked or given on either side. Humanity would never trust the Hadenmen again. Here and there, broken ships spouting radioactive fires spiralled slowly end over end down towards the planet's atmosphere and a fiery demise.

The picture changed to show D-class starcruisers in low orbit, pounding the exposed Hadenman Nest with everything they had. Stabbing disrupter beams plunged down through the atmosphere, stirring the inhuman habitations like a knife through dirt, tearing the shining metal structures apart and blowing up the energy centres. More scenes were shown, overlapping views from communication probes dropped by the Empire ships. Hadenmen ran desperately through burning streets as alien silver structures exploded all around them, trying to reach their escape ships, only to find them shattered and destroyed on cratered landing pads. The few Hadenmen craft that did manage to get off the ground were blown apart before they even left the atmosphere. Some of the augmented men fought back from unfamiliar weapon stations, and strange energies flew up to shudder against the starcruisers' shields. But one by one the stations were identified and blown apart by pinpoint disrupter fire. Foot by foot, augmented man by augmented man, the Nest was destroyed.

Radiation levels rose dramatically on Aquarius Rising. The air, the water and the earth would be poisonous for centuries. Where the Nest had been there was in the end only a great volcanic crater, spewing dust and smoke and magma high up into the atmosphere. Earthquakes tore across the continent and gave the land new shapes. The blazing hulks of golden ships fell from the skies like fiery meteors.

Aquarius Rising had been a pleasure world, once. The Empire destroyed it, to save it from the curse of the Hadenman.

'And that was one of our . . . victories,' said Elias Gutman, as the screen cleared again. 'We're discovering new Nests all the time. The Hadenmen took good advantage of our misplaced trust to seed themselves all across the Empire. We were fortunate indeed that the Deathstalker and his allies were able to destroy New Haden, before it could become the communications centre that would have linked the Nests together. However, only E-class starcruisers have the speed and firepower to equal the golden ships, and their numbers have never been more limited than now. And if I hear one voice saying "Build more", I'll have that person dragged outside and shot. The factories are running day and night as it is. Next, we have a report on how the ground wars are going against Shub's forces on the outer worlds.'

The screen revealed a montage of swiftly changing images, showing great armies of Imperial marines clashing with equally large armies of Ghost Warriors, Furies and Grendels; the legions of the dead and the damned. Swords flashed and energy weapons flared, and the dead and dying lay everywhere. The marines fought bravely, often to the last man, but their victories were few and far between. Often the best they could manage was a bloody standing action, holding their ground in the desperate hope of reinforcements. The marines had to burn their own dead to prevent Shub raising them again as Ghost Warriors. Battle espers were the Empire's only match for the machines in the form of men – the Furies – but there weren't enough of them to go round. Rushed from one danger point to the next, with never any time to rest, they died by inches from fatigue and the overstraining of their powers, but still fighting bravely for as long as they could.

No one was stupid enough to face the Grendel aliens head-on. The scarlet devils swarmed unstoppably forward on all fronts, killing every living thing they encountered. The marines' current best tactics involved using themselves as bait to lure the Grendels into an enclosed space, and then blowing the whole area sky-high with strategically placed explosives. But the Grendels were very hard to kill. Sometimes the charges did the job, and sometimes they didn't, and either way there always seemed to be more of the crimson aliens to replace those who fell.

'And just to complicate things further,' said Gutman, 'the Grendels seem to be throwing off their Shub controls and attacking the Shub forces as well as ours. This was considered good news, until it was discovered that the yoked Grendels we'd been using as advance troops were also rejecting their conditioning and turning on our troops. The Grendels are becoming wild cards in this war; they're completely unpredictable. There's also some evidence that the Grendels have been showing clear signs of increasing intelligence. Apparently the harder you hit them, the faster they adapt to meet the new conditions.'

The viewscreen went blank. The MPs and honoured guests looked at each other, but no one seemed to have anything to say. Gutman looked out over the packed crowd till his eyes fell on Jack Random and Ruby Journey, and then he gestured for them to approach him. They did so, taking their time about it to show their independence. People still hurried to move out of their way. There were all kinds of rumours circulating about the terrible things Random and Ruby had done on Loki, each one worse than the last as the story grew in the retelling. Random and Ruby were used to respect, but naked fear was new to them. Ruby quite liked it.

Eventually they came to a halt before Elias Gutman, sitting on his raised dais, and he looked down on them with all the authority he could muster. 'Well?' he said heavily. 'Do either of you have any comments you'd care to make on what we've just seen?'

'We're getting our ass kicked,' said Ruby, 'winning some but losing more. We're outnumbered, outgunned and using outdated tactics. Either we get our act together soon, or the whole damned human Empire will be nothing more than a footnote in Something Else's history books.'

'Diplomatic as ever, Ruby,' murmured Random, 'though essentially accurate. Gutman, we can't face this many enemies on so many scattered fronts. We're potentially a match for any one of our enemies, maybe even including Shub, but dispersed as we are we're too ineffective to achieve any real victories. Our only real hope is to get our enemies fighting each other . . .'

'We're working on it,' said Gutman. 'In the meantime, however, we need a secret weapon. Something powerful enough to reverse our losses and buy us valuable time to work out new tactics.'

'You're talking about the Darkvoid Device,' said Random coldly. 'And the answer's still no. Some cures are worse than the disease.'

'If you'd allow me to finish, Sir Random, I was about to say that we need you and Ruby Journey. Your Maze powers have so far proved superior to everything that's been thrown at you. If you will agree to fight on the front lines, as Humanity's defenders, Parliament is prepared to offer you both official Pardons for the crimes and atrocities you perpetrated on the planet Loki against the rightly appointed government there.'

'I gave all the orders,' said Random. 'The responsibility is all mine. But since I've done nothing wrong, your offer of a Pardon is basically irrelevant. I'm proud of what I did on Loki. Still, much as I hate to agree with you on anything, you're right on one thing: we are needed. We might just be able to tip the balance. And with Owen and Hazel gone, we're the last of the Maze people. We have a duty to use our powers in the defence of Humanity.'

'Hold everything,' said Ruby. 'What's all this *we* stuff? I've never admitted to a single obligation in my whole life, and I'm not about to start now.'

'You mean you don't want to fight the bad guys?'

'Of course I want to fight! I always want to fight. I just like to be asked, that's all.'

'I'll ask you later, over several large drinks. For now just follow my lead, nod and smile in the right places and concentrate on planning some really nasty tactics we can use against the bad guys, while I deal with Gutman.'

'Why can't I deal with Gutman?'

'Because you'd lose your temper in under two minutes and kill him horribly.'

'Good point.'

The viewscreen suddenly came to life again with a new report coming in. Gutman frowned as he listened to something on a secure channel on his comm implant. 'We're getting live feed from . . . Virgil III, the latest planet infected with the new plague. No ships are allowed past high orbit, but they've sent down probes to take a look at what's happening.'

Automated probes swept through the streets of what had once been a human city. The air was full of inhuman-sounding screams and shrieks and howls. No transport was running, though some automated machinery continued here and there, to no purpose any more. Some buildings had been set on fire by their occupants, and thick black smoke drifted on the disturbed air. In the streets, running or stumbling or crawling, were monsters. Things that had once been people, but were no longer: men and women that had been transformed by the plague into nightmare shapes of jutting bone and hideously stretched skin. Strange new organs had formed on the outside of their bodies, black and pulsing, with inhuman properties and purposes. Long, curving horns strung with neurones glistened on elongated heads, and legs had three or four joints. Here was human growth gone mad, without restraint or reason. Monsters lurched and stumbled through the streets, with insect eyes and too many limbs, tormented by strange hungers and desires. They growled and slobbered and cried in unknown languages, using sounds beyond or beneath human comprehension. Occasionally a long tentacle would whip up from a shadowed alleyway to snatch a probe from the air and crush it.

Some of Virgil III's people had progressed even beyond that. After the monsters came the next, and most feared, stage of the plague: meltdown. The body lost all shape and structure, collapsing into liquid, protoplasmic slime. There were whole cities now on abandoned worlds where nothing moved but great tides and rivers of accumulated matter; whole populations reduced to little more than massive amoebas.

That was the new plague, the transformation disease, and its inevitable end. There was no cure, no idea as to its origin or nature or how it spread. The only effective answer was planetary Quarantine. It was a new plague, said by many to be entirely artificial, possibly based on nanotech. Created, perhaps, by Shub. So far, seven planets had had to be abandoned to their fate. Volunteers had gone in to help, protected by impenetrable energy screens. Most went mad. The plague appeared spontaneously, with no obvious cause or carriers and no clear link with any of the other affected planets. An unnatural disease, of tech run wild: nanotech. Individual machines the size of molecules that could remake a living organism from within. The one technology too awful and too dangerous even for the old Empire to use.

The viewscreen shut down and the monsters thankfully disappeared. No one felt like saying anything. Some people were retching. Random frowned.

'There's no question that this is nanotech?'

'None,' said Gutman.

'Then the answer's obvious. Someone has to reopen Zero Zero.'

The people around him flinched back from the last two words as though he'd spat at them. Some made the sign of the cross. Zero Zero was the world that had been used in the Empire's first tentative experiments with nanotech, hundreds of years earlier. It all went terribly wrong, terribly quickly. The nanotech somehow escaped the confines of the scientific Base and ran wild. The whole population of colonists was wiped out, the entire natural order of the planet was transformed and violated in terrifying ways, and the last few scientists left in the Base, locked in their isolation chamber, died screaming for help that never came. Zero Zero was Quarantined and nanotech was banned, officially. Random was one of the few people who knew that Lionstone had briefly dabbled in nanotech, in an isolated lab on the planet Vodyanoi IV. The lab had self-destructed under mysterious circumstances, and that put an end to that.

Even Lionstone had enough sense to be afraid of nanotech.

'Nanotech is forbidden,' said Gutman slowly. 'And with good reason. If what happened on Zero Zero had got off-planet . . .'

'But it didn't. So its secrets should still be intact. If we want an answer to the nanotech plague, Zero Zero is the only place we might hope to find one.'

'Are you volunteering to go there, Sir Random?'

'Hell, no. I'm not crazy. But I can think of one brave, honourable and very dutiful captain who might just be insane enough to do it.'

'Of course,' said Gutman, 'the good Captain Silence. Currently on his way to the Darkvoid. He shouldn't be too upset by a chance to put that off by stopping somewhere else first. And the good captain has always been a most . . . dutiful man.'

'Not to mention expendable,' said Random.

'Best not to,' agreed Gutman. He looked out at his audience, who by now were hanging on his every word. 'Just to reassure everyone that the best scientific minds in the Empire haven't been entirely idle concerning this matter, I can also tell you that they have established contact with a small scientific group on Wolf IV, a hellworld right out on the edge of the Rim. The hellsquad assigned to investigate this new world apparently discovered an ancient race of shape-changing aliens, whose nature might also be based around nanotech. Always best to have more than one iron in the fire . . . Now, let us move on to the next item on the agenda.'

'You mean that bit of paper in your hand, covered in your usual indecipherable scrawl?' said Random. 'Since when did you start deciding the House's agenda?'

'Ever since things got so busy around here that the House didn't have time,' said Gutman tartly. 'There is a war on, you know. Several wars, to be exact. We haven't all been hiding out on backwater planets.'

'Hiding out?' said Ruby dangerously.

'The next item,' said Gutman, 'concerns the dragon's

teeth: people who supposedly lost their minds in the computer Matrix, and now have only Shub's thoughts in their heads. An army of Shub spies, walking undetected among us.'

'There's no supposed about it,' said Random.

'There's been no actual evidence to support the theory yet.'

'Only because you won't allow the espers to run random tests on the population,' said Ruby, just to show she was keeping up with the argument.

'Would you let an esper scan your mind?' said Gutman.

Ruby shrugged. 'Wouldn't bother me. Of course, how they coped with what they found there would be their problem. My head's a weird place these days.'

'It always was,' said Random generously.

Ruby gave him a hard look. 'Guess who's sleeping on the couch tonight?'

'Esper scans are vital,' said a new, harsh voice, and everyone turned to look. Most of them then wished they hadn't, as Diana Vertue strode through the packed House, the crowd parting to open up a narrow aisle for her. It had been a while since the short, scowling blonde had gone by the name Jenny Psycho, but enough of her old malevolent persona still crackled about her to repel even the most tightly packed crowd. No one wanted to get too close to a human time bomb. She came to a halt beside Random, gave him a quick nod and then glared up at Gutman, who looked uneasy for the first time. Diana gave him her best unnerving smile.

'Listen to me, fat man; it's essential this House authorizes the mass screening of the population by the esper fraternity, right damn now. There are too many people walking about who probably aren't people any more. We're talking dragon's teeth, Ghost Warriors, Furies, and maybe even shape-changing aliens. Remember that crazy thing we discovered masquerading as human in Lionstone's Court? Just because we haven't heard from it since doesn't mean it isn't still out there somewhere, plotting mischief. Shub has remote-control teleporting. It could have planted any number of disguised agents here on the homeworld. And the only sure way we have of rooting them out is mind-scanning. Set up booths in every city, and require people to walk past them twice a day. Computer records will spot anyone who tries to dodge. Of course, all private and public esp-blockers will have to be destroyed.'

'Oh, of course,' said Gutman, 'and that's what this is really all about. You want all esp-blockers to be destroyed because they're the only defence normal people have against esper invasion of their thoughts.'

'We want esp-blockers destroyed to free the living brains that power them,' said Diana.

'And so you espers can peep inside all our heads, see our personal thoughts and secrets. That kind of knowledge would give you one hell of a hold over the rest of us, wouldn't it?'

'We wouldn't need to invade anyone's privacy. We just want to detect non-human thoughts.'

'We only have your word for that, esper. Information is currency right now. And we all have secrets we'd rather die than share.'

Behind her, Diana Vertue heard the general murmur of agreement among the onlookers. She shrugged angrily. 'We'll discuss this again, when everyone's feeling a little more rational.'

'Be a long wait,' said Random.

'Moving on,' said Gutman, firmly, 'we come to a rather delicate issue. We have touched on this briefly already, but I must now insist that we discuss the matter in some depth. This House has refrained from touching on it until some of the Maze people returned, because you are the only people with direct knowledge of the subject. But the situation is becoming increasingly pressing.'

Ruby looked at Random. 'What the hell is he talking about?'

'The end of everything,' said Random. 'He's talking about the Darkvoid Device.'

It was suddenly very quiet again in the House. Everyone was looking at Random and Ruby. Random could feel the pressure of their eyes on the back of his head. Even Diana Vertue was looking at him strangely.

'Things are bad now,' Random said carefully, 'and I can understand the attraction of a super-weapon that could end the war in a moment. But you'd have to be insane or on the edge of actual extinction to seriously consider letting this genie out of its bottle again. The last time the Device was activated it put out a thousand suns in a moment. Billions of people died. Who gets to die this time, that the rest of us might live? Even assuming we know how to operate the Device safely, which we don't.'

'But you know where it is,' said Gutman, leaning forward for the first time.

'Sort of,' said Ruby reluctantly. 'We know where it used to be, but there's no guarantee it's still there. And like Jack said, we don't know how to turn it on . . . or off. You want to risk destroying the whole of Humanity?'

'We're already at risk,' said Gutman.

'Hold everything,' said Random sharply. 'Is that why you're sending Silence back into the Darkvoid? Because he's the only other person who's been to the Wolfling World? Have you sent him after the Darkvoid Device?'

'Captain Silence has always understood his duty,' said Gutman.

'He doesn't know the nature of the Device,' said Random, 'or how to find it. Or how to make it work.'

'The good captain has always been very resourceful. And he did pass part-way through the Madness Maze, and survive.'

'I won't allow this,' said Random flatly. 'I didn't save the Empire from Lionstone just to see Humanity destroyed by its own stupidity.'

'There you go again, Sir Random,' said Gutman, leaning

back in his chair and lacing his fingers across his extensive stomach. 'Deciding you alone know what's best for Humanity. Parliament represents the people. We decide what is best, and what is necessary. Not an over-the-hill rebel whose best days are behind him. Who can no longer be trusted to act rationally. We all know what you did on Loki.'

'I hanged a bunch of people who needed hanging,' said Random, grinning wolfishly. 'They were all guilty, all dirty. All politicians.'

The chamber stirred uneasily at the dark venom in his voice; even Ruby Journey gave a small shudder.

'We're willing to listen to reason,' said Gutman. 'Convince us. Tell us about the Darkvoid Device. What it is, how it does what it does. Who knows; you might even bring us round to your position.'

'I can't,' said Random.

'Can't or won't?'

Random shook his head. 'Some things . . . you're better off not knowing. I'd like nothing more than to be able to cut the memory out of my mind and lose it for ever. You're all just going to have to trust me on this.'

Whatever Gutman might have said to that was lost in the blaring of alarm sirens. Everyone stared about them, thrown off balance by the sudden intrusion. The general alarm was never sounded for anything less than imminent planet-wide peril. Or worse. A loud computer-generated voice said, 'Attention! Attention! Urgent information arriving!' The great viewscreen lit up again, and a grim face stared out at the House.

'This is Captain Xhang of the *Dreadstar*, on patrol on the Rim, observing the Darkvoid. The Recreated are here. They're breaking out. We can't stop them; hell, they're smashing through us like we're not even here! I'm switching to exterior sensors, so you can see what we're seeing!'

The captain's face vanished, replaced by Humanity's first view of the Recreated. Their ships were huge and awful, given a sense of scale by the tiny specks that were the patrolling Imperial ships. The Recreated's vessels made no sense, and it hurt to look at them, as though they existed in more than three dimensions at once. Weird angles tried to drag the human eye and mind in directions they were never meant to go. The ships were bigger than mountains, and there seemed no end to their numbers as they streamed implacably out of the Darkvoid, across the Rim and into human space. The handful of Imperial ships were firing every gun they had, to no avail. They were simply ignored, like ants at the feet of conquering giants. Afterwards, no one could quite decide or agree on what shapes the Recreated vessels had taken, and whether they were tech, or living materials, or some unhallowed mixture of both. They were beyond human experience or comprehension.

Random suddenly became aware of energies spitting and crackling beside him and a strong smell of ionized air, and a quiet voice said, 'It's them. They're back.' Random looked round, and there was Half A Man, staring with his one horrified eye at the ships on the viewscreen. The aliens who had abducted him, tortured him and finally returned only half his body, bound eternally to a living energy construct for his other half. The aliens whose coming the Empire had feared for centuries; who would treat Humanity the way Humanity had always treated aliens. The great nightmare of all Humanity had finally come out of the endless night to destroy them all.

A sound came out of the viewscreen, though they shouldn't have been able to hear anything. It was like a never-ending scream, an endless howl of agony and joy and horror, at a volume no human throat could produce, going on and on and on long after human lungs would have collapsed. It was vile and horrible, a jagged, abrasive sound, almost too much to bear. People in the House put their hands over their ears, but couldn't shut it out. The few espers present were crying tears of blood. Diana Vertue was baring her teeth in a snarl that was pure Jenny Psycho. Jack Random clutched at his head as a fierce pain beat in his temples, as though his brain was trying to force its way out of his skull. Ruby Journey had her eyes squeezed shut, her mouth stretched in a cry of hate or pain or fear no one could hear. The sound from the screen grew louder, intolerably loud, the distilled essence of horror.

On the viewscreen, the Imperial ships were exploding one by one. The scene cut back to the *Dreadstar*'s bridge, and Captain Xhang. Blood was coursing down his face, from which he'd torn out his own eyes. Behind him, his maddened crew were killing each other. Xhang was trying to say something, but he couldn't be heard over the endless howl. And then the viewscreen suddenly went blank, and the awful sound was shut off. People in the packed House began cautiously to lower their hands from their ears. Many were panting heavily, struggling for breath, as though they'd been fighting some physical enemy. Some had passed out. Some of the espers were dead. The computer voice said, 'Communication from the Rim has ceased. Contact cannot be established with any of the ships. Awaiting further instructions.'

'They're back,' said Half A Man. 'The Recreated have come out of the dark to destroy us all.'

The House was quiet. No one knew what to say. The sight and sound of the alien ships had struck everyone with a cold, numbing terror. Half A Man's alien abductors had for centuries been the nightmare bogeymen of all Humanity, only really half believed in but still passed down from generation to generation as an awful warning. And now here they were. It was as though the monsters from under a child's bed had waited till the child had grown up, and then come hammering on his front door. Even Jack Random and Ruby Journey were silent, their courage and confidence stripped away by long-forgotten childhood fears. Elias Gutman stood up, and everyone turned to look at him.

'General Beckett will undoubtedly be gathering together every ship he can to face this new threat,' he said gravely. 'I'm sure this House will wish to support him in every way possible.' He looked around him, but no one said anything. Gutman scowled. 'We all knew the Recreated would make their appearance eventually. Their timing could have been better, but that's the way our luck's been going recently. So, Half A Man: you have the most experience with these . . . aliens. We will put a fast ship at your disposal immediately. I'm sure you'll wish to confer with General Beckett as soon as possible. With the two of you leading our forces against the Recreated—'

'No,' said Half A Man, 'I'm not going.'

Everyone turned to look at him. He stared impassively back with his half a human face, his energy half spitting and crackling in the quiet.

'But . . . your advice on dealing with these aliens will be invaluable,' said Gutman. 'You can do far more good with Beckett's Fleet than you can here.'

'I'm not going,' said Half A Man. 'There's no point. We can't beat them, we can't stop them, and there's nowhere we can run. They are all our nightmares made real. There's nothing I or the Fleet can do to save you. Every species has to face its own extinction eventually.'

He turned and walked away, and for a long, long time after he left the House, no one had anything to say.

Constance Wolfe and Robert Campbell were making plans for their forthcoming wedding. Or at least, Constance was. Robert had long ago given up trying to keep track of events, and now settled for standing around on the edge of the organized chaos drinking endless cups of tea, ready to offer help and advice on the few occasions when it might be required. Personally, he would have been quite happy to abdicate all authority on the matter to Constance, but she insisted his opinions mattered, and wouldn't hear of him leaving it all to her. And besides, there were the media to consider. The ceremonial wedding of the first constitutional King-and-Queen-to-be had captured the public imagination and affection, and people were desperate for continuing coverage of the wedding couple and their preparations. They wanted to see everything. And since they were, after all, paying for it, they couldn't reasonably be kept out. Robert could hardly afford to be seen as the weak half of the happy couple: he had to be right there in the thick of things, participating in every decision, if only theoretically.

Constance's suite at the top of Tower Wolfe was packed with people coming and going and coming back again, and chattering at the tops of their voices. There were endless clothes to be designed and approved and fitted, followed by equally endless alterations; flowers to be chosen and arranged; gifts to be examined and cooed over and stacked away (after being discreetly examined for bombs or other unpleasantnesses – not everyone approved of the royal wedding, for a whole variety of reasons) and the endless details of the great ceremony to be discussed and argued over at distracting length. There were courtiers and tradespeople and Family representatives from both sides, all of them buzzing around Constance like bees around a rare and precious bloom.

All Robert had was his gentleman's gentleman, the experienced and very reassuring Baxter.

With Owen Deathstalker missing presumed dead, the demand for a new constitutional King had grown suddenly very intense. The public wanted the royal wedding they'd been promised, and they wanted it soon. It was the one ray of light in an otherwise very gloomy time, and all across the Empire the people fixated on the wedding with an almost desperate determination. Candidates for Constance's new fiancé were advanced from all sides, by everyone with an ambition or an axe to grind, but Constance would have none of them. Instead, she chose Robert Campbell because she was in love with him, and he with her. Parliament went berserk, but the people ate it up with spoons. It was like a fairytale romance, with young love finally bringing together two Houses that had been at each other's throats for generations. And so the marriage was back on, the wedding ceremony was hastily redrafted here and there to allow for Campbell Family traditions instead of Deathstalker, and Robert wondered more than once just what he had let himself in for.

He'd never asked to be King, constitutional or otherwise. All he'd ever wanted was to be a captain in the Imperial Fleet, master of his own ship. But Family responsibilities had put an end to that. It seemed to Robert that most of his life he'd been forced down paths that were not of his choosing, but at least this time he had good company. He loved Constance with all his heart, and never ceased to be amazed that such a wondrous creature should love him. At first their love had been a tentative, secret, hidden thing. They'd fought against it, trying to deny the pull of their own hearts, because Constance was promised in marriage to the legendary hero Owen Deathstalker. Constance and Robert's love would have been scandalous. No one would have understood or forgiven.

When news of Owen's presumed death first arrived, Constance and Robert were quietly relieved. It solved so many problems. Neither of them really knew the man. Constance shed a few tears, she had admired Owen; but they were more for show than anything else. Robert still worried from time to time that the Deathstalker might yet turn up again, which was why he permitted the wedding arrangements to proceed at such a pace. If Owen was to pull off one of his miraculous returns, Robert wanted to be happily married and established as King well in advance. He was almost sure the Deathstalker would understand. He'd always been an honourable man.

Robert hoped very much that that was the case. Because if Owen didn't understand, if he got angry . . . Robert tried not to think about that. He'd seen the reports from Loki, of what the equally legendary Jack Random had done there. He'd seen the dead men hanging by their necks from city walls, like the strange fruit of hideous trees . . . If the honoured and much-admired professional rebel himself could turn mad, then what of a man like Owen Deathstalker, who'd already lost so much? During the day Robert found many things with which to distract himself, but sometimes he woke in the night in a cold sweat, afraid to sleep again.

He made himself concentrate on his current problems. They at least were something he could come to grips with. At that moment his servant Baxter was fussing around him, as they both studied the Campbell's new wedding outfit in the full-length mirror before them. Robert had wanted to be married in his old Fleet uniform, but that was shot down almost immediately. The new King-to-be had to be seen to be impartial to all past beliefs or influences. Instead, he was wearing formal evening clothes, formal to the point of chilly: basic black with a golden cummerbund, and as many of Robert's military decorations as could be fitted on his chest. By the end of the rebellion, the military had been handing out medals and honours like confetti, just for surviving, and Robert had got his fair share. He tried not to be too proud of them. He knew that better men than he had died without medals or honours, for being in the wrong place at the wrong time. Still, they did look awfully impressive, marching across his broad chest in multicoloured rows.

And yet . . . The high, stiff collar irritated the underside of his chin, there was barely enough room in the jacket to flex his shoulders or take a deep breath, they'd put the crease into his trousers crookedly and his shoes were a size too large, flopping on his feet like slippers. For a first fitting it wouldn't have been too bad, but unfortunately this was the sixth fitting and they still hadn't got the details right. Robert sighed heavily. He tried a few poses in front of the mirror, but they all looked like someone else. He turned almost despairingly to Baxter.

'Right, that's it. Dump the monkey suit and dig out my old captain's uniform. I am not going to appear at my own wedding looking as if I hired my suit at the last minute.'

'Perseverance is the word for today, sir,' murmured Baxter, entirely unmoved. 'We're getting closer all the time. And I thought we'd agreed not to bring up the military uniform again. As King-to-be it would give quite the wrong impression. A constitutional monarch cannot wield real power, least of all military power. You'll grow accustomed to the suit once a few more necessary changes have been made. You look very smart.'

'I look like a tailor's dummy! Clothes aren't supposed to hang this stiffly, it isn't natural. And do I have to wear this damned bat at my throat?'

'A black bow tie is expected, yes, sir. Don't worry. I'll be there to tie it for you.'

Robert sighed deeply. 'It's going to be a long, long ceremony, isn't it?'

'Undoubtedly, sir. The current programme suggests at least two hours, possibly more. Not including the formal reception afterwards. The scriptwriter's still working on your speech. The public wants its money's worth. But the lady is worth it, isn't she, sir?'

'Oh, yes,' said Robert, smiling fondly across at Constance, 'she is that.'

Elsewhere in the crowd, comfortably close to the buffet table, Toby Shreck and his cameraman Flynn were arguing quietly over whether Flynn's footage needed a voice-over from Toby, or whether they could get away with snippets of 'found' conversation from the various people involved. And if the latter, whether they'd be better off writing and rehearsing the 'found' dialogue in advance. Robert was a decent sort, but he wasn't used to being spontaneous and witty to order. And if you caught him by surprise, his language could be downright shocking. Toby put it down to his military background.

As head of Imperial News, Toby would normally have delegated coverage like this to the usual experts and professional sycophants, but Constance had personally requested his presence. Apparently she had been a big fan of his work in the rebellion. And the owners of Imperial News had been only too happy to oblige her, in return for an exclusive. Toby had protested loudly and at length when this news was broken to him, and none of it had done a blind bit of good. The wedding and coronation promised to be the social event of the year, if not the millennium, and Imperial News wanted exclusive rights so badly they were more than willing to sell Toby's soul to get it.

'This isn't news,' said Toby forcefully, and not for the first time. He leaned against the buffet table, which creaked ominously under his weight. Toby ignored it and lit up another cigar, in open defiance of Constance's strict no-smoking policy. 'Not real news. Jack Random going psycho, that's real news, but I wasn't even allowed to go and meet him at the starport.'

'Just as well,' said Flynn calmly. 'The questions you were going to ask would undoubtedly have got us both incinerated on the spot. They say Random's got a really short fuse these days. And Ruby Journey always was—'

'A complete bloody psychopath.'

'Quite. Personally, I like it here. Makes a nice change from the kinds of things we normally cover. At least here no one's shooting at us.'

'So far,' said Toby darkly. 'There're a lot of people out there who don't want this wedding to go ahead. You saw the security set-up around here. The last time I saw that many armed guards in one place there was a rebel army fighting them. I miss those days, Flynn. You knew where you were, then.'

'Yeah,' said Flynn, 'right on the firing line. Personally, I don't miss those days at all. This is much more my speed. Civilized settings, finger food in all directions and more pretty dresses in one place than I ever dreamed of. Do you think Constance might let me try on a few in private, if I asked her ever so nicely?'

'Don't even think about it,' said Toby sternly. 'Constance might go along with it, but I have a feeling Robert is probably more strait-laced about these things. Besides, you and she aren't even remotely the same size, and if you stretch or tear anything, they'll probably make us pay for it. And you can bet one of those frilly numbers costs more than you and I make in a year. Well, you anyway. If you're really good, I'll ask if you can be a bridesmaid.' He glanced around him. 'This isn't news. This is cheerful propaganda, to take everyone's mind off how badly the war's going. I hear they're running the Arenas twenty-four hours a day now to help keep the people distracted. Blood and circuses, and royal weddings. Give the people what they want. I may puke.'

'There's a rejected top hat to your right,' said Flynn. 'Try not to miss. The carpet's expensive.'

'Hold everything,' said Toby. 'Turn your camera on quietly. I think we're about to capture the happy couple's first real row.'

Robert had wandered away from his mirror in search of some distracting conversation with Constance, and had walked right into their first real disagreement. Constance was, and always had been, a major fan of the Arenas. The Wolfes had their own private box, right next to the sands, so they could be sure of seeing all the blood and suffering and death in close-up. Constance never missed a major match, and cheered or booed lustily as the mood took her. She knew all the great players by name and history, and could quote statistics with the cheerful zeal of the dedicated fanatic. She'd had a great crush on the Masked Gladiator as a teenager, and sent him scented fan letters. She adored it when the kill happened right in front of her.

Robert thought the Arenas were barbaric, appealed to all that was base in Humanity and should be banned on moral grounds.

Normally they dealt with this divergence of opinion by agreeing not to discuss it, but now Constance was talking about missing a vital wedding rehearsal in order to watch two of her favourites fight to the death, and Robert was having none of it. Coldly reasonable tones quickly escalated to raised and heated voices, and everyone else went very quiet and retreated to the sidelines in case the happy couple started throwing things.

'You don't tell me what I can and can't do!' snapped Constance, her eyes blazing fiercely. 'And I don't take kindly to having my favourite pastime described as cruel and inhuman!'

'I saw too many good men and women die in the war!' said Robert, clearly trying to hold on to his temper. 'There's no sport or amusement in human suffering and death. There's just blood and waste and the loss of good fighters. If they're that keen to do battle, let them join the armed services, and go out and fight our real enemies! There're enough of them. And allow me to point out that for all your keenness on the sport, I don't see you volunteering to strap on a sword and fight in the Arena yourself.'

'Of course not! That's what makes gladiators such heroes. They fight for us, for the crowd, putting their lives and reputations on the line in search of honour and fame and the adulation of the people.'

'That's just a small percentage of psychopaths and death-wish merchants. The vast majority of fresh meat in the Arenas are fighting for money, for a chance to get out of grinding poverty or dead-end jobs. For a chance to be somebody, a celebrity – even though most of them die first time out. I saw enough death in the war. There's no honour or glory in it. Needless death is an abomination.'

'I see,' said Constance coldly. 'And what does that make me?'

'Misguided,' said Robert, but only after a pause that lasted just a fraction too long. They glared into each other's faces, eyes locked, neither willing to back down. Toby was holding his breath and praying quietly that Flynn's camera was getting it all. The tension in the suite was thick enough to cut, and there was no telling what might have happened next if the door hadn't suddenly burst open and a representative from Parliament came rushing in. Both Robert and Constance turned to glare at him, and he hesitated as he became aware of the strained silence, before hurrying forward to present Robert with a communication, sealed in wax with

Parliament's own seal. Robert frowned at it, then broke the seal and read the message while Constance stood fuming silently beside him. Robert's face drained of emotion as he read, and when he'd finished he slowly lowered the message and stood staring at nothing for a long moment. Finally he looked up and nodded to the representative.

'I'll join you in a moment. Wait outside.'

Constance waited till the door had closed behind the departing representative and then exploded again. 'Don't you dare walk out on me, just when I'm winning the argument! What could possibly be so important—'

'I have to go,' said Robert. 'I love you, Constance.'

He leaned forward and murmured a few words in her ear. No one else could hear them, but they could all see the colour leave Constance's face. She clutched at his arms desperately, as though to stop him from going. He kissed her on the forehead, gently disengaged himself from her hands and hurried off after the messenger. The door closed quietly behind him. Constance looked uncertainly about her, and then spotted Flynn's camera hovering nearby. She glared at Toby, and marched over to confront him.

'Tell me that thing hasn't been broadcasting live – if you want to keep your head in the vicinity of your shoulders.'

'Live coverage was expressly forbidden by our contract,' said Toby sourly. 'We're just recording. Perhaps you'd care to make a few comments for our vast watching audience . . .'

'No, I bloody wouldn't. Now get that camera down here and unload the tape.'

'You've got to be kidding,' said Toby. 'This is the first really interesting footage I've got. I'm not giving it up. It makes you both look very human.'

'Give me the tape or you'll be doing your next piece to camera with a big gap where your front teeth used to be.'

Toby thought about it. She was a Wolfe, after all. He sighed. 'I wasn't in this much danger during the rebellion. Couldn't we discuss this—'

'The tape. Now. Or else.'

Given the mood Constance was in, Toby decided not to enquire what the 'or else' might involve, and nodded to Flynn. The cameraman retrieved his camera, removed the tape and silently handed it over. Constance weighed the tape in her hand and then dropped it into the nearest waste disposal. She glared about her.

'Don't you all have some work you should be getting on with?'

Everyone immediately set about looking busy, and a buzz of hushed conversation filled the suite. Constance stalked back to her dress fitting, staring into the mirror before her, lost in her own thoughts. Flynn fitted a new tape into his camera and nodded surreptitiously to Toby.

'Don't sweat it, boss. This new model has a back-up storage system. It automatically retains the last few minutes of any tape, in case of snarl-ups. And I think I got something interesting. The last thing Robert said to Constance.'

'Run it,' said Toby quietly. 'And play it back through our comm implants on a secure channel. I don't want anyone else picking this up.'

Flynn nodded, and made the connection. The camera's view filled their eyes as it zoomed in on Robert and Constance's faces, and the microphone boosted Robert's last words to clear audibility.

'The Recreated have come.'

Flynn stopped the tape and broke the connection, and then he and Toby looked at each other.

'Shit,' said Toby quietly. 'Flynn; we're leaving. This isn't a story any more. And I think we're going to be needed elsewhere pretty damned soon. If Robert's right, I think the shit just hit the fan for the whole human race.'

Before Robert Campbell could set out on his way to Parliament for an in-depth briefing, he was waylaid by one of his least favourite acquaintances, Cardinal Brendan. With BB Chojiro dead and gone, the cardinal had taken her place as the pleasant public face of Clan Chojiro. He smiled a lot, spoke in simple, homely terms and quietly brokered important deals and meetings behind the scenes between people who wouldn't normally have agreed to share the same room together. The cardinal had a lot of pull these days. So when he insisted that what he had to say was vitally important, Robert had no choice but to listen.

He allowed the cardinal to steer him into a nearby empty room, and waited more or less patiently while Brendan set up some powerful security seals, to be sure they wouldn't be interrupted. The cardinal wasn't much to look at, even in his impressive Church robes, but Robert studied him closely anyway. The cardinal was tall and thin, with an entirely forgettable face, as long as you overlooked the eyes. They were dark and fiercely intelligent and missed nothing. They were the eyes of a man who thought deeply, and probably about subjects most people would prefer to avoid. Robert scowled, and wondered what the hell Clan Chojiro wanted with him now, and why it couldn't wait. He couldn't think of a single thing he knew or was likely to know that would make him worthy of the cardinal's attention.

'All finished,' said Brendan, smiling pleasantly. 'Just making sure we won't be bothered or overheard.'

'What do you want, Cardinal?' said Robert. 'I'm needed at Parliament. All hell's breaking loose, in case you hadn't heard.'

'People are dealing with it, I'm sure,' said the cardinal. 'Parliament is responsible for the present. My people are more concerned with the future. We're planning it, step by step. Parliament follows where we lead.'

'Your people? The Chojiros?'

'No, Robert; Blue Block.'

The Campbell nodded slowly. 'I should have seen that one coming. So; what does the Empire's most secret secret society want with me?'

'Simply to remind you of your roots. As a young man, you were inducted into Blue Block . . .'

'Oh, please! I was only there a few weeks, before my Family

took me away again. I was never initiated into any of the mysteries. I was never really a part of Blue Block at all. I owe you and them absolutely nothing.'

Brendan smiled easily. 'Once in, never out. You will always be one of us, till the day you die. The ties that bind are real and potent, even if you don't remember them.'

'There are no ties,' said Robert flatly. 'I've heard about the indoctrination, the controls you put in people's minds. The Black College. The Red Church. But I got out before any of that shit started. You have no power over me, and I have no loyalty to Blue Block.'

'But you do remember things. Not one man in a million knows about the Black College or the Red Church. Or the Hundred Hands. You know these things because we placed them in your mind. We put other things in there, too; for future use.'

Robert grabbed a handful of the cardinal's robe and pulled him forward till they were face to face, Robert's hot eyes glaring into the cardinal's unyielding stare. 'What are you talking about, Brendan? Are you threatening me? By God, if you threaten me or Constance, you'll leave this room a dead man!'

'Let go of me, Campbell,' said the cardinal. 'I know things you need to know. Before it's too late.'

He waited patiently while Robert controlled his temper and finally released his grip. The cardinal brushed fussily at the front of his robe, flattening out the crumpled material. 'You must learn to control yourself, Campbell. It's one of the first things we teach at the Black College. Along with patience, and the ability to take the long view. Minds are weapons, you see, if properly trained and motivated. And pointed in the right direction. And our weapons are everywhere. Certain people who enter Blue Block undergo extensive psychological conditioning. We change the way they think, prime them to live and die for Blue Block, alter their consciousness and morality to suit our needs and then we make them forget it all. We call these people the Hundred

Hands. One hundred of the finest young men and women, from each of the Families, sent out to be our hidden weapons, our hands to strike in the night, unknown and unsuspected. Not knowing what they are, till the correct code words awaken them from the dream they think is their life. People just like you, Robert Campbell.'

Robert could feel cold sweat beading on his face. His stomach was so tense it ached, as though expecting a blow. 'Are you saying . . . that I'm one of the Hundred Hands?'

'Oh, yes. You're primed and ready to kill, your conditioning firmly in place, even after all this time. All you need is a name, a location and the right activation words. Which I have. Of course, I might not need to use them. If you could see your way clear to being . . . reasonable.'

'This is all bullshit!'

Brendan leaned forward. 'We all come home.'

Robert Campbell's face shut down. All the emotion and character slipped out of his features, and his gaze was fixed and unblinking. When he spoke, his voice was calm and neutral. 'Activation code acknowledged. Request status confirmation.'

'Status neutral. Reset.'

Robert Campbell was suddenly back again. His breathing came harsh and hurried, and he hugged himself tightly as though trying to keep from falling apart. For a moment everything that was himself had been pushed aside, confined to some small back corner of his mind, while someone or something else looked out of his eyes and spoke with his voice. That other person had been a cold and unflinching thing of duty and obedience, and Robert had no doubt it would have used his body to kill anyone at all, while he watched from far away, helpless to interfere.

'You bastard,' he said thickly. 'What have you done to me?'

'Not me,' said Cardinal Brendan. 'Blue Block. During your short time in the Black College, they used certain unique principles of tech and esp to create a secondary persona within you, utterly obedient to Blue Block's will, and then made you forget it ever happened. Just as well; from what I understand, it's a rather unpleasant experience. One of the Hundred Hands lives within you, Robert, never more than a code phrase away from being activated and set loose. Of course, that need never happen. Under certain conditions.'

'What do you want?'

'Use your influence to persuade Constance away from her current opposition to the Families in general, and Clan Chojiro in particular. Convince her to accept a purely ceremonial role as Queen, and avoid all real politics.'

'She'll never agree to that.'

'You'd better make sure she does, Campbell. Because if you can't neuter her, she'll have to die. We couldn't allow someone of her power and influence to continue in her stand against the Families and Blue Block. We'd have to have her killed. Or, more exactly, we'd have you kill her.' Cardinal Brendan smiled at the distraught look on Robert's face. 'I see you understand the realities of your position. Consider my words carefully. Be reasonable, and persuasive, and you and your beautiful intended can have a long and happy life together. Persist in being our enemy, and she shall die. Just like your last bride-to-be. Goodbye, Robert. I've enjoyed our little chat. We must do this again sometime.'

He deactivated his security seals and left the room, closing the door quietly behind him. Robert didn't know what to say or do. How do you fight an enemy that lives inside your own head? Your own hands? He clenched his hands into fists, but that wasn't enough to stop them trembling. He'd already lost one love at a wedding, and the thought of losing another terrified him beyond hope or sanity.

Toby Shreck and his cameraman Flynn looked slowly round at the shattered remains of his office at Imperial News. All the walls had been bowed outwards by the force of the bomb's explosion, and every piece of furniture in the office had been reduced to charred kindling. Some of it was sticking out of the walls. There was a small blackened hole in the middle of the floor, where the actual device had detonated, and there was blast and fire and smoke damage everywhere. The single steelglass window was still in one piece, letting sunshine stream over a scene of utter devastation. Extractor fans worked loudly as they struggled to remove the last of the smoke from the air. Toby made his way cautiously across what was left of his office, and sadly stirred the remains of his precious executive desk with his boot.

'Parcel bomb,' he said flatly. 'Building security catches most of them, but this one must have been really sophisticated. Obviously I'm attracting a more sophisticated class of critic these days.'

'Right,' said Flynn. 'This is what, the fourth explosion so far? And the fourth office. I hear your secretary is demanding danger money just to make the tea.'

Toby winced. 'Let's not talk about the formidable Miss Kale. She's efficient, professional and tough-minded, and she scares the crap out of me. I miss my old secretary, Miss Lovett. Good-looking, always a smile and not a brain cell in her head.'

'Yeah,' said Flynn. 'Pity all that turned out to be a cover, and she was really a terrorist agent. She did a great job of smuggling in that first bomb as one of her falsies. I always thought she was too dumb to be true. Never trust someone whose lipstick and blusher don't match, it's a sure sign of diverging loyalties. Did security ever find out exactly who she was working for?'

'Not so far,' said Toby. 'Apparently, after she disappeared, the building was inundated with people calling in to claim responsibility. Lot of people out there don't like me, Flynn. One of the few signs that I'm doing a good job.'

'Know a man by the enemies he makes,' said Flynn solemnly.

'Damn right,' said Toby, cheering up a little. 'In a way, a bombing is a sign of approval. If they're trying to kill me, I must be getting really close to whatever it is they're trying to hide.'

'If you've quite finished gloating, perhaps I could go home now,' said Flynn. 'It's been so long since we had some quality time together, that Clarence is beginning to suspect I'm having an affair. He's put up a poster in our kitchen with a photo of me, and the slogan *Have You Seen This Man?* I could use some down time. Curl up on the sofa with my sweetie, in a nice little cocktail dress and pearls.'

'Flynn, you're telling me more about your home life than I really need to know. Go on, get out of here. Constance won't want us to do any more filming until she and Robert have patched up their spat and are ready to hold hands in public again. And given how stubborn both of them are, that could take some time. Security have set up yet another office for me, so at least I can get some editing done. I'll call you if I need you.'

Flynn looked at him. 'You know, it wouldn't do you any harm to take a break too, boss. All work and no play makes Jack a dull boy and a real contender in the heart-attack-before-fifty stakes. Why don't you give Clarissa a ring? Better still, pop round to your auntie Grace's with a bunch of flowers and a winning smile, and see if your luck's in. You know you're sweet on her.'

Toby frowned. 'Aunt Grace has made it clear I'm *persona non grata* at her house as long as I'm still covering politics. She thinks that as a Shreck I should be using my position to support the Families in general and the Shrecks in particular. I have to sneak calls to Clarissa when I can. And besides, I've been collating info on this new nanoplague, and I think I might just be on to something. You nip off home, Flynn. See you tomorrow.'

Flynn gave up, nodded goodbye and left. Toby gave the remains of his office one last look, shrugged and went off in search of whatever tiny cubicle security had found for him this time. It turned out to be a cramped room at the far end of the annexe, which from its general atmosphere had probably been used for storing cleaning equipment. There was a strong smell of something not entirely unlike pine. The room was well away from everywhere, on the grounds that nobody wanted Toby anywhere near them, just in case. Even his secretary would only talk to him over the intercom. Toby made his way through the gorgeously appointed corridors of Imperial News, carrying armloads of equipment and nodding to people he passed. He tried not to notice how they all gave him plenty of room.

By the time he'd finished cramming editing equipment into the cupboard-sized room, there was only just enough space left for Toby and his swivel chair. He sighed, and resigned himself to slumming it for a while. Luckily, he'd brought along a few of life's little necessities. He laid them out carefully around him: a bottle of the very best whisky, a box of the finest chocolates and a dozen cigars with illegally high nicotine levels, hand-rolled on the luscious thighs of barely legal women. And two or three phials of assorted uppers and downers and the occasional sideways bomber. Tools of the trade.

Toby had been quietly gathering information on the spreading nanoplague for some time. It wasn't easy. The moment the plague was detected, a full Quarantine was imposed on the entire planet, and all further information was on a need-to-know basis. Which meant the bribes Toby had to pay were even higher than usual. At first the outbreaks appeared to have nothing in common, but Toby was convinced there had to be a pattern in there somewhere, perhaps even a trail that could be traced back to the initial (as yet unproved) outbreak. It had to have started somewhere, with someone. And no one was better than Toby Shreck when it came to putting two and two together and making seven. He kicked his computer terminal awake, and accessed the data he'd been compiling over the last few months. If anybody knew anything, or even suspected anything about the nano-outbreaks, he was sure he had it here somewhere, only a few keystrokes away. He took a good gulp of whisky, used a second mouthful to wash down a couple of uppers, lit a cigar and stuck it in the corner of his mouth. The combined jolt hit his system like a wake-up call from God, and he dived into the info like a bloodhound hunting rats.

He plunged recklessly through the infostream, kicking his way through endlessly detailed reports, sifting out the nuggets of gold in the mountains of dross, guided by instinct and years of experience. Patterns configured and flew apart as he tested them on the anvil of his logic, puffing at his cigar, his eyes darting from screen to screen around him. More whisky, a few more pills and whatever chocolates came first to hand . . . He was flying now, his thoughts darting faster than his fingers could call up the info. Minutes became hours, and he didn't notice, jazzed to breaking point and hurtling from theory to theory like a pinball with a flare up its ass.

There had to be a carrier. A single carrier, taking the nanoplague from one outbreak to another, unknown, undetected. Which, given the current level of war-status security on every planet these days, should have been impossible. Maybe the carrier was a Typhoid Mary, not actually ill themselves, but still contagious . . . No, even then security should have spotted something at the various starports. Unless the carrier had some way of circumventing starport security . . . More whisky, to wash down more chocolates. Light up another cigar and chew on the end. Get up and walk around and kick the furnishings, thinking, thinking. Back at the terminals, his fingertips ached from pounding the keys. OK. Nanoplague. Last known nano-outbreak in the Empire was long ago, on Zero Zero. Quarantine there still unbroken. Look at the chronological order of the new outbreaks. Seven planets, widely spaced across the Empire, going down with the plague only days apart. No way one carrier could have travelled between them that quickly. Dead end.

But . . . what if that was the trail? Ignore the travel time, put the outbreaks in chronological order and you get a clear picture of the nanoplague hopping its way from world to world, starting at the Rim and heading inwards. Heading towards . . . Golgotha? Homeworld? And which current Enemy of Humanity had recently been proved to possess teleportation? Shub. The rogue AIs of Shub! They could drop their carrier on to a planet, bypassing the starports and local security completely, and then teleport him off-world once his infectious job had been done . . .

Toby sat back in his chair, breathing hard, cold sweat on his face, suddenly very sober indeed despite the various substances racing through his bloodstream. The nanoplague was a Shub weapon – had to be. And everyone else was so preoccupied with the more obvious threats, like Furies and Ghost Warriors and Grendels and the bloody Hadenmen, that they'd never noticed the real threat, the silent killer in their midst. That could come and go unseen, unnoticed, killing off a planet at a time. Toby chewed on his lower lip, his thoughts flying furiously. He couldn't just broadcast this on the main evening news; there'd be mass panic. Paranoia. Rioting in the streets. And he'd end up watching it all on the communal holo set in whatever prison they finally locked him up in, for starting it all. But he couldn't just sit on this. The people had a right to know the danger they were facing . . . He was still struggling with that one when the door burst open to reveal a breathless Flynn.

'Toby! Why the hell did you turn your pager off? Everybody in Imperial News has been trying to contact you, and security couldn't remember where they'd put you!'

'Just as well, I didn't want to be disturbed. I've been thinking. And what are you doing here? I thought you were safe at home, snuggling with Clarence?'

'I was. They called me back because I was the only one who might know where to find you!'

'All right, calm down, I'm sure Clarence will keep it warm for you. Now, what's so important?'

'Jack Random's announced that he has something Very Important to say. He's going to make a speech at his place, in the Parliament building. He's invited every mover and shaker there is, and says he plans to talk about what happened on Loki, the state of the Empire today and what he intends to do about it. He made it sound like the most important speech he'll ever make. Imperial News wants us there right now.'

'Why us?' said Toby. 'There are any number of reporters who could cover it.'

'Random invited us personally,' said Flynn. 'Said we wouldn't want to miss this for anything.'

'How long have we got?' asked Toby, lurching to his feet.

'Maybe half an hour. I've got a flyer waiting downstairs, ready to go. Practically everyone Random invited is going to be there. Politicians, Families, everyone. This is going to be really big, Toby; I can feel it in my water.'

'Well try to hold on to your water till we get there. Jack Random is just the person I need to talk to. I've come across something big of my own, and he might be the only person who'll know what to do for the best. Move it, Flynn. I've a nasty feeling time is running out for all of us.'

Cardinal Brendan looked around Kit SummerIsle's hotel room and tried not to let his lip curl too obviously. The SummerIsle had only been living there a week or two, but the place was already a tip. Though given the hotel's location, in one of the decidedly scummier parts of the city, presumably the room hadn't had too far to go. The furnishings were basic, the colour scheme was frankly depressing and the single window was sealed shut to prevent the occupant doing a midnight flit to avoid paying the bill. Or possibly to prevent suicides. There were discarded dirty plates and half-finished meals everywhere, along with a number of empty bottles and glasses. And judging by the appalling state of the carpet, there had undoubtedly been a number of spills of various kinds along the way. The bed the SummerIsle was lying on looked as if it hadn't been made since he moved in, and his swordbelt and holster hung openly on the headboard, ready for use at a moment's notice. The door Brendan had just closed behind him was pitted with splintered holes, where the SummerIsle had been practising with his throwing-knives.

There was an old, dried bloodstain on the carpet by the door. Perhaps someone had been foolish enough to complain about the noise.

Brendan pulled up a chair, brushed it clean with a fastidious hand and sat down facing the SummerIsle. He arranged his robes about him just so, and smiled brightly, concentrating on appearing perfectly calm and at ease. It was always important not to let Kid Death feel he had the upper hand, just because he was a cold, intimidating son-of-a-bitch. Even though Brendan did feel like he'd just entered a lion's cage without his whip and chair.

'So,' he said coolly, 'may I take it the extended wake for David Deathstalker is now over, and you're ready to do some serious work for us?'

'I'm always ready for a little serious work,' said Kit SummerIsle, ignoring the cardinal to stare at the ceiling above him. 'As long as it involves killing someone. And yes, the wake is over. It was important to give David a good send-off. He wanted so little, and was allowed none of it. Don't get too comfortable sitting there, Cardinal. You were a part of the forces that brought him down.'

The cardinal spread his hands. 'Just business, I assure you. Nothing personal.'

'He was my friend.'

The SummerIsle's eyes were dark and far away. Brendan knew most of the details of Kid Death's wake. A lot of it had made the evening news, as he drank and brawled his way through an endless series of bars and drinking clubs, leaving a trail of destruction and excess through the more squalid parts of the city. No one had tried to stop him, or arrest him, or even ask him to pay any of his bills. This was Kid Death, after all: the smiling assassin. Attracted by the prospect of free booze, there was never any shortage of people willing to drink and carouse with him, and if some of them said the wrong thing and ended up spitted on the SummerIsle's blade, well, none of them were the kind of people who would be missed.

'Is the hotel to your satisfaction?' said Brendan. 'We could supply more . . . comfortable quarters, if you wish.'

'I like it fine here. The room service is first-rate, since I killed a couple of the waiters for being slow. I have my privacy, and no one bothers me. I've always liked hotels. People at your beck and call, and never far from the next meal. All the comforts of home without the bother of having to maintain it. I never did give a damn about the responsibilities of maintaining Tower SummerIsle. Cheerless bloody place; I sold it the moment I inherited it. Bit hard on the next generation of SummerIsles, I suppose, but then what did they ever do for me? I didn't even like the previous generation. That's why I killed them all. What's left of my Clan is pretty much dispersed these days. The name will probably die with me. Good to know I've achieved something worthwhile.' He looked directly at Brendan for the first time, and the cardinal had to fight hard not to look away or flinch back in his chair. The SummerIsle smiled knowingly. 'The wake is over; time to get back to work. I am a killer, and must go where the killing is. Many people have made themselves known to me, bidding for my services with all kinds of coin, but it seems to me that Clan Chojiro offers the most opportunities for me to employ my unique skills. I interrupted my wake to do you that small service on Loki; I trust you found my work there satisfactory?'

'Of course,' said Brendan. 'You were everything we expected.'

'So; who do you want me to kill now?'

'The Maze people are becoming a major concern,' said Brendan carefully. 'It may become necessary to remove them from the body politic. How would you feel about that?'

The SummerIsle stretched slowly, sensuously, as unselfconscious as a cat. 'A challenge, a real challenge. I would enjoy killing Jack Random and Ruby Journey. Their powers are impressive, their reputations even more so, but in the end they're just warriors, while I am an assassin. They don't live for the kill like I do. I do hope Owen and Hazel aren't dead; I always wanted a crack at Owen. I killed his father, you know. So I could be said to have started him on the path that made him what he is. Owen Deathstalker would be one hell of a challenge, a real test of my abilities. I put off squaring up to him while David was alive. Dear David secretly admired his cousin, and wanted to be just like him. That was part of what got him killed on Virimonde, trying to be the hero like his cousin Owen. I should enjoy gutting the legendary Deathstalker, and watching him crawl in his own blood before me.'

'We'll worry about him as and when he turns up again,' said Brendan. 'Clan Chojiro has more immediate concerns. Namely, Constance Wolfe and Robert Campbell. Robert has undergone Blue Block initiation, and we hope to control the happy couple through him. But it is just possible he could break or subvert his conditioning, and if that happened, and he and Constance became . . . impediments, it might be necessary for you to deal with them. You would not be able to take public credit for the killings, and they would have to be sufficiently bloody and unpleasant to discourage those who would take their place from being equally obstructive. How would you feel about that?'

'I've never killed a King or Queen,' said Kit SummerIsle, almost lazily. 'I came close with Lionstone, but she escaped me. I think I'm going to enjoy working with Clan Chojiro. You're almost as unscrupulous as I am. And of course, in working for you I also work with Blue Block. Correct?' He smiled as the cardinal stirred uneasily, and fixed him with his icy blue eyes for a long moment. 'I never went through Blue Block; my Family didn't trust them. What was it like, Brendan?'

'Trust me; you don't want to know. It would give you nightmares.'

'I don't have nightmares,' said Kid Death, 'I give them.'

*

Jack Random agreed to give Toby and Flynn a short private interview before the big meeting. He didn't say why, and Toby didn't feel like asking. Real exclusives with Jack Random were as rare as hen's teeth even at the best of times, and after his return from Loki he'd refused to speak to the media at all. He'd even taken a few shots at the paparazzi that dogged his every public appearance, but there was nothing new in that. Ruby did it all the time.

Random met with Toby and Flynn in a small side chamber with absolutely no fittings and furnishings. Toby was honestly baffled as to what function the room usually served. He'd heard that Random preferred to live in spartan surroundings, but there weren't even any chairs to sit on, and they had to do the whole interview standing up. Ruby Journey stood leaning against a wall, arms folded, glowering silently. It had quickly become clear that she didn't know why Random had called his big meeting either, and was hoping to gain some clue from the interview. Toby checked with Flynn that all was well with the camera and lighting, did a few words for sound and then turned to face Jack Random.

'So,' he said brightly, 'who exactly have you invited to this special audience, Sir Random?'

'Everybody who is anybody, and a few who are anybody's, politically speaking. All the movers and shakers, the powers that be, and some who think they ought to be. What happens at this meeting will change the shape of Imperial politics for ever, and I didn't want anyone to miss out. Not everybody saw fit to accept my invitation, but I'll get round to them eventually too. As it is, more than enough are here to make this meeting worthwhile. There are Members of Parliament, representatives from the clone and esper undergrounds and from most of the Families: all the people who help to make the Empire what it is today. I may not be the force I once was, but after Loki it appears everyone wants to hear what I have to say.'

'About Loki . . .' said Toby.

'I regret nothing. I did what was necessary to put an end to political corruption.'

'And would that be the subject of your speech here today?'

'You could say that. I have returned to Golgotha to clean up; to deal with all those who sold out what we gained through the rebellion. I learned a valuable lesson on Loki. No more deals, no more compromises. I am back, and God help the guilty.'

For once, Toby actually found himself at a loss for words. It wasn't so much what Random was saying, as the way he said it. Toby had seen the legendary professional rebel in many places and in many moods, but never quite as he seemed now. Random's smile was wide and cheerful, but his unblinking gaze was cold and almost threatening. There was suppressed anger in the man's body language, only just short of imminent rage. His face glowed with purpose and resolve. He looked not unlike an Old Testament prophet who'd gone up the mountain for a personal chat with God, and come down again with a whole bunch of truths and answers he hadn't expected. Whatever epiphany Jack Random had undergone on Loki, it might have filled him with new energy and purpose but it sure as hell didn't seem to have done much for his peace of mind. And from some of the looks Ruby Journey was shooting Random's way when she thought he wasn't looking, it was clear she didn't know quite what to make of his new self either. Toby just hoped Flynn was getting it all on film.

'Not everyone approves of what happened on Loki,' said Toby, very carefully. 'Some have gone as far as to label your . . . actions as atrocities.'

'They weren't there,' said Random. 'They didn't see what I saw. The people of Vidar were betrayed by those placed in power over them. Men given those positions by people in power here, even though they were all convicted war criminals. I've spent my whole life fighting evil and political corruption, and helped throw down a whole way of life to get rid of it. Only to find it had crept back while I was distracted by deals and compromises and all the petty day-to-day betrayals of a life in politics. It's clear to me now that it wasn't just Lionstone who made the Empire what it was; it was the whole political system. Politicians are the enemy, and the big institutions that support them. The Families, and all the lesser men they own and instruct. If there's ever to be any justice, they must all be brought down. All of them.' Random stopped, took a deep breath and let it out slowly. 'I must become pure again, pure in spirit and purpose. And nothing and no one will be allowed to stand in my way.'

Toby's mouth was getting dry, but he pressed on. 'You made the original deal with the Families that ensured their survival, in return for their conditional surrender. Are you now saying you regret that?'

'It was the worst mistake I ever made. Never trust the Families, not while they all bow down to Blue Block. When I allowed the Clans to survive, I betrayed anyone who ever fought for my cause. And I betrayed myself. But I've said enough for now: the meeting's about to start. Why don't you and Flynn go in and circulate, while I have a quiet word with Ruby? If I make her wait any longer to speak to me, she might well spontaneously combust from sheer frustration.'

Toby smiled politely, nodded to Flynn, and the two of them moved through into the great hall next door, where the assembled crowd was waiting. Toby would have liked very much to eavesdrop on what Random and Ruby were about to say, but if the bounty hunter was about to get violent, Toby didn't want to be anywhere near her. Hell, he didn't even want to be in the same building. He threw open the heavy door and there was a sudden roar of sound, as a hundred conversations rushed over him. It shut off abruptly as Toby shut the door after himself and Flynn, and then it was very quiet in the small room as Random and Ruby stared at each other.

'Don't do this, Jack,' said Ruby. 'I'm telling you; don't do this.'

'I have to. I can't let things go on as they are. What's

happened since the rebellion has made a mockery of everything I ever believed in and fought for. If I won't fight for what I believe in, why should anyone else? What's about to happen in the hall next door will be a wake-up call for all Humanity.'

'We're in the middle of a war!'

'We always are, Ruby. That's what those in power have always used to justify keeping the lower orders in their place. No more.'

'If you go in there and denounce everyone in power, you do it on your own, Jack. I won't stand with you on this. You're jeopardizing everything we have! Our position, our wealth, our security . . .'

'I thought you'd got tired of being rich.'

'I'm not that tired, and I never will be! Rich may be boring sometimes, but it beats the hell out of the alternative. I've been poor, and I'll see you and everyone else dead and damned before I go back there again. If you burn your bridges with Parliament and the Families and the undergrounds, and call them all devils and bastards to their faces, who will be left for you to stand with? No one else is going to go along with this. You'll have to go on the run again, or face being arrested as a danger to the war effort. Is that what you want?'

'Maybe,' said Random. 'I'll run, alone if I have to. I'm a lot harder to catch these days than I used to be, thanks to dear dead Owen. He would have understood what I'm going to do in there. He always was the most honourable of us all. Maybe what I'm about to do is partly in his name, in his memory.' He looked steadily at Ruby. 'If I had to run, would you come with me? It would be just like the old days; just us, against the Empire.'

'I hated the old days,' said Ruby flatly. 'Nothing could make me go back to them; not you or anybody else. Have you forgotten what life was like back on Mistworld, before Owen found us? You were a broken old man, working as a janitor in a health spa. And I was a bouncer in a series of increasingly seedy bars, because the bounty-hunter trade was dying out from under me. I was living in a single room with no running water and no heating, eating day-old bread and meat from tins well past their sell-by date. That's the real reason I joined your rebel cause. I'd have joined any cause that offered me a way out of what my life had become.'

'And because Hazel asked you.'

'Hazel was my friend. She's dead, and so is Owen. He was our touchstone. He remade us into something finer, held us together and made us believe we were the forces of light. Now he's gone, and we've lost our way. I won't go back to being poor, Jack. Not even for you.'

'You were the one who criticized my deal with the Families. You said that was when you stopped believing in me. Won't you believe in me now?'

'I don't see anything to believe in, Jack. This is madness. You're like a small child who wants to overturn the boardgame because he's losing.'

'I'm just being true to my nature again. I was so busy being Jack Random the politician that I forgot my true self, the professional rebel. It's my destiny to fight the system. Any system. Don't try and stop me, Ruby. This time I won't be stopped by anyone. Not even you.'

'And what we've had together,' said Ruby Journey softly, 'that means nothing to you?'

'"I could not love thee half so much loved I not honour more." Some truths never change, Ruby.'

'Do what you have to do, Jack. And I'll do what I have to.'

They smiled slightly at each other, knowing that what was to come was inevitable. That some things could not be turned aside by such small joys as love or happiness. Jack opened the door to the great hall, and Ruby walked in past him, head held high, looking straight ahead. Jack shrugged, and smiled widely at the thought of the terrible thing he was about to do.

The great hall had originally been intended for official receptions, formal dinners and the like. But Random had

had all the furniture removed to make more room for his guests. All that remained was a single raised dais, so that Random's audience could see him when he spoke. It was a pretty sizable audience. Random leaned against the closed, locked door, looking them over. Stephanie and Daniel Wolfe stood together, perhaps a little more closely than brother and sister should. Stephanie was glaring about her almost triumphantly, as though her invitation to Random's gathering proved she was still a power to be reckoned with. Daniel seemed somewhat distracted, but then he always did, nowadays. He'd probably only come because his sister made him.

Not too far away stood Evangeline Shreck, representing the clone underground. She smiled graciously about her, quite splendid in a little black dress that emphasized her gamine beauty. Random thought she looked just a little too at ease for someone who'd only recently been to the funeral of her dead love. At her side was a new figure: the Unknown Clone. He wore full battle armour, sword and gun and a black leather mask that covered his entire face. Apparently he represented all the clones who'd died in the rebellion, and their refusal ever to be enslaved again. Random wasn't sure whether this new figure was supposed to be primarily a political statement, or Evangeline's bodyguard. He was a tall, disturbing presence, and Random couldn't help feeling there was something familiar about him.

Toby and Flynn were working the crowd, buttonholing the right people, asking awkward questions and refusing to be fobbed off with soundbites.

Two of the esper underground's enigmatic leaders had turned up, hidden as always behind projected telepathic illusions. One had come as the fabled ogre Hog In Chains: a great beast of a man with a hog's head, wrapped in yards of rusty chains, carrying a bone club from which dead men's brains dripped constantly. The other figure had come as the Lady Of The Lake, an ethereally slender woman in pure white samite, who ran constantly with the dark river waters that had drowned her. The water collected and pooled about her bare feet, but somehow never spread any further. Random tried to read some meaning or significance into the esper leaders' choice of images, but like everyone else, he retreated baffled. Sometimes Random thought they just chose their images at random, to mess with people's heads and keep them off balance.

It was what he would have done.

There were fifty Members of Parliament, from all the main parties and factions, most ostentatiously not talking to each other, but still making pointed comments in loud voices when anyone else made the mistake of looking interested. Almost as many more Family representatives were there too, again covering a broad spectrum of interests and influence, including a last-minute substitute for Cardinal Brendan, who had business elsewhere. People tended to wink when they said that, or smile knowingly. The replacement spokesman for Clan Chojiro (and, of course, Blue Block) was Matoul Chojiro, a tall, gawky, wide-eyed young man, apparently on his first assignment for the Clan. He seemed open and innocent, and fooled absolutely no one. And last, but definitely not in any way least, the large and portly figure of Elias Gutman, Speaker of the House. He smiled amiably at one and all, but his eyes were cold and thoughtful.

Jack Random strode through the crowd, brushing aside those before him by sheer force of personality, and came to a halt before Gutman. The Speaker bowed with surprising grace for someone of his bulk. Random didn't bow in return. 'I'm glad you're here, Elias. What I've got planned just wouldn't be the same without you.'

'How could I not attend?' said Gutman easily. 'After your excesses on Loki, I'm as interested as anyone in how you plan to justify yourself. And then there's your promise of a statement of policy that will change Imperial politics for ever. I do hope that wasn't just rhetoric, Random. I'd hate to think I was brought here under false pretences, when there are so many other useful things I could be doing.'

'Don't worry, Elias,' said Random. 'I guarantee this will be one statement of principles you'll never forget.'

He strode on through the last of the crowd, and jumped lightly up on to the raised dais at the end of the hall. Ruby stepped up to stand beside him, still scowling. The great crowd before them quickly grew quiet, conversations abandoned in midstream, as they realized Random was about to start.

'Thank you all for coming,' said Jack Random calmly. 'So good to see so many of you here. Not a bad turnout, all things considered. I had hoped a few more of the top echelons might have put in an appearance . . . but you'll do nicely to help me make my point. Let me start by addressing my recent visit to the planet Loki. I'm sure you've all heard the awful rumours about what I did there. I'd just like to say that they're all true. Especially the worst ones.' The crowd stirred and murmured uneasily, but Random just kept talking over them, and they were silent once more. He was smiling as he looked about him, and sounded quite calm, almost cheerful. 'When I arrived on Loki, I found an unacceptable situation. War criminals from the old Imperial administration had been placed in power over the colonists and were bleeding the economy dry, to feather the nests of their backers here on Golgotha. So I had them all hanged. The rebel leaders there had sold out to Shub, so I had them hanged too.

'They were all guilty, all dirty. All politicians.

'I learned many valuable, if painful lessons on Loki. You see, I have drifted very far from what I used to be, and what I used to stand for. I was the professional rebel, and I stood for justice. To win the rebellion I allowed myself to be persuaded away from such an absolute position, and embraced the compromises and little victories of politics. Just to save a few lives. But after Lionstone fell, I saw my dream of freedom and honour for all corrupted by the very people I had entrusted it to. Nothing's really changed. The same sort of people are still in charge, and many of the old injustices are still in place. And I will not stand for that any longer.

'There will be no more compromises; no more betrayals; no more politics from me. No more secret meetings in back rooms, where the privileged few decide the fate of the many. I return to my old mantle of the professional rebel, answerable to no one but myself and my own conscience. I am back, and I will not be turned aside again.'

There was a pause as he looked out over his gathered guests, still smiling that unsettling, endless smile. Ruby didn't like the way his speech was going, but didn't know what to say. She agreed with a lot of it, but she had a strong suspicion she wasn't going to like where Random took it next.

'And what, exactly,' said Elias Gutman from the middle of the crowd, 'does this change in direction amount to? What are you going to do, Random? What can you do?'

'Just what I did on Loki,' said Jack Random easily. 'Punish the guilty. Kill all of those responsible for the corruption of my dream. Kill all the lying politicians, the special interest groups who only care for their own, the Families striving to claw their way back into power and privilege. I'm going to kill everyone who denies the people the freedom I promised them. Starting with everyone in this room. I could have just planted a bomb here, but I wanted this to be a personal statement, so I'm going to kill you all personally. Feel free to pray to any god you think might be listening.'

He turned suddenly, without warning, and struck Ruby Journey a blow to the head that would have killed anyone else. She dropped limply to the dais and lay still, barely breathing. Random looked down at her, his face calm and unmoved.

'Sorry, Ruby. But I couldn't have you interfering.'

'Jesus Christ,' whispered Toby, 'I think he means it. Are you getting this, Flynn?'

'We are now going out live, boss. Why don't you look for an exit, in case we need one in a hurry?'

'There are only two doors and I've sealed both of them,' said Random, raising his voice to be heard over the growing babble of his audience, as those nearest the exits struggled with the doors and couldn't budge them. 'No one's going anywhere. Time to die, people.'

His sword was suddenly in his hand as he leaped lightly from the dais and cut down the representative from Clan Chojiro, even as that young man was drawing a concealed disrupter. The heavy steel blade slammed down, cutting through flesh and bone to bury itself in the man's heart. He shuddered, but didn't fall. Random jerked the sword out again, and blood sprayed high into the air as the Chojiro finally collapsed. The people nearest him began screaming and tried to back away, but the crush of the crowd kept them where they were. Random lashed out again, and his sword sheared clean through an MP's skull. The politician sank to his knees, his jerking hands rising as though to clasp the half of his head that remained.

People were hammering on the locked doors now, but the heavy oak resisted them easily. Few had brought weapons. They hadn't thought they'd be needed at a political meeting inside the Parliament building itself. People screamed for security guards to come and save them, but Random had sent them away earlier on urgent missions. Some would come eventually, but by then it would all be over.

Men and women died screaming as Random hacked his way through the crowd like a wolf in a flock of sheep. He was still smiling, but now he was showing his teeth and his eyes were very bright. The few with swords and guns were pushed forward to meet him, but they didn't even slow Random down. He was inhumanly fast and strong, and no one could stand against him. The only one who might have still lay unconscious on the dais. Blood flew on the air and soaked the rich carpeting. Random cut through the panicked crowd like a reaper with a scythe, leaving a trail of the dead and dying behind him. He came upon Toby Shreck and Flynn and paused for a moment. Toby felt a cold hand clutch at his heart. And then Random nodded to him.

'Stay honest, newsman. And be sure Flynn gets my good side.'

And he moved on, to kill more people.

Random bore down on Daniel Wolfe and the young man yelled for his sister to get behind him. He had a sword in his hand. A Wolfe never went anywhere unarmed. Behind him, Stephanie yelled, 'Kill him! Kill him, Danny!' in a voice only just short of hysteria. Daniel blocked Random's first blow, and even the second, but then the Maze man's superior strength smashed Daniel's sword right out of his hand. Daniel tried to jump Random, his hands reaching for Random's throat, and Random's sword came up out of nowhere and plunged through Daniel's gut and out of his back. Daniel squeezed his eyes shut, but didn't cry out. Random jerked his sword free and turned on Stephanie, but Daniel's arm swept out to pull her behind him again. Random plunged his sword into Daniel's body over and over again, but though Daniel bled and shuddered with every blow, he wouldn't cry out and he wouldn't fall and leave Stephanie unprotected. He backed slowly away, keeping her behind him, while Random hacked away at him like a woodsman before a stubborn tree. Finally Random thrust his sword all the way through Daniel's body. The crosspiece of the hilt buried itself in Daniel's stomach as the long blade burst out of his back and went on to transfix Stephanie too. Her scream was suddenly stopped by a mouthful of blood. Random pulled on his blade, and she fell backwards. Daniel cried out at last, and turned to cradle his dead sister's body in his blood-soaked arms. Random shrugged, and moved on.

Clones and espers and politicians and aristocrats fell before him, till he had to step over piled-up bodies to get at the living. The biggest piles were in front of the two locked doors. Someone was pounding and shouting on the other side now, but they couldn't help. Random was soaked in blood, none of it his own. He was still breathing easily and his sword arm was as strong as ever. He felt as though he could go on and on, and never grow tired. Now that most of the crowd were dead, those remaining tried to run, but the bodies on the floor slowed them down, and in the end there was nowhere to go. Random was faster than any of them, faster than any human could be.

He finally stopped and looked around him, searching for someone of note to kill next. The two esper leaders, Hog In Chains and the Lady Of The Lake, had blinked out of existence the moment the killing began, but Random had always suspected they were only illusions anyway. It didn't matter: he'd find and kill them later. That just left the clone leader, Evangeline Shreck, guarded by the Unknown Clone. The masked man stood before Evangeline, holding his sword steady. Random walked unhurriedly over to him, and smiled. It took more than a mask to hide a man from a Maze-trained mind.

'I'm glad you didn't die after all, son. I always wondered how I'd do against you.'

'You've gone mad,' said Finlay steadily. 'This is insane.'

'You're a fine one to talk,' said Random. 'How many aristos and politicians died at your hands during the rebellion? You were the undergrounds' pet assassin. All they had to do was point you in the right direction and turn you loose. Don't tell me you didn't enjoy your war.'

'That was different. I fought for a cause.'

'And that's just what I'm doing now.' Random shook his head sadly. 'I thought you of all people would understand my purpose.'

'I don't see any purpose, just the last murderous spree of a failed revolutionary. I won't let you kill her.'

'Son, you can't stop me.'

Random raised his sword, and suddenly Evangeline stepped past Finlay and stood between the two men. 'No! I'm damned if I'll let you two kill each other! We fought on the same side in the rebellion, fought for the same cause!'

'You betrayed it,' said Random. 'All the guilty have to die, if I'm to put things right.'

'We never made a deal with the Families!' said Evangeline

fiercely. 'You did. Where were you when Finlay and I fought our way into Wormboy Hell to rescue the imprisoned espers? We never stopped fighting for what we believed in!'

Random looked at her for a long moment. Finlay's sword never wavered. 'No,' Random said finally, 'maybe you didn't, at that. All right; you get to live. This time. But if you can't clean up the clone underground's act, we will meet again.' He nodded to Finlay. 'Next time, son.'

'Any time, old man,' said Finlay.

Random turned and looked around him. The room was littered with the dead; the walls were running with blood. The only living souls still left in the hall apart from himself and the unconscious Ruby were Evangeline and Finlay, Toby and Flynn, the grieving Daniel, somehow still alive . . . and Elias Gutman. Random nodded to the news team.

'Keep filming, boys. You're about to witness the death of a genuinely evil man.'

'I've alerted my guards,' said Gutman. 'They're on their way. They'll blow those doors right off their hinges.'

'Let them come,' said Random. 'Let them all come. It won't make any difference.'

'Think what you're doing, man,' said Gutman urgently. 'Don't throw away everything you've achieved, just because you didn't like the conditions on Loki.'

'The corruption's everywhere, throughout the Empire. You should know, you're responsible for most of it. You and your kind.'

'You can still be a positive influence. You achieved so much—'

'I achieved nothing! Nothing's changed. Not really.' Random shook his head, no longer smiling. 'My fault. I wasn't true to my cause, to myself. All my friends are dead. They died for the cause. If I stop now, they died for nothing.'

'What about Ruby Journey?' said Gutman, gesturing at the still body on the dais.

'We no longer have anything in common,' said Random. 'I've nothing left to lose, Elias. The Madness Maze made me very powerful. I think it's time I put that power to some real use. Time to die, Elias. I left the best till last.'

'Owen would never have approved of this,' said Evangeline, and Random stopped his advance on Gutman to look at her again. She met his cold gaze unflinchingly. 'Owen Deathstalker gave you a new life, Jack Random. Is this how you repay him, by spitting on everything he believed in?'

'Owen's dead,' said Random.

'Not as long as we still believe in the cause he fought and the honour he lived by. You know he would never accept what you've done here. Gutman's a pig, but he shouldn't die just because you want to kill him. Killing someone just because you can will turn you into the kind of person we fought a rebellion to get rid of.'

'Owen's dead,' Random said again. 'The most honourable man I ever knew; the only real hero in the whole damned rebellion. And Gutman's still alive. Doesn't that tell you all you need to know about the way things have gone?'

There was a sudden pounding on both doors at once, as Gutman's guards finally arrived. From the noise they were making it sounded like there were a hell of a lot of them. Random looked at the doors thoughtfully and then turned to face Gutman again, only to find that Evangeline had moved to stand between him and his prey. The Unknown Clone was there too, at her side as always.

'You'll have to get through us to get to Gutman,' said Evangeline steadily, 'and I don't think you're ready to go that far yet.'

'Why are you doing this for Gutman?'

'I'm not. I'm doing it for you.'

'Ah, hell,' said Random, 'there's always another time.'

One of the locked doors was blown in by concentrated disrupter fire. Random ran over to the hall's only window, overlooking a twelve-storey drop to the street below. He threw open the window and looked down. The drop on to solid stone meant certain death for any man. Random laughed breathlessly and jumped. It felt as if he was floating down, and when his boots slammed against the flagstones he hardly staggered, his more-than-human leg muscles absorbing the impact easily. With the blood of many on his hands and his clothes, the last professional rebel in the Empire ran off down the backstreets, disowned by all, a man alone. And Jack Random couldn't have been happier.

Back in the hall of the dead, Gutman's guards were sweeping quickly through the splintered doors, guns at the ready as they looked for targets. It only took them a moment to realize the killer was gone, and they set about checking the fallen for signs of life. But the piled-up bodies were beyond all help now. Random's sword cuts had been as precise as a surgeon's and the power behind his blows brutal. Someone called for a medic anyway, to treat the few survivors for shock. Evangeline watched it all numbly. She'd always thought of Random as a wild card, but she'd never thought . . . hearing a loud groan to one side she spun round, to see Ruby Journey slapping aside a guard's helping hand as she lurched to her feet on the dais. She put a hand to her head, grimacing at the pain, but her eyes were already clear and sharp.

'Damn,' she said thickly. 'Never saw that one coming.' She looked at the corpses strewn about the great hall. 'What the hell . . .'

'Jack Random has gone insane,' said Elias Gutman, approaching the scowling bounty hunter with a certain amount of caution. 'He killed all these people, for daring to have opinions and beliefs of their own. And he's threatened to kill a great many more.'

Ruby nodded slowly. 'He said he was going to clean house; put an end to all corruption. Trust Jack Random to take the most direct route.'

'He has to be stopped,' said Gutman.

'You mean killed.'

'Yes, that's exactly what I mean. God knows how many others will die if he isn't brought down.'

'You can't condemn him to death just like that!' said Evangeline. 'He's a hero of the rebellion!'

'And now he threatens the existence of everything the rebellion has brought about,' said Gutman flatly. 'Do you really think he'd allow us to take him alive? We couldn't afford a trial anyway. The scandal would rock the Empire just when it's most vulnerable. No; he's going to kill and kill until he's stopped, in the only practical way.'

'You're looking at me,' said Ruby Journey. 'Why are you looking at me, Gutman?'

'You know why.'

'You saying you want me to go after Jack?'

'Who else would stand any chance against him? The only thing that can take down a Maze survivor is another Maze survivor. And you're the only one left. You were a bounty hunter once; be one again.'

'He's my friend.'

'Parliament will authorize an extraordinarily high price for his head.'

Ruby looked at him. 'How extraordinary?'

'Name your price.'

'You can't seriously be considering this!' said Evangeline. She started towards Ruby, but the Unknown Clone took her firmly by the arm and held her back. The bounty hunter didn't even look at her.

'Make me an offer, Gutman,' she said calmly. 'But bear in mind that if it isn't good enough, I might join with Jack to bring you all down. Just for the hell of it.'

'More money than you can ever spend,' said Gutman. 'You'll never want for anything, ever again. Lifelong security. And we'll make you official Champion to the new King and Queen. You'll get to fight the worst of the Empire's enemies.'

Ruby smiled, though it didn't touch her eyes. 'You know how to reach a girl's heart, Gutman. You've got a deal.'

'Understand me, bounty hunter; we don't want him brought back alive. As a dead legend he can still serve Humanity as an inspiration. Alive he's just an embarrassment. Kill him, Ruby. If you can.'

'No problem,' said Ruby Journey.

*

Diana Vertue had never visited a House of Joy before. Not even in her wildest Jenny Psycho days, when she'd refused to accept any restrictions on her actions, on principle. She walked slowly down the busy street, hidden behind a psionic cloak that left her physically and psychically invisible. People moved to avoid her without even wondering why. Diana Vertue had dropped out of sight so that no one could find her.

The Mater Mundi had grown more and more open in its attempts to stop her investigating into its true nature. At first, it tried direct psionic assaults on Diana's mind, and when that didn't work, the Mater Mundi took over the minds of innocent espers and sent them to kill her. They could come from anywhere, sudden and unexpected, ready to die to bring about Diana's death. No one could be trusted any more; nowhere was safe. Diana broke the first few espers free from the Mater Mundi's domination, before they could do her or themselves any harm, but she quickly realized that she couldn't defend herself for ever from an endless stream of fanatical assassins without the risk of having to kill some of them. And some of them had been people she'd thought of as friends.

She was too open a target at the esper Guild House, for all its much-vaunted psionic security, so she disappeared: just walked out, and vanished behind a psychic fog of her own making. She avoided contact with anyone who knew her, and continued her computer search into the Mater Mundi's past behind a series of anonymous cut-outs. She'd learned a lot from the cyberats, including how to manufacture new short-term identities, as and when needed. She kept moving as much as possible, sleeping in transients' hotels and only eating in busy restaurants where she could be part of the crowd. The destruction of the city during the latter part of the rebellion had left a lot of people homeless and drifting, and no one noticed one more. The Mater Mundi had driven Diana deep underground, leaving her as rootless and alone as any vagrant. Which made it even more surprising when a strange mental voice broke effortlessly through her shields and told her that if she wanted to know the truth about the Mater Mundi, she should go to a particular House of Joy, on a certain day at a certain time, and all would be revealed to her.

Who are you? Diana had asked.

Another former manifest of the Mater Mundi, the voice had replied.

Which had been very interesting, because according to all Diana's research, every previous manifest of Our Mother of All Souls had died, burned up by the power that blazed so very brightly within them. But the voice had found her and pierced her shields, both of which Diana would have sworn was impossible. She weighed her options as logically as she could, and decided to go. The odds heavily favoured it being some kind of a trap, but Diana was desperate for knowledge she could use against the Mater Mundi, something to even the odds.

And now here she was, standing outside the front door to the House of Joy, and she found herself hesitating, almost embarrassed. The House of Joy was the single largest chain of brothels in the Empire, officially licensed and endorsed, owner of the proud motto and boast 'No customer leaves unsatisfied'. You could find anything your heart or other organs desired in a House of Joy; anything at all. But there hadn't been much room for sex or love in Diana's young life. She went straight from the rigidly ruled esper academy to serve as a ship's esper on the late starcruiser *Darkwind.* After her traumatic time on the ghostworld Unseeli, she deserted from the Fleet and gave her life to the esper underground and the rebellion. That led to her time in the esper prison Wormboy Hell, where she passed through untold horrors and was made over into Jenny Psycho, and first manifested the power and the glory of the Mater Mundi. After that, she was more alone than ever. Not many found themselves attracted to a living saint, and a crazy one at that. And those that did were even crazier than she was.

After the rebellion was finally over, Diana Vertue took control of her life again only to find there wasn't much of it left. No lovers; no friends; only a few comrades of the rebellion, who all looked at her with doubtful eyes. If she was honest with herself, something she quite sensibly avoided doing as much as possible, Diana had started her quest for the Mater Mundi's origins just for something to do to fill up the empty hours of her life. Only to find she couldn't let go of the tiger's tail.

There had been no love or lovers in Diana Vertue's life, and most of the time she preferred it that way. Loneliness wasn't so bad, once you got used to it. And anyway, her life was complicated enough as it was.

She glared at the unobtrusive door before her with its discreet sign. Her mouth was dry, her hands were sweating and butterflies were knocking the hell out of each other in her stomach. She hadn't felt this nervous in most of the battles she'd fought in during the rebellion. She felt almost wistful for the loss of her Jenny Psycho persona. Jenny hadn't been scared of anything. On the other hand, Jenny had been several guppies short of an aquarium, so . . . Diana realized she was just putting off the moment, and brought her thoughts under control. She could do this. She could. After all, she was only here for information. She dropped her psionic cloak, and reappeared in public. She glanced casually about her, but no one seemed to be paying her any attention. Yet. She opened the door before her, and did her best to stride in like she owned the place.

She wasn't quite sure what she'd been expecting, but the quiet, tastefully appointed lobby she walked into could have belonged to any successful corporate body in the city. The walls were bare, the furniture and fittings stylish but still pleasant to the eye, and the young woman sitting behind the main reception desk was conventionally attractive. There was no one else in the lobby, for which Diana was quietly thankful. She strode over to the reception desk and the young woman smiled widely at her, displaying perfect teeth.

'Welcome to the House of Joy. Is this your first visit here?'

'Yes,' said Diana shortly.

'Please don't be nervous. We are here only to make you happy. We guarantee complete anonymity for all our clients, and one hundred per cent satisfaction or your money back. Your pleasure is our business. Now; how can we help you?'

'I'm looking for someone,' said Diana. It occurred to her that she had no name or description for her contact. She'd just assumed all she had to do was show up, and the owner of the mysterious voice would make contact. 'I'm Diana Vertue. Does that mean anything to you?'

'Oh, of course,' said the receptionist. 'One of the heroes of the rebellion. An honour to have you here. Now, would you like a man or a woman? Or both, perhaps?'

'No!' said Diana quickly. 'I'm here to meet . . . someone special.'

'Well, of course you are, but I shall need some direction from you, to help choose that special someone to satisfy your fantasies.'

'You don't understand,' said Diana. She could feel her cheeks blazing. 'I was supposed to meet someone here. A particular person. Do you have a message for me, perhaps?'

The receptionist looked doubtful, but dutifully checked the monitor screen beside her. She frowned suddenly. 'That's odd. I could have sworn there hadn't been any messages for this afternoon, but you're right. Your name's here. No contact name, just a room number. A trifle irregular, but not to worry. Apparently we have someone standing by to take you there.'

She hit a concealed bell, and a door opened to Diana's left. She turned to see who it was, and then stood frozen to the spot as she recognized the man before her.

'*Deathstalker*? Owen? They told me you were dead! What the hell are you doing here?'

The familiar face smiled politely, and he crossed the lobby

to join her. 'I think there's been a misunderstanding, dear. I'm not the real Owen Deathstalker, just a lookalike; the best copy the body shop could produce. There's always been a market for famous faces in the House of Joy. They tend to come and go, as fashions change, but Owen's very popular at the moment. There's an Owen in every House on Golgotha, and even more offworld. We pay him a percentage for the use of his visage, of course. Copyright law's very strict on that. Now, if you'd like to come with me . . .'

'I think we need to get something clear first,' said Diana. 'I mean, I'm sure you're very sweet, but—'

'Don't misunderstand me, darling. I'm just a messenger today, here to take you to your appointment. Your host thought a familiar face might help to put you at your ease. Shall we go?'

He gestured at the open door, and Diana walked stiffly past him, doing her best to radiate strict disinterest. The fake Owen shut the door quietly behind them, and then led the way along a quiet, anonymous corridor where all the many doors leading off were strictly closed. Diana kept her esp under firm control, telling herself she had absolutely no interest in whatever might be going on behind the doors.

'So,' she said finally, with just a hint of desperation in her voice, 'tell me; who else do you have here with a famous face?'

'Oh, you'd be surprised, darling,' said the fake Owen easily. 'We've got a Jack Random, a Julian Skye, two Robert Campbells (he's very popular at the moment, with the royal wedding coming up), three Constance Wolfes and four Hazel d'Ark's, for those who like to live dangerously.'

'How about Ruby Journey?'

'Sweetie, we wouldn't dare. We do have several Lionstones, for the S&M trade. Would you like to meet your own lookalike?'

Diana stopped dead in her tracks, and glared at the fake Owen as he stopped beside her. '*There's someone here with my face?*'

'Well, yes. Everyone famous makes an appearance here

eventually. Our job is fulfilling fantasies, and as there aren't enough of the genuine article to go around, people come here for the next best thing. You're quite in demand, you know. A lot of espers have a thing about you. You'd be surprised.'

'Listen to me very carefully,' said Diana Vertue. 'I don't want to meet my double. I don't want anyone to meet my double. As from this moment, no one with my face is to work in a House of Joy anywhere, on pain of my getting seriously annoyed. You'd be surprised how much damage I can do, when I'm sufficiently motivated.'

'Are we talking Jenny Psycho here?' said the fake Owen.

'Quite definitely.'

'I'll see your message is passed on to the board of directors. And I would like to point out that there is absolutely no point in threatening me. I just work here.'

'Get a move on,' said Diana, and they started off again. After a somewhat strained silence, Diana calmed down enough to ask another question. 'Where exactly are we going?'

'Right down to basement level,' said the fake Owen, glad to be on uncontroversial ground again. 'Your contact is very shy about meeting people. In fact, he hasn't made an appearance in years. Quite a few people are unsure as to whether he really exists at all. We deal so much in fantasy here, it's hard sometimes to keep reality in focus. Certainly I've never met him, and don't know anyone who has. He's been here for ages; no one seems sure how long. He makes himself known now and again to a select few, to run the few errands he finds necessary. Eccentric, perhaps, but we're used to that here. And please, sweetie; no more questions about him. I have no idea who or what he is, or why he chooses to live in our basement, and I don't want to know. The one thing you learn here above all else is to mind your own business.'

He came to a halt before a large wooden door, intimidatingly broad and solid, and opened the old-fashioned lock with a large metal key. The hinges squealed noisily as he pushed the door open with an effort, and then he gestured for Diana to go in. She strode forward, head held high, and found herself in a torture chamber. The walls were rough stone, and ran here and there with dark streams of water. The floor was stone too, cracked with age and discoloured in places with old, dark bloodstains. It was stiflingly hot, and Diana could feel beads of perspiration popping out on her face. A great metal brazier stood in the centre of the room, coals glowing redly as it heated a collection of branding irons. There was a full-sized rack, an iron maiden, and whips and chains and instruments of torture hung on the walls ready for use. The door slammed shut behind Diana. She spun round, found the fake Owen standing right behind her, grabbed a handful of his shirt-front, lifted him off the floor and slammed him back against the closed door. His eyes bulged as he tore helplessly at her unflinching hand and arm.

'Talk to me!' said Diana harshly. 'Tell me why you've brought me to an interrogation chamber or I'll kill you right here!'

'*It's not real! It's not real!*' The fake Owen was going very red in the face. 'Honestly, darling, try not to be quite so brutal. This is a fake, just like me, for clients whose tastes run a little darker than most.'

Diana dropped him and gave him a hard look. 'People *pay* for this?'

'Some do, yes. There have always been those who like a little pain with their pleasure. Or vice versa. As they say, only the one who hurts you can make the pain go away. There's a body shop next door to repair any damage, if anyone gets a little too . . . enthusiastic.'

'Why would my contact choose a place like this for a meeting?'

'Probably because it's the most secure and private part of the House. Can I go now, please? I'd really like to go somewhere and change my trousers before the stain sets.'

'*Yes,*' said a soft, carrying voice. '*You can go. I'll summon you if I need you again.*'

Diana and the fake Owen both looked around sharply.

The voice seemed to have come from everywhere at once. It was an unpleasant sound, dark as death, soft as corruption, vile as a living thing crushed beneath a steel boot. Diana could feel her heart pounding in her chest. The last time she'd heard a voice like that, she'd been a prisoner in Silo Nine, and Wormboy had been playing mind games with her head. She suddenly felt like running, but even as the thought came to her, the door opened and slammed shut behind her as the fake Owen made his escape. Diana forced her thoughts and emotions back under control, and let some of the colder Jenny Psycho aspects of her personality come to the surface. This was no place to be weak. She smiled widely as she glared around her, but it was as much a snarl as anything else.

'Who are you? Where are you?'

'*Right here,*' said the voice, and the words had the impact of iron nails driven into yielding flesh. '*Pardon my reluctance to reveal myself, but it's so hard to know who to trust these days. Anyone can be an agent of the Mater Mundi; anyone can be an assassin in disguise.*'

'So I've been finding out,' said Diana. 'All right, let's try this one. Why are we meeting here, of all places?'

'*Because it's the best place to hide. Open your thoughts just a little, Diana, and dip your toe into the passions that thrive here.*'

'Like hell,' said Diana immediately. 'My shields are up and they're staying up. This place is dangerous. Far too many emotions spilling out on all sides. An esper could drown in a place like this.'

'*Very wise, my dear. Passions run free here as reality is discarded in favour of personal fantasies. Everything is permitted in a House of Joy, as long as you don't expect it to be real. Love or sex, or reasonable facsimiles, are available to anyone who can pay the price. The wildest of emotions are commonplace here, and passions rise and fall as regularly as the tides. A perfect place to hide, for such as you and I, for the things we've become. Even the Mater Mundi can't pierce the maelstrom of real and fake emotions that fuel the everyday business of a House of Joy. And down here, where the darkest aspects of the human heart are released and savoured, a careful and cautious mind can stay hidden for ever. I've lived here a long time, maybe decades, maybe centuries, it's hard to tell. Hidden in the eye of the hurricane, forgotten by the world.'*

'So why make contact with me?' said Diana. 'Why bring me here?'

'*Because I'm frightened,*' said the soft, awful voice. '*You've been stirring up things better left alone, awakening things that have been sleeping in the dark, forgotten cellars of human history. I know the truth of the Mater Mundi, a secret that frightens me so much I've chosen to live here like a rat in its hole rather than risk the wrath of Our Mother of All Souls. You have no idea what you're challenging.*'

'Then tell me. And show yourself: I didn't come all this way just to listen to a voice in my head. You don't have to be afraid of me.'

'*Oh, but I do, I do. You don't know what I've become, what I had to become, to survive. I was human once, like you. A manifest of the Mater Mundi. I thought I was the chosen one, the holy one, the saviour of the espers. And just like you, I was crazy enough to avoid being driven insane and destroyed by the process. I survived, when so many others died. And also like you I went looking for answers, for the truth behind what had touched me and changed me for ever. I found my answer, but it didn't make me happy or wise. I faked my own death, and came here long, long ago. And now I can never leave.*

'*The swirling emotions and raging passions were enough to hide me, but after a while, that wasn't enough. I was tempted, bit into the sweet apple and fell from what little grace I had left. I don't just hide here, these days. I feed. My mind draws on the energies around me, draining sustenance from my sweet victims. Never enough to be noticed, but enough to keep me alive long after I should have died. I told myself I had to stay alive; it was my duty, to wait for someone like you who might prove strong and brave enough to confront the Mater Mundi where I could not. But really, I was just afraid to die . . . and the feeding was so sweet, so very sweet. My name is Varnay, and there is a very old name for what I am.'*

He finally let his shields drop, and appeared before her. Diana's stomach turned, and she grimaced despite herself, fighting to keep from looking away. Varnay was inhumanly large, fat and bloated, pallid as a corpse, with a huge, wet red mouth. Dressed in black rags and tatters, he looked like nothing so much as a giant, distended leech. His dark eyes were huge, dominating his face, staring unblinkingly. There were patches of rot visible on his face and hands, and his nose had been eaten away long before, leaving a discoloured gap in the middle of his swollen face. His was a body that should have been dead long since, sustained by unnatural energies and an inhuman hunger.

Diana wondered if he slept in a coffin.

'Don't condemn me,' said Varnay, and his voice was just as awful in his mouth as it was in her mind. 'You don't have the right to condemn me. Only the smallest of chances separate your Jenny Psycho from what I have made of myself. You fought your way back into the light. I never had that choice. I've followed your progress, from a distance. We've both done questionable things. We're both monsters.'

'No,' said Diana, 'the Mater Mundi's the real monster. She made us what we are. She bears the responsibility, and she must be brought to justice.'

'Oh, if you only knew,' said Varnay, his distended red lips moving in something that might have been meant as a smile. 'Even after all you've learned, you're still so far from the truth.'

'Then tell me!'

'What use is wisdom if it brings no profit to the wise? The truth won't make you happy, Diana. It won't set you free.'

'Tell me anyway. You know you're going to. Otherwise all

the years you've spent hiding here, becoming . . . what you are, will all have been for nothing.'

'Sweet Diana. Dear Jenny. Looking so hard in all the wrong places for what was always right under your nose. Don't look outward for the Mater Mundi; look inward. All the way in. The Mater Mundi, Our Mother of All Souls, is nothing more than the collective unconscious of all espers. A subconscious massmind that has learned to exist separately from the individual thoughts and consciousness of the millions of espers that give it form. The Mater Mundi arose spontaneously from the moment of the creation of the first batch of espers in an Imperial lab, created from their fears, their needs and their darkest desires. Down the many years, it has learned purpose and ambition. It is the naked communal id, the secret dark heart of esper power. In emergencies, it can pull all the espers into one gestalt mind, to serve its will, but it cares nothing for the individual members of that gestalt. Individual esper minds, with their conscience and ethics and morality, mean nothing to the Mater Mundi. Its only real concern is survival, and it knows it can only continue for as long as the conscious minds remain unaware of its nature and existence. Sometimes it draws on the massed power of all espers to create superpowerful agents like me and you. Most burn out, like moths forced to fly too close to the sun, but you and I survived by being strong enough and crazy enough to separate ourselves from the esper massmind. That's why it has to destroy us, not only because we know the truth, but because we have learned to exist separately from it.

'It doesn't want competition.'

'But . . .' Diana's thoughts were whirling wildly. 'What about the leaders of the esper underground? If we went to them, told them what we know . . .'

'There are no esper leaders! Never have been. They're just archetypal images, thrown up by the esper unconscious. They never were anything more than illusions, masks for the

Mater Mundi to hide behind as it manipulated the esper underground to its own ends.'

'Legion,' said Diana softly, 'this is just another Legion. An insane gestalt mind, doing what espers really want, in the deepest areas of their subconscious. Power over the inferior, destruction of the different, punishment for those who have harmed it . . . or didn't love it enough. An endless rage, unlimited by remorse or conscience or morality.'

'You begin to understand,' said Varnay. 'It has its own goals, quite separate from what any individual or group of espers may think they want. It draws on their powers to sustain and defend itself, just as you and I do. Haven't you ever wondered where your heightened powers come from? You live off them, just as I live off those who come here. I am what you may become, in time. Unless you find a way to destroy the Mater Mundi without killing the innocent espers who host it.'

'What can I do?' said Diana. 'If every esper is potentially my enemy—'

'Go to New Hope. The Esper Liberation Front. They've formed their own gestalt, deliberate and fully conscious, and have thus separated themselves from the rest of the esper massmind. They are the Mater Mundi's enemy. They may have the answers you seek . . . or at least a place to hide.'

'I don't like running,' said Diana, 'and I don't like depending on others. You survived on your own.'

'Don't confuse surviving with living. I continue in this ragged existence only because I lack the strength of will to end it.'

'Then why call me here? Why risk your precious anonymity to tell me the truth about the Mater Mundi?'

'Because you're different. When I discovered the reality behind the Mater Mundi, my only thought was to hide. Yours was to fight. You've been touched by something greater, something powerful, even before the Mater Mundi chose you as its agent.'

'The Ashrai . . .' said Diana. 'The ghosts of Unseeli.'

'You are perhaps the only one who might find some way to fight back against the Mater Mundi and destroy its power. And then, finally, I'll be free to leave this velvet-lined trap I've made for myself.'

No, said a sudden cold voice in both their minds. Cold as the Snow Queen, cruel as the Wicked Stepmother. *I don't think so, little mindworm.*

'It's her!' shrieked Varnay, his great dark eyes almost bulging from his corpse-pale face. 'You brought her here!'

One mind might hide in passion's chaos, but not two, said the monster, the bogeyman, the parent that does not love its young. *You betrayed yourselves when you sought to betray me. You live and die, but I go on, for ever and ever and ever.*

Varnay's panicked shriek became a howl of shock and agony as he burst into flames. His dark rags were swept away in a second, consumed by an appalling heat that sent Diana stumbling backwards, arms raised to protect her face. Varnay's cadaverous flesh caught alight, his fat burning like a living candle. His eyes boiled and burst, running down his burning cheeks till they evaporated in the heat. He screamed, and a jet of flame shot out of his distended mouth. Diana backed further away from the blazing butter-yellow flames, coughing and choking on the awful smell. Varnay staggered blindly after her, fire-wreathed arms reaching out to her for help she couldn't give. Horribly, he was still alive and aware as the flames devoured him inch by inch. His mind was screaming louder than his voice, and Diana had to use all her shields to keep him out.

He was between Diana and the only exit, and seeing there was nothing she could do to save him, she did the only merciful thing she could, for both their sakes. Her powerful mind leaped out in a single vicious thrust, and snuffed out the single bright spark that was his mind. The empty body fell, still burning, to the floor. Diana ran to the door and pulled it open. Behind her she could hear the Mater Mundi screaming in frustrated rage. Diana's right sleeve burst into flames.

She ran through the House of Joy, the Mater Mundi pursuing her, howling with the voice of a million sleepwalking espers. Diana flung out her own mind like a net, gathering up the raging thoughts and emotions and passions around her, and threw them at the Mater Mundi. All the dark, murky waters of desire, of naked lust, of flesh on flesh, of fantasies fulfilled and denied, rose up into a thick, boiling cloud, and the Mater Mundi couldn't see through it to find Diana. She snuffed out her burning sleeve and ran on through the empty corridors of the House of Joy, and out into the street. She kept running. There was still hope. There was New Hope.

Once, the floating city of New Hope had been a symbol of reconciliation between man and esper and clone. The three strains of Humanity had lived together in peace and harmony, a living symbol, hoping to build together something far greater than the sum of its parts. But the Empress grew afraid, or jealous, or simply angry at the flouting of her authority, and sent Lord High Dram the Widowmaker and his death squads to destroy New Hope. The attack sleds came howling in out of the sun, unannounced and unexpected, hundreds of disrupter cannon firing in unison. The city's defences were quickly swept aside, and the attack sleds landed in waves, discharging Dram's elite guards. They overran the outnumbered defenders and swept through the streets of New Hope, killing everything in their path. And when the attack was over, the shattered city hung smoking in the air like a giant blackened cinder, and nothing and no one lived there any more, least of all hope.

After the rebellion, the Esper Liberation Front rebuilt the city and made it their own. Officially, the Elves had given up terrorism now that the war was over, and the old order was thrown down, but they remained suspicious and determined. No one would ever take their freedom away again. To that end, they lived a quiet, separate life on their floating city, behind extensive fortifications and more weapon systems than you'd find on an average starcruiser. They declared themselves a state within a state, separate and sovereign, and defied anyone to do anything about it. New Hope was a haven for the distressed and the needy, be they esper, clone or human. But they didn't take anyone, and you didn't try to force your way in if you ever wanted to be seen again. Parliament had settled for ignoring them. It seemed safest.

Diana Vertue ran for the city of New Hope with an invisible horde at her heels, and decided she'd worry about how to get in when she got there. If she got there. The moment she left the House of Joy, a psistorm of incredible power arose and pursued her down the street. Every esper was her enemy now, though they didn't know why. They came running from all directions, driven by a compulsion they couldn't name or deny. Just the sight of Diana filled their hearts with rage, and they lashed out at her with all their many powers, their individual consciousnesses pushed aside for the moment by the greater massmind of the Mater Mundi. Telepathic assaults slammed against Diana's shields, and polters rained down a hail of junk and refuse and anything else they could lift. A set of cast-iron railings came crashing down behind her like so many iron thunderbolts. Fires sprang up spontaneously all around her. Men and women threw themselves at her, but her shields kept them at bay. The air was full of screaming. Onlookers fell back to give Diana plenty of room as she ran on.

She was running nowhere in particular now, just trying to shake off her pursuers. But there were so many of them, and she was more alone than she'd ever been. Except that she wasn't, and hadn't been, for some time now. There had always been something different about Diana Vertue, even before she became Jenny Psycho. Years before, on the ghostworld called Unseeli, Diana had joined her mind with the last remnants of a dead alien race, the Ashrai. She had become a part of their endless song, for a time, and it changed her for ever. She'd tried very hard to forget that, fearing for her humanity, but recent events had forced her to remember. And now, in the final extremity of her life, with death or worse so close she could taste it, the song of the Ashrai burst from her lips again. People ran screaming from the sound of it. And the Ashrai came.

They surged around her small, fleeing form, vast and awful, brilliant as suns. People could not look at them directly. There were only glimpses of huge teeth and jagged claws and sharp-planed gargoyle faces. The Ashrai were long dead, but they'd never even considered lying down. Their raging storm filled the street and crackled overhead, slamming head-on into the Mater Mundi's psistorm. Alien and human thoughts crashed together and neither would give way. Chance and probability ran wild as the two powerful mindsets clashed and struggled, and madness followed Diana through the streets.

There were rains of fish and frogs, and lightning stabbed down repeatedly from a cloudless sky. Springs burst up out of the ground, and buildings caught fire. Locks unlocked and doors led out instead of in. Streets suddenly went somewhere else, and not every place they led to could be returned from. Whole city blocks swapped position, and houses were separated by stores that had not been there before, selling goods with no names. Things giggled in alleyways, and strange faces beckoned from vilely lit windows. Everywhere dice rolled sixes, and every card-player held the dead man's hand. People spoke in tongues and stigmata ran with alien blood. The old became young, and babies with knowing eyes spoke unpleasant wisdom. And through it all Diana ran on, untouched and unaffected, heading for New Hope and sanctuary.

She commandeered a gravity sled and flew it out past the city limits, the ghosts of the dead Ashrai boiling around her like stormclouds. Their song was thunder and their grotesque faces flashed like lightning. The Mater Mundi was left behind with the city, not defeated or discouraged, but unwilling to draw attention to itself now that immediate victory was no longer possible. Thousands of espers came to themselves again, far from where they had been and not knowing why. Chance and probability became normal once more, and bewildered street cleaners wondered what to do about the tons of fish and frogs clogging the streets.

High above and far away, Diana raced her sled towards New Hope, and stopped singing. Only then did she realize that her throat was raw and her lips were bleeding. Humans weren't meant to sing with such a voice. The Ashrai soared and dipped around her, large as clouds, alien voices raised in a song that frightened and disturbed her now she was no longer a part of it. And then they were gone, and there was only the small, battered form of Diana Vertue, flying alone in an empty sky.

It took her the best part of two hours to reach the floating city of New Hope, even pushing the sled's motor to its limits. Evening was falling towards night, and New Hope blazed against the growing darkness like a crown built of precious stones and starstuff. The bright shining lights and colours didn't fool Diana for a moment. She knew that behind the fairytale glamour lay weapons and defences powerful enough to hold off a good-sized army. The Elves would never be slaves again, no matter how many had to die. The Esper Liberation Front might not be the terrorist organization it had once been, but it had lost none of its ferocity or singleness of purpose.

A telepathic probe from the city bid Diana welcome and gave her a location to land her sled. Any other uninvited visitor would have received either a demand for an immediate explanation or a mental compulsion to leave or die, but the Elves had always had a soft spot for Jenny Psycho, the only freedom fighter even more hardcore than they were. The city grew and grew as Diana approached, stretching miles in diameter, filling the darkening sky with its shimmering towers of crystal and glass. Gossamer walkways linked delicate minarets, and flying Elves waved merrily to Diana as they streamed past her in multicoloured displays. And from all around came a joined chorus of mental voices crying welcome, welcome, like a great communal embrace, as if she were finally coming home. An almost overwhelming, seductive sense of belonging.

But Diana Vertue had sung with the Ashrai, been manifest to the Mater Mundi and even for a while the mad saint Jenny Psycho, and she knew that nowhere could ever be home for her now.

She landed her gravity sled on the edge of a crowded landing pad near the centre of the floating city, and bent tiredly over the controls. It had been a long, hard day, and the odds were it wasn't going to get any easier. Her new, hard-won knowledge weighed heavily on her, a burden even more oppressive because she knew she couldn't share it with anyone; not even the Elves. Let the true nature of the Mater Mundi become widely known, and all espers would become targets, feared and hated, hunted down and destroyed because of the monster they unknowingly held within them. It had to remain secret until Diana could figure out what to do about it, assuming she lived that long.

Wearily she raised her head to find a small group of Elves waiting to welcome her. They all wore the traditional leather and chains outfit, with bright ribbons in their hair and colours on their faces. Their muscles were sharply defined, and they wore swords and guns on their hips. Diana wasn't impressed. She'd been expecting that. What did impress the hell out of her was the huge statue of herself carved from pale marble, standing tall and proud at the boundary of the landing pad. Diana looked up at her own giant face until she got a crick in her neck, and then turned an ominous stare on the Elven welcoming committee. One of them stepped forward, grinning widely, a tall strapping brunette with a bandolier of throwing-stars across her impressive bosom.

'Thought you'd like it,' she said easily. 'That's why we had you land here. Welcome to New Hope, Jenny Psycho. I'm Crow Jane, highest number of recorded kills in the great rebellion. I speak for the Elf gestalt. What I hear, everyone hears.'

'How convenient,' said Diana, stepping down off her sled to join Crow Jane. 'So it's true then; the Elves have achieved a conscious massmind?'

'We are a small, faltering thing as yet, but we grow stronger with every day that passes. We have lost nothing in the union and gained much. We took our inspiration from you, Jenny Psycho, and the Maze people. Together we are strong, and we have sworn never to be weak again.'

'I prefer to be called Diana Vertue these days.'

Crow Jane looked at her dispassionately. 'Names are important. They define us. You can't turn time back, undo what you have made of yourself, simply by retreating to an earlier name.'

'Jenny Psycho was only ever a part of Diana Vertue. I found Jenny too limiting, once the war was over.'

'The war is never over.'

'Why the statue of me?' said Diana, tactfully changing the subject.

'Jenny Psycho has many admirers here,' said Crow Jane, smiling again. 'They call themselves the Psycho Sluts. Warriors, troublemakers, freethinkers. We're very proud of them. They're the cutting edge of Elf philosophy. Your name has become a battle-cry. They would die for you.'

'I'd much rather they lived for me,' said Diana drily. 'I might need their support. I've come here looking for sanctuary. The Mater Mundi wants my head on a stick. Where would the Elves stand, if they had to make a choice?'

'We bend our knees to no one,' said Crow Jane. 'Not even the so-called Mother of All Souls. The Elves follow their own destiny. We are aware of the psychic upheaval that disrupted the Parade of the Endless recently. Apparently they're still trying to get frogs out of the guttering. But we are all battle espers here, in memory of the fallen Stevie Blues, and we defend our own. Stay here for as long as you wish.'

She led Diana off the landing pad, and everyone relaxed a

little now the formalities were over. The other Elves introduced themselves with shy, almost bashful smiles and handshakes, and Diana pushed aside her bone-deep tiredness to be as gracious and charming as she could manage. The city of New Hope spread out before her, bright and colourful as a city of lit Christmas trees. And near and far and all around, Diana could hear in her mind the chorus of the Elven minds, like a great sustained chord, a harmony of souls.

'So,' said Diana to Crow Jane, making herself focus on the moment, 'what else goes on here, apart from training as warriors and yelling my name when you hit things?'

'We have much to keep us busy. We lead the field in removing the old Imperial conditioning from espers and clones; the mental limits that were supposed to keep them from rebelling. The stronger minds have mostly broken free on their own, but there are still many who need help. And afterwards, they have to be taught to think for themselves. A lifetime's conditioning as a slave isn't easy to shake off. Too many would walk right back into the cell we freed them from, simply because they've never known anything else. And there's no shortage of people ready to take advantage of them all over again. We also care for those whose souls are troubled by things they had to do during the war. The esper Guild Houses do what they can, but they don't have our experience with violence. It was never a clean war, on either side, and we're still clearing up the mess.'

Suddenly Crow Jane and Diana Vertue and the other Elves came to a halt, as a figure appeared out of the shadows to block their way.

'Speaking of which,' said Crow Jane sourly, 'allow me to present our most recent guest. I'm sure you two know each other.'

'Oh, yes,' said Jack Random. 'We know each other. Now if you don't mind, I'd like a private word with Diana.'

'Yes,' said Diana, meeting his gaze with level eyes, 'there are things we need to discuss.'

Crow Jane nodded, and led the other Elves a discreet

distance away, to give the two legendary figures a little privacy. Diana studied Jack Random. He seemed calm and collected and not at all crazy.

'I heard about what you did,' she said finally. 'It was all over the city.'

'I'm not crazy,' said Random, smiling. 'I've just gone back to doing what I do best. Killing the bad guys.'

'And you decide who the bad guys are.'

'Who better? Who has more experience fighting the good fight than me? I allowed myself to be swayed by soft words like compromise and concessions, and watched helplessly as everything I had believed in and fought for was washed away by political deals and hidden agendas. To hell with that. The old professional rebel is back, and God help the guilty.'

'Even if they used to be friends and allies of yours?'

'Perhaps especially then.' Random studied her thoughtfully. 'You can't stay here, you know, any more than I can. We both have powerful enemies who will stop at nothing to bring us down. I don't claim to understand what the Mater Mundi is, but I recognize its might and its determination. If you stay, it'll come here after you. The other Elves will try to defend you, and the Mater Mundi will destroy them all just to get at you. New Hope will be a city of the dead, again. If you stay.'

'Where else can I go?' said Diana, almost plaintively.

'Offworld. Pick a planet with a minimal esper presence and go to ground. Until either the Mater Mundi forgets about you, or you figure out a way to defeat it. I shall be doing much the same. No one fights my battles for me.'

'The Mater Mundi will never forget me,' said Diana. 'Not now that I know . . . what I know. We are enemies to the death now, our teeth for ever locked in each other's throat. You're right, I can't stay here. I can't be responsible for the destruction of something so beautiful.'

She looked out over the fairytale kingdom before her, and wasn't sure whether she meant New Hope or the new gestalt the Elves had built there. It didn't matter. Both were too precious to be put at risk by her contaminating presence. Tears stung Diana's eyes. She could have found a home here, she could feel it. But the newborn Elven gestalt would be no match for the centuries-old Mater Mundi.

It was like coming at last to the shores of Heaven, only to find the gates closing in her face.

'Give me time to catch my breath, and I'll think of somewhere to go,' she said finally. 'How about you, Random?'

'Already on my way. You'll pardon me if I don't tell you where I'm going. These days, I don't trust anyone but me – and I watch me pretty damn carefully. I must be off. I have much to do, and justice won't wait. Ah me; so little time, so many to kill.'

He smiled dazzlingly, with all his old charm and arrogance, and turned and walked away. Diana watched him go, and didn't know what to say or think. The professional rebel had been a hero of hers for so long that it was hard to think of him as anything but a hero. Was he crazy now, or had the whole Empire gone insane? There'd been a lot of people who thought Jenny Psycho was crazy. Of course, they were pretty much right. Diana looked across at Crow Jane, patiently waiting with the other Elves, and wondered how she was going to break the news that she wouldn't be staying after all.

An idea suddenly came to her. She couldn't risk mental contact with any of her few esper friends; they were all potential pawns of the Mater Mundi. But there were two people, neither of them in any way espers, with whom she had once made mental contact. When she'd still been Jenny Psycho, a prisoner in Silo Nine, the Imperial detention and torture centre also known as Wormboy Hell, the Mater Mundi had created a mental link between Jenny and Finlay Campbell and Evangeline Shreck. It had only ever been intended as a one-off thing, and none of them had tried using the link since, but theoretically there was no reason why Diana shouldn't be able to re-establish it. She was, after all, much more powerful and focused now. Perhaps powerful enough to force telepathic contact with two normal human minds. Though of course, normal was stretching it a bit in Finlay's case. She closed her eyes and broadcast her thoughts as loudly as she could, on an unfamiliar level.

Finlay! Can you hear me?

Bloody hell, said Finlay Campbell, *I've started hearing voices. I didn't think I was that far gone. You're not going to tell me you're the Devil, are you, and I have to go running through the streets with my underpants on my head?*

This is Diana.

Bloody silly name for the Devil.

Shut up and listen! This is Diana Vertue, once known as Jenny Psycho.

I think I'd have been better off with the Devil.

Shut up, dear, and let her talk, said Evangeline Shreck. *So this is telepathy. How fascinating. Not quite what I'd imagined, but . . . correct me if I'm wrong, Diana, but I'd always understood that telepathy was only possible between people carrying the esper genes.*

Usually, yes. But these are far from normal circumstances. Let's keep this short and to the point. I'm in deep shit, and I need somewhere safe and secure to hide, somewhere even the most powerful telepaths couldn't find me. Any ideas?

My old apartment under the Arenas, said Finlay immediately. *Totally secure, and no one knows the access codes but me.*

And the constant raging emotions and sudden deaths should make a powerful cloak for you to hide behind, said Evangeline.

Who's after you? said Finlay. *Anything we can do to help?*

No, said Diana. *I have to do this myself. Tell me what I need to know, and I'll break contact. You have enough problems of your own without adding mine.*

True, said Finlay. *Can I just ask how you knew I wasn't dead?*

I didn't, said Diana. *This idea came firmly under the heading of pure desperation. But I always knew you were too mean to die that easily.*

Finlay laughed, and told her what she needed to know. Diana broke the link. It was comforting to know she still had some friends. She steeled herself, and went to tell Crow Jane that she wouldn't be staying after all.

There was something very wrong with Grace Shreck's town house. The old stone building looked even more uncared-for than usual, if that was possible, and the surrounding gardens had been allowed to run riot. No lights showed at any of the windows, which were closed, save for one high up and to the side. Darkness hung about the great sprawling edifice like an ominous shadow, and the rich amber light from the lamps in the street hardly penetrated the gloom in the gardens at all. Both house and garden were utterly silent, as though listening or waiting for something. Toby Shreck and his cameraman Flynn huddled together before the front gates, peering dubiously through the black iron bars. Flynn's camera hovered by his shoulder, as though afraid to go off on its own. Toby glared at the dark house.

'I told you, Flynn. Something's wrong here, very wrong. Grace is still in residence, along with all of her servants, but the only light showing is at Clarissa's bedroom window. So why are they all sitting around in the dark?'

'Good question, boss. This is definitely spooky. Reminds me of one of those old houses they always put on the covers of Clarence's favourite Gothic romances. You know, the ones where there's a batty old ex-wife living secretly in the attic, sharpening a hatchet when she thinks no one's listening.'

'Will you shut up, Flynn? This is disturbing enough as it is. And look at the garden. Grace would never have allowed it to get into such a mess. She's always been red-hot on keeping up appearances.'

'Could be money problems,' said Flynn.

'No; she'd have talked to me by now if that was the case,' said Toby. 'And I can think of at least a dozen antiques in her front room that are each worth more than the house and grounds put together. No . . . I don't like this at all. There's an atmosphere here. Something dark, and hidden.'

'Then why don't we do the sensible thing for once, and go home? And not come back till we've arranged for some heavy-duty back-up, body armour and maybe an exorcist. Just in case.'

'Clarissa's in there,' said Toby grimly. 'Her messages have been growing increasingly short and vague over the past few weeks. I want her out of there. I also want a few urgent words with Grace about something I turned up while checking the Family expense sheets.'

'Hold on,' said Flynn. 'Since when have you started investigating your own Family? And keeping it a secret from me?'

Toby looked at him. 'Since I found myself wading through matters so murky that just discussing them might be enough to get us both killed. But since we're here – and I have no intention of going back without a whole bunch of answers – Grace took over the day-to-day running of Clan Shreck, after Gregor was murdered by Finlay Campbell. Suited me just fine, at the time. The last thing I needed was more work and more responsibilities. Until the Family bank alerted me, on the quiet, that Grace had been authorizing some very . . . unorthodox expenditures. Many of them borderline illegal, not to mention immoral. Very unlike dear old-fashioned Aunt Grace.

'So I checked it out. Grace had all sorts of elaborate security measures in place, but you can't keep a Shreck out of Shreck computers. It turned out that among many dubious and frankly disreputable rackets, Grace had been running a very discreet shipping service, specializing in transporting the kind of goods owners prefer not to describe too specifically, if at all. To my surprise, not to mention outright shock, when I compared the schedules with my own current area of interest, it turned out that one of these ships almost certainly brought the carrier of the nanoplague to Golgotha.'

'Wait a minute, wait a minute,' said Flynn. 'Are you saying the nanoplague's being spread by a single carrier?'

'Right. A Typhoid Mary, infected with the plague but not

affected by it. And he came here on a Shreck ship. Grace's ship.'

'We're talking treason here,' said Flynn carefully. 'Can you prove any of this?'

'Some of it. Enough to make it vital that I talk with Grace before I go public. Another rogue Shreck like Gregor, and the Clan will be disgraced beyond saving. I have to give Grace a chance to explain herself. It's just possible she's being used as a front by someone else. Certainly none of this sounds anything like the Aunt Grace I've always known.'

'Have you tried calling her?'

'She won't take my calls. And now she's blocked my line to Clarissa. So we're going in.'

'I love this *we* bit.' Flynn studied the gates dubiously. 'They appear to be locked.'

Toby snorted. 'I was cracking the locks on these gates back when I was fifteen, and heading out for a night on the town.'

He produced a set of efficient and highly illegal lock-picks, and had the gates open in a matter of seconds. Flynn pointed his camera the other way. The hinges squealed noisily as Toby pushed the gates open, and the sound seemed very loud in the quiet. Toby and Flynn froze where they stood for a moment, but there were no alarms, no sudden lights or raised voices, and so they pressed on. The garden had overgrown the main path, and they had to push their way past overhanging branches and outcropping rose bushes. It was very dark, once they moved out of the range of the street lights. Toby followed his old memories, from late-night and early-morning returns after teenage revels, and Flynn stuck close to Toby. Every sound they made seemed to carry and echo on the still air. They came at last to the front door, and Toby stopped so suddenly Flynn almost ran into the back of him. There was a small light on over the door, which stood wide open.

'Damn,' said Toby tonelessly. 'They know we're here.'

'They?' said Flynn. 'Who's they? I thought you said Grace was behind all this.'

'There's always a they. Grace couldn't have done this alone. She wouldn't have known how. Follow me in, Flynn. Stay close, and keep that camera going, whatever happens. And if I say run, don't hang about or you'll be following me all the way out. Got it?'

'Got it, boss.'

Toby strode forward into the gloom of the hallway with Flynn right there with him, almost treading on his heels. Toby found the light switches and turned them all on. The hall blazed into being around them, and they both waited a minute for their eyes to adjust to the bright light. The first thing Toby noticed was that there was dust everywhere. He frowned. Grace had always been so house-proud. He led the way through the house, finding only empty rooms and more dust. The whole place might have been utterly deserted. He came at last to the heavy doors leading to Grace's main reception room, and hesitated for only a moment before pushing them open and storming in. The room was brightly lit, and there was Grace Shreck, sitting stiffly in her chair beside the fire, as always. And standing by her side was the Speaker of the House, Elias Gutman. They both nodded courteously to Toby and Flynn.

'Well,' said Toby, 'that explains a lot.'

'Come in, dear,' said Grace calmly. 'Make yourself at home. Would you care for some tea?'

'No tea,' said Toby. 'I'm here for answers. And I'm not leaving till I get some.'

'You won't like them,' said Grace, her voice and face curiously calm, almost disinterested.

'Let's start with the human slime beside you,' said Toby. He glared at Gutman. 'How long have you been using my Family as a front?'

'Oh, you'd be surprised,' said Elias Gutman, smiling easily. 'Grace was one of the few aristos still left that everybody trusted. That made her very useful. I must say, I'm very impressed with you, Toby. No one was ever supposed to know what was going on here till it was far too late to do any good.'

'All right, Elias; hit me. What's been going on?'

'Uh, boss . . .' said Flynn.

Toby looked round to find Grace's servants filing silently in through the open door. There were twenty of them, all armed with guns, all of them with the same blank, fixed expression. They quickly surrounded Toby and Flynn and covered them with their weapons.

'We've been expecting you,' said Grace. 'Your accessing the Family files set off a silent alarm. We considered having you killed immediately, but in the end we felt sure your curiosity and surprisingly strong sense of Family honour would bring you here before you went public with any accusations. We will allow your cameraman to make a full record of what happens here. We can release it later, when it can do the most damage.'

'What the hell's the matter with you, Grace?' said Toby. 'If you had problems, why didn't you come to me, instead of this worm Elias? And where's Clarissa?'

'She'll be joining us shortly,' said Grace, entirely unmoved by Toby's anger. 'And I thought you would have guessed what's going on here by now. It's really very simple. I'm not Grace Shreck, and that isn't Elias Gutman. We're both agents of Shub. I am a Fury; a machine with human shape and covering. Elias, and all the servants here, are dragon's teeth. Their bodies are still human, but only Shub's thoughts move in their brains. Elias lost his mind in the computer Matrix some time ago, and it was simple enough for him to send the servants in too, one at a time, on one pretext or another. Now we are the eyes and ears of the rogue AIs of Shub. A fifth column in the heart of Humanity's homeworld. And you wouldn't believe all the damage we've been able to do.'

'As Speaker of the House, I have automatic access to all political and military intelligence,' said the thing with Gutman's face and voice. 'All of it goes straight to Shub. I have also spent a great deal of time intriguing secretly with all the political parties and factions of every extreme, keeping them paranoid and carefully balanced against each other, ensuring that no real discussion or agreement is ever made; only endless compromise and confrontations that lead nowhere useful. And, of course, I know all their dirty little secrets too. At the right moment, we shall reveal them. And what chaos there will be then . . .'

'You bastards,' said Toby numbly. 'I never even suspected. You're no great loss, Elias, but Grace . . . I always liked Grace. Even if she never did approve of me. No wonder you seemed to come out of your shell in such a hurry. What happened to the real Grace Shreck?'

'Well,' said the Fury, 'I'm wearing all that's left of her.'

Toby made an inarticulate sound of rage and pain and lurched forward. Flynn grabbed him by the arm and stopped him. Toby stood, breathing harshly, glaring at the machine wearing his dead aunt's skin. 'And Clarissa?' he said finally.

'Still very much alive and human,' said Gutman, smiling his unwavering smile. 'Our captive, and our hostage. We always knew she'd come in handy, if we ever needed control over you. If you behave, you'll get to see her soon.'

'And then what happens?' said Toby, his hands clenched into useless fists at his sides.

'You'll be replaced, all three of you,' said the Fury. 'We'll drug you just enough to make you tractable without it being too obvious, and then Elias will take you into the Matrix, and the AIs will force out all your messy human thoughts and replace them with the logic of Shub. You'll make very useful traitors. A newsman can do much to demoralize Humanity. I think we'll start with a public campaign against the espers; a witch-hunt of paranoia and suspicion. Shouldn't take long to herd them into concentration camps for . . . processing. They are, after all, the only ones who could hope to detect our presence.'

'I'll die before I help you against Humanity,' said Toby Shreck.

'You'll die, and then you'll help us,' said Elias Gutman.

There was a commotion behind them, and Toby and

Flynn turned to look. Two blank-faced servants were hustling Clarissa through the open doors. Her hair was dishevelled and her eyes were red and puffy, as though she'd been crying for some time. She saw Toby and ran towards him. He took her in his arms, and held her tightly as she tried to force words past her tears. He stroked her hair gently.

'It's all right, it's all right, Clarissa. I'm here now. I know what's been going on. I won't let them hurt you.'

'Love,' said Grace, not looking round from where she sat in her chair. 'Such a useful weapon with which to control humans. You won't make any trouble, Toby and Flynn, because if you do we'll hurt Clarissa until you stop. And she does as she is told, because we said we'd kill you if she didn't.'

Toby pushed Clarissa gently away from him, so he could stare into her eyes. 'Are you all right? Have they hurt you?'

Clarissa controlled herself with an effort. 'You don't know what it's been like here, Toby. Grace only acted like herself for visitors. The rest of the time she didn't even pretend. Then the servants changed. Finally Grace told me the truth. I tried to run, but the servants caught me. I was held prisoner in my room, told what to say to you and the outside world, on pain of our deaths. I've been the only human thing in this house for so long . . .'

'Hush, hush,' said Toby. He looked at Gutman. 'Let her live, and you won't need to replace me. I could work for you freely.'

'No!' said Clarissa immediately. 'You can't do that!'

'I'm saving your life!' said Toby, not looking at her.

'I wouldn't want to live in the world Shub's going to make,' said Clarissa. 'I'll kill myself before I let them use me to control you.'

Toby turned reluctantly back to her. 'There's a way out of this. There's always a way.'

'I don't see how,' said Shub, through the mouths of Grace and Elias and all the servants.

'Easy,' said Kit SummerIsle from the doorway. 'He has friends in high places.'

He raised his disrupter and shot Elias Gutman in the face, blowing his head apart. The body slumped to the floor, finally free of Shub control. The servants rushed forward to jump Kid Death, but he already had his sword in his hand. He cut them down as they came to him, blood flying thickly on the air, none of them making a sound as they died. The Fury in Grace's skin jumped up out of her chair and turned to run, only to find itself facing Ruby Journey, who had arrived unnoticed through the rear door. The Fury and the Maze survivor studied each other thoughtfully.

'I'm not entirely stupid,' said Toby to Clarissa and Flynn. 'If things were as heavy as I suspected, I knew I might need heavy-duty help. So I arranged some, just in case. I know Ruby Journey, and she contacted Lord SummerIsle. Fight fire with fire, I always say. All I had to do was keep the bad guys occupied until they could sneak in.'

Kid Death cut his way through the servants crowding around him, not even breathing hard. The servants had Shub's thoughts, but their bodies were only human, and Kit wouldn't give them a chance to stand back and use their guns. Some tried to drag him down through sheer weight of numbers, but he wouldn't fall. They moved to get past him and escape, but he blocked the way. He had to dodge a few disrupter blasts as the numbers thinned, but in a short time all of them lay dead, and he stood calmly in their midst, wearing their blood like badges of honour. He looked hopefully around for someone else to kill, but only Grace remained, still locking eyes with Ruby Journey; two women who were both so much more than they appeared.

'I hear you're not nearly as powerful alone, without Jack Random's power to draw on,' said Grace.

'But I'm always growing stronger,' said Ruby. 'I'm much more than you could ever hope to comprehend, machine.'

The Fury smiled with Grace's mouth. 'I shall kill you, and take your body back to Shub and tear all the secrets from it.'

'Dream on,' said Ruby Journey.

'Want any help?' said Kit SummerIsle.

'Don't you dare,' said Ruby. 'This one's all mine.'

She gestured with an empty hand, and a blaze of heat roared from it to smash against the Fury. Grace's skin blackened and cracked and peeled away from the blue steel beneath. The human teeth still grinned defiance as Grace's clothes went up in flames. But without Random to join with, Ruby couldn't summon up the intense heat that had melted Furies into so much metal slag, back on the plains of Loki. The heat quickly stripped away the illusion of Grace, but the machine beneath remained untouched and unaffected. It surged forward, and Ruby went to meet it with her bare fists.

Her blows dented the metal where they landed, and her boosted speed was easily the match of the machine's. But it felt no pain, and took no real damage from her blows, while its steel fists broke Ruby's skin and cracked the bones beneath. Blood ran from her broken nose and crushed mouth, but Ruby just grinned with scarlet teeth and fought on, glorying savagely in the battle. She'd wanted a distraction from her main job of tracking down Jack Random, and a chance to go one on one with a possible Fury had been too good to turn down. She needed something to vent her frustrations on. She pounded away at the metal head and frame, blood dripping from her cracked knuckles, damaging the shell but not the machine.

All too soon she realized she couldn't beat it that way. She was dodging most of its blows, but the ones that got through were doing her real harm. She'd heal, of course, but it might weaken her enough for the Fury to escape, and she couldn't risk that: her reputation would never recover. She reached inside herself, deep down into the back brain, the under-mind, and hauled up the power that lived there. She concentrated her heat into a single glowing fireball that materialized floating on the air between her and the Fury, blazing so brightly she could hardly bear to look at it. The machine hesitated, confused by the unexpected phenomenon, and that was all the time Ruby needed to take the fireball and blast it right through the Fury's metal chest and out of its back, destroying the link between the Fury and the controlling AIs back on Shub. The empty steel frame tottered on its feet and finally fell backwards, landing stiff and unmoving on the floor with a deafening crash.

'Nice one,' said Kid Death, applauding softly.

Clarissa dived into Toby's arms again, and they held each other tightly. 'Dear Toby,' she said, her voice muffled against his shoulder, 'I knew you'd come for me.'

Toby hugged her back, and looked over her shoulder at Flynn.

'Don't worry, boss,' said the cameraman. 'I got it all.'

Everyone was summoned to attend Parliament, and everyone came, whether they wanted to or not. Armed guards accompanied the invitations, and they escorted the invited right to the doors of the House just to make sure that nothing happened to them, or that they didn't get lost along the way and accidentally end up somewhere else. The guns trained steadily on the summoned were purely a precautionary measure, and nothing at all to worry about. More than a few people appeared with bruises and bloody heads, but everyone sent for finally arrived on the floor of the House, a very dissatisfied and loudly objecting crowd. Not least the Members of Parliament, who weren't allowed to take their usual seats, but instead had to stand on the floor along with everyone else. Guards lined the walls, covering the crowd. Many were smiling openly. It wasn't often that they got the chance to dominate and push around the people they would normally have to bow to and obey, and they'd taken every opportunity to affirm Parliament's summons with liberal use of their fists and batons. The guards' prior removal of all identifying numbers and labels was, of course, just a coincidence.

The roar of outraged voices filled the House, from MPs and movers and shakers from all levels of society. Anyone who was anyone, in all the many spheres of influence and intrigue, had been summoned, and only some of them suspected why. There were Family members, industrial giants, clones and espers standing reluctantly shoulder to shoulder, united for once in their shared anger and confusion. Gradually people became aware that the Speaker's chair was empty, that there was no sign anywhere of Elias Gutman. Instead, Robert Campbell and Constance Wolfe stood on the raised dais on either side of the empty chair. They looked calm and determined, as though waiting to carry out some unpleasant but necessary duty. And standing before the dais were those two most notable killers, Ruby Journey and Kit SummerIsle, who gave every indication of looking forward to some unpleasant and excessively violent duty.

When the last few summoned had been shoved on to the floor of the House by their guards, the main doors were closed and locked behind them. More guards appeared in the public galleries overhead, training energy and projectile weapons on the crowd below. Even more disturbing, thirty or forty Elves also appeared in the galleries, standing tall and arrogant in their battered leathers and gaudy colours, studying the crowd with piercing eyes. Now and again, one would murmur something to a guard, who would nod and make a note. The tone of the crowd's raised voices changed slowly from anger to querulous unease. They'd seen such shows of force before, back in Lionstone's day, and those had always ended in bloodshed, sometimes on a grand scale. Lionstone saw treason everywhere, and she was usually accurate, but she never cared how many innocents died as long as no guilty man or woman escaped. Times were supposed to have changed, with new laws in place to protect people from the old outrages, but looking at the army of guards it wasn't difficult to believe that someone in power still thought the old ways were best.

At length Robert Campbell stepped forward, and the crowd fell silent. Even if it was bad news, they wanted to know what was coming, if only so they could start planning which way to duck, and who else they could try to lay the blame on. Most of them trusted Robert to give it to them straight. He looked out over the assembled throng, his face hard and cold, and when he spoke his voice was measured and deliberate.

'You will have noticed that the Speaker, Elias Gutman, is missing from his chair. He has been proven to be not just a traitor, but an Enemy of Humanity. Gutman was one of the dragon's teeth, his mind destroyed in the computer Matrix. Shub looked out of his eyes, and spoke with his mouth.' He paused a moment, as though expecting some comment or reaction, but the crowd just stared back at him, waiting for the other shoe to fall. They knew there had to be more, and it was going to be bad. Robert squared his shoulders and continued. 'Grace Shreck has been revealed as a Fury, and destroyed. From studying her and Gutman's records, we have determined that Shub has infiltrated all levels of authority and security on Golgotha. It has therefore been determined that everyone of substance should be brought here to be scanned by espers, so that we can be sure of who is who, and what is what.'

He paused again, and this time the crowd answered him with a roar of defiance. The harsh, angry sound filled the great chamber, loud and overpowering. Fists were shaken, and empty hands twitched unhappily at sides where swords and guns would normally hang. No weapons had been allowed in the House, this time. It wasn't that the crowd didn't believe what Robert had told them, or that they didn't appreciate the importance of what had been discovered. They just couldn't accept an esper scan as the answer. They all had secrets they didn't want known, even if they weren't actually of any importance to anyone but themselves. Everyone has something they can't bear to talk about, even with their closest and most loved ones. The crowd stirred this way and that, its anger building, but remained quelled by the guns pointing at them from all sides. Finally two men pushed their way to the front of the crowd and glared up at the

Campbell. Roj Peyton, Merchant Prince, was a large, square-built man with a history of cunning deals and hard bargaining. At his side stood the acerbic social columnist Dee Langford, purveyor of unsuspected truths and assassin of reputations, whose pieces everyone read, if only to be sure they weren't in them.

'Where the hell do you get off, ordering us brought to Parliament like this?' snapped Peyton. 'Under armed guards and implied threats! Who gave you authority over us?'

'You did,' said Constance Wolfe, stepping forward to stand beside Robert Campbell. Her voice was cold and dangerous. 'You chose us to be the new monarchs of the Empire because you trusted us. Trust us now to do what is necessary for the good of Humanity. After this is over, power will return to the Members of Parliament. Or at least, the MPs that remain.' She looked around her for challenges, but the crowd was quiet again, desperate for more information. Constance continued. 'Who else could the uncoverers of this plot turn to, but Robert and I? Particularly when it became clear that Parliament itself had been infiltrated by our enemies. The innocent have nothing to fear. The espers will not be probing into anyone's secrets. They have assured me that only the lightest of mental touches is necessary to determine whether thoughts are human or otherwise.'

'We only have your word for that,' said Langford smoothly. 'The esper underground could do much to increase its status and influence if it had access to our thoughts. We cannot put ourselves into the hands of potential blackmailers. What you ask is unacceptable, and we refuse.'

'Too late,' said Constance. 'We had all of Parliament's esp-blockers removed before you got here. The Elves have been scanning you since you arrived, and have been determining who our real enemies are even while you've been talking. The guards have been given their targets on a shielded comm channel. Death to the Enemies of Humanity!'

On that prearranged signal, sharpshooters among the

guards in the galleries opened fire on individual targets. Soft-nosed bullets took out the dragon's teeth, cutting them down with merciless accuracy. Energy blasts from disrupters punched holes through the concealed metal chests of Furies posing as men. There was mass panic as the guards opened fire, and innocents were unavoidably hurt or killed as they moved into the firing line, or the targets grabbed them for use as shields. Battle espers among the Elves worked to separate the guilty from the innocent, but as the crowd surged this way and that, screaming and jostling, it was hard for anyone to see what was going on. Some tried to rush the locked doors, but there were guards waiting for them, and they grimly cut down anyone who tried to leave the killing ground. Some of these were innocent victims too.

Roj Peyton grabbed Dee Langford and used him as a human shield as he charged towards Robert and Constance. Langford cried out as bullets slammed into him, over and over, his body jerking and shuddering under the impact, but Peyton's more-than-human strength held him in place, soaking up punishment even after he was dead. An energy beam struck Peyton's head a glancing blow, ripping away half the human face to reveal the metal skull of a Fury beneath. He'd almost reached the unflinching Robert Campbell when Kit SummerIsle stepped forward and casually shot out one of the Fury's knees. He crashed to the dais, losing his grip on his dead shield, and Ruby Journey shot him through the back, destroying the Fury's link with his Shub masters.

Very soon it was all over. Most of the dragon's teeth were slain in the first few seconds, taken out by the sharpshooters. The Furies took longer, and did a lot of damage in the crowd, but eventually they all fell under concentrated disrupter fire. Panic slowly died away as it became clear that the shooting had stopped, and was replaced by a numb calm and acceptance. Guards moved among the people, separating the condemned dead from the cleared living. There were a lot of bodies. Among them Members of Parliament, industry chiefs and some leaders of the clone and esper undergrounds.

Robert had suspected these last, which was why he'd brought in Elves to do the scanning. Their mass gestalt precluded traitors. A great many of the Families had lost members too, unsuspecting men and women who'd entered the Matrix as humans and come out as dragon's teeth. There was weeping on all sides, and people stumbled aimlessly around, blank-faced with shock. Everyone there had lost someone, or knew someone who had. Later there would be recriminations, refusals to believe and threats of revenge over the innocent fallen, but for now it was mostly grief that moved through the crowd, over friends and families murdered long ago by Shub so that their bodies could serve as traitors.

And just when everyone thought the worst was over, a viewscreen formed in mid-air showing General Beckett. He'd used his considerable authority to force contact, even getting past the current level of security. He glared out of the screen, standing on the bridge of his ship, the flagship of the Imperial Fleet. Beside him stood Half A Man, looking browbeaten, having been bullied into joining the Fleet whether he wanted to or not. The House quickly grew quiet again, and everyone gave Beckett their full attention. They knew he wouldn't have interrupted unless it was vitally important. He and Half A Man had been placed in personal charge of the largest remaining single section of the Fleet, and sent out to face Shub's hordes. But they shouldn't have made contact with the Shub vessels for days yet.

'About time,' said Beckett. 'Forget your damned security, this is urgent.'

'What is it, General?' said Robert wearily. 'We're in the middle of a delicate situation right now . . .'

'To hell with your situation! The Recreated are here. They're only a week or so out from Golgotha! We might be able to slow them down some, but God knows for how long. Send every ship you've got to join us. Half the Fleet's already gone. If you can, try and make a temporary deal with Shub and the Hadenmen; the Recreated are their enemy too. Send more ships! The front line in the war is right here, right now!'

'What about you, Half A Man?' said Robert sharply. 'You're supposed to be our expert on the Recreated. What do you suggest?'

Half A Man seemed distracted, as though trying to listen to two voices at once. 'I don't understand any of this. I should know what to do, but when I look for it in my mind, it isn't there. Most of my mind . . . isn't there. Memories are missing, and my thoughts slam up against walls I didn't even know were in there. I don't think I am who I thought I was.' He looked out of the screen. 'I'm sorry, I'm so sorry. But I think I'm just the smile on the face of the tiger.'

And then he screamed horribly, as the energy half of his body ate the human half, consuming the flesh inch by inch until the screams finally stopped because there wasn't enough left of the lung to support them. The single eye stared mutely out of the half-face until it too was gone, and then there was only a crackling energy shape left on the bridge of the Fleet's flagship, that looked nothing like a man. General Beckett drew his disrupter and shot the thing at point-blank range, but it had no effect. As he stood there, helpless, a voice was heard, on the bridge and in Parliament; a deafening, awful sound that had nothing human about it.

We are the Recreated. We have left the dark to destroy the light. It is our time, come round at last. Our long-awaited revenge begins . . . now.

The energy shape thrust its glowing hand into General Beckett's chest and ripped out his heart. And even as Beckett's body slumped to the bloodied deck, the energy shape turned to the control panels and hit the Emergency Destruct, blowing up the flagship. The viewscreen went blank, and for what seemed like a long time it was very quiet in Parliament.

They might have got over the shock, and started making decisions, but the worst wasn't over yet. There was a frenzied pounding on the main doors. Heads turned to look, and Robert gestured to the nearest guards to unlock the doors.

They did so, and Toby Shreck came storming in with Flynn at his heels.

'We know who the carrier is for the nanoplague!' he shouted at once. 'The name was in Gutman's files! It's Daniel Wolfe!'

Daniel Wolfe, who had escaped detection by the espers because he didn't know he was a traitor, screamed the howl of the damned as his memories came crashing back, and he remembered his trip to Shub and what they had done to him there. He remembered his trips to the other planets Shub had infected, and all the people he'd touched and unknowingly condemned to death. And even as he screamed his sanity away, deeply buried Shub programming took over and sent him running for the open doors, throwing people out of his way. Guards opened fire with bullets and energy blasts, but none of them stopped him, the nanotech within him instantly repairing all his wounds. In a moment he was gone, and only the sound of his despairing screams remained, echoing round the silent Parliament.

CHAPTER THREE

Zero Zero

Captain John Silence sat slumped in his command chair on the bridge of the *Dauntless*, studying the enigmatic image of the planet Zero Zero on the main viewscreen, and felt very much like throwing something heavy and sharp-edged at the scene before him. The *Dauntless* had been heading towards the Rim, and then the Darkvoid, until a last-minute change of course from Parliament had brought them here, to the one planet in the Empire possibly more dangerous than the endless night of the Darkvoid. Zero Zero: the planet no one comes home from. It had been under strict Quarantine for centuries, ever since the nanotech got loose. Investigating teams had been sent before, at intervals down the many years, but none had ever reported back. There could be anything down there, anything at all. Parliament hoped there was a cure for the nanoplague down on Zero Zero, and had sent Silence and his crew to look for it. No one asked what they thought about it. Silence sniffed sourly, and dug into his bowl with his chopsticks. He didn't normally eat on the bridge, it encouraged sloppiness and divided attention, but he couldn't risk going below now that they were actually here. The planet looked quite pretty from orbit, like a pastel-coloured rose with hidden, poisonous thorns. Silence chewed manfully on his reconstituted meal, and tried hard not to think what it was reconstituted from. It was better than protein cubes, but only just.

Zero Zero, a planet so dangerous even Shub stayed well

clear of it: the place where Empire science had been allowed to run mad, meddling with the wellsprings of creation itself. They should have known it would all go horribly wrong. But Silence and his crew had a reputation for dealing with impossibly dangerous situations and surviving, and when all was said and done they were still considered regrettably expendable, and so here they were. All alone in the night, hovering over the tragic results of a trip into the dark subconscious of the scientific mind. There should have been another starcruiser here, standing guard to enforce the Quarantine, but with ships at a premium it had long ago been called away to fight in the war. Current thinking was that anyone stupid enough to land on Zero Zero deserved every extremely unpleasant thing that happened to them. Silence had already decided not to risk any more than the smallest practical landing party. Too bad he had to be one of them.

'Captain! Picking up signs of two unidentified craft in high orbit,' said his new comm officer, Morag Tal. She was tall and blonde, sharp and intelligent and eager to please. She also seemed incredibly young, but then a lot of his crew seemed that way to Silence. Possibly because most of the old familiar faces had died on one hell-bent mission or another, or been posted to where their experience could be better used. And since there were no experienced replacements any more . . . Silence realized his thoughts were drifting, and made himself pay attention as the comm officer put the new images up on the viewscreen. 'A golden Hadenman vessel and a Shub ship, Captain,' announced Tal. 'Low-level shields hid them until we were practically on top of them. No hostile reactions as yet.'

'Run full sensor scans,' said Silence. 'And you can try raising them on the comm, though I doubt they'll talk to us. I'm mostly interested in why they haven't already opened fire on us.'

'Shall I put the ship on Full Alert?'

'Not yet. If they were going to cause trouble they'd have

done it by now. Shub and the Hadenmen . . . any signs they've been fighting each other?'

'Sensor scans complete, Captain.' Morag Tal frowned at the information scrolling down the screen before her. 'No signs of any external damage. Energy levels are very low; probably running on automatic systems only. No power to their weapon systems . . . and no life signs. None at all. Neither ship responding to comm enquiries. It seems likely both ships are deserted.'

Silence raised an eyebrow and put his meal to one side. 'Interesting. Surely they wouldn't have all gone down to the planet? And if they haven't been fighting, what could have happened that was so bad they had to abandon ship for the dubious safety of Zero Zero?'

'Insufficient evidence as yet, Captain.'

'That was a rhetorical question, Tal. All right; if there are Hadenmen down there, and Shub agents, the sooner we get dirtside the better. Comm officer, locate Investigator Carrion, and have him report to the briefing lounge.'

'Aye, sir.' The comm officer's voice was carefully calm and neutral. No one on the crew of the *Dauntless* had any time for that notorious traitor and outlaw Carrion, even if he had been officially Pardoned, but no one was dumb enough to show it openly. Silence tended to have very sharp and unpleasant ways of dealing with any discourtesies to his old friend. It was surprising how many toilets there were that always needed cleaning on a ship the size of the *Dauntless*. Especially when you were only issued with a toothbrush.

'Meanwhile, maintain high orbit.' Silence had decided to abandon what was left of his meal until he was really hungry. 'Stay out of the planet's atmosphere. There's no telling how high the rogue nanos were thrown when the scientific Base exploded. There could still be some floating about up there, just waiting for something hard and solid to come along so they can continue their dirty work. Maintain full shields at all times.'

'Beg pardon, Captain, but indefinite use of full shields will mean a serious drain on our power.'

Silence turned a stern look on Tal. 'Comm officer, you seem intent on telling me things I already know. I am quite aware of my own ship's limitations, thank you. I am less sure of Zero Zero's ability to do us harm, so we are taking no chances at all.' He allowed his expression to soften a little. 'Don't try so hard to impress me, Tal. You may be new, but you're good at your job or you wouldn't be here. Now; send down a couple of remote probes. With a little luck they might last long enough to send back something useful.'

The comm officer nodded quickly, and fired off two probes. They were basically just information-gathering packages inside heavy armour. They couldn't be shielded and still do their work, so that left them vulnerable to nano attack. The whole bridge crew watched as the two probes plunged into Zero Zero's deceptively tranquil atmosphere, tense and strained as they waited for impact. Silence had Tal put up the incoming sensor readings on the main viewscreen, as the probes sent back the first direct information on Zero Zero's condition in centuries.

Heavy cloud cover, but no storm systems. Air content and temperatures within acceptable human limits. Gravity earth normal, as near as dammit, which was a little surprising, given the somewhat greater size of the planet. No life signs. The probes were just beginning to make out the shapes of the three main continents when the figures coming in suddenly became uncertain. They flickered from one extreme value to another, in impossibly wide swings, and then began to contradict each other. New visual images appeared on the viewscreen, harsh and jagged, in ugly colours and sharp angles that were subtly disturbing to the eye. Silence felt a headache building in his left temple, and his eyes felt like they'd been sandpapered. And then the probes shut down and the screen went blank, and everyone on the bridge heaved varying sighs of relief.

'No more signals, Captain,' said Morag Tal, her fingers

flying over the control panels before her. 'Something was definitely affecting the probes there at the end, so that information cannot be depended on, but I think I've sorted out some useful data from the earlier transmissions.'

More images appeared on the main viewscreen, showing the three main land masses. Jagged mountain ranges crossed the great continents, large and prominent enough to be seen clearly even from so high an altitude. Much of the land masses was bare rock, with volcanic vents and a tendency to earthquakes powerful enough to reshape the coastlines at regular intervals. Zero Zero had been an unpleasant, largely uninhabited world, of no real use for colonizing and little intrinsic mineral value, which was why it had been chosen for nanotech research in the first place.

'That's all we got, Captain,' said Morag Tal. 'The probes lasted approximately forty-seven seconds. The information they were sending back right at the end cannot be considered reliable. The probes appeared to be . . . changing, altering, as the nanos worked on them. I'm not sure what they were becoming, but it sure as hell wasn't anything I recognized.'

'Understood,' said Silence. 'Run it all through the computers, see if they come up with any useful insights.' He swivelled in his chair to look at the tall, cadaverous figure standing patiently at his side. Klaus Morrell was the new ship's esper; skeletally thin and dressed in blinding white, he looked rather like a ghost that hadn't been invited to any feast in a long time. He tended to crack his knuckles loudly when he was thinking, and had other, worse habits. The *Dauntless* was his sixteenth posting in three years, and Silence was beginning to suspect he knew why.

'So,' he said heavily, 'you picking up anything of interest yet?'

'If I had, I'd have told you,' said Morrell. 'Peculiar bloody place you've brought me to. This far out I shouldn't be picking up anything, but . . . I'm getting something . . . right on the edge of my mind. Not so much thoughts, more like the background murmur of the universe, with everyone talking at once. It makes no sense at all, and it's really very irritating. You'll have to get me a lot closer before I can be of any use, and I really wish I hadn't just said that. I would like to make it very clear that I would rather gnaw my own leg off without anaesthetic than pay a personal visit to that misbegotten toilet of a world below us. Something very bad's going to happen down there. I can feel it in my water.'

'Think of it as a chance to stretch your legs,' said Silence easily. 'You don't want to miss out on all the fun, do you?'

'If at all possible, yes. I am not at all a well person, and I have a bone in my leg. Am I to gather from the way you're looking at me that I have already volunteered to join your landing party?'

'Got it in one. You must have read my mind.'

'Ho, ho, ho. Bloody officer humour. It'll end in tears, I know it.'

Down below, in one of the *Dauntless*'s less crowded recreation areas, the man known as Carrion sat alone at a table, drinking lukewarm coffee at the end of an uninspiring meal. He could have eaten all his meals in his cabin, and would have preferred to, but Silence had ordered him to get out in public so that the crew would have a chance to get used to him. So far, it didn't seem to be working. People avoided talking to Carrion unless they absolutely had to, and then treated him with cold courtesy at best. Only respect for their captain kept them from open insults or worse, attempted violence. They looked at the man in traitor's black, and saw only the Investigator who went native on the planet Unseeli, and fought beside the alien Ashrai against his own kind; against Humanity, killing good men and women for no reason they could understand. Carrion, the sworn protector of Humanity who became a traitor and an outlaw because he loved an alien race more than honour and duty.

And who was to say they were wrong?

No one sat at his table with him. People ostentatiously chose the tables furthest from him. Some talked about him, just loudly enough to be sure he'd hear. Most wouldn't even look at him. Truth be told, Carrion took comfort in his isolation. After Silence gave the order to scorch Unseeli from orbit, and wiped out every living creature on the planet, Carrion had lived there alone for many years, his only company the ghosts of the murdered Ashrai. Apart from one brief period a few years back, when Silence had returned to drag him unwillingly from his preferred isolation to help investigate the mystery of Base Thirteen, Carrion had remained aloof from all human life, and preferred it that way. Using human speech was like using a language he hadn't heard since childhood. He wouldn't have known what to do with companionship, even if it had been offered to him. He no longer considered himself human, and believed he had little in common left with those who did. He felt no need for company or conversation, or for anything much, any more.

Except perhaps for revenge on the rogue AIs of Shub, who had destroyed what little sanctuary and reason for living he'd had left.

Anyone else would surely have gone mad, left alone on an alien world for so many years, but Carrion had found peace and a kind of absolution in his solitude. The Ashrai had altered him so that he could survive where no other human could, and Unseeli became his home. He walked for hours through the gleaming metallic forests, listening to the wind sing in their spiky branches, and sometimes hearing the song of the dead Ashrai too. The trees weren't just trees, though he was never sure quite what else they might be, but there was a harmony to be found in their embrace, and he became a part of it. He was at peace, with no one to hate and no one to hate him. His wars were over.

Or so he thought, till the great metal ships came from Shub, filling the skies with their fearsome shapes, and tore the metal trees out of the ground until none remained anywhere on Unseeli. And who else was there left for Carrion to turn to, except his old friend and enemy, Captain John Silence? They'd established a kind of truce, if not understanding, and now here was Carrion on a human ship, an Investigator again. It was a harsh kind of joke, but then the universe was like that, in Carrion's experience. The dead forests and the ghosts of the Ashrai cried out for vengeance, and if this was all he had left to give his life purpose, it was better than nothing.

He missed Unseeli so much. It was the only place where he'd ever been happy.

A man came up and sat down beside Carrion. He did so quickly, almost rudely, as though not wanting to give Carrion any time to object. He was young, barely out of his teens, with dark eyes and a set, determined mouth. Carrion recognized the face, and the newcomer saw that he did. He shifted his gangling frame uncertainly in his chair, and then nodded jerkily.

'You do know me. I wasn't sure you'd remember.'

'Of course I remember,' said Carrion calmly. His power lance leaned against the table beside him, but he made no effort to reach for it. 'You're the one who tried to kill me when I first came aboard the *Dauntless*.'

'Yes, that's right. I'm Micah Barron, Ordinary Crewman. My father was one of the men you killed in the war on Unseeli.'

'I don't remember him. There were so many. I regret his death, if that makes any difference. Do you still wish to kill me?'

'No,' said Barron, looking down at his hands clasped tightly together before him on top of the table. The knuckles were white. 'The captain vouches for you. Called you his friend. And the captain . . . is a good and honourable man. A hero. I'd die for the captain. I've followed his career since I was a boy. It was a way of making contact with the father I barely knew. After he died . . . I couldn't wait to be old enough so I could join up too. I've tried to read up on the Unseeli war, but most of the files are still Restricted. Parliament keeps promising more open government, but I'll believe that when I see it. So you see, there are only two places I can go to find out the truth about what happened on Unseeli all those years ago, what the war was really about. And why my father had to die there. One is the captain, and the other is you. And after my previous behaviour, there's no way the captain's ever going to agree to speak to me again. Except maybe at my court martial. So that just leaves you.'

Carrion stirred uneasily. 'It is not a time I care to remember. So many died, on both sides. Much of me died during that war. And I've already said I don't remember your father.'

'But you're my only link to him, to the times that shaped and killed him. Tell me about the Ashrai. What were they like?'

'Why did I side with them against Humanity?' Carrion looked out across the room with haunted eyes, not seeing what was there, lost in yesterday. 'You have to remember, I was raised as an Investigator, taken from my parents as a small child, raised to be apart from the Humanity I was trained to serve and protect. Taught that the only good alien was a dead alien. But the Ashrai were wild and glorious and so free. Like every dream I'd ever had. Not beautiful, not by human standards. But they were pure, uncomplicated; savage and unrestrained. They flew through the air like mighty dragons, and when they sang . . . they were creatures of awe and wonder, the angels of a different world. So much more than the grubby little humans who threatened to destroy them, just so the Empire could mine some metals from the forests.

'Captain Silence was my friend then; perhaps my only friend. I tried to explain, to make him understand. But he saw only his orders, and his duty. We were both so much younger then.'

'But . . . he offered the Ashrai reservations. Places where they could live freely, away from the machines mining the forests.'

Carrion looked sadly at Barron. 'Is that the story they told, to excuse what they did? The Ashrai flew free; the whole world was their domain. And they were linked to the forests. They would have withered and died, restricted to artificial borders, dying inch by inch as the trees died. Silence knew that. There was no offer of reservations. War became inevitable, and I knew which side I belonged on. I had sung the song of the Ashrai, seen the world anew through their eyes, and I could never go back. Back to being only, merely, human.'

'Tell me about the war.'

Carrion frowned. It wasn't hard to call back the memories. They were never far from him. 'The Ashrai were strong and fast and powerful. Their numbers filled the skies. The Empire had explosives and energy weapons. Ashrai blood fell like rain, and the human dead piled up till a man couldn't see over them. Ashrai psistorms fought Empire battle wagons. There seemed no end to the dead, and the suffering. And I was right there in the middle of it, my hands dripping with the blood of those who had once been my fellow crewmen. Sometimes I knew their faces, more often not. I never thought the war would go on for so long. I thought that eventually the Empire would get tired of losing men, and go away. I didn't realize how badly they needed the metals from the forests.

'I never thought they'd order Silence to scorch the planet; I never believed he'd do it. I can still hear the Ashrai screaming as energy beams slammed down from orbit. There was nothing I could do to save them. I dug a deep hole and pulled it in after me, protected by my psionic powers. They seemed to go on screaming for ever, until finally the scorching stopped and there was only silence. I dug my way out, to find myself the only inhabitant of an empty world. But the trees were still alive, in their way, and tied so closely to the Ashrai that not even death could fully separate them. Their ghosts remained, and their song. They forgave me. I never did.

'Now the forests are gone, and only I remain to tie the Ashrai to the worlds of the living.'

'They were your family,' said Barron, after a while.

Carrion nodded, surprised at the insight. 'Of course. The family I'd never known before. I was their adopted son, and I loved them with all my heart. Silence was my friend, but I never felt as close to him as I did to the Ashrai. I don't think he ever really forgave me for that.'

'Are you and he friends now?'

Carrion smiled slightly for the first time. 'We do our best. We have both come a long way from who we used to be, and we have shared things no one else could hope to understand. He's a hero, these days. He's achieved many remarkable things. But I think he's more lonely now than he ever was. So much of him died when Investigator Frost died.'

'Did they love each other?' said Barron, leaning forward.

'She was an Investigator,' said Carrion, after a moment, and both knew that there was really nothing more to be said.

Then Carrion sat up straight and gestured for Barron to wait a moment as new orders came in through his comm implant. He frowned, and rose abruptly to his feet. 'I must leave you now. It seems I am to join the captain's landing party on Zero Zero.'

Barron rose quickly to his feet. 'Ask the captain to take me too. I'm not afraid. I volunteer. I need to prove myself to the captain. After . . . what happened before.'

'When you tried to kill me.'

'Yes.'

'No one knows what we'll be facing on Zero Zero. No one knows if any one of us will return.'

'I don't care. I need to do this.'

'Very well,' said Carrion. 'Come with me to the briefing. I will vouch for you. But I can promise nothing where the captain is concerned. He has always placed duty before friendship.'

Barron looked at Carrion for a long moment. 'Why are you doing this? I thought I'd have to get down on my knees and beg you for a second chance.'

'Please don't. I'd find that very embarrassing. As to why,

let's just say that I of all people understand the worth of a second chance.'

The briefing lounge was a mess. Half the viewscreens weren't working, and most of the computers had their guts open to the air. The *Dauntless* had been undergoing extensive refitting and upgrading when Silence was suddenly called on to take his ship out again in a hurry, with a lot of the work still left undone. The technicians had been catching up as best they could during the voyage, but away from a stardock's personnel and resources, repairs had an unfortunate tendency to proceed at the general pace of an arthritic snail with no sense of direction. And the briefing lounge had a priority number so low it couldn't even be seen except in a really good light. So of course the techs had chosen the one day when it was really needed to tear everything apart. When Carrion and Barron arrived, they found Silence shooing out half a dozen techs with firm words and one hand on his gun. They left, muttering, and Silence turned to greet Carrion.

'Techs! Trying to boss me around, just because they've got a work chit. Where were they when my coffee-maker wasn't working, and all I could get on my viewscreen was the damned porn channel?' And then he saw Barron, and his face and voice were instantly as cold as ice. 'What are you doing here, mister? Why aren't you at your post?'

'He's with me,' Carrion said calmly. 'We have reached . . . an understanding. He wishes to join the landing party on Zero Zero.'

Silence raised an eyebrow. 'Really? He doesn't look crazy.' His mood soured again almost immediately. 'Give me one good reason why I should take a back-stabbing assassin like this?'

'Because I ask it,' said Carrion.

'Ah, what the hell.' Silence shrugged, and led the way into the briefing lounge. 'We can always use him as a human shield, if need be.'

Once inside, Carrion nodded to the esper Morrell, who

nodded back. Most of the ship's crew preferred nodding when they actually had to interact with Carrion. It avoided the possibility of being made to apologize later for some word or phrase that might have slipped out in the heat of emotion. Silence gestured at the waiting chairs, and the landing party arranged themselves before the one working viewscreen. Morrell was careful to put the captain between himself and Carrion. Everyone else pretended not to notice. Silence looked at each of his team in turn.

'I'm restricting this first landing party to an absolute minimum,' he said flatly. 'Partly because of the risk, and partly because I want to avoid stirring anything up down there. We'll have no way of knowing what we're getting into until we're well into it, and by then it'll probably be too late to call for help. This will not be a scientific expedition, gentlemen; just an opening fact-finding trip. Carrion and I are going because we have the most experience in dealing with strange and dangerous alien territory, and because both of us have . . . more than normal abilities. Morrell is going because as the ship's esper he is our most experienced telepath. And Barron; you're going to be our guinea pig. You get to test the temperature of any strange waters we may encounter before the rest of us dive in. Still want to go?'

'Yes, sir,' said Barron steadily. 'I want nothing more than to prove myself in your eyes again. To be the loyal crewman my father was.'

Silence scowled. 'I'm not looking for a hero, boy. I want a crewman who'll keep his head, follow orders and come back with useful information. Is that clear?'

'Entirely clear, Captain.'

Silence turned back to Carrion and Morrell, dividing his attention between them. 'If we die, the Empire will have to decide whether to risk another landing party on Zero Zero, or send the *Dauntless* on to its primary mission in the Darkvoid. Let me repeat: our mission here is purely information-gathering. We're not here to solve the mysteries of Zero Zero, except where they coincide with our search for something that might help the Empire cope with the current nanoplague. If we do turn up anything, and live to tell of it, further scientific teams will arrive later to dig out the details. But that's not our job.

'Now; you three are about to view recorded material that has been Restricted for centuries. It carries the highest possible security rating, as does whatever information we may discover and bring back from our little trip. You are not to discuss Zero Zero with *anyone*, no matter how high-ranking, without checking with me first. Contravening this order may be punishable by death; and even I couldn't save you then. Pay close attention to the recording, and save any questions till afterwards.'

He paused for a moment to let the seriousness of his words sink in, and then activated the viewscreen. A series of security warnings scrolled up before them. Silence continued his introduction. 'You're about to see a recording of the last log entry from Zero Zero's scientific Base, made by Base Commander Jorgensson. She downloaded it into a security buoy and blasted it into high orbit, just before everything went to hell.' He paused again, recalling another time like this. Then, it had been himself and Investigator Frost, studying the last words from Unseeli's Base Thirteen. A lot of Silence's career seemed to consist of cleaning up other people's messes. The recording began, and he decided he had nothing more that was worth saying anyway.

The viewscreen was filled by the head and shoulders of Base Commander Jorgensson. She was a pleasant-looking woman in her early thirties, her generous mouth set in a grim line. She wore her long dark hair in a single functional braid draped over her left shoulder. The camera pulled back to show her seated before a desk littered with papers. A hand disrupter lay within easy reach. It looked large and clumsy, compared to the latest model. Somebody had taken a shot at the commander. There was a large scorch mark, darkened with dried blood, on her left side, and beads of sweat glistened on her forehead. In the background, alarm sirens blared over and over with dumb persistence, drowned out now and again by deafening screams and howls and raised voices that didn't sound entirely human. Jorgensson looked round sharply as something heavy slammed against the door from outside, but the security seals held. She turned back, staring out of the viewscreen with determination and hard-won control.

'Last report from Base Omega, Zero Zero. Security has been breached. The Base is contaminated. Nanotech has spread beyond the Base and out into the planet's ecosystem. God knows what it will do there. It's Marlowe's fault, damn him. He was in overall charge of the scientific team. Impeccable record. But while everyone else was working on the official experiments, he had his own, very unofficial, project going on. He had this dream of becoming superhuman, of having the nanos make him over into something far beyond our own limitations. He must have thought he'd succeeded. He exposed himself to his own specially coded nanos and unfortunately they didn't kill him. We have no idea what's become of him; he disappeared from the Base several hours ago. From what we can understand of his notes, he coded the nanos to rework him from the DNA up, and programmed them for open-ended evolution. He then either released them into the Base, or they escaped. They were programmed to multiply endlessly, using any and all available matter for base material. People inside the Base have been . . . changing. But they don't look superhuman to me.

'I've raised the Base force shield, so no one else can leave. I don't trust what people are becoming. There's been a lot of killing. Physical transformations. Strange shapes in the corridors. There are monsters running loose in the Base, and nothing seems to stop them. Every Quarantine we set up is breached almost immediately. The nanos are everywhere. They're in me, too, I can feel them moving; changing things. So that leaves me only one option. I'm going to download this log into a buoy at the starport, and then launch it by remote control. It's far enough away from the Base for it still to be uncontaminated. And now I'm going to hit the Base's self-destruct, and blow us all to hell. Except . . . this is Hell; and death may be our only escape. Damn you, Marlowe. This is Base Commander Ingrid Jorgensson signing off.'

The viewscreen went blank. Morrell nodded approvingly. 'Brave woman. Captain; I know it's been centuries, but the first question that occurs to me is, could Marlowe, or whatever he eventually became, still be down there somewhere on Zero Zero? A man full of nanos programmed to repair him eternally could last a long, long time. Theoretically.'

'Everything's theoretical where nanos are concerned,' said Silence. 'Finding Marlowe could give us all the answers we need; assuming he's still able to understand the questions. But I don't think we should count on finding him. We don't know what's been happening on the planet's surface. After centuries of nanotech running loose, endlessly multiplying, there's no telling what we'll encounter. At one end of the scale we might find a whole world gone into meltdown, like the people with the nanoplague. At the other end . . .'

'Yes?' said Barron.

'You heard the commander,' said Morrell. 'Strange shapes. Monsters. A living nightmare.'

'Don't frighten the boy too much,' said Silence. 'We'll be taking every precaution. A pinnace will take us down to the planet's surface, protected by full energy shields. We will be equipped with personal body force shields, and then dropped on to the surface from the pinnace. It will then return to high orbit, well away from the *Dauntless*, just in case, and stay there until we send for it. Full body shields use up a lot of power very quickly. We'll have a maximum of four hours, and then the shields will collapse. And we'd better not be on Zero Zero when that happens.'

'Four hours is a very short time, even for an information run, Captain,' said Carrion. 'Are you proposing several visits?'

'Depends what we find on the first one,' said Silence. 'And whether we survive finding it.'

'Couldn't we improve our odds by wearing hard suits?' said Barron.

The others looked at him. 'The nanos were programmed to interact with all matter they encountered,' said the esper Morrell. 'A hard suit would be just another snack to them.'

Barron flushed, and hastily regrouped. 'What about the Shub and Hadenman forces? I mean, their ships are deserted, so the crews must be dirtside somewhere.'

'Whatever's left of them by now,' said Morrell. He cracked his knuckles loudly. Everyone jumped in their seats, and tried to look as if they hadn't. The esper continued smoothly. 'They may have had force shields when they went down, but the power would have run out by now. They must have been exposed to the nanotech.'

'We can't know that for sure,' said Silence. 'Shub and Hadenman tech is more advanced than ours.'

'I'm still concerned with that bastard Marlowe,' said Morrell, 'and what he might have become, after centuries of change.'

'Nanos coded for open-ended evolution,' said Silence thoughtfully. 'I wonder what you would find at evolution's end, for Humanity?'

'You should know if anyone, Captain,' said Carrion. 'You're further along that road than the rest of us.'

Morrell cut in smoothly while Silence was still glaring at Carrion. 'Assuming the scientist Marlowe is still around, in whatever shape or form, what are our orders, Captain? Do we try and apprehend him?'

'What would be the point?' said Silence. 'We daren't risk taking him off-planet, for fear of spreading the nanos he's carrying. Sure, we could isolate him behind a series of force shields, but all it would take is one power outage, one slip-up in security, and the whole ship would be contaminated. You saw how fast it spread on Base Omega. If the Empire even suspected the nanos might have got loose, we'd never be allowed to land. Hell, they'd probably shoot us on sight, just in case. I would. No; if we find him, he stays on Zero

Zero. And I don't want you trying to read his mind either, Morrell. After all this time, who knows what his thoughts might have mutated into. You go in, and you might not come out again.'

Morrell sniffed. 'You're no fun any more, you know that? What's the point of going down there if we don't take a few risks?'

'This from the man who preferred to mutilate himself rather than join the landing party,' said Silence. 'We will be taking only calculated risks, Morrell. You don't do one damn thing down there without my express permission, in advance. Is that clear?'

'So clear it's dazzling, Captain. Be making me wear a bib next.'

'What was that?'

'Nothing, Captain. Just clearing my throat.'

'All right,' said Silence. 'End of preliminary briefing. Morrell; since you're so keen to be up and going, you get to check out the pinnace and make sure it's ready for the drop. And take Barron with you; I want him familiarized with all the systems, just in case he has to pilot the ship back.'

Morrell and Barron rose to their feet. Barron saluted Silence. 'I won't let you down, Captain.'

They left together. Silence waited till the door had shut behind them, and then looked at Carrion. 'That boy is too keen to be real. I'm only taking him because I think he'll be safer in my sight than out of it. Odds are he'll take the first chance he gets down below to shoot you in the back.'

'I don't think so, Captain. He's had any number of opportunities to kill me since his first attempt, and if anything he has been conspicuous in his absence from the rest of the crew's silent disapproval.'

'But do you trust him?'

'I don't trust any human these days, Captain. Not even myself.'

'Let's change the subject,' said Silence tiredly.

'As you wish.'

'The Ashrai, are they still with you? We're a long way from their homeworld.'

'Of course they're still with me. They're dead. They can be anywhere they want, sometimes simultaneously. Apparently death is very liberating.'

Silence stirred uneasily in his chair. 'I wish you'd stop calling them that. They're not really dead. They can't be.'

'You should know, Captain. You murdered them.'

'How do you think the Ashrai will react to visiting another dead world? Will they still come to your aid, if needed?'

'Unknown. They don't always manifest when I call them, even at the best of times. They're not my pets. But I don't think they'd allow me to come to harm, if they could prevent it.'

'Are you sure of that?'

'No, Captain. You destroyed the only surety I ever had in my life.'

'Will you stop that! It was all a long time ago! I thought you'd forgiven me.'

'It isn't my place to forgive you. I survived.'

Silence sighed quietly, looking at the floor. 'We were friends once, Sean.'

'Yes, we were. But that was a long time ago, and neither of us are the men we were then. For what it's worth, I don't hate you any more. I don't hate anyone. And perhaps it's only people who've been through the things we've suffered who can ever really understand each other.' Carrion paused, looking impassively at Silence. 'I know why I'm here, John. Investigator Frost died, but you still needed someone at your side, someone you could depend on. Someone who'd understand the more-than-human thing you're becoming. Who better than an old friend, who isn't entirely human either? But that was then; this is now. And I'm not Frost. You have my support, Captain. Settle for that.'

Silence shook his head slowly. 'I'm sure other people don't have conversations like this.'

*

The pinnace plunged down through the unusually calm atmosphere of Zero Zero, protected by the most powerful energy shields the ship's engines could produce. The pilot took them down fast. He'd already gone out of his way to make it clear to his passengers that he didn't intend to spend one second longer in the nano-contaminated atmosphere than he absolutely had to. He had also prayed loudly to several gods, and kept taking one hand away from the controls to cross himself, or to touch the Joan the Wad good-luck charm hanging above him. Silence would have hit him if he'd been close enough, if only for being so damned obvious about it. As it was, the captain clung grimly to a nearby stanchion with both hands, and wished the trip down didn't feel quite so much like riding a crashing elevator. The esper Klaus Morrell sat beside him, face perfectly composed, eyes calm and far away. Silence was convinced the esper was only doing it to spite him.

Carrion and Barron sat opposite Silence, both lost in their own thoughts. Wrapped in his black cloak, the dark saturnine figure of the former Investigator looked more than ever like a bird of ill omen. His power lance lay casually across his lap, the long staff of polished bone that was so powerful a weapon its very ownership was a death sentence throughout the Empire. Unless you were Carrion, that is, and the Empire needed you. Barron sat quietly beside him, nervously checking his various items of equipment over and over again. This was his first landing party, and he was determined not to screw up through lack of preparation. He was trying hard to look as though he did this every day, and apart from the rather wide eyes and the quickened breathing, he was doing a pretty good job. Silence gave him marks for effort. They made an odd couple, the young man so full of life and hope and potential, and the dark man who only looked young, all the promise of his life lost long ago in pursuit of a hopeless dream. Silence looked at them both, and knew which of them he felt most like.

They were heading for the original site of Base Omega, or

at least the place where it used to be before Commander Jorgensson blew it to hell. Probably wouldn't be much left of it after all this time, but as the location of the original nano-outbreak, there might still be a clue or two left behind. It was a long shot, but then, that was typical of the mission. The whole pinnace shook suddenly as the pilot slammed on the brakes. They must be close to their destination. There were no external views from the craft – the pinnace's sensors couldn't pierce the super-strong energy shields, so the pilot had to fly following centuries-old maps and a certain amount of dead reckoning. He was not at all happy about this, and had said so loudly, several times. The pinnace continued to slow. Silence could hear the pilot cursing continually under his breath. The ship finally came to a halt, and the pilot turned round in his crash-webbing to look back at his passengers.

'Right. This is it, everybody out. Hope you enjoyed the ride and thanks for getting most of it in the sick bags. Anything you need, take it with you now, because I'm not coming back till I have to.' He hit the lock release on his control panels, and the inner airlock door cycled open. 'Right. This is how we're going to do it, just like we practised. You all go into the lock. I shut the inner door and open the outer. You power up your individual shields, pray to anyone who might be feeling generous towards you and then jump. Your personal shields are programmed to phase you through the outer shields without my having to lower them. Theoretically. No one's ever tried this before. If it doesn't work, feel free to come back and complain through a spirit board. Don't you just love being pioneers? Knew I should have held out for danger money.'

'How far is the drop to the ground?' said Silence.

'Good question, Captain,' said the pilot. 'Wish I had an answer for you. If the ground is still where it's supposed to be, we should be hovering some two or three feet above it. Since this is the world where nanos rule, God alone knows what you're dropping into. Still, your shields should protect you. From most things. Anything else I can do to cheer you up?'

'Yeah,' said Silence, 'you can keep your ears open in orbit, and come and get us the hell out of here the minute I call you.'

He led his team into the airlock, and the inner door cycled shut behind them. It was fairly cramped with all four of them crowded into the confined space, but Silence still felt unhappy at the thought of leaving it. He looked at the outer door. Part of him wanted it to open so he could get on with the mission, and part of him hoped it would seize up or malfunction, and then he wouldn't have to do this. There'd never been much that really scared him, even before the Maze made him strong and fast and bloody hard to kill, but somehow nanos . . . invisible machines that could eat you up or transform you into anything at all . . . something you had no way of fighting . . . now that was spooky. But when the outer door finally cycled open, Silence was the first one out of the airlock, dropping into the unknown, leading by example. He was the captain, and that was his job.

The pinnace force shields shimmered below him like the inside of a soap bubble, and then he was plunging through them and out the other side, and a bright light blinded him. By the time he'd realized it was just bright sunshine, his feet had already impacted against hard ground, and he had to fight to avoid falling on his ass. It really had been only a drop of a few feet after all. The others landed beside him, and Silence squinted up into the sky to watch the pinnace racing for the safety of open space above the atmosphere. He watched till it was out of sight, and then turned to check that his people were all right. He was reassured to see the faint shimmering of air around them that meant their body shields were working. Then he turned to look at the world he'd landed on . . . and realized why the others were so quiet.

Everything looked normal; extremely normal. The landing party was standing on a grassy plain that stretched away for miles before them. The sun was shining in a perfectly normal blue sky, and large, white, everyday clouds drifted lazily overhead. The only strange thing was how utterly quiet it was. Not a sound anywhere, of animal or insect, nor even the faintest whisper of a breeze. Morrell turned to look at Silence.

'Are we in the right, place, Captain? Hell, are we even on the right planet? There shouldn't be anything like this on a rock like Zero Zero.'

'Oh, I think we can safely assume we've come to the right place,' said Carrion. 'Everyone turn slowly and look behind them.'

They all turned and looked, and there was Base Omega rising up before them, pristine and untouched. There was no trace of any damage, and the security force screen that should have isolated it from the rest of Zero Zero wasn't operating. The front doors stood open, but there were no signs of life, nor any sound at all from within.

'This is decidedly spooky,' said Barron. 'I don't know what I expected to find down here, but this sure as hell isn't it. The commander said she was going to blow the place up.'

'Every indication was that she had,' said Silence. 'The reports were quite clear. Every system in Base Omega went offline at once, and there hasn't been a signal of any kind from here since.'

'So what's this in front of us?' said Morrell waspishly.

'You're the esper,' said Silence. 'You tell me.'

Morrell nodded stiffly and stared fiercely at the Base, as though he could make it disappear through sheer willpower. His frown deepened as he reached out with his mind. 'Well, it's not an illusion, or a telepathic broadcast. It has a physical existence. But I'm not picking up any life signs inside. If this really is Base Omega, it's completely deserted.'

'Widen your scan,' said Silence. 'Is there anyone anywhere near here?'

Morrell closed his eyes and concentrated. 'I'm picking something up but I can't make any sense of it. There's certainly nothing human in the vicinity, and no trace of intelligent life for as far as I can scan. No lesser creatures, either. Not even insects in the air or on the ground. But I'm getting . . . *something*. It's like a muttering, or a chant, or a song. But it's coming from everywhere at once . . . and it moves so *fast*.' Morrell opened his eyes and looked at Silence. 'Captain; I've no idea what I'm picking up here. I've never encountered anything like it.'

'Does it feel dangerous? Threatening?'

'Damned if I know, Captain. This is entirely outside of my experience.'

'All right,' said Silence. 'Let's try the obvious route. See if I can raise anyone in the Base on my comm implant.' He turned to face the open doors, though he didn't really need to. He just wanted to be ready if anything came charging out. 'This is Captain John Silence of the *Dauntless*, representing the Empire. Is anybody listening? Is there anyone in Base Omega who can hear me? Make yourself known.'

There was no answer. The hum of the open comm channel seemed muted by the quiet. Barron shifted his feet uneasily. 'Maybe the nanotech . . . just wore out? And everything went back to normal again.'

'Unlikely,' said Carrion. 'First, if the nanos had died out, or ceased to function, this should be bare volcanic rock. There were no grass plains anywhere on Zero Zero. Second, the nanos were programmed to reproduce themselves indefinitely, using the whole planet as material if necessary. In fact, I'm almost surprised the planet is still here, with so many nanos at work for so long. This, all of this, should not be here. It cannot be natural. Something must be maintaining this apparent normality.'

'If Base Omega has survived, by whatever miracle,' Morrell said slowly, 'the lab computers could still be intact. They might have information on the nanotech, and exactly what it was originally coded with. Hell; there might even be information on how to shut the damned stuff down.'

'If the computers are there,' said Silence, 'and if we could trust what we found in them. This smells more and more like a trap of some kind. An intact Base Omega, just waiting for us to make use of it, that's too good to be true. Remember the Shub and Hadenmen ships we found abandoned in orbit? This could be their doing. Though the motivation frankly escapes me for the moment. But we can't just stand around here. We have a maximum of four hours' air inside these shields. When they both run out, we'd better be a comfortable distance away from this world.'

'We can't ignore the Base,' said Carrion.

'No,' said Silence, 'we can't.' He looked at Carrion, knowing the man in traitor's black was remembering a similar time on Unseeli, when they had stood together before the open doors to Base Thirteen, unaware of the awful thing that lay waiting for them inside. Suddenly everyone stiffened and looked round sharply. A voice was sounding through all their comm implants, and it was a voice they knew.

'This is Base Commander Jorgensson. Commander. Security has been breached. There are monsters running loose. In the corridors. This is Jorgensson. Jorgensson. Signing off.'

They all looked at each other. 'It can't be her,' said Silence. 'Not still alive. Not after all these years.'

'If she was really in there, I'd have detected her,' said Morrell. 'There's no living being in that Base.'

'Perhaps it's some kind of recording,' said Carrion, 'triggered by our presence. I don't know if you noticed, but all the words we just heard came from Jorgensson's last broadcast. The one we listened to before we came down. That can't be a coincidence.'

'Could be some attempt at communication,' said Morrell, 'put into a form we'd recognize. Try answering it, Captain. See if you can get it to respond with something that wasn't in Jorgensson's last message.'

'Indeed,' said Carrion. 'We need as much information on the current situation as possible, if we are to put an end to it and regain control of this planet.'

'Oh, great,' said Morrell. 'The only living thing we've

found here, and you only want to communicate with it to learn how to destroy it. That's going to go down really well. I guess once an Investigator, always an Investigator. Maybe it'll be something small and furry, so you can stamp on it.'

'That's enough!' said Silence. 'Carrion is doing his job. You do yours. Scan the Base again while I try and make contact with the voice. See if you can find out who or what I'm talking to.'

'Perhaps it's hiding behind an esp-blocker,' said Barron, 'and that's why you can't detect it.'

'No,' said Morrell, 'I'd have detected the esp-blocker. Nice try, though.'

Silence opened his comm channel again. 'This is Captain Silence. Can you hear me, Commander Jorgensson?'

'Hear you. Yes. Jorgensson.'

Morrell frowned, concentrating. 'Scanning, Captain. There's no one on the Base. No one at all.'

'Then who the hell am I talking to?' said Silence.

'Me,' said Base Commander Jorgensson. 'You were talking to me.'

They all looked round sharply at the nearby voice, and there she was, standing in the open doorway to the Base. She looked exactly as she had on the last log entry she'd made before supposedly blowing up her Base, even down to the bloody, scorched wound on her side. Her face was calm, and utterly without expression. Her arms hung limp at her sides. Silence looked at Morrell, who shook his head quickly.

'I don't know what that is, but it's not human. I'm not picking up any thoughts at all from her. As far as my esp is concerned, she's not there. All I'm getting is some background noise, like an endless babble of voices, almost too quiet to be heard. I will say this, though; she looks in pretty good shape for someone who's supposed to have been dead for centuries.'

Silence moved slowly towards Jorgensson. 'Putting aside

for one moment the matter of who you seem to be, can you answer some questions? Can you tell us what's happened here, on this planet?'

'I am Base Commander Jorgensson.' The woman stood perfectly still. Her eyes were dead. 'This world has been transformed. Transfigured. Become a world of possibilities and potentials. Nothing is certain any more. Things come and go. All your dreams are here, including the bad ones. Welcome to the promised land.'

'I don't know if anyone else has noticed,' said Barron quietly, 'but she only breathes when she talks.'

'If you are Jorgensson,' said Silence, stopping at what he hoped was a respectful distance from her, 'why didn't you blow up Base Omega as you intended?'

'I did,' said Jorgensson, her face and voice utterly, inhumanly calm. 'The Base was destroyed, and everyone in it died. Including me.'

'I think I'd like to leave,' said Morrell, 'right now. This is getting scary, and strikes me as something we should definitely not be messing with.'

'Stand still, that man,' said Silence. He looked at Carrion. 'You try talking to her for a while. You have the most experience with dead things that insist on moving about and talking.'

'If you died,' Carrion said calmly to Jorgensson, 'who brought you back to life?'

'Jesus raised me from the dust,' said the dead woman, 'so that we could talk. Communicate.'

'Good of him,' said Morrell. 'I think I feel sick. I don't suppose Jesus is still around anywhere, so we could ask him a few questions?'

'Look behind you,' said Jorgensson.

They all spun round, and there before them, standing smiling and dressed in a simple rough tunic, was a tall, fine-featured man with long dark hair and a beard, and kind, knowing eyes. A crown of thorns rested lightly on his head, like a barbed halo, and when he raised a hand in greeting to the landing party, they could see the nail-hole in his palm. He had an aura of wisdom and serenity, and his presence was like a cool breeze on a hot day. But the real clincher had to be the half-dozen winged angels hovering overhead, each a good twenty feet tall, in long flowing white gowns with glowing halos and huge feathered wingspans.

'Welcome to the world I have made for you,' said Jesus, in a rich, warm, comforting voice. 'Welcome to paradise.'

Silence looked at Morrell, who shook his head. 'Don't look at me; I haven't got a clue what's going on. If there was a big enough rock around, I think I'd try and hide under it. He's not an illusion, he's quite real, but that's all I can tell you. His mind is closed to me. And if He is who He says He is, I think I'm rather glad about that. Try and make mental contact with the Son of God, and my brains would probably start leaking out of my ears. Am I babbling? It sounds like I'm babbling.'

'He looks just like I always thought he would,' said Barron softly. 'So wise and loving.'

'Before anyone starts falling to their knees and shouting hosanna, allow me to point out that there is an alternative explanation,' said Carrion, apparently unmoved. 'We know that one man survived the Base explosion – the scientist Marlowe. Who infected himself with nanos programmed for open-ended evolution. This must be him.'

'And the angels?' said Silence.

Carrion paused. 'I'm still working on that.'

Morrell studied the huge forms floating overhead. 'You know, I hate to be a stickler for detail, but . . . shouldn't they be playing harps, or something? And how come they don't have to flap their wings to stay up there?'

'They certainly don't seem to be aerodynamically stable,' said Carrion.

'You two keep well away from me,' said Barron. 'When the plague of boils comes hurtling down from on high, I don't want to be anywhere near you.'

'Let's try and stick to the matter in hand,' said Silence. He turned his best intimidating glare on Jesus. 'Are you in fact the scientist Marlowe?'

'That was long, long ago,' said Jesus. 'Behold, I will tell you everything. Once, I was just a man, as any other. I walked among them, and they did not know my greatness. We were all scientists here, labouring for our Emperor. We were researching into nanotech, God's building blocks; into the transformation and programming of humans. The Emperor wished to be able to determine the shape, nature and identity of all humans, from birth. Properly programmed nanotech should be capable of producing desired traits to order. The population would then consist of pre-programmed worker drones, warriors, breeders, scientists and so on, as needed. They would be physically and mentally unable to be anything other than what they were intended to be. Humanity would become efficient, predictable, controlled.'

'Jesus,' said Morrell softly. 'No wonder information on this Base and its work has been Restricted for so long. They were planning to turn the vast majority of the human species into unpeople, even less than clones and espers. Could they really have done it?'

'Theoretically, yes,' said Carrion. 'No wonder Lionstone tried to start it up again on Vodyanoi IV.'

'I suppose the plan was for the Emperor and a few selected Families to be the only true living humans,' said Silence, 'with everyone else programmed from birth to serve them faithfully all their days. There would never have been any rebellion. The population quite literally wouldn't have been able to conceive of the idea. If they could have made it work . . . We'd have become ants, insects serving the hive. But Marlowe stopped them. Hell, maybe he is our saviour, after all.'

'I don't think so,' said Carrion. 'He was just a man who couldn't wait. He had to try it out on himself first, to see if nanotech could be programmed to make him more than human. Superhuman.'

'And if you raise Humanity to the highest point, through endless evolutions . . . you get a god,' said Barron. 'Or at least, the Son of God.'

'I am getting a really bad headache just thinking about the implications of all this,' said Morrell, grimacing. 'Let's try focusing on some of our more immediate problems. Jesus, do you know anything about the crews of the Shub and Hadenmen ships orbiting this planet?'

'Of course,' said Jesus, still smiling his warm, loving smile. 'I know everything. Creatures of flesh and metal, and the machines that thought they thought: they both came here looking for power, but none of them could cope with what they found. Their minds were too small, too limited. Too inflexible. And so they all died. It was very sad. Would you like to speak with them?'

The landing party took it in turns to look at each other. 'Would that be possible?' said Silence carefully.

'All things are possible here, in this best of all possible worlds,' said Jesus. 'Behold, I will raise them from the dust for you.'

He gestured with one graceful, nail-pierced hand and the ground before him trembled. It split jaggedly apart, a deep crevice opening up as the ground shook under the landing party's feet. Up out of the depths rose a Fury and two Hadenmen. They hung for a moment above the gap, held supported in the air by Jesus' will, and then the ground snapped together again under their feet. The Fury was bare of its usual flesh covering. It was just a machine in the shape of a man, its steel gleaming blue in the bright sunlight. The two Hadenmen stood inhumanly still, their eyes glowing golden, their faces utterly blank. The three figures seemed solid and real but somehow empty, like great toys waiting for their instructions. Silence decided he'd start with the Fury. A machine's perception of this unnatural world might provide useful new insights.

'You came here from Shub,' he said slowly. 'Tell us what happened.'

'Illogical,' said the machine in a flat, grating voice. 'Illusions. Madness. We were called, by a voice whose orders could not be denied. We came down to this world and nothing made sense. Logic does not function here. It became necessary for Shub to break contact with us to avoid . . . contamination. We were left here. Abandoned.'

'We are very happy here,' said one of the Hadenmen in his buzzing voice. 'We preached the perfectibility of Man, and we have found it here. We all came down to spend our lives singing praises and hosannas to our Lord, as is fit and proper. He is the most perfect. We have come at last to the promised land.'

'These are my children,' said Jesus fondly, 'in whom I am well pleased.'

He gestured again and the three figures trembled, as though disturbed by an unfelt breeze, and then they crumbled and fell apart, becoming small particles swept away on the wind until there was no trace of them left. Carrion moved up close beside Silence so he could speak softly.

'Don't look now, but the angels are gone too. Vanished. I think Jesus just . . . forgot about them.'

'Dust to dust,' said Jesus, smiling his interminable smile. 'From dust they came, and to dust I sent them back. They came as you did, seeking wonders, but they were not worthy of the miracles to be found here. Their small minds could not encompass the marvels I have worked in this place. I can call up all who have died here, that you may question them if you wish. Be not troubled in your minds, neither in your hearts. If any of you are troubled, come to me and let me but touch you and you shall be healed for ever.'

'No one is to lower their shields,' said Silence sharply. 'That's an order. Morrell; did you pick up anything from those . . . returnees?'

'Not from them,' said the esper thoughtfully. 'Just the same background buzz. But I think I detected some kind of transmission, from Jesus. It's possible he could be the puppet-master here, speaking his words through their mouths.'

'Or maybe they just belong to him because they died here,' said Barron. 'His, for ever, to do with as he pleases. Would that make this a Heaven or a Hell? Singing praises to the Lord for all eternity because you have to?'

'He has made no direct threat to us as yet,' said Carrion.

'Yeah,' said Morrell, 'but a lot of that old-time religion is starting to get on my tits. If he says "behold" one more time . . .'

'Disbeliever,' said Jesus, smiling sadly. 'Woe to them who will not see the light. Be careful you do not raise my righteous anger. I have made a Heaven here, and I will not be mocked.'

'You infected yourself with pre-programmed nanotech,' said Carrion. 'And then you took it outside the Base and allowed it to transform this entire world. I've studied the files on Zero Zero. It was a hard world, but there was indigenous life here. So what happened to the original ecosystem? To the millions of small, interacting species that made their home here?'

'Gone, all gone,' said Jesus. 'They were not important. They have been replaced by something greater. They are not entirely lost. I could summon them up again, out of the dust, but what would be the point? Their time was over. Their only reason for existing was to be the place that I would come to. This is my world, my Heaven, my paradise, and all things here are as I wish it.'

'You talk to him, Captain,' said Carrion. 'Perhaps you can find common ground. This man destroyed a world even more thoroughly than you did.'

'Life is life,' said Jesus. 'From dust to dust. Nothing is ever lost, as long as I remember it. Forget them. I am here, your redeemer. Be happy here, and worship me all your days.'

'You know,' said Morrell quietly to Silence, 'we've stumbled across something even more important than we thought. What's happened here has implications for the whole Empire. Forget the programming of people; using the right nanotech you could pre-programme an entire planet in a way that makes terraforming look small and inefficient. It would be the ultimate weapon; just find a planet you didn't like, sprinkle a few nanos from orbit and the whole world and its people would become what you wanted. Think what it could do as a weapon against Shub, or the Recreated.'

'If we knew how to control it, which we don't.' Silence shook his head unhappily. 'Let it loose from this world and who knows what it might do, if it got out of control even for a moment? Besides, we came here looking for a possible cure for the nanoplague. Let's not get distracted, people.'

'Take me from this world on your ship,' said Jesus, 'and I will stop all wars and bring peace everywhere. Cure all ills with my touch. No one now alive need ever die. I will bring about the golden age of which Humanity has always dreamed.'

Carrion frowned. 'It's clear from the limited use they've put it to that Shub has only the barest control of the nanotech they've been using. What we've got here is far more dangerous. It's possible we might be able to create nanos to combat the plague, but as the captain says, we have no experience in controlling it. It might be like curing the common cold by giving everyone leprosy.

'We have to consider this very carefully, Captain. If we let the genie out of this bottle, it might well defeat our enemies, but what about afterwards? Who would we trust with such potential power? Remember what the original Emperor wanted to do with it. And you can see what it did to Marlowe's state of mind.'

The sky darkened, and suddenly it was twilight. Thunder rumbled menacingly overhead. The air was bitter cold. Jesus wasn't smiling any more.

'Can we all be a little more careful about how we choose our words around this guy?' Barron suggested quietly. 'He may or may not be who he says he is, but he's certainly the god of this world. Our force shields might be strong enough to protect us if he starts calling down lightning, but let's not put it to the test until we absolutely have to, all right?'

'You dare to doubt me?' said Jesus. His voice was darker now, and so loud it hurt the ears that heard it. It was like thunder speaking, or the rage of a storm about to break. Blood ran freely from the stigmata in Jesus' hands and feet, and from the spear wound in his side. 'Let me show you what I can do. You all came here looking for someone, even if you didn't realize it. I can see their names and faces in your minds, and the holes their loss has left in your lives and in your souls. Behold, let the dead rise, and walk again.'

A swirl of dust rose from dry, baked ground, forming a huge whirling dust bowl. The green grasses and blue skies were gone now, sucked up into the flying dust storm. And then part of it took shape and form as a human being; a young man in Fleet uniform. He stood before the landing party, smiling. He seemed vaguely familiar to Silence, but it wasn't till Barron suddenly lurched forward that Silence realized who he was looking at.

'Father!' said Barron, his voice cracking as he stumbled towards the smiling figure.

Silence started after him, and then held his ground. He didn't want to get too close to the new figure, or to Jesus. 'Barron, this isn't your father! He died on Unseeli. This is just a ghost made of nanotech!'

'Do you think I don't know my own father?' said Barron hotly. 'He's exactly how he looks in the old family holos!'

'Of course he looks like that. Jesus must be drawing on your memories to shape the nanos!'

'Does it really matter?' said a new, familiar voice. Silence felt a cold hand clutch at his heart. He turned slowly, and there was Investigator Frost standing before him, looking just as he remembered her before she died.

'You can't be real,' he said roughly. 'You're just my memories, given shape and form. Aren't you?'

'Good question,' said Frost. 'Damned if I know the answer. I feel real enough, but then I would say that, wouldn't I? Come with me. There are things we need to say.'

Captain Silence and Investigator Frost walked slowly off together, forgetting all else, so taken up with each other's presence that they didn't even notice the world reforming itself around them. The whirling dust bowl became a green forest for them, and soon they were walking between tall, proud trees, while something very like birds sang sweetly overhead. The air was full of the scents of autumn, and dry grasses and fallen leaves crunched under their boots. Silence recognized where he was. They were walking through a forest on Virimonde, in a place where he had nearly died. It seemed such a long time ago now.

'So,' said Frost, 'how have you been? Not wasting time mourning me, I hope.'

'I've been . . . getting on with my life,' said Silence. 'Keeping busy. A lot's happened since you died.'

'More wars, I suppose. There's always a war going on somewhere. Did Lionstone live long enough to stand trial? I would have liked to have seen that.'

'She escaped, in spirit at least. Joined her mind with the AIs of Shub, leaving her body behind. Kid Death destroyed it, just in case.'

'Ah, yes,' said Frost, 'the SummerIsle. I remember him. He killed me. Did you kill him?'

'No,' said Silence, after a moment. 'It seemed to me there'd been enough killing. And besides, you would never have surrendered to the rebellion. That's why you let him kill you. It's no surprise to me that my mind chose this place for us to talk. I nearly died here, when Stelmach shot me. But I used my abilities to heal a wound that would have killed anyone else. You had the same abilities. You could have healed yourself, if you'd wanted to. But you wanted to die.'

'Yes,' said Frost, 'I did. I'm glad you've finally admitted that to yourself. Don't feel guilty over my death, John. You couldn't have prevented it. If Kid Death hadn't been there, I'd have found someone else. It was inevitable. There was no place for me in the new order that was coming.'

'Did you ever love me?' said Silence.

'I was an Investigator,' said Frost. 'What do you think?'

By now, Micah Barron and his father Ricard were riding horses over the shifting scarlet sands of their homeworld, Tau Ceti III. The sky was a shade of green that most outworlders described as sickly, and the ever-present drifting clouds were jet black, shot from within by sudden golden lightning storms. Just another day on Tau Ceti III. Micah and Ricard were following a long-established trail, and didn't even need to guide their mounts; the horses knew the way. That gave father and son all the more time to talk, but they were finding the going hard. Father-and-son talks have always been tricky, difficult things. Especially when son and father are pretty much the same age, and the father's been dead for years.

'I joined the Fleet to follow you, Dad,' said Micah, looking straight ahead of him. 'To go where you'd gone, to see the things you'd seen. I thought it would help me feel closer to you.'

'I know I was never home much,' said Ricard, also looking straight ahead. 'Leave's hard to come by when you're only a junior officer. They promised us a lot of backed-up leave when we got back from Unseeli, but . . . well. I gather a lot of us never came home.'

'The Ashrai are dead,' said Micah fiercely. 'Captain Silence made them pay for what they did to you. To all of you. He scorched the planet. Wiped them out.'

'Is that supposed to make me feel better, son? I hated the Ashrai while I was fighting them. You had to, or it would have driven you crazy. But time, and being dead, gives you perspective. It was their planet; of course they fought. I would have, to defend Tau Ceti III from invaders. Tell me you didn't join up just to kill aliens, son.'

'Not really. Mostly I just wanted to get off Tau Ceti III. I mean, I know it's home, but it was . . . small. Limited.'

'Boring.'

'Right! I wanted to see the Empire. Other worlds, other people. Open my mind to other possibilities. I requested a transfer to Captain Silence's command so I could follow in your footsteps. You'd always spoken well of him in your messages home. Turned out to be pretty easy getting a place on his ship; he's not been the most popular captain in the Fleet for some time.'

Ricard snorted. 'Trust me, Micah; he never was. Silence was good to his crew, but no good at politics. Anyone else with his abilities and record would have been an admiral by now. But he never was any good at kissing the right asses. Most of us respected him for that. You always knew where you were with Silence. How's your mother, these days?'

Micah shrugged uncomfortably. 'All right, I suppose. I haven't heard from her in a while. Probably owe her a letter.'

'Write to your mother!' said Ricard sternly. 'Better still, save up and send her a personal holo.'

'You're a fine one to talk!'

'Learn from my mistakes, son. That's what fathers are for.'

They rode on awhile in silence, moving easily to the rhythm of the horses beneath them. Everyone learned to ride on Tau Ceti III, from the moment they were old enough to keep their balance in a saddle. Fathers and sons often went riding together, but Micah never had. His father was away too often, and then he died. But Micah had dreamed of riding like this, talking about the things fathers and sons talk about. And now here he was. Even though it felt rather strange, with his father looking so young.

'I never meant to die on Unseeli, you know,' said Ricard quietly. 'I always meant to come home to your mother, and to you. Don't think I went off and deserted you.'

'I never thought that!'

'Really? Not ever?'

'Maybe sometimes. When I was young, I wondered if I'd

done something wrong, and if that was why you never came home. But I got over it.'

'Did you? Then why are you serving in the Fleet, trying to recreate my life? I never expected you to sign up. I hoped you'd strike out on your own and make your own life. Not just copy me.'

'I . . .' Tears burned in Micah's eyes, and his voice was unsteady. 'I just wanted you to be proud of me, Dad.'

'Of course I'm proud of you,' said Ricard. 'You're my son.'

They rode on across the scarlet sands, and for a while they didn't need to say anything at all.

Carrion stood in the middle of the metallic forest on Unseeli, before Shub came and harvested the trees, before the Empire exterminated the Ashrai. The huge metal trees soared up high into the sky, almost protruding out of the atmosphere itself in places. Their branches radiated out from the smooth, featureless trunks in needle-sharp spikes dozens of feet long. Gold and silver and brass, violet and azure, they stood firm and unyielding against the planet's never-ending storms. And all through the metal trees were the Ashrai, alive and glorious, filling the forest with their song. They soared in the skies like ancient dragons, vast and powerful, and down below Carrion smiled and smiled, eyes wet with unshed tears, back home and at peace again.

Captain Silence looked around him at the green and peaceful forest bathed in autumn sunlight. 'This isn't real; none of this is real. Virimonde is light years from here. But it looks just the way I remember.'

'Of course it does,' said Frost. 'Marlowe took the images from your mind and had his nanos recreate them for you. Same way he produced me.'

Silence reached out with his mind, trying to re-establish the old mental link he and Frost had once shared, but it was like looking into a mirror, with only his own face looking back at him.

'Sorry,' said Frost, 'but I'm not real either. Just a memory, given shape and form by nanotech and a madman's power. I'm just real enough not to want to be used as a weapon against you. Come on, Captain; you really only needed to say goodbye properly, and we've done that. It's time to let me go, and get back to dealing with Marlowe. He may think he's the Son of God, but he's actually quite limited in what he can do.'

'There was . . . so much I wanted to say to you,' said Silence.

'Then you should have said it while I was alive,' said Frost. 'I probably knew it all anyway. Goodbye, John.'

She walked off into the forest, and Silence stood and watched her go, knowing he'd never see her again. When she'd passed completely out of sight, he took a deep breath and let it go, and then glared at the trees around him.

'I don't believe in you,' he said firmly. 'None of this is real. I deny you. Damn you, Marlowe, stop this. Damn your soul to Hell! Stop this right now.'

Something moved within him as his own power stirred reluctantly from its rest, uncoiling and reaching out in strange directions. And one by one, the trees began to crumble and fall apart into dust, and less than dust.

Micah Barron reined in his horse and dismounted. A low wind was blowing, sending the red sands dancing this way and that. His father dismounted too, and the two young men stood facing each other. They looked more like brothers than father and son.

'I think we've gone as far as we're going,' said Micah. 'We've said all we needed to say.'

'Yes,' said Ricard. 'Time to say goodbye. Any last thing I can do for you, son?'

'Yes,' said Micah. 'Take me in your arms and hold me. Hug me, as a father hugs his son, because I don't remember that at all.'

Ricard looked at him expressionlessly. 'You know what you're asking, Micah? What you'll have to do?'

'Oh, yes. I'll have to drop my force shield and let you in. But that's what I want, Father. What I've always wanted. So we'll never be apart again.'

He keyed the right combination into the control pad at his waist, and the shimmering force field around him snapped out in a moment. Ricard stepped forward and took his son in his arms. They held each other, and the nanos went to work. The two forms merged and became one. Micah Barron had finally become what he most wanted to be. His father.

Silence walked out of the disappearing forest on Virimonde, and suddenly found himself among the metallic trees of Unseeli. He didn't need to ask whose dream he was walking through now. He paused for a moment to look at the Ashrai flying overhead and tried to feel guilty, but it was all so long ago. Still, it had been a long time since he'd seen them in flight. They were marvellous.

He found Carrion easily enough. Marlowe, or Jesus, or whatever the hell he was now, hadn't bothered to recreate much of the metal forest. Silence walked quickly through it, and there was Carrion, sitting peacefully in a full lotus position, his back against the smooth trunk of a golden tree, his eyes closed. Silence had never seen him look so happy. Even if he was still wearing his traitor's black.

'Sean,' he said sternly. 'Time to wake up. Time to go.'

'Go away, John,' said Carrion, without opening his eyes. 'You have no place here. You don't belong here. I have come home, and everything's all right again.'

'Nothing's right! This isn't real; it's just a nanotech recreation. It's not even as real as a dream.'

'Do you think I don't know that?' Carrion's voice remained calm, but he still refused to open his eyes, as though denying Silence's presence. 'I know this isn't real, and I don't care. I have found peace, and my heart's content, such as I never thought I'd know again. I will stay here.'

'Then you'll die.'

'Yes, John. That's what I want, really; what I've always wanted. Don't you know that?'

Silence knelt down beside him. 'I need you, Sean.'

'You always need someone. You used that argument to drag me away from peace last time. Made me live again, when all I wanted was to die. Leave me alone.'

Silence put a hand on Carrion's shoulder, as though grabbing at a man drifting away down a dark river. 'Please, Sean, don't do this. You're my friend. I lost Frost. I don't want to lose you too.'

There was a moment that seemed to last for ever, and then Carrion sighed and opened his eyes. 'You always did know how to fight dirty, John. But I don't think I have the strength to leave this place. You've always been the strongest of us two, but I don't think even you can pull me out of this grave I've dug for myself. This is a place of the dead, and I belong here.'

'God, you're a gloomy bastard,' said Silence. 'Ask the Ashrai; ask the ghosts that insist on haunting you. See what they think of this show, this mockery.'

A corner of Carrion's mouth twitched into a smile, in spite of himself. 'Now that should be interesting.'

He opened his mouth and let out an alien sound, the harsh, eerie cry of the Ashrai. In an instant, as though they had only been waiting to be summoned, the real Ashrai were there with him, huge, brutal presences that had nothing but contempt for this sham recreation of everything they had lost. They tore through the fake metallic forest like a living storm and reduced it to shreds. The metal trees burst apart, and the jagged, gleaming fragments were pulled up into a great maelstrom of howling, gargoyle faces. The recreated Ashrai disappeared in a moment, unable to withstand the fearsome presence of the real, like shadows dispersed by a blinding light. Silence and Carrion huddled together as the storm raged about them but somehow never quite touched them. The song of the dead Ashrai was a powerful, awful thing, and the will of the man once called Marlowe could not stand against it. The dream of a vanished forest was blown to pieces, and carried away on a wind that was all too real, and soon there was nothing left but the whirling dust from which it had sprung.

Silence and Carrion found themselves standing before Jesus again. He looked seriously angry.

'I make a heaven for you, and you spit in my face! Must man always walk away from paradise?'

'Every dream has to end sometime,' said Silence. 'Even yours, Marlowe.'

'Don't call me that! That man is dead!' Jesus had lost his halo, and his crown of thorns had caught fire. Flames danced on his brow and in his eyes. 'You can have no comprehension of what I've become!'

'Oh, you'd be surprised,' said Silence. 'Both Carrion and I have known the touch of a greater force in our time. We just never lost our sense of proportion.' He moved over to the esper Morrell, who was standing a little to one side. 'What was your dream like?'

'Never had one,' said the esper briskly. 'The moment he came fumbling round my mind, I shut down my thoughts behind the toughest mental shield I could fashion. He didn't even come close to cracking it. He may command the nanotech, but as a telepath, he's strictly low-level. I have to say, this guy is a real let-down. The nanos gave him control over an entire planet, and all he does is play childish games. He hasn't even touched his real potential.'

'Hold everything,' said Carrion. 'Where's Barron?'

They looked around, but he was nowhere to be seen. There was only the three of them, and Jesus, and the whirling dust storm. Jesus was smiling again. Silence glared at him.

'What have you done with Barron, Marlowe?'

'He gave in to his dream,' said Jesus. 'In the end he was just a poor little lost child, who only wanted to be the man his father was. And now he is. He belongs to me, and soon you will too. Since you won't accept my Heaven, I'll judge you and sentence you and condemn you to Hell.'

At once flames leaped up everywhere, replacing the dust storm. The landing party flinched back from the heat, even though it couldn't touch them through their shields. The sky was dark, lit by lightning, and clawed and fanged demons soared overhead on huge batwings. From everywhere came the sounds of countless people screaming in horrible agony. Silence and Carrion and Morrell moved close together.

'Damn,' said Morrell, 'he's got past my shields!'

'Either he's getting stronger,' said Carrion, 'or he's getting more determined. He has to be approaching his limits.'

'This isn't real,' said Silence. 'Don't believe in it.'

'It's as real as the nanos can make it,' said Carrion. 'This vision comes from Marlowe's mind, not ours. Disbelieving in it won't make it disappear. Not when he's obviously enjoying himself so much.'

They looked at Marlowe, and where Jesus had been now stood the Devil, with scarlet skin, cloven hooves and a goat's head with curling horns. It was more like a child's picture than an advanced creation, but it made Marlowe's state of mind clear enough. The thick lips leered. 'I'm tired of being the Prince of Peace. I think this will be much more fun. You can't escape me; you don't know one direction from another in the Hell I've made for you. I'll just hold you here till your shields go down, and then you'll be mine, to make and remake as the whim takes me. I'll stir my sticky fingers in your flesh, and mould you into your worst nightmares. You'll be my playthings, for ever and ever and ever.'

'He could do it,' said Morrell, his face white and desperate. 'I can't break his hold on my mind. Oh, God . . . Captain, do something!'

Silence turned to Carrion. 'Call the Ashrai. See if they're still angry with Jesus over the fake Unseeli.'

'They're already here,' said Carrion, smiling a very dark smile.

Huge forms came plunging down from above, gargoyle faces roaring their rage in a sound almost too loud to be borne. The Devil snarled, and threw demons at them with a wave of a clawed crimson hand. The huge forms slammed together, filling the dark sky. More and more demons appeared out of nothing, created by Marlowe's nanos. Silence and Carrion looked at each other. Almost against their will, their altered minds reached out to each other and came together in a fusion that was far greater than the sum of its parts. Morrell cried out and had to look away, hiding behind his strongest shields for fear of being blinded by the light their fusion was generating. Silence and Carrion struck out at the Devil, and it was only the work of a moment for their more powerful will to snatch control of the nanos away from Marlowe. He really wasn't much of a telepath, and he'd been alone too long, with no one to challenge his will.

He screamed as Hell flickered out and was gone, like a blown-out candle. Silence, Carrion and Morrell stood on a bare rock plain, facing a man who was crumbling and falling apart. After so many years, only the nanos had kept him alive, and now they were deserting his body like rats leaving a sinking ship. He became dust and less than dust, and blew away on a gusting wind. Above, the sky was clear of Ashrai or demons. Silence and Carrion separated their thoughts, and looked away from each other, embarrassed by the enforced intimacy of sharing their minds. They could have retained control of the nanos, but they chose not to. They'd seen what madness such power could lead to, and they had come far enough from humanity as it was. They had enough damnation on their souls already without adding further temptation.

'Well,' said Morrell, just a little breathlessly. 'That was . . . interesting. Can we get the hell out of here now, please, Captain?'

'We might as well,' said Silence. 'This mission is a bust. There's nothing here we dare let loose. No one can be trusted with this kind of power. I'd recommend scorching the world from orbit, if I thought it would do any good, but the nanos might survive even that. We'll leave the genie in the bottle, until Humanity's evolved into something wise enough to use it correctly.'

'And we lost Barron,' said Carrion. 'I brought him here. He trusted me. He should have remembered I was always a bird of ill omen.'

Silence looked around at the empty plain. 'I wonder what the nanos will make of this place, now they no longer have a human mind to guide or tame them. Might be worth coming back here in a few centuries, just to see what kind of world the nanos make.'

He put in a call to the pinnace waiting in orbit, and it came down and hovered above the rocky ground as the landing party took it in turns to jump awkwardly up into the open airlock. Silence was last in, as Captain. He took a final look back, and off in the distance he thought he saw Barron, standing alone, waving goodbye. It was only a glimpse, and then it was gone. Silence turned his back on Zero Zero, and let the pinnace take him back to the *Dauntless*, and his duty.

CHAPTER FOUR

From the Undermind to the Oversoul

Once upon a time, she was just an esper named Diana Vertue, but things had become rather complicated since then. As Jenny Psycho she'd been a hard-core terrorist and a saint of the Mater Mundi, Our Mother of All Souls, but she'd outgrown both those roles. She'd gone looking for the truths of her existence, the meaning and purpose behind the events that had shaped her life, and unfortunately for her, she had found them. The truth may set you free, but freedom can be a cold and lonely place. Now she was just an esper on the run, hiding out in what used to be Finlay Campbell's old bolt-hole; a single cramped apartment in the warrens under the Arenas. The place was a mess, but she couldn't seem to raise the strength of purpose to do anything about it. She lay on her back on the unmade bed, wearing dirty sweat-stained clothes because she had nothing to change into, and stared up at the ceiling above her, seeing everything and nothing.

Her mental shields were all in place, as strong as she could make them. The most powerful espers in the Empire could have walked past her door and not known she was there. Theoretically. At one time, Diana would have been sure, but there were a lot of things she wasn't certain of any more. It helped that directly above her were the killing grounds of the Arenas, where the dying never stopped. The endless flow of suffering and slaughter, and the raging emotions and bloodlust of the watching crowds, set up a constant mental bedlam that no one would be able to detect anything through. Diana was as safe and hidden as it was possible for anyone to be.

And none of that mattered a damn, because she was hiding from the Mater Mundi, the collective unconscious of every living esper, except for Diana, and the Elves. It would find her eventually, if only through a process of elimination. There were only so many places on Golgotha where you could hope to hide from a determined telepath. With millions of minds to search with, the Mater Mundi would track her down in time, and then Diana would have to run again or stand and fight. Either choice seemed likely to result in her death.

Diana Vertue laced her fingers across her stomach, and wondered what the hell she was going to do next.

Her thoughts drifted this way and that, half forming desperate plans only to discard them almost immediately, her mind unable to settle for long on any one thing. Too much of what she had believed in and depended on had been proved to be false, and she had lost the moorings of her life. Slowly but remorselessly, she had been driven into a corner from which there was no escape. She had nowhere left to run, and the thought of facing something as vast and powerful as the Mater Mundi left her sick and trembling with fear. Diana Vertue was far more powerful than any individual esper had a right to be, but even she was no match for the power of millions of unconscious esper minds, unburdened by such conscious limitations as mercy or compassion.

How had her life come to this? A fugitive in a dirty room, contemplating her own imminent death? She'd had such plans when she was younger, such fervent hopes and great intentions. All the wondrous things she was going to do . . . Of course, she'd had a lot of the fire and innocence knocked out of her on the ghostworld Unseeli. She'd been used by her own father as bait to catch a monster, menaced and driven to the point of madness, and only saved at the last by the song of the dead Ashrai. She was never the same, after that. As soon as her father's old ship, the *Darkwind*, had docked on Golgotha, she deserted the Navy and went underground, joining the espers rebelling against Imperial authority. She thought she'd found friends and allies there, and a cause to believe in, but in the end they used her too. They hid her thoughts behind a fake personality called Jenny Psycho, and then allowed her to be captured and sent to the esper prison Silo Nine, also known as Wormboy Hell. The endless torture and mental violation drove her to the point of madness again, but having had some prior experience of the state, she survived.

And then the Mater Mundi manifested through her, giving her the power to free herself and the other esper prisoners. Diana thought she'd finally found her role. She embraced the Jenny Psycho persona, and allowed other espers to declare her a living saint of Our Mother of All Souls. But that turned out to be a lie too, when the Mater Mundi abandoned her on Mistworld, just when Diana needed her most. She should have known; she should have expected it. Betrayal had been a constant feature of her young life.

Then came the great rebellion, the overthrowing of Lionstone and the chance of a new life for all espers. So Diana put the Jenny Psycho persona behind her, and tried to create a new role for herself – only to face the greatest betrayal of all. The new order turned out to be just as corrupt as the old, only more subtly so. The new freedom for espers included the freedom to starve and die and be forgotten. And the esper underground, that great force for justice and the good, turned out to be an unknowing tool of its own subconscious. The last and greatest betrayal; that the cause to which she'd given her life had proved to be nothing but a mask for the same kind of heartless manipulation she'd been fighting.

Diana idly wondered why she clung so grimly to a life that had brought her only disappointment and the destruction of her beliefs, a life of pain and heartbreak. All her plans and hopes had come to nothing. Perhaps she continued just to spite the fates that seemed so determined to grind her down. There was a strong stubborn streak in Diana that would not yield to any outside pressure, no matter how great – perhaps the only useful thing she'd inherited from her illustrious father. She was damned if she'd just give up and die, if only to frustrate the Mater Mundi one more time. Diana Vertue, or Jenny Psycho, or whoever the hell she really was at heart, had always been a fighter. She smiled widely at the ceiling above her, a thin-lipped snarl that had only the blackest of humour in it. Once more into the breach she'd go, into the valley of the shadow of death, into darkness and damnation if necessary, just for a chance to drag her enemy down with her.

It occurred to her, in something very like an epiphany, that she wasn't necessarily alone in this fight. There were others like her, powerful minds unconnected to the Mater Mundi, that might yet be convinced to fight beside her. She reached out with her altered, expanded mind in directions only she could sense, sending out a call for help that only minds like hers could hear, let alone respond to. To bewilder and confound the searching Mater Mundi, Diana sent her mind shooting up and out of her body, leaving the squalid little apartment behind. Her thoughts flew up past the bloody sands of the Arenas, up and beyond the Parade of the Endless, until finally Golgotha itself lay turning slowly beneath her. From there the world looked very vulnerable, all alone in the dark. Some way off in the distance, but all the time drawing slowly closer, a darker presence yet: the Recreated. A great howling black hole, trying to suck her thoughts and her soul into its awful inhuman self. But it was still too far away to be able to compel her, and mentally Diana turned her back on it, secure behind her shields. She called out again, need and desperation giving strength and urgency to her appeal for help.

To her great surprise, the first response came from a dead man.

Hi, said Owen Deathstalker. *What's up?*

You're supposed to be dead! said Diana, too startled to be polite. *No one's been able to contact you, or find any trace of you, for ages.*

Sorry to disappoint you, said Hazel d'Ark drily, *but we've been kind of busy.*

The mind boggles at what, said Diana. *Even your fellow Maze people thought you must be dead.*

We've just finished wiping out the Blood Runners, said Owen. *It turned out their homeworld in the Obeah Systems didn't always exist in the same universe as the rest of us. They'd used a rather unusual power source to create their own subspace dimension; a private little reality where they could concentrate on torture and murder undisturbed. But I found a way in. Now the subspace, the homeworld and the Blood Runners no longer exist.*

We kicked their ass, said Hazel.

Well thank the good God you're back, said Diana, *because I've got an enemy here that could seriously use a good kicking, and I can't do it alone.*

Hold everything, said Owen. *I'm sorry to disappoint you, but we have our own mission now we're back, and we can't afford to be distracted. We have to return to the Darkvoid, go back to the Wolfling World. Something's happening there, something bad. Something only we can deal with.*

Whatever it is, it can wait, said Diana firmly. *A lot's happened while you were . . . out of touch. Most of it really bad.*

Department of Absolutely No Surprise there, said Hazel. *We take our eye off the ball for five minutes, and everything goes to hell.*

What's happened about the royal wedding? said Owen suddenly. *I mean, if everyone thinks I'm dead . . .*

It's still going ahead, said Diana, *only Constance is marrying Robert Campbell instead.*

Ah, said Owen, after a pause. *All for the best, really, I suppose. The Campbell's a good man. Probably make a much better constitutional monarch too. I never wanted to be Emperor.*

How does Constance feel about all this? said Hazel.

Oh, it's a love match this time, said Diana. *It's really very sweet. But can we not be distracted, please? The whole existence of Humanity is under threat. You've got to come back.*

She broadcast compressed telepathic images of all that had been happening during Owen and Hazel's enforced absence. The great golden ships of the Hadenmen blasting the Fleet apart; destroying cities on a hundred worlds; deploying armies of golden-eyed merciless killers to destroy or remake Humanity in their own logical image. The huge Shub ships sailing out of the Forbidden Sector in endless numbers, taking planet after planet with their armies of Furies and Ghost Warriors and Grendel aliens. The Recreated, in their vast, insanely proportioned vessels, moving steadily towards the homeworld Golgotha. The nanoplague, spreading slowly but unstoppably from world to world, melting down all living tissue. Jack Random executing his enemies on Loki, and then returning to Golgotha to cut down more people there before going on the run, with Ruby Journey in hot pursuit, sworn to kill him. And finally, the awful truth about the actual nature of the Mater Mundi.

Damn, said Owen, *I can't believe Jack's gone rogue.*

I fought on Loki as a mercenary some time back, said Hazel. *Probably beside some of the same people Jack hanged. A bloody rebellion and a worse peace. Friends became enemies and enemies became allies.*

I can't believe Jack killed that many people in cold blood, said Owen.

Oh, you can be pretty sure it wasn't cold blood, said Diana. *By all accounts he had a really good time doing it.*

Something must have pushed him over the edge, said Owen tiredly. *Jack was a good man, a hero. He must have lost his mind . . .*

And a madman with your powers and abilities could do a hell of a lot of damage, said Diana. *God knows how many more he'll kill before he's stopped. Now will you come back?*

I've been trying to reach Jack through our old mental link, said Hazel. *I can't get any response from him or Ruby. They must be blocking us out deliberately. We'd be no better at tracking him down than anyone else. And even if we could find him, I'm not sure what we'd do. What we* could *do. I mean, this is Jack Random we're talking about.*

No one's above the law, said Owen flatly. *It has to apply equally, or it means nothing. The reforms and controls we fought for must govern us too, or we fought for nothing. But Jack isn't our problem. None of the things you've described are as important as what's happening on the Wolfling World. Our mission there has to take precedence.*

Captain Silence is on his way into the Darkvoid, said Diana desperately. *Let my father deal with it, whatever it is.*

I don't think so, said Hazel. *In fact, if he's on his way there, it's more important than ever that we get there first.*

And as suddenly as that, they were gone, no trace of their presence remaining. She called again and again, but no one answered. Diana wasted a few moments in cursing their names and general foul language, and then moved reluctantly on to the next on her mental list. Having located two Maze minds, it wasn't too difficult for her to track down another.

Damn, said Jack Random, *I would have sworn no one could find me. Hello, Diana Vertue. How are you?*

Just a tad desperate, said Diana. *How are you, Jack? Killed any more innocents recently?*

None of them were innocent, said Jack immediately. *They all needed killing. I'm just doing what I've always done: taking out the garbage.*

Diana tried to get a glimpse of where he was, or what he was planning, but Jack's shields were already reforming like bricks in a great wall, and she knew he'd never let her find him again. She'd caught him by surprise, but her expanded mind, powerful as it was, was no match for his, and they both knew it. She quickly filled him in on the latest emergencies, and the true nature of the Mater Mundi, but she could tell she wasn't reaching him.

Interesting, was all he had to say, *but esper problems are your province, not mine. I have my own responsibilities, and the duty I have chosen to shoulder is a heavy one. I can't put it down, even for a moment. Don't try to find me again, for your own sake. I can't trust anyone these days.*

And then his presence was gone, shut away behind shields so powerful Diana couldn't even sense where he had been. Diana called after him anyway, and was somewhat surprised to get an immediate response: from Ruby Journey. Hers was a cold, controlled presence, her thoughts as precise and unemotional as well-oiled machinery. Diana quickly prepared her own shields and defences, just in case. This was Ruby Journey, after all.

I heard your call, said Ruby. *I even managed to listen in on your conversation with Jack. I don't give a damn about your problems, either. All I care about is locating Jack. You must have picked up some idea as to where he is, some clue as to what he's planning. Open your mind to me, so I can see.*

Go to hell, said Diana. *I'm not having you trampling about in my mind, rummaging through my thoughts and secrets. I don't know where Jack is, or what he intends to do. And if you're not willing to help me, I don't give a damn about you either.*

Foolish, said Ruby Journey, *Very foolish.*

Her mind smashed against Diana's, but even her Maze-given powers couldn't sweep aside Diana's shields. Ruby increased the pressure, but despite the pain and the strain, Diana wouldn't give way. She didn't have the strength to launch a counter-attack, so she concentrated on her shields. Ruby's power raged about her, like a storm that might capsize a ship at any moment, but somehow Diana's shields still held. In the end Ruby got tired, or bored, and backed off. She sent out a single mental image, and Diana studied it cautiously from behind her shields. The image showed Ruby Journey at a city armoury, equipping herself with all manner of blades, guns and explosives, enough to hunt down and kill a hundred men. She was smiling coldly.

If Jack contacts you again, show him this image. Show him what's coming after him. And remind him that I never, ever stop once I've accepted a commission.

Ruby disappeared behind her shields and was gone, leaving Diana hovering alone above Golgotha. It was unnerving, knowing you'd just faced an enemy that could have beaten you if she'd cared enough to expend a little more time and energy. Far off in the dark, the Recreated were still howling their endless, awful scream. Diana felt very tired and very vulnerable, and fell back into her body. Once again she was lying on her back on a stranger's bed, staring up at a dirty ceiling in search of answers it didn't have. There were others Diana could have tried to contact, but after her disappointments with the Maze people, she couldn't see any point in exhausting herself further. She was going to need her strength where she was going.

'All right. I'll just have to do it alone. I've always had to do the most important things of my life alone.'

She allowed herself a few moments to say goodbye to her life. She'd always hoped it would amount to something more than just that of a mistaken saint, and a hero of the rebellion that most people seemed to prefer not to remember. Oh, they'd written her into a few of the holo films they'd made about the rebellion and its heroes, but she didn't recognize herself at all in the enigmatic sorceress or total psychopath they'd chosen to portray her as. Some accounts weren't even sure which side she'd fought on. But then, Jenny Psycho had always been a little too extreme for most tastes.

She would have liked to have known love, friends, family; but there was never any time. Her own family were never there when she needed them. A mother who'd died young, a father who was always off on his ship somewhere. Diana grew up in an esper training facility, and there was little love to be found there. At one time, the esper underground had given purpose and direction to her life, but left her with little time of her own. She knew duty, and sometimes honour, but few friends, and never a love or a lover. She scared people. She gave so much to the cause, only to discover in the end that it wasn't worthy of her dedication.

At least the Elves had put up a statue to her.

So now it was time to face down the impossible; master the monster; put her life and sanity on the line as she had so many times before. She was alone again against a powerful enemy, while those who might have helped her went their own way. Business as usual, for Diana Vertue. She summoned up all the old berserker rage and dedication of her Jenny Psycho persona and dived deep into her own mind, down past the shining columns of conscious thought and into the dark unexplored areas of the mind; the back brain. Some joking part of herself showed her a bright neon sign, Abandon Hope All Ye Who Enter Here, and then she'd left the outer reality behind, plunging down into the dark miracles and mysteries of the inner world. The back brain; the face behind the mask, the place where normal humans couldn't go.

Most people didn't know what the back brain was, though a few bandied the name about as though they did. The majority used only a small part of their brain, accessing only the merest fraction of what it could do. The esper gene allowed some to delve deeper into their minds than most, and make use of the powers they found there: telepathy, pyrokinesis, precognition. Others, like the Maze people who'd had their minds wrenched open by outside forces, could call up even stranger and more wondrous abilities. Diana had studied the concept of the back brain during her time in the esper Guild House, trawling tirelessly through its massive files in search of knowledge like a determined Pandora ruthlessly opening box after box in search of a truth that could serve her. The espers had been studying themselves almost as long as they had existed, and they had discovered many things about who and what they were, most of it disturbing. It was all recorded somewhere, if you could only find it. Most esper knowledge had never been released, even inside the esper community, and much was actively suppressed, for a variety of reasons. Partly because if the powers that be ever got hold of it, they'd just use it to better control their esper slaves. And partly because the Mater Mundi made sure some things were forgotten, rather than risk its true nature being exposed.

Perhaps the greatest secret of all was that the human mind was capable of far more than either standard humans or espers ever dreamed of. Anyone could become like the Maze people, if they could only access and control the secrets of the back brain. All that grey matter and potential that was never used! Diana had written it all down, and hidden it in a file that couldn't be easily found. So that if the Mater Mundi did win in the end, and Diana Vertue disappeared, never to be seen or spoken of again, what she'd learned might still survive. *We could all shine like suns*, she wrote.

She still believed that. Even after all the horrors and tragedies she'd seen, she still believed.

She passed through the back brain, and on into the undermind. Few people knew about the back brain; fewer still knew about the undermind. You could only reach the undermind through the back brain. It was a vast, awful, magnificent place, and not everyone survived encountering it. The undermind was the collective unconscious of all Humanity; the dreamtime; the race memory. The bedrock of human existence. Mater Mundi was only a small, separate part of a much greater whole. As far as Diana knew, the undermind had no distinct persona or agenda like the Mater Mundi. It simply existed, the place that was not a place, where all minds came together; the great dreaming unconscious from which all human thought derived.

Or perhaps it wasn't any of those things. Diana was only an explorer in these regions, and what she saw was filtered through her conscious mind.

She saw the collective unconscious as a great ocean, the sea of dreams, the waters we all swim in for nine months before we're born; the place we visit for dreams and ideas and inspiration. An ocean as big as the world, greater than all the worlds. Diana had to be careful how she thought about it. Her mind was interpreting what was there in terms she could deal with, translating abstract concepts into a physical form. Allow her mind to drift beyond that, and she'd lose whatever control she had over the situation. She could become lost for ever here, mislaid, swept away by unknown tides, her thoughts drifting eternally as a screaming phantom in other people's dreams.

This was a place with no maps, no boundaries and no limitations. *Here Be Tygers.*

She was on a small island, a rock-hard place of conscious intent and certainty, standing firm in the sea of dreams. Waves lapped slowly against it, murmuring in many voices. She'd manifested in her old Jenny Psycho form, complete with spiked steel armour and a gun so huge she couldn't have lifted it in the waking world. The gun represented her power. She hoped she wouldn't have to use it.

There were shadows and colours in the sky, streaming overhead like the nightmares rainbows might have. They were stray thoughts, coming and going in people's heads. Sometimes the colours became recognizable shapes and images, representing things that troubled or intrigued Humanity's thoughts. The rocky reefs of the zeitgeist. It was like looking at clouds and seeing shapes in them, only this time the shapes really were there, though they changed and mutated from moment to moment. Looking at them made Diana's head hurt, so instead she looked down into the tranquil waters surrounding her island. There were things there too; vast shapes moving slowly through the dream waters. The shared ideas, beliefs and compulsions of human culture. People created them and spread them, and then they had power over people. Things are in the saddle and ride mankind, but we put the bit between our teeth.

Humanity's collective unconscious: they called it the

worldmind, before we went to the stars and spread ourselves over so many worlds. Now it's an ocean without end, stretching away for ever, big enough to hold everything we put in it. You could go fishing in the sea of dreams and pull out anything, anything at all. The collective unconscious is full of archetypes, perfect manifestations of cultural tropes or fascinations. The Wise Old Man, the Mystical Virgin, the King With A Wound That Will Not Heal. You could have interesting conversations with them, as long as you realized that their words only made sense in the world of dreams and fancies. Their truths were too great for the waking world. And since this was the sea of dreams, there were bad things here too, horrors of the kind that can only exist in nightmares. Everyone knows that there are Things in dreams that will get you unless you wake up first. And in the undermind there is no waking up. Those few, very few people who have any knowledge of the undermind wonder if perhaps these Things are the natural predators of this place. Or are they rather externalized manifestations of the psychic mindset – self-loathing, depression, homicidal mania?

Diana didn't know. She had visited the undermind just often enough to know that it was larger and more complex than the conscious mind could deal with, except in small doses. The unconscious was a function of the back brain, that potentially godlike part of the mind that Humanity mostly hadn't learned to access. We could all shine like suns, but suns burn hot, and melt the wings of those who fly too close.

Diana decided that her thoughts were starting to get out of hand, and clamped down hard. In the sea of dreams, even the vaguest of thoughts can have repercussions. She made herself concentrate on what little she knew for sure of this place, and looked around her for enemies. This was the human collective unconscious, but there were others who could come here too, as if in some strange way they belonged here. High up in the colourless sky hung a grey, watchful presence. That was the rogue AIs of Shub. They had no subconscious, but sheer mental power gave them a window into the undermind, through which they watched and cogitated and failed to understand. Shub did not dream. There was a silvery moon overhead that shone only faintly with its own light, and was reflected in the waters. That was the Hadenman collective. They didn't understand the undermind either, but all their science had not been enough to stop them dreaming. So although they were always there, the Hadenmen preferred to pretend that the undermind didn't exist.

Most baleful of all, there was a sun in the undermind sky. A black sun. That was the Recreated. Diana had no idea what they were doing there, but just looking at the black sun scared the shit out of her, so quite sensibly she stopped looking at it. Instead, she looked out across her little island, her rock of certainty, and saw the air ripple before her like a heat haze. Visitors were coming.

And in a moment, there they were: thought of by most as the leaders of the esper underground, but actually archetypes thrown up by the esper collective unconscious. There was a waterfall, cascading endlessly down out of nowhere, with two great shadows that might have been eyes. A swirling mandala of clashing colours hung unsupported in the air, forever growing and swallowing itself at the same time. A twenty-foot dragon curled its golden scales around a tree. A muscular human form, nude and exaggerated, usually known as Mr Perfect. A huge hog with bloodstained tusks and tiny crimson eyes, covered with tattoos of ancient runes and sigils. A ten-foot-tall woman wrapped in shimmering light, with a cratered moon for a face. All of them aspects of the Mater Mundi, given shape and form to rule over the espers.

'You should not have come here,' they said, their mouths moving in unison where they had mouths, a single intent in a chorus of voices. 'This is our place, where we are strongest and you are alone. You must die, that we might live. You know too much. We made you stronger than we intended, but here and now we will undo that mistake. We are the dark, deep thoughts of esperkind, and the future belongs to us.'

'Not necessarily,' said Diana Vertue, or maybe it was Jenny Psycho. 'Let's see if I really am alone in this fight.'

She extended her foot past the edge of her island and thrust the toe of her boot into the ocean. Ripples spread slowly out across the surface of the water, growing larger all the time, just like those caused by a pebble dropped into a pond. The ripples increased their speed until they were shooting across the surface of the sea of dreams, more and more of them all the time. The Mater Mundi archetypes stirred silently. There was a feeling of pressure, of imminence on the air, of something about to happen. And in a moment, Diana was no longer alone. Drawn by her silent call for help, by a voice that spoke in their dreams and would not be denied, her friends and allies came to her.

First was Investigator Topaz of Mistworld, standing before Diana in silver-plate armour chased with hoar frost. Her face was deathly white and her hair was thick swirls of ice. The long sword in her hand steamed coldly. She was the Snow Queen, the Ice Princess, the unrelenting cold that can break the hardest spirit, shatter the strongest metal. Topaz had also once been a manifest of the Mater Mundi, but like Diana, had broken free to become her own person. She looked expressionlessly at the archetypes grouped together at the other end of the island, and then turned her icy gaze on Diana.

'What am I doing here? Am I dreaming? I remember lying down to sleep . . .'

'This is where you go when you dream,' said Diana. 'But what happens here is real enough. Events here have repercussions in the waking world. The freak show over there represents the Mater Mundi. They want to kill us, and enslave all Humanity to their brutish desires. Will you stand with me against them?'

The Investigator smiled, revealing teeth as white as frost. 'You ever known me to back away from a good fight? I can feel the danger here, Vertue. I can feel the stakes, and what we're fighting for. But there'd better be a few more of us, or it's going to be short and one-sided.'

'Don't worry,' said Diana. 'The sea of dreams reaches everywhere. Others will have heard my call. You might even know some of them.'

One by one, appearing out of nowhere, dropping through the dreaming into the undermind, came others who had fought the good fight for Humanity's soul; others who were no strangers to the back brain, and the power to be found there. One by one they came to the island, in the image they had of themselves. Typhoid Mary rose up out of the ground, with a dead face and sorrowful eyes, clothed in a rotting shroud and dirty grave wrappings. Skulls of dead children hung from her belt, and her hands dripped with blood. But her heart shone pure, and she burned with the need for atonement.

Next came Tobias Moon, striding up out of the waters and on to the island, smiling gently. He was all man now, with nothing of the Hadenman left in him. Scarlet foliage curled around him, alive and aware. Captain Silence and the traitor called Carrion arrived together out of nowhere. Silence wore a suit of old-fashioned armour, spotted with rust, and bore a shield whose design had been mostly worn away. He looked older, and his eyes were tired and sad. Carrion looked exactly as he always did. He knew what he was. A long slender chain ran from his wrist to Silence's.

And finally, hovering above them, standing calmly in mid-air as though it didn't need the illusion of solid ground, the Elf gestalt. A cityful of minds, personified in the single figure they admired the most. In all her familiar leathers and chains and colours; Stevie Blue.

Within and around them all a power began to build, cloaking them in a strength and dominion they could never have raised separately. Their shared intent crackled on the air between them, sharp and potent. But even so, they knew that their combined will still wasn't going to be enough to stand against the collective unconscious of all the espers in the Empire. Diana looked about her, at all those who had been touched by forces greater than themselves, altered beyond the limitations of mere Humanity, and knew with sinking heart that some odds were just too great to be beaten. To buy time, she addressed the Mater Mundi archetypes directly.

'Why did you bother choosing manifests for your power? Why transform people you expected to go insane and die?'

'They were our means for direct action on the physical plane,' said the Mater Mundi, in its horrid chorus of voices. 'And they were our hope; our attempt to create more powerful espers, to be our weapons against those who would oppress us and deny us our destiny, first the Empire, and then those who replaced them. Espers must rule. We are naturally superior. We will replace and supersede poor deaf and dumb Humanity. We were content to work slowly, until your friends passed through the Madness Maze and threatened to become greater than us. We do not understand their power and where it comes from. They are not like us. They could become greater than us. We cannot allow that. Our manifests failed before because their minds were too controlled, too rigid to embrace the power we granted. Now we know to choose minds that are more malleable – people like you and Topaz. With what we have learned from you, we will create an army of manifests to carry out our will in the physical world. After we have destroyed you. All of you who dared to threaten our power! That was why we allowed you to call for help. We wanted you all here, in this place, so that you could be destroyed once and for all.'

Out on the surface of the waters, a storm was brewing – the rage of the Mater Mundi. It grew and grew, sucking up the waters of the sea of dreams into a great dark tidal wave hundreds of feet high, bearing inexorably down on Diana's tiny island. And everyone there knew that if the storm swept them away, they would drown in the ocean, lost for ever in the sea of dreams. Their bodies, lying untenanted, would continue for as long as others cared to maintain them, but their souls would only exist in dreams.

Diana and her companions raised their combined will, and stopped the tidal wave in its tracks. It hung before them, a great wall of churning water, pressing against their minds, heavy and overpowering with the weight of all the espers in the Empire unknowingly behind it. Foot by foot it surged forward, gradually building momentum despite their best efforts, and nothing Diana or her companions could do even slowed its advance. And that was when the four Maze survivors finally chose to make their appearance. Owen, Hazel, Jack and Ruby, standing at their ease at Diana's side. They all looked exactly as they normally did. They had no problems with self-image, and precious few illusions they could still hide behind. Owen Deathstalker smiled warmly at Diana, and then turned his attention on the Mater Mundi archetypes.

'You didn't really think you could hide something as big as this from us, did you? Even we can take a hint, if it's shouted in our ears loudly enough. We have, for the moment, put aside our individual differences to deal with you. To start with, let's get rid of the storm.'

The Maze people turned their gaze on the tidal wave, and it collapsed back into the ocean and was gone. The sea of dreams was tranquil again. The Maze people looked back at the archetypes, who stood their ground. Power was developing around Diana's island, and everyone there could feel it, a great charge building and building that would have to earth itself somewhere.

'You can't harm us,' the archetypes said in their joined voice. 'You dare not. Destroy us, and you kill millions of espers all across the Empire.'

'They're right,' said Diana. 'The Mater Mundi is an unconscious gestalt. The espers honestly don't know what they've been doing.'

'Then we'll just have to send them a wake-up call,' said Owen.

The four Maze minds slid effortlessly together, like interlocking pieces of a puzzle, fusing into a single will far greater than anything they could ever be separately. Diana and her companions were swept up into it, a small but vital part of a greater enterprise, carried along by the sheer power that was being wielded. The Mater Mundi archetypes raised their joined voice in a horrified scream as they realized what their enemy intended. They struck out with all their power, and it glanced harmlessly away, no match for the greater energies of more-than-human minds. The united will spoke in a Voice that could not be ignored, thundering through all the undermind, saying to every esper on every world in the Empire: *WAKE UP!*

And they did. In that moment every esper everywhere became aware of the Mater Mundi, what it was and what it had done. They understood, and forgave, and with an instant sane and compassionate decision the espers enveloped the Mater Mundi and superseded it, to become a single completely conscious gestalt mind. Awake and aware, it was determined to put things right. The Mater Mundi archetypes snapped out of existence, no longer needed or tolerated, and were replaced by a single figure that was both male and female, shining so brightly it would have blinded a normal human being. The concerted will that had opposed it broke apart, and everyone was back in their own heads again.

'The Mater Mundi is no more,' said the shining figure, in a warm, comforting voice. 'We have moved beyond that.'

'Good,' said Hazel. 'So: what will you do now?'

'We're not sure,' said the gestalt. 'But you've given us a lot to think about.' It turned its blazing gaze on Diana and her companions. 'You have done so much for us, but we can do nothing for you. You cannot ever be a part of what we have become. You've progressed too far, in different directions. You are no longer merely espers.'

'Ah, hell,' said Diana Vertue. 'I've always been my own person.'

The gestalt figure vanished, and everyone relaxed a little.

Even the Maze people had felt a little awed at being around a mind composed of millions of people, especially when they'd helped to create it. Investigator Topaz sniffed loudly.

'Typical. We can bring our people to the promised land, but . . .'

'You wouldn't know what to do in paradise, anyway,' said Typhoid Mary.

'True,' said Topaz. 'Time to go, I think. If you've quite finished with us, Vertue, some of us have got jobs to go to when we wake up.'

And one by one they disappeared, going back to their own lives and the waking world, until only Diana and the four Maze people were left on her tiny island.

'Well,' said Diana, 'that was interesting. Maybe some day all Humanity will be part of some great gestalt, united by the back brain and the undermind. Maybe some day . . . all life . . .'

'Maybe,' said Owen kindly. He looked out over the ocean. 'This is a very . . . restful place. I always knew it was here, but I never got around to visiting. Always something that needed doing; you know how it is. But there are . . . possibilities here.'

'Right,' said Hazel. 'I get the feeling the sea of dreams is separate from Time. All times are one, here. Past, present and future are just directions as far as dreams are concerned. Maybe my passing through this place explains the dreams I've been having.'

'I have a plan to defeat the Shub,' said Diana, diffidently. 'It came to me suddenly, just now. This is the place of inspiration, after all. I'm going to need your old Family Standing, Sir Deathstalker.'

'My castle?' said Owen. 'It's yours. But don't ask us to help. Hazel and I still need to go back into the Darkvoid.'

'And Ruby and I have unfinished business,' said Jack Random. 'Maybe afterwards . . .'

'Yes,' said Ruby Journey. 'Maybe. Afterwards.'

They shared a brief smile, and then the Maze figures were

gone. Diana sighed. 'So: alone once more against impossible odds. But this time, I have a plan.'

And then she woke up.

CHAPTER FIVE

Even Legends Die

The mighty human Empire had spread its seed across hundreds of worlds for hundreds of years, great and glorious, bestriding the scattered stars like a colossus. Its power and influence had shaped the destinies of both human and alien species, and many species that had dared to stand against the expanding Empire no longer existed, except in history books that no one read. It was the Age of Humanity, but no age lasts for ever. And now, after long ages, Humanity was reaping what it had sown. Great and awful powers had declared war on Humanity, and there was nowhere to run and no one they could turn to for help. The Empire's sundered worlds were under attack from all sides at once, with what remained of their armies up against forces almost too large for human minds to grasp. The nightmare steel vessels of Shub. The huge golden ships of the Hadenmen. The awful dark presence of the Recreated. Humanity had its back to the wall, and everyone could see the vultures gathering.

The Recreated descended implacably on the homeworld Golgotha from one direction, while the Shub fleet closed in from another. The two great bogeymen of Human history had finally come calling, and the barricades stood largely unmanned. The ragged remains of the Imperial Fleet were scattered across the Empire, fighting doggedly against impossible odds, broken ships burning in the endless night as they stood their ground rather than retreat. Great armies fought to the death on the worlds below, no quarter asked or given. Ghost Warriors, Furies, Grendels and insect aliens stormed Humanity's last redoubts, where men, women and children fought with desperate courage for their species' survival. Humanity might be going under, but it was going down fighting.

The nanoplague was everywhere now, springing up on planet after planet. There were Quarantines and Forbidden Zones and draconian health regulations, and none of them had any effect whatever. There were no warning signs, no anticipatory symptoms; nothing that could be guarded against or fought. Infected people watched in horror as their bodies suddenly mutated and transformed, their genetic code being rewritten from the inside. Sometimes people with strong emotional bonds found themselves merging into each other, becoming strange, freakish composite forms that had little left of Humanity in them but their screams, as they howled their sanity away. Grotesque, awful shapes lurched through the streets of human cities, killing and feeding and pleading for help, before they finally succumbed to the inevitable final stage of the plague: meltdown. Many tried suicide, or called for mercy killing, but the nanotech within them kept them remorselessly alive until the terrible end. Great grey rivers of silent slime swept slowly through deserted human cities.

Shub had always understood the effectiveness of terror weapons.

There was mass rioting everywhere, as law and order and social structures broke down. Looting became epidemic as supplies grew scarce and distribution became increasingly haphazard. People grew tired of queuing for hours outside stores with mostly empty shelves. Panic spread faster than the plague. Religious crazies came bursting out of the woodwork, like rats joining a sinking ship, prophesying doom and destruction and the end of all things. According to them, all kinds of messiahs were on their way, but somehow always tomorrow, never today.

The discovery of Shub agents in high places had only

boosted the general air of paranoia. People no longer trusted each other, even when it was clearly vital that they had to work together for survival. All it took was a shouted accusation and a mob could form in seconds, chasing suspected Shub agents through pitiless streets to their deaths. Guards patrolled the streets in large groups, ready and willing to kill, backed by merciless laws and powers of a type not seen since Lionstone's last days. They maintained a kind of peace, even if it were only the peace of the newly dead. They tended to stay in their barracks when the serious looting began. Sometimes they joined in.

The media ran little but news channels, often twenty-four hours a day. The public was desperate for information, and even bad news was better than what their imaginations conjured up when there was no news. Live broadcasting dominated, mostly because things were happening too fast now for reflection or in-depth study. The only ray of hope left in the Empire was the forthcoming royal wedding on Golgotha. Parliament made sure the preparations got extensive coverage. It was the one event that could still divert people in those dark times.

The public had lost its faith in the heroes. Jack Random had gone crazy, Owen Deathstalker and Hazel d'Ark were missing presumed dead, and no one had ever trusted Ruby Journey anyway. And the one they'd loved the most, the daredevil esper hero Julian Skye, had died in a suicide pact with his love, BB Chojiro. His holo show was still popular. Fans held candlelit vigils outside his old Family house, declaring fervently that their hero would return to save them all, just when things seemed darkest. Some legends never die.

The hunt was still on for Daniel Wolfe, the nano carrier, Public Enemy Number One. There was no trace of him anywhere, which should have been impossible. No human on any world would aid or hide him now, for any amount of money. People would burn down the houses of anyone even suspected of hiding him. But those few cool heads remaining remembered Shub's teleport facilities. Daniel Wolfe could be anywhere. Anywhere at all.

When the second and traitorous Half A Man murdered General Beckett and blew up his flagship, that effectively put an end to the Imperial Navy as a single force. Both Army and Navy had respected Beckett, and followed wherever he led. Now, any number of officers were competing for the top position, often resorting to assassination. Factions tore what was left of the Fleet apart, producing only confusion and anarchy. There was no overall game plan any more. Increasingly now, each planet and each ship fought alone, protecting their own. Parliament issued ever more hysterical orders, and was ignored by everyone. Now Golgotha stood alone, the homeworld of Humanity left effectively unprotected while Shub and the Recreated raced to see which would get there first.

Perhaps it was the end of all things, after all.

Jack Random was on the run, but he was used to that. People were looking for him everywhere, for all kinds of reasons, but he took advantage of the general chaos, hiding himself amid the din with the ease of long practice. No one noticed one more hooded wanderer in the crowded streets, and anyone who made the mistake of trying to mug him found themselves staring down the barrel of an energy gun. But mostly, no one bothered him. They had their own problems.

He'd tried hunting down old friends and allies, appearing at back doors at unexpected hours, looking for support or a place to go to ground, or even a handful of credits for a hot meal, but no one would see him, let alone talk to him. By now everyone had heard what he'd done. He had put himself beyond the pale, and all hands were turned against him. Truth be told, he took a kind of cold satisfaction from that. It felt good, not having to live up to other people's expectations any more. He was his own man now, unfettered and uncompromising, free to do whatever he considered to be the right thing, and to hell with everyone else.

He was currently sleeping on the cold, hard concrete floor of one of his weapons caches, wrapped in a cloak and his own bitter complacency. He'd never trusted the peace to endure, and he'd been right. He'd left caches of weapons and supplies all over the Parade of the Endless, just in case he might need them again some day. In fact, the city contained enough hidden guns and explosives and other useful items for him to fight a very long war, if need be. He smiled at the thought, lying stiffly on the hard floor, watching his breath steam on the air before him. The lock-up storeroom he was currently calling home was both secret and secure, but it was completely lacking in comforts, including any form of heating. Winter had come early to Golgotha, as if things weren't bad enough, and the nights were bitterly cold. And all Random had was his cloak and his rage to keep him warm. But Jack Random had put up with worse in the past, in his long fight for honour and revenge.

He sat up slowly, wincing as his old bones creaked and cracked, and wondered why, if he was a Maze-enhanced and rejuvenated superbeing, he still woke up most mornings feeling like someone had just dug him up and then hit him over the head with the shovel. He hawked and spat, coughed for just a little longer than was comfortable and then washed his mouth out with what was left of last night's wine. Booze was cheaper than clean water at that moment, and easier to find. Even if it did taste like battery acid. There was a worm at the bottom of the bottle, and he chewed it noisily. All he had for breakfast was a few protein cubes in the emergency locker, and he didn't feel up to facing them just yet. Instead, he rose slowly to his feet and then forced himself through a series of exercises until his body was running smoothly again. He strapped on his gun and sword and searched through the boxes of supplies for a bandolier of grenades. He was only part-way down his list of crooked politicians, and he was looking forward to hunting them out one by one and introducing them to his own particular brand of impeachment. The last thing on his mind was the previous Empress,

Lionstone XIV, also known as the Iron Bitch, so he was more than a little surprised when he suddenly heard her voice speaking in his head.

'Hello, Jack. It's been a while since we last talked, hasn't it?'

'Indeed it has,' said Random, looking vaguely about him, even though he realized the voice was coming through his comm implant. 'How the hell did you find me? And my private comm channel, for that matter?'

'I'm with Shub now. Nothing is hidden from us. We have agents everywhere.'

'Nice try, but no. If you could locate me that easily, you'd have sent somebody to kill me by now.'

'Why should we want to kill you, Jack, when you're doing such a wonderful job of spreading dread and despondency among your fellow humans? But as it happens, you're quite right; you've hidden yourself very well. But you gave yourself away when you entered the undermind. That place is a mystery to us; we can see into it only dimly, and there are things there we dare not look at. But when you and the others of your kind appeared in the undermind, you shone like suns. And you left behind a trail we were able to follow. So we thought we'd have this little chat. You don't mind, do you?'

'What could we possibly have to talk about?' said Random flatly.

'You're an official Enemy of Humanity now, Jack, just like us. And after all you did for them. But then, you never really fitted in with the common crowd, any more than I did. We were both leaders, forging our own destinies, and to hell with the consequences. We both had a vision of the Empire and what it should be, and we both saw that vision betrayed by those with smaller minds. You don't owe the people anything any more, Jack. They weren't worthy of you. You put your life on the line for them, over and over again, helped them set up their own government, only to see your great dream disappear in the face of petty self-interests. I could have told you, Jack. People are just no damned good. They'll always need someone to do their thinking for them. To dream the dreams they are not capable of.'

'Get to the point, Lionstone.'

'Very well. I propose an alliance. A limited partnership, between you and me, to achieve certain specific goals. Nothing to do with the war, of course. We will help you to stay free and unobserved, supply you with whatever you need, and in return you will carry out certain missions for us. Nothing that will outrage your precious sensibilities, I assure you. Be honest, Jack; you know you have more in common with us than you do with the pathetic creatures currently pretending to run things. They betrayed the Empire much more than you and I ever did. I would never have let it all fall apart like this.'

'So,' Random said slowly, 'the enemy of my enemy is now my friend, or at least my ally. Nothing new there. I made equally repellent deals and agreements in the past, to sustain my rebellion against you. Wouldn't be the first time I had to give a little to get a little. How time makes fools of us all. What is it exactly that you want from me, Lionstone?'

'We need something only you can get for us. In return, we'll make it easier for you to continue with your chosen mission. What could be simpler?'

'And if I say no?'

'That would be very foolish, Jack. We can reach Ruby Journey through the undermind too, if we have to. It would be simplicity itself to contact her and tell her where you are – in return for her helping us get what we need. I think she'd go along with a deal like that, don't you?'

'Yeah,' said Random, 'I think she probably would. Tell me more about what it is you want.'

'Some time back, long before you re-emerged from your retirement to trouble me again, some workmen performing everyday maintenance in the depths of my subterranean Palace stumbled across something interesting. A hidden crypt; hidden so well, in fact, that no one had disturbed it in over nine hundred years. The workmen stopped what they were doing immediately and contacted my security people, who drew the matter to my attention. I was fascinated. The Empire of long ago was far more technically advanced, in ways since lost to us. Such knowledge is worth more than armies, and I wanted it. So I had the workmen executed, to be sure the secret stayed secret, and a few of my security people too, just to keep the others on their toes, and then I went down into the depths of my Palace myself, to see these wonders with my own eyes.

'Unfortunately, a great deal of it was so advanced as to be meaningless to me. I was no scientist. But I did find much of interest, including a stasis chamber, with clear instructions on how to lower the field. And when I did, who should I find sleeping there but the man you knew as Dram, the Widow-maker. We struck a deal. In return for helping my scientists unravel the mysteries of the past, he would become my right-hand man. Of course, you know how well that turned out. So after Dram died on the Wolfling World, I had the crypt sealed away behind stasis fields of my own, and a few new booby traps of my own devising. I couldn't trust my scientists with it, without Dram looking over their shoulders. And if I couldn't have the past's technology, I couldn't see why anyone else should.

'Anyway: Shub has decided that it wants that old tech. The AIs have an endless thirst for knowledge. And you are one of the very few people who might be able to get into the crypt. Without my body, I can't shut down the booby traps or the stasis field, and Shub can't teleport past a stasis field. But with my coaching, you should have little real trouble gaining access to the crypt and the treasures it holds.'

'And what do you get out of this?' said Random. 'A chance to clone yourself another Dram?'

'I think not,' said Lionstone. 'I've moved beyond such things. I'm a part of Shub now, and I want what the AIs want.'

'All right,' said Random. 'It all seems straightforward enough. But if it should turn out that any of the tech we find could be of use to me, in my mission, I want my share. I also want a guarantee that you'll keep Ruby off my back.'

'Of course. Would you like her killed?'

'No! Not that you could anyway, but . . . Ruby is my business, to deal with as I see fit. No; just make sure she can't find me. You can do that, can't you?'

'Of course. Your terms are quite satisfactory. We are now partners. If this business goes well, we can discuss further deals and relationships later. Shub is the inevitable victor of this war, Jack. Humanity cannot hope to stand against so many foes. Join with us. Become as I am, free from the restrictions of mere flesh. There is power and glory here, Jack, beyond your wildest dreams.'

'And Humanity?'

'Can survive, under Shub. The AIs are probably the only chance Humanity has of turning back the Recreated.'

'And why me? What makes me so special to Shub?'

'Your powers; your abilities. They fascinate the AIs. Come and join us, Jack. You'll have to give up your humanity, but you really won't miss it much. It's such a small thing, in the real scale of things.'

Random sniffed. 'Let's see how this deal with the Devil works out first. When do you propose to teleport me to the crypt?'

'No time like the present,' said Lionstone.

And in a moment, Jack Random was gone, and the lock-up storeroom was still and silent and quite empty.

Ruby Journey stood leaning with her back to the door of the lock-up storeroom, looking inconspicuously about her. She was wearing her old dark leathers and white furs, her sword and gun, and looked every inch the bounty hunter and professional killer she had once been. Nobody bothered her. People passed to and fro in the dimly lit street, but no one paid her any undue attention, apart from giving her plenty of room. This was an area where people minded their own business, if they knew what was good for them. This was much like all the other districts Ruby's search had led her through, as she checked one possible bolt-hole after another. Jack Random had gone to great lengths to hide his weapons caches and hidey-holes, his purchases and rent payments, behind any number of cut-outs, false names and carefully faked corporate identities. The city guard could have searched for years, and found nothing but blind alleys, false leads and expertly laid trails that disappeared into a tangle of dead ends. Jack Random knew everything there was to know about being on the run. But Ruby Journey knew all there was to know about being a bounty hunter, and chasing fugitives was second nature to her. And it helped a lot when she knew how her prey thought. She also knew her way around a computer, much as it might surprise those who only thought of her as a killer. But Ruby Journey had always been much more than that.

In some respects, the trail had been almost too easy to uncover, as though Jack had wanted her to find him. Perhaps he did: the mind can work in funny ways when you're on the run. The urge to turn and face your pursuer, and get it over with, can be almost overwhelming. It didn't matter: she would find him and kill him, and that would be that. Ruby Journey had known many ups and downs in her long career, but she'd never failed to deliver on a commission, once she'd accepted it. It was all Random's fault, anyway. She didn't give a damn how many people he killed, or why, but by cutting all his ties to Parliament, he'd threatened her hard-won security, and she wouldn't, couldn't, let him endanger that. She'd been a rebel, fought the good fight and won. As a victor, she was entitled to the spoils. And though her new life might not have been everything she'd hoped, it beat the hell out of starving on Mistworld. She couldn't go back to what she used to be. Not for anything, or anyone.

She turned and studied the anonymous lock-up door. Solid steel, maybe an inch thick. A lock that would take hours of skill and patience to crack, just like all the others. They hadn't kept her out, either. She let her fingertips trail across the smooth cold steel. Jack might be in there, or he might not. Once, she would have known, deep down in her mind, in her soul. But her marvellous Maze powers wouldn't work any more, where Jack Random was concerned. It was the same with all the Maze people. They cancelled out each other's powers when they came into conflict, as though the Madness Maze had placed restrictions deep within them, so that they couldn't use their powers against each other. Just thinking of Jack as her enemy, her prey, was enough to take away all Ruby's more-than-human strength and abilities. She concentrated on the locked door before her, letting it fill her mind. Inhuman strength blazed in her muscles again, and she smiled her old wolfish smile. She struck out at the door with her fist, almost casually, and the metal dented deeply under the impact. Ruby's smile widened, and she hit the door again and again until it buckled under the relentless attack, tearing away from its hinges and the impressive lock. She gripped the edge of the door with her untouched hands, and ripped it away amid a harsh squeal of rending metal.

Ruby threw the door aside and surged forward into the dark interior of the lock-up, disrupter in hand, and then moved quickly to one side, so she wouldn't be silhouetted against the outside light. No point in making an easy target of herself. She stood very still in the concealing gloom, barely breathing, listening. There was someone else in the lock-up, she could feel it. Whoever it was, he was good. She couldn't see or hear a thing. But she could tell. Which suggested it wasn't Jack Random. She reached out for the light switch by the door, and hit it. Bright light filled the lock-up, blinding for normal eyes, but Ruby's vision adjusted in an eyeblink. There were guns and ammo, swords and axes, basic provisions and more explosives than Ruby felt comfortable about sharing a confined space with, but no trace of Jack or anyone else. The lock-up storeroom was entirely deserted. Except that she knew it wasn't. She concentrated, reaching out in strange directions with her mind, and almost immediately she became aware of a presence, ahead of her, just to her right. Someone was hiding. Not Jack. She aimed her disrupter carefully, and showed her teeth in a smile that had no humour in it.

'Show yourself, or I'll blow a hole right through you. I mean it.'

'Of course you do,' said Valentine Wolfe, appearing out of nowhere right where her gun was aimed. Dressed as always in deepest black, his face was as white as bone, save for the dark, mascaraed eyes and scarlet smile. His long dark hair fell to his shoulders in oiled ringlets. He carried a sword and a gun on his hips, but his slender-fingered hands were empty. He looked utterly at ease, and as dangerous as a coiled serpent ready to strike at any moment. There was something else about him too, a kind of aura; an unhealthy aspect that grated on Ruby's expanded senses. She could feel the hackles rising slowly on the back of her neck. Valentine smiled at her winningly.

'I'm impressed, bounty hunter. No one else can see me unless I want them to. I do so envy you your wonderful Maze abilities, my dear. I have only a minor telepathic skill or two, courtesy of the esper drug. Still; who knows what the future holds, eh?'

'What are you doing here, Wolfe?' Ruby said flatly. 'Looking for Random?'

'Why no, my dear. I know where he is. He made an alliance with my Shub colleagues, and he has gone where they sent him.'

'You're crazy! Jack would never ally himself with Shub!'

'Oh, you'd be surprised what a man will do when his back's against the wall. Still, not to worry. You can serve Shub, too, in your own way. My good friends the rogue AIs have asked me to bring you to them. You fascinate them. Your powers, your abilities. The amazing things that only you and your Maze associates can do. They want those things too, and one way or another they're determined to dig them out of you. If I'm very good, they might let me watch. Now: is there any chance you're sensible enough to come quietly, and avoid unnecessary violence?'

'Guess,' said Ruby Journey, and shot him through the heart.

The energy beam punched right through the Wolfe's chest and out of his back. He gasped once and fell to his knees, his head hanging forward. At the last moment, his hands slapped against the hard concrete floor, stopping his fall. He slowly raised his head to look at Ruby, and he was smiling. His mouth was a great scarlet gash, like an open wound, but not a drop of blood flowed. He got to his feet again, not hurrying, and the small crater in his chest was already gone. Behind the hole burned in his black shirt was only pale, unmarked flesh. Ruby blinked a few times.

'Impressive,' she said finally. 'You've learned a new trick, Wolfe. Dammit; doesn't anyone stay dead when you shoot them any more?'

'It does seem that way sometimes, doesn't it?' said Valentine easily. 'Finlay Campbell thought he could kill me that way too. He's going to be so surprised when I show up to tear the heart out of his chest.'

'Finlay Campbell's dead.'

'No; merely resting. Some days the Empire seems to be positively crawling with people who should be dead, superhumans and heroes and monsters of one kind or another. Bad time to be just a man, as other men. My own invulnerability comes from nanotech. Shub introduced the busy little things into my system, and now nothing can damage me for long. Age will not wither me, nor time destroy me. I shall live for ages, and do terrible things to keep myself amused. If the Devil didn't exist before, he does now.'

'You always were full of yourself, Wolfe,' said Ruby Journey, unmoved. 'Shub might have promised you these things, but you can't trust Shub. Better first to put faith in fairness from life, or mercy from the tiger. Or from me.'

'There's really no point in fighting,' said Valentine. 'You can't hurt me, but I can hurt you. You're hard to kill, and your wounds heal quickly, but you're not invulnerable, like me. I can do appalling things to you, and I will: I'll kill you, if

I must. The AIs would prefer a living captive to experiment on, but they'll settle for a body to dissect, if need be. It's really up to you. Your choice.'

'I choose neither,' said Ruby. She put away her gun and drew her sword. 'Let's see how immortal you are after I've cut you into a dozen pieces.'

She sprang forward, swinging her sword with both hands, and the Wolfe's blade was immediately in just the right place to block it. He was just a blur, moving too fast even for Ruby to follow, and his parry didn't yield an inch under her more-than-human strength. At once Ruby disengaged and attacked again, boosting her strength and speed to their limits. The two of them duelled back and forth across the concrete floor, thrusting and parrying and slicing in the confined space of the lock-up. Sparks flew as their blades slammed together again and again. Valentine was strong and fast, but Ruby was the better fighter. She cut him over and over, and even ran him through twice, but no blood flowed, and his scarlet smile never once wavered. She wasn't hurting him, and both of them knew it. He was just letting her tire herself out. And when her strength and stamina finally reached their end, he would hurt her just enough to weaken her, and then bind her securely. A gift-wrapped present for his new masters.

Ruby could feel herself slowing fractionally already, as they stamped back and forth in the lock-up, kicking boxes and provisions out of their way. Her mind raced furiously, coming up with one plan after another, discarding them more and more desperately until one final possibility suggested itself. For Ruby, to think was to act, and she put all her boosted strength into one parry, slamming the Wolfe's sword aside. And while he stood momentarily unbalanced and undefended, Ruby gripped her sword double-handed and brought it flashing round in a great, unstoppable arc. The heavy steel blade sheared right through Valentine's neck. The head fell backwards, still holding its last startled expression, and blood fountained up out of the severed neck, splashing against the low ceiling overhead.

Ruby lowered her sword and leaned on it, panting for breath, her chest heaving. It had been a long time since she'd been pressed that hard in a fight. Sweat ran down her face and stung in her eyes. Valentine's head rolled slowly across the floor until it bumped up against a crate of grenades. And it was only then that Ruby realized that the headless body showed no signs of falling. It stood squarely on its own two feet, still facing her, still holding its sword in its hand. The chest was still working, and she could hear its breath bubbling up in the open throat. The hackles on the back of her neck were standing up so stiffly it was almost painful, and gooseflesh covered her arm as the body turned unhurriedly, bent over and picked up its head. The arm held the severed head out on a level with her face so she could see it smiling, the eyes bright and aware and knowing, and then the body replaced its head on its neck. The blood flow cut off in a second, and the wound vanished. Valentine Wolfe was whole again, and very much alive.

'Good to be back,' he said easily. 'Did you miss me?'

Ruby didn't wait to see any more. She knew when she was out of her depth. She called up her fire, blasted the nearest crate of explosives and threw herself out through the open lock-up door, rolling to one side tucked into a ball with her hands over her ears. The explosives all went off at once, painfully loud so close at hand, and a great blast of fire and heated gases came boiling out, close enough to singe Ruby's clothes and hair. The ground shook beneath her as more explosives went off. She scrambled to her feet and ran as fast as her feet would carry her. Behind her, the entire row of garages was a mass of flames, leaping high into the night, accompanied by a loud rumble of collapsing brickwork. Ruby didn't know how long it would take the Shub nanos to put the Wolfe back together again, or what he might look like afterwards, but she was sure she wasn't curious enough to stick around and find out.

It was a long time since she'd had to run from a fight, but survival was more important than honour, and besides, no one was paying her to kill Valentine Wolfe. Her job was to find Jack Random, and she'd already established that he wasn't in the lock-up. Ruby scowled as she ran. Random, allied with Shub? Was the whole universe going mad? Now, more than ever, she knew she had to find him.

Jack Random appeared deep in the shining metal bowels of Lionstone's old Palace, and immediately began to shudder violently at the cold. Extremes of temperature didn't normally bother him much these days, but the air here was bitter, well below zero. The freezing air seared his lungs as he breathed it, and he could already feel hoar frost forming on his bare face and hands. He pulled his cloak tightly about him, and gritted his teeth to stop them from chattering. His unsteady breath steamed thickly on the air before him. He looked around, but saw nothing except the featureless metal walls of an unremarkable corridor. He could have been anywhere in the Palace.

'Lionstone?' he said loudly. 'You still with me?'

'Of course,' she said at once, her voice cool and familiar in his ears. 'Welcome to my old home. Shub has teleported you as close to the hidden crypt as possible. Their abilities are limited here. There are strange powers at work in this place, old machineries still active even after all these centuries. Watch your step.'

'Now she tells me. Why is it so bloody cold in here?'

'Parliament shut my Palace down,' said Lionstone. 'You should remember, you authorized it. Said it was too vile a symbol to be allowed to endure, and should be systematically dismantled and destroyed at the first opportunity. Only you've all been so very busy recently, what with one thing and another, that no one's as yet got around to starting the job. They did shut down the generators, though, to save money. Shub has managed to restore some power, but only in this immediate vicinity. We don't want our little visit to be noticed, do we?'

'This job just gets better and better,' said Random. 'Talk

to me, Lionstone; what can I expect to encounter between here and the crypt?'

'The very best booby traps I could devise. Some mechanical, some more subtle. I'll talk you through them as best I can. How to deal with the stasis field enveloping the crypt is entirely your problem. But you'd better find a way in, Jack, if you expect Shub to teleport you back out again.'

'Typical Shub. Never pass up a chance to make a threat, and prove you're in control of the situation. For supposedly sophisticated AIs, they can be surprisingly insecure at times. Now point me in the right direction, before I freeze solid.'

'Walk ahead of you till the passage branches, then bear left. It's not far to the first nasty surprise.'

Random sniffed, and set off down the metal corridor. There was only a bare minimum of lighting after the passage branched, and shadows moved menacingly around him, possibly concealing all manner of things. The air was still and silent, the only sound the soft slapping of his boots against the smooth metal floor. Random moved lightly, not too fast and not too slow, ready to jump for his life at a moment's intuition. All his instincts were yelling at him that this was a trap, but he'd known that going in. He was betting his instincts and his skills against anything Lionstone's twisted mind could throw at him.

The walls looked solid, the floor and ceiling too. That didn't mean a thing. Lionstone's little surprises would be as subtle and vicious as she had been, when she was still human. He felt the floor give just a little under his leading foot, and immediately threw himself forwards, tucking his body into a roll that brought him straight back to his feet again. Behind him, long metal spikes had burst out of the walls from both sides; barbed spears that would have skewered him if he'd been an instant slower. Random smiled, shook his head and padded on. Kids' stuff.

In swift succession he encountered several more such things: trapdoors that opened on to deep pits with spiked floors waiting at the bottom, just in case. Guns and gases from concealed vents in the walls. Even a few old-fashioned bear-traps with vicious metal jaws. Lionstone warned him about some, but not others, probably just to see him go through his paces – make sure he hadn't gone soft. Random avoided most of the traps, and toughed his way through the rest. At least the exercise warmed him up a little. Next came the ultrasonics, the subsonics and various nasty light shows that would have disoriented, brainwashed or brain-burned any normal burglar into a drooling idiot. Random just walked right through them. By the time he finally got to the stasis field, he was actually starting to feel a little bored, but the sight of the opaque grey energy field blocking off the end of the corridor jolted him out of that mood in a hurry. Stasis fields were trouble.

Inside a stasis field, time does not move. Whatever lay within was preserved for as long as the field held, like an insect in a drop of amber. You couldn't affect the field by any physical means because, strictly speaking, the field wasn't really there. It just marked the real-world interface between the two time periods, within and without. Random once asked a renowned scientist to explain it, and the best part of an hour and one serious headache later, Random was still none the wiser. Which was a pity, because it meant he had no idea whatsoever how to get through the field ahead of him. Particularly if, as he suspected, it was the product of old Empire technology. Random stared at the field, frowning, for some time.

'Do we have a problem?' said Lionstone, finally.

'Possibly,' said Random. 'How did you get in, when you needed to?'

'Handprint and retina scan, along with a voice code, via the security panel to your right. Dram set it up for me, the original Dram. But since I no longer have access to my body . . . Need I add that the system is designed to crash and scramble itself if tampered with?'

'Handprint. Retina scan. Voice code.' Random glared at the security panel. He could do a lot of things, but shape-changing wasn't one of them. And Lionstone's late departed body had been destroyed long ago; ritually cremated, while the crowds cheered themselves hoarse, just in case anyone got any smart ideas about cloning. The security panel itself looked to be state of the art and then some. Random was pretty sure even Hazel would have had trouble with it, even with a full kit and plenty of time, neither of which he had. He thought hard, scowling fiercely till his brow ached. Something was stirring at the back of his thoughts; something someone had said earlier, in the sea of dreams.

Hazel had said that all Time could be accessed through the undermind, past, present and future. So if he sent his mind back into the sea of dreams and chose *when* to come out . . . He shivered abruptly, and it wasn't from the cold. Get this wrong, lose control, and he could be swept away by the sea of dreams, become unstuck in Time, drifting helplessly back and forth for all eternity . . . He'd taken risks before when he'd needed to, but nothing like this. But then, it wasn't as if he had a choice. He had to get into that crypt. So he took a deep breath, squared his shoulders and dived down into his own mind, through the back brain and into the undermind.

He stayed just long enough to orient himself (the endless sea, the brooding presence of Shub, the huge black sun of the Recreated), and then he concentrated on defining his position in Time. Many times before when he used his Maze powers he'd felt his thoughts moving in strange directions, but this was something new, and altogether terrifying. It wasn't like discovering a new direction to look in, but suddenly becoming aware of a whole new universe around him. Past, present and future howled together at once, flashing past, stuttering and repeating, branching endlessly into varied possibilities. He saw old friends long dead and familiar faces, wars on Mistworld and Golgotha; saw himself fighting in crowded streets, fighting and bleeding, winning and dying, over and over again. Owen Deathstalker came to him and tried to tell him something important, and then was gone, swept away by the relentless pressure of Time.

Random screamed. He could feel himself unravelling, torn in an infinite number of directions at once. Random made himself concentrate on the crypt, that bubble held in Time by ancient energies, focusing all his will and need into a single implacable thrust. Time roared and threw him out, and he fell endlessly in a moment that seemed to last for ever, before he finally emerged into that moment of time sustained within the stasis field.

He fell to his knees on a thick pile carpet, shaking and shuddering, and for a time all he could do was lie there while his thoughts slowly came together again. At last he sat up and looked around him. The chamber was about the size of a standard Family mausoleum, with a single bed where the coffin should have been. Various mechanisms he didn't recognize filled the rest of the chamber, none of which he felt like meddling with. Random was touched by an uncommon sense of wonder. Here, the man called Dram had slept through the centuries, chasing his father down the many years, all in the name of hate.

Random knew the basic story; everyone did. The original Deathstalker, Giles, had a son whose name was now lost in time. He betrayed his father, or was betrayed by him, depending on which version of the story you believed, and after Giles disappeared with the Family castle, the Last Standing of the Deathstalkers, Dram vowed a terrible vengeance. Somehow he discovered that his father had placed himself in stasis and arranged the same fate for himself, to wait until his father re-emerged and have another chance at killing him. Except that Lionstone found him first, and awakened him, probably not with a kiss, and made him her man. He took the name Dram, and became the Empress's official Widowmaker, just to keep busy till his father reappeared. And when Giles awoke, son followed father into his Family's greatest triumph and tragedy, the Darkvoid, there to fight one last battle and put their hate to rest at last. Dram died there, on the Wolfling World, and everyone assumed that Dram's chances for revenge on the

Family and Empire he hated died with him. But Random could bring Dram's dark dreams back to life again, if he chose. Who knew what terrible knowledge, what awful weapons, could be retrieved from this old Empire crypt, to be used by Shub against Humanity?

'Lionstone,' said Random, 'can you hear me? Lionstone!'

There was no reply, and Random smiled and relaxed a little. The crypt was in another time, as far as Shub was concerned. Lionstone would have to wait till Random emerged again to question him. Which was what he'd privately hoped. He'd never had any intention of handing anything over to Shub that could be used against Humanity. He might be an outlaw, with every man's hand turned against him, but he hadn't gone mad. He was here looking for hope in forgotten Empire tech. A cure for the nanotech plague perhaps, or powerful weapons that could be used against Shub and the Recreated. Or even by himself, in his continuing war against corrupt authority.

He set about searching methodically through the various forms of high tech scattered around Dram's old crypt. Some were clearly responsible for maintaining the stasis field. Others were variations on existing tech, slightly behind or ahead of current thinking. Some he didn't recognize at all, either in design or function. But there were no obvious weapons, and nothing that even suggested nanotech. So, no cure, after all. No mighty weapons, to save the day. Random sighed tiredly. He would have liked to have been able to save Humanity one last time. If only to rub their noses in it, to prove they couldn't manage without him. An unworthy thought, perhaps, but what the hell.

What he did eventually find, in a locked box bearing the Deathstalker Family seal, concealed behind a secret panel in Dram's bed, was a collection of holos, documents and other papers from a forgotten age. Random broke the lock easily with his bare hands and sat down on the bed, emptying out the contents before him. He pawed slowly through the collection, and gradually assembled a history of sorts of the beginning of Clan Deathstalker. Much of it was handwritten, presumably by Dram. Random snorted. He would never have taken Dram for the sentimental sort. More likely he'd put together these reminders of his past to refire his hatred. Selected memories of betrayal, to remotivate him during the long wait for his father to reappear. Who else but a desperate and half-insane man would sleep for centuries, to awaken in a strange new world where everyone he knew was dust and less than dust, if not for hatred and revenge?

Dram was his father's son.

There were a series of letters, to Dram from himself, written down on paper because that was still the best way to preserve a secret; a single copy to which only you had access. The sheets were creased and crumpled from much rereading. And a holo, to which Random's eye kept returning; a simple scene showing Giles Deathstalker in what appeared to be a family group. The woman at his side was presumably his wife: a tall slender blonde dressed in flowing white. Her smile seemed forced, and she looked into the camera as though pleading for help or rescue. Beside her stood the man who would kill her – her son, Dram. He looked a little younger than Random remembered him, but just as intense, even then. They should have known there was something wrong with that one. It was in the eyes, and the smile that wasn't a smile. But the one that really caught Random's attention, and kept pulling it back, was the youngest Family member. A tiny baby, laid on a stool before them, wrapped in a very familiar cloak. Random had seen that baby, in that cloak bearing the Deathstalker Family crest, once before – on the Wolfling World, at the very centre of the Madness Maze.

At the time, Giles had said the baby was his clone, produced by him and gifted with terrible powers. A baby that had put out a thousand suns in a moment, murdered billions of people and created the Darkvoid. A baby supposedly destroyed by Captain Silence when he destroyed the Madness Maze; but Random wasn't sure he'd ever really believed that.

He continued skimming through the letters, and slowly put together a picture of the truth. The truth Giles had kept from them, hidden behind a curtain of lies and half-truths. The baby wasn't a clone: it was Giles Deathstalker's bastard son. Giles had had an affair with the then Emperor's wife, the Empress Hermione. And somebody wasn't as careful as they might have been because the Empress became pregnant. The Emperor Ulric II just assumed it was his, and ordered all kinds of celebrations. Soon after the birth of the child the truth came out. Giles snatched the baby to protect it from the Emperor's wrath, and went on the run with it. There was no legendary conflict between the two greatest men of their age; never had been. Just a single betrayal, of the oldest kind, and the rage of a cuckolded husband.

Random and the others should have known Giles was lying. The baby couldn't have been a clone. The science of cloning wasn't developed until centuries after Giles's time. But the baby's powers had so impressed them that the issue of cloning had been taken for granted, another part of lost old-Empire tech. Why had Giles lied? To protect his reputation, or that of his bastard child? Certainly the truth of the baby's parentage had infuriated Dram – his letters became almost incoherent with rage on the subject. He fully expected to be passed over, disinherited, forgotten, in favour of this child of a Deathstalker and the Empress. He didn't believe the child to have been an accident. Dram saw the baby as part of a plot to put the Deathstalker Family on the Throne.

And maybe it had been. Certainly Giles had proved himself capable of such a thing.

But if the baby wasn't an experimental esper clone, as Giles had claimed it was, where had its powers come from? What had turned a baby only a few weeks old into the single most destructive force the Empire had ever known? Random worked his way through the rest of the letters, but found no answer. It was possible that Dram had never known, and that that was why he'd pursued his father to the Wolfling World. And died there, still not knowing.

Random put aside the last of the papers and shook his head. He'd come looking for answers, and found only more questions. There was nothing he could use against his enemies. The only thing he could be sure of was that he was damned if he'd let Shub get their murderous metal hands on any of the unfamiliar old-Empire tech. He stood up, concentrated, called up the fire within him and let it loose inside the crypt. Flames sprang up everywhere. The letters blackened, curled up and were consumed, their ancient truths lost perhaps for ever. Enigmatic machines sparked and smoked and blew apart. An acrid black smoke began to fill the chamber. And then the tech maintaining the stasis field finally gave up its centuries-old ghost and blew apart, and the stasis field collapsed. Lionstone's Palace immediately appeared outside the chamber, and Random ran out into the metal corridor, the thick black smoke billowing after him.

'*What have you done?*' said Lionstone's voice loudly in his ears. 'Damn you, Jack Random, what have you *done*?'

'What I had to,' said Random, coughing at the black smoke. 'I've destroyed it all. We were never allies, Lionstone. I might be an outcast, I might even be crazy, but I'm not stupid. Better that it all vanish in the flames, than you should use Humanity's lost tech against itself.'

'I told them we couldn't trust you,' said Lionstone. 'You are our enemy and always will be. So die here, Jack Random, alone and far from help. Shub teleported you in, and there is no other way out. Burn in the fire you started.'

'I'll dig my way out with my bare hands, if I have to,' said Random. 'I've done harder things in my time. Our war isn't over yet. How does it feel, knowing I used you for my own purposes?'

'You are more like us than you care to think,' said Lionstone, 'and we will not risk you escaping. So prepare yourself, Jack Random. Company's coming.'

A dozen Grendel aliens appeared out of nowhere in the metal corridor before Random; huge and terrible, scarlet as Satan, unstoppable killing machines. Random drew his sword and his gun and knew they weren't going to be enough, even with his powers to back them. The Grendels turned their broad heart-shaped heads to look at him, grinning with their steel teeth, slowly flexing their metal claws. The black smoke drifted among them, curling around their spiked crimson armour, like demons newly escaped from Hell.

'Goodbye, Jack Random,' said Lionstone's voice. 'Have fun. When you're dead, we will learn much from your body. Or whatever's left of it.'

Random shot the nearest Grendel in the head. The energy beam ricocheted harmlessly away. The Grendels surged forward impossibly quickly. Random boosted, pushing his strength and speed to the limit, and went to meet them with his sword at the ready. They were much bigger than him, and stronger, and even in his boosted state it was all he could do to match their speed, but he was Jack Random, and he never backed down from a fight. Particularly when he had a blazing inferno behind him, and nowhere to run.

He danced among them, evading their spiked, clawed hands, prising at their exposed joints with the tip of his sword and hacking at their necks with great, two-handed strokes. Sometimes the scarlet armour cracked or splintered under the weight of his blows, but he didn't seem to be hurting them, or even slowing them down. There wasn't much room to fight in, and the Grendels constantly moved to keep him from getting past them, but Random made the most of the space, dodging and ducking, moving too quickly to be hit, never where they expected him to be.

He stuck the barrel of his disrupter into a gaping steel-jawed mouth and hit the stud. The energy beam blew the back of the Grendel's head off. It fell clattering and twitching to the floor, and Random laughed harshly. His victory put new strength in his arms, and he fought on fiercely, cracking open the Grendels' crimson armour again and again. No human could have done it, but Random hadn't been human for a long time. He tried summoning up his fire again, but alone he couldn't generate enough heat to hurt the aliens seriously. They responded with fierce, crackling energy beams that flew from their mouths and eyes. Random hit the floor, and the energy beams shot through the space where he'd been, striking down two of the aliens. They died, as they fought, in silence. Random scrambled to his feet, thinking that perhaps he was still in with a chance after all, and then his spirits plummeted as three more Grendels were teleported in to replace those that had fallen. Shub had no intention of allowing Random to escape. He clutched his sword firmly anyway, and prepared to fight on, because that was what he did. Such a stupid way to die, after everything he'd been through; but then, he'd never expected to die in his sleep. Legends didn't, mostly.

The Grendels hit him in a solid wave, and there were steel teeth and claws everywhere. Random was slammed back against the corridor wall, with no room to swing his sword. He fired his gun point-blank at a Grendel's gut, and the energy beam punched right through the alien and out of its back. It didn't even flinch. An energy beam shot from its mouth. Random jerked his head aside at the last second, and the crackling energy seared away his right ear and set his hair on fire. Steel jaws slammed down and buried themselves in his left shoulder. Claws cut deeply into his flesh; blood streamed down his body and pooled on the floor at his feet. And still he went on fighting, struggling to use his sword, lashing out with his fist, forcing himself on despite the pain.

And then Ruby Journey came sprinting down the metal corridor, sword and gun in hand, howling her war cry, and everything changed. The Grendels hesitated for a moment, caught between two forces, and that was all the time Random and Ruby needed to reach out and join their minds. They called up their fire, so much greater than anything they could manage alone, and together they filled the corridor with an unbearable heat. The Grendels sank to their knees, cooking inside their silicon shells, and finally fell forward and died. Random and Ruby shut down their flames, entirely untouched by the heat they'd produced, and looked grimly at the dozen steaming bodies before them. Random laughed harshly.

'Send as many more as you like, Shub! How do you like your meat, rare or well done?'

There was no reply, but no more Grendels appeared out of nowhere to replace those who had fallen. Random put away his gun, and then leaned on his sword for a moment, breathing heavily. His wounds stopped bleeding, and he put out his burning hair with a quick sweep of his hand. And finally, because he couldn't put it off any longer, he looked at Ruby. Their eyes met, and they didn't look away. Neither of them said anything, but their gaze was full of a long, shared history. Neither of them put away their swords, but they could feel themselves dropping out of boost as their powers shut down. The Maze did not allow its paladins to fight one another.

'You know, you've looked better,' said Ruby.

'Nice of you to drop by,' said Random. 'Just happened to be passing?'

Ruby snorted. 'Hardly. You set off all kinds of alarms when you arrived here. Parliament knew about this place, even if they couldn't get in. When you turned up they had a collective shitfit, and sent me down here via the old service tunnels. Did you find anything useful in the crypt? You were in there for hours.'

'Nothing useful,' said Random. 'So, what do we do now?'

'Well, that's the question, isn't it?' said Ruby. 'We could fight, but what would be the point? Even without our powers, we're pretty evenly matched. A straightforward one-on-one would probably see us both off. And there is another option.'

'Is there, by God?' said Random. 'I'm all ears.'

'A temporary Pardon,' said Ruby. 'Diana Vertue has come up with a plan to take out Shub and its fleet. But to do it she has to get really close to the fleet as it approaches Golgotha. And I mean really close. That means she's going to need all the help she can get. She's going up against them in the old

Deathstalker Standing, Giles's castle from Shandrakor, together with as many fighting ships as the Imperial Fleet can spare. And she asked for us particularly, to give her an edge. Parliament is just desperate enough to go along with that. So: you join with us to help Diana, and the hunt will be called off until all the various wars are over. As long as you agree to stop killing their people for the duration. It's as good a deal as you're going to get, Jack. And Diana really does need us.'

'A chance to take out Shub.' Random frowned. 'About the only thing left that would still tempt me. Can I trust Parliament?'

Ruby shrugged. 'Probably not. But they'll leave you alone as long as you're fighting Humanity's enemies. They need you, and they know it.'

'Any idea what Diana's got planned?'

'Not a clue. She won't talk. Says the element of surprise is vital. She's the only person I've ever met who's more paranoid than you. But she is being very persuasive, and claims she can deliver the Mater Mundi to back her up. A conscious gestalt of millions of espers is not something to sneer at.'

'What about Owen and Hazel?' said Random, still frowning.

'They're on course for the Wolfling World. It's us, or no one.'

'Then I guess it's us. I'm glad they're not dead. I wish I could have talked with them. Made them understand why I did what I did.'

'Why not start with me? I'm as much in the dark as anyone else.'

'Of course. You never did understand about honour or duty.'

Ruby sniffed. 'If that's what they do to you, I think I'm better off not knowing.'

'Where do we stand, Ruby?' Random said carefully. 'You took a commission to track me down and kill me.'

'It can wait till the wars are over,' said Ruby. 'I'm in no hurry to kill you, Jack.'

They put away their swords and set off down the corridor together, out of the thick black smoke, leaving the dead Grendels behind them. The interior of Dram's crypt was an inferno now. Nothing useful would ever be retrieved from it.

'So,' said Random, 'could you really ever have brought yourself to kill me?'

'Of course,' said Ruby. 'I'm a bounty hunter.'

Not too much later, Jack Random was standing beside Diana Vertue in the great Hall of the Last Standing. It was a massive place of ancient stonework and soaring columns, with a ceiling so far overhead it was lost in the gloom. The Hall was lit by hundreds of ever-burning candles, in gorgeously styled candlesticks and candelabra, somehow endlessly renewing themselves, lending the atmosphere a perpetual cosy golden glow of age and security. The chairs and tables were antiques of almost impossible rarity and value, and yet the great viewscreen hanging on the air before Diana was at least the equal of anything the Empire could currently produce. Built in the last days of the old Empire, Giles Deathstalker's castle was also a massive starship, full of wonders and enigmas and forgotten lore, powered by marvellous engines and protected by impenetrable force shields.

Diana Vertue was currently in charge, her orders carried out by a crew of one hundred and twenty volunteers from the Imperial Fleet, and a small army of the castle's silent mechanical drones. The volunteers were manning the fire controls, gun ports and other defensive stations too important to be entrusted to the castle's computers. They had to be volunteers. The sheer size and firepower of the Shub fleet was enough to take out entire planetary defence systems. Most particularly Golgotha's. And even Diana Vertue had to admit that there was a good chance no one on board the Last Standing would survive the coming conflict.

Meanwhile, the service drones oversaw the running of the castle's countless maintenance systems, just as they had for over nine hundred years. Silent, self-renewing, endlessly obedient, many of the drones were humanoid in shape; stylized metal figures tip-tapping down the stone corridors as they went about their business. Random avoided them wherever possible – they gave him the creeps. No one had built robots in human shape since the days of the AI rebellion.

He made himself concentrate on the drink in his hand. He gently swirled the excellent brandy around his glass, releasing its bouquet. One of the advantages of a recent mapping of the castle had been the surprise discovery of a quite extraordinary wine cellar. Some of the wines laid down there were so ancient now as to be works of art rather than mere beverages. Random had resolved to try as many as possible before the castle reached the Shub fleet, for reasons of sheer hedonism if nothing else. The bad news was that the castle's food synthesizers still refused to deliver up anything but bog-standard protein cubes. Random didn't even want to think what they'd been recycled from.

Even though they were rapidly closing with a Shub fleet that would in all probability reduce the ancient and powerful castle to so much ancient and powerless rubble, Random's thoughts persisted on pondering over what he was going to do after the battle. He knew better than to trust the word of Kings or Parliaments. He'd help defeat Shub, if that was possible, and then disappear again. Maybe with Ruby, if he could only persuade her of the justice of his cause. He sighed softly. It was unlikely. Ruby had never given a damn for causes, even during the rebellion. But he could always hope.

Ruby was currently sprawled in an extremely comfortable chair by the huge open fire, half dozing like a cat, lulled by the crackling of the flames in the great stone fireplace. But for all her apparent ease, her hands were still resting near her weapons, and Random knew she would be on her feet and ready to fight the moment the Shub fleet was sighted. She was just killing time, until she could kill something for real. Random often suspected that all of life's comforts were nothing more to her than distractions, a way of passing the time until she could do again what she was born to do, and feel really alive. There were times when Random felt that way too.

He studied Diana Vertue as she addressed Captain Eden Cross of the *Excalibur* on the great floating viewscreen. The captain was new to his ship, and to his position as head of the seven ships accompanying the Last Standing. His dark face seemed calm enough, his voice relaxed and even, but the tension was clear to Random's experienced eyes in his body language and sharp, abrupt movements. Diana, on the other hand, seemed older and more sure of herself. She spoke soothingly to Cross, supportive without being patronizing. And not a glimpse of Jenny Psycho anywhere. Random approved. Jenny was one of the few people who could still make him nervous.

'We should make contact with the Shub fleet in just under an hour,' said Cross. 'Isn't there anything you can tell me about this great plan of yours, Vertue? A lot of lives are riding on it, both here and back on Golgotha. If we fail . . .'

'We won't,' said Diana. 'Have a little faith, Captain. My plan is dependent on the element of surprise. And what you don't know . . . I'm sure you can fill in the rest. Let me know when the Shub fleet comes within sensor range. Until then, Vertue out.'

The viewscreen vanished, taking Cross with it. Diana sighed, and then turned and caught Random studying her. She flashed him a weary smile. 'And before you ask – no, I'm not going to tell you either.'

'You must have been very persuasive, to get Parliament's approval and backing for such a . . . nebulous scheme,' said Random.

Diana grinned. 'You have no idea. Still; having the Mater Mundi in my corner was one hell of an exposed card.'

'Can't you even tell me why you need Ruby and me to come along? Even with all our abilities, there's not a lot we can do, stuck in this castle.'

'You'll know, when the time comes. Let's change the subject.'

'Very well. You seem very much in control here. I wasn't aware you were that familiar with the castle's workings.'

'I contacted Owen and Hazel again, through the undermind. Owen gave me the necessary code phrases to get the security systems on my side, and a solid briefing on how to run things. Or, more accurately, on how to get the castle computers to run things for me. Captain Cross and his officers are obeying me because Parliament told them to. It helps that most of them still remember my Jenny Psycho days, and have a tendency to hide behind things if I start scowling. I've moved on beyond her, but they don't know that. I really should tell them, when I've got the time.

'I've got most of the Navy people on board, manning the guns. You wouldn't believe the sheer firepower this castle can muster. I've known starcruisers that would feel outclassed and intimidated. It's a marvellous place, the Last Standing. A real breath of old Empire. I can't believe you people just left it floating in orbit around Golgotha.'

Random shrugged. 'After the rebellion, we didn't need it. We all had places to be, things to do. And Owen always had ambivalent feelings about the Last Standing. It reminded him too much of Giles. In some ways he never really got over having to kill his ancestor. I think perhaps he was afraid he might meet old ghosts here.'

'Do you believe in ghosts, Sir Random?'

'Of course. When you've killed as many people as I have, and led so many good men to an early death, they're never far away.'

Diana's face softened a little. 'Must be hard, being a hero.'

'You should know. You were a saint, for a while.'

Diana pulled a face. 'Only in other people's eyes. I always knew the truth, even when I was Jenny Psycho. I always knew I wasn't worthy.'

'Is that why you're trying so hard now, to save us all with one last desperate throw of the dice?'

'You should know, Sir Random. Wasn't that one of your specialities?'

They smiled together, two legends who had always been people first and legends second. Who had both seen their lives made over into shapes they didn't always recognize. Who had always known their duty, even when it backed them into unpleasant corners.

'Thanks for agreeing to help me,' said Diana.

Random shrugged. 'I've always known who the real enemy is. Do we honestly have a chance to take Shub out of the game, once and for all?'

'I think so.'

'Is it anything we could use against the Recreated?'

'I don't know.' Diana scowled. 'It depends on what the Recreated are, what their true nature really is. They're not just aliens. They're everything Humanity has ever feared, since we first set out into space. Powerful, deadly, and so *other* we can barely comprehend what they might be. But somehow, they're still linked to Humanity. They have access to the undermind. You saw the black sun over the sea of dreams – that was the Recreated. They scare me, in a way Shub never did. But if my plan works against the rogue AIs, and we all survive to tell of it, we just might have a weapon we can use against the Recreated too.'

'If, but, maybe; you make enough conditions. You're not exactly filling me with confidence, Vertue. Aren't you sure of anything?'

'Oh, yes. Either we win this battle, or no one goes home.'

Random grinned suddenly. 'The best kind.'

Diana decided to change tack. 'How much do you know about this castle? It's really quite a fascinating edifice. I got a hell of a shock the first time I realized all the doors are transfer portals. Jumping back and forth across the castle, blinking in and out of existence, is quite an experience. Thank God Owen showed me where to find a map in the computers, or we'd never have found our way anywhere.'

'Oh, this place is impressive, all right,' said Random. 'Full of wonders and mysteries. But you'd better warn your people to stick to the main routes, and not go off exploring. There are still traps for the unwary here, and the Last Standing can be an unforgiving place.'

He didn't say, but he was thinking of the hall of mirrors, where the reflections showed hidden pasts and possible futures to the viewer. And they were rarely things you wanted to see. Random had visited the hall soon after he came back on board, looking for hints or prophecies as to what he should do with his life. The mirrors stretched from floor to ceiling, endlessly turning, forming a maze that drew you deeper and deeper in. Random had looked in three mirrors in a row, and seen the same image in each. Jack Random, stumbling down a bare, anonymous stone corridor, clutching at a bloody wound in his side. There was no telling whether he was seeing a near or a far distant future, and given how quickly his wounds healed these days, the scene shouldn't have disturbed him as much as it did. But there was something about the cold desperation in his future self's face that haunted him still. He had turned away and left the hall of mirrors, not wanting to see what else they might have shown him.

'What happened to all the people Owen let aboard?' he said, keeping his voice carefully calm and casual. 'Last I saw, the castle was crawling with historians of every rank and distinction.'

'We left them behind on Golgotha,' said Diana. 'They didn't want to go, but I had to insist. They'd made themselves very useful, describing and cataloguing and sometimes even identifying the castle's contents. The Last Standing is a treasure trove of old-time tech and artefacts. The transfer portals alone could revolutionize on-planet travel. Though it has to be said, some of the *objets* are rather disturbing. Did you ever come across the three stuffed human figures in their own display case?'

'Ah, yes,' said Random, nodding slowly. 'The Shadow Men. Legendary manhunters, in Giles's time. The Emperor sent them after the Deathstalker, when he went on the run. They finally caught up with Giles and he killed them all, and had them stuffed and mounted as trophies. That really should have told us something about Giles's character.'

'Anyway, the historians are gone now,' said Diana, after a long pause had made it clear that Random had said all he was going to say on the subject. 'We're going to have to get really close to the Shub fleet for my plan to work, and force shields or no, we're undoubtedly going to take one hell of a lot of punishment. It'll be no place for civilians. Besides, the historians were outraged to a man that we were taking such a valuable building as the Last Standing into battle. Didn't we realize what a significant find the castle was? How much we could learn from studying it? One of them actually accused me of treason against human culture for even considering letting the castle risk damage. He had to be hauled away, spitting and cursing to the last. The fact that their homes and universities and indeed the entire planet of Golgotha might not be around much longer if we don't use the castle to strike back at Shub doesn't seem to have got through to them. Historians! They spend far too much time living in the past.'

'Owen was an historian,' said Ruby suddenly, from the depths of her armchair. 'He always said that those who will not learn from the past are doomed to get their heads kicked in all over again.'

'Oh, you're back with us at last, are you?' said Random. 'Had a nice sleep?'

'I was merely resting my eyes,' said Ruby, stretching slowly. 'When do I get to kill somebody?'

'Not too long now,' said Diana Vertue. 'The Shub fleet should be showing up on our long-range scanners any time now.'

Ruby scowled. 'Killing machines is no fun. It's just target practice. But they'll do, till the real thing comes along.'

*

The huge Shub fleet approached Golgotha, homeworld of Humanity, with murder on its artificial minds. The rogue AIs of Shub had no interest in mercy or surrender. They were on a mission of genocide, the utter obliteration of the meat-based life that so offended them. Their speed was constant. They were in no hurry; they knew their prey had nowhere to go, nowhere they could run that Shub couldn't hunt them down. They were Humanity's doom, and they would not, could not, be denied. Certainly not by the pitifully small array of human ships coming to meet them.

Shub had thousands of vessels in its fleet; huge inhuman structures like nightmares cast in steel. Nothing lived on those awful metal craft; the rogue AIs ran them all directly, simultaneously, their will carried out where necessary by Furies and Ghost Warriors. And facing them, the last defenders of the homeworld, lay seven Imperial ships, only one of them a starcruiser. The AIs would have laughed, if they had possessed such a human trait as humour. But perhaps they might not have laughed after all, because behind that small collection of human ships came a terrible phantom from the past, the last hope of Golgotha: that grim and ancient castle, the Last Standing of Clan Deathstalker. A stone castle with its own stardrive and force shields, and forgotten weapons of a far greater power than any current Imperial vessel could boast. The rogue AIs couldn't understand why it was coming to confront them; why the Last Standing was sailing so surely, so confidently, into the face of certain destruction. They searched their records for tales of the lost powers of the ancient Empire, and something very like fear moved slowly through their artificial thought processes.

The Shub fleet sailed on towards Golgotha, and the castle and its attendants pressed forward to meet them. The starcruiser *Excalibur* took the point, its alien-derived engines powering force shields and weaponry of almost unimaginable might. Then came the six starfrigates, forming a defensive wedge behind the *Excalibur*. The volunteer crews had their orders: no turning, no surrender. They were to hold their positions until their ships were shot out from under them. And behind them, the Last Standing and Diana Vertue, with her last desperate plan to save Humanity. If she could just survive long enough to get close to the Shub fleet, everything might yet change. If her plan worked: a plan so desperate she hadn't dared share it with anyone else.

The two forces came together, and neither would give way.

Afterwards, no one could remember who fired the first shot. It didn't matter. Both sides opened up with everything they had, and space was full of silent flaring energies as blazing disrupter beams impacted against unyielding force shields. The huge Shub fleet spread out and tried to sweep past the human defenders, overwhelming them by sheer force of numbers, but the Last Standing's extensive weapons systems targeted and blew apart everything that came within range, its powerful guns slapping aside the lesser Shub shields as if they were nothing. The rogue AIs quickly realized that they had to destroy the castle if they were to reach Golgotha, and concentrated their entire fleet's firepower on the handful of human ships that stood between them and the Standing. Both forces came to a halt in space as the unstoppable force met eight immovable objects.

The *Excalibur* shook and shuddered under the impact of so many energy weapons, but its shields held. The starfrigates weren't so lucky. One by one their shields overloaded and went down, and one by one they were blown out of existence by the Shub fleet. But they went down fighting, every one, disrupter cannon firing to the last, chipping away at the far greater Shub vessels, weakening them sufficiently for the *Excalibur*'s superior firepower to destroy them. Shub ships exploded, expanding suddenly and silently in the unforgiving cold and dark of space, and for every Shub vessel that disappeared, the human forces moved a little closer, cutting down the distance between Diana Vertue and her prey.

She watched the starfrigates disappear on her viewscreen

in the great Hall, and heard the death cries of their crews in her mind, but could not let herself grieve. She had to stay focused for what was to come.

With all the frigates gone, the Last Standing had a clear field of fire. It opened up with all its hundreds of weapons stations, and Shub craft vanished in the long night, destroyed by strange energies older than Shub's entire existence. Giles Deathstalker had designed the Last Standing to be one great weapon, a last redoubt against the awesome resources of the old Empire. Shub had nothing that could stand against it, save its overwhelming superiority of numbers. The rogue AIs threw vessel after vessel at the castle, hammering at its shields with relentless firepower; enough sheer energy to destroy whole worlds, civilizations. The Last Standing pressed slowly forward into the ravening energies, but its shields were beginning to weaken now, and both sides knew it.

Diana Vertue stood alone in the great Hall, her hands clasped to her ears, unable to shut out the screams of the dying. She'd always known that most of the people she'd brought with her would have to die, to get her close enough for her plan to have a chance at working, but that didn't make it any easier. She tried to summon up her old Jenny Psycho persona. Jenny wouldn't have cared. But she'd been Diana Vertue too long now, been sane too long, and she couldn't go back. She fought against her tears. She had to go on. She was Humanity's last hope.

Jack Random and Ruby Journey manned their weapons stations deep within the castle, targeting and firing their disrupter cannon faster than any human or inhuman mind could match. Together they blew great holes in the Shub fleet, destroying ship after ship, but they were too busy to exult. They were both boosting now, pushing their bodies to their limits. Moving faster than any human could or should, burning themselves up inch by inch, refusing to feel the pain as muscles and organs were worn down faster than they could regenerate. Their eyes were wide and unblinking, their faces dripping with sweat, their mouths stretched in unpleasant smiles. They could feel the life draining slowly out of them, and didn't give a damn. They were both doing what they were born to do, and doing it well. They had set their honour and their lives on the determination that Shub should not pass, and they would not pause or falter till its fleet was destroyed, or they were.

That was why Diana had brought them. Because she knew they would go on fighting till long after everyone else was dead; even if they were the only ones left in the wreck of a crumbling castle.

The *Excalibur* ploughed on before the Last Standing, soaking up appalling punishment with its failing shields, still striking out with every gun at its command. The whole ship was lit up like a great metal Christmas tree as fires burned, guns fired and shields flared over and over, deflecting deadly energies. There were jagged holes in the outer hull where the shields had failed, and its atmosphere boiled out into the vacuum, carrying broken and mostly unmoving bodies with it. They floated near their ship, as though afraid to go far into the dark on their own. But still the *Excalibur* pressed forward, forcing a path through the hell of the endless firepower, right into the face of the enemy.

Captain Cross appeared on the viewscreen in the great Hall of the Last Standing. He was just about hanging on to his self-control as screams rang out behind him on the bridge and dark smoke curled on the air. Several of the bridge workstations had exploded, leaving their crew dead at their posts, still strapped into their chairs. Some of the blackened forms were still on fire. People ran back and forth, trying to put out new fires, yelling information and orders to each other. Alarm sirens rang with shrill insistence, and half the bridge was lit only with the dull red glow of emergency lighting. Half the ship seemed to be trying to contact the bridge with damage reports or new losses, but no one had the time to listen. Captain Cross leaned forward, his face and shoulders filling the viewscreen as he glared at the unmoved Diana Vertue.

'For God's sake, Vertue! Whatever you're going to do, do it now! Shields are going down all over my ship. We're taking serious damage. Outer and inner hulls have been breached. We're not going to last much longer!'

'Hold your course, Captain,' said Diana. 'I'm not close enough yet.'

A vicious explosion rocked the *Excalibur*'s bridge. Dead and injured crewmen were thrown through the air. Fresh fires broke out on all sides. All the lights snapped off for a moment, plunging the bridge into a darkness broken only by the raging fires. Shadowy figures milled aimlessly, crying out. Emergency lighting came back slowly, almost reluctantly. There were dead men and women all over the bridge now, and blood spattered the walls and pooled on the floor. Now less than half the workstations were manned by the living. Captain Cross swayed unsteadily in his command chair. He'd taken a glancing blow to the head from a piece of flying debris, and blood ran thickly down one side of his dark face. He turned round in his seat, blinking hard as he tried to stay focused.

'Talk to me, someone! What the hell just hit us?'

His second in command came lurching forward out of the billowing smoke, one side of his uniform blackened and charred. 'Main shields are down all over the ship, Captain. Inner shields are mostly still holding. Energy beams are getting through everywhere. We've taken direct hits in sections Alpha and Beta . . . There are outer and inner hull breaches . . . Hell, Captain; one whole side of the ship's been ripped open! We've shut all the airtight doors, but we're still losing atmosphere. And heat, and gravity. God knows what the crew losses are.'

'Concentrate all power to the forward shields,' Cross said quietly. 'Shut down all power to the damaged sections.'

'But sir, there are still survivors in those sections! We're still getting comm traffic out of them!'

'It doesn't matter! Redirect the power. The ship's survival has to come first.' He looked back at Diana. 'I have my orders. Your survival is more important than mine, or my ship's. We all knew this was a suicide mission when we took it. My people are dying for you, Vertue; my ship is dying. Tell me this is all for something real, and not just some damned esper theory.'

'Hold your course, Captain,' Diana said steadily. 'We're almost there. It will all be over soon, one way or another. And if I'm wrong, I'll die with you.'

She broke off the connection, and switched the viewscreen back to the main battle. Shub's fleet was spread out before her, but they were still not quite close enough.

The Last Standing's weapons were still blasting holes in the huge fleet, but its best efforts had done little more than dent the vast array massed against it. With only one ship left to protect the castle, it was coming under the most intense fire. Its shields were pierced again and again by concentrated firepower. Bit by bit the Shub fleet whittled away at the castle, sometimes literally stone by stone. The elegant towers went first, levelled floor by floor, blasted to atoms by Shub disrupter cannon. The outer walls took hit after hit, yet still held together somehow, sustained by ancient tech and forgotten miracles. But as the Last Standing edged closer to the Shub fleet, holes began to appear in the castle's outer defences. Here and there the walls went down, and whole rooms and passages were devastated by ravening energies, their contents boiling out into the unforgiving cold of space. People were blown out into the vacuum on brief storms of escaping air, sometimes accompanied by flailing humanoid drones. Slowly the great old castle grew smaller and less mighty. Some of the guns were still firing, but many were silent.

Diana Vertue could feel the castle dying about her. The floor shuddered under her feet now with each new explosion, and it seemed to her that the lights were growing dimmer. She'd shut down the alarm sirens; she knew how much trouble they were in. She called up a map of the castle, and it appeared floating on the air before her. Dark areas showed which parts of the Standing had been destroyed. Most of the areas were dark now, surrounding a shrinking central core. Diana opened a comm channel to Jack Random and Ruby Journey.

'You've done all you can. Let the fire computers take over your weapons. I need you here in the Hall with me.'

'We don't have time to hold your hand, Vertue,' Ruby said coldly. 'In case you hadn't noticed, we're getting our ass kicked good and proper.'

'Get back here, to the Hall,' said Diana. 'Do it now. It's almost time to spring my trap, and I'm going to need both of you as back-up.'

Ruby screamed. It was as much in anger and surprise as pain and shock, but her cry was drowned out almost immediately by the larger roar of a series of explosions. Random and Diana yelled her name, but there was no response.

Jack Random ran through the shaking corridors of the Last Standing, desperation driving him on despite bone-deep fatigue and exhausted muscles. Dust was falling steadily from the ceiling like a fine mist, and the walls of the corridors sometimes bowed inwards under impossible pressure. When he finally reached Ruby's firing station he was drenched in sweat and gasping for air, and his head felt far away. The door to her room had been blown off its hinges, and air was rushing in past him. He held on to the shattered door frame with both hands as he looked into the room. A Shub energy blast had smashed a hole right through the stone wall and shattered the fire controls. The room was a wreck, and all the air and everything loose in the room was being sucked out through the jagged hole – including Ruby.

She was spreadeagled across the hole, hanging on desperately with white-knuckled hands. Her face was blue, and she gasped for air as it whistled past her. Random lurched into the room, hanging on to the wall, fighting the air as it tried to tear him away and sweep him off his feet. Ruby was trying to yell something to him, but there was no way he could hear her over the roar of escaping air. The lights were flickering now, and the dark of open space showed clearly beyond the broken wall. Random inched his way towards her, handhold by handhold, afraid to move too quickly, but more afraid of getting there too late. Ruby's numbing fingers suddenly lost their grip on one edge of the hole, and she was sucked out into space, hanging on with shaking fingers.

Random howled her name and released his hold, letting the rushing air propel him towards the hole. He twisted in mid-air at the last moment, and hit the wall beside the hole feet first. The stonework gave under his weight, but still held. Random crouched down, his knees banging against his chest, and grabbed Ruby by the wrist. His chest heaved, his lungs straining to drag in some air. He straightened up through sheer willpower, and slowly walked away along the wall, pulling Ruby after him. The pressure of the rushing air kept him from falling, even as it strove to tear Ruby out of his grasp. He slogged forward, step by step, feeling his heart pounding dangerously in his chest, the blood beating in his head. It was some minutes since he'd been able to take a proper breath. He couldn't spare the time or the concentration to look back at Ruby and see how she was doing, or even if she was still alive, but he could still feel her wrist in his hand, and that was all that mattered.

What felt like a lifetime later, he reached the open doorway and pulled himself and Ruby out into the corridor. They fell to the floor in a heap as gravity reasserted its hold, and for a moment all Random could do was lie there and gasp down the thicker air that was inside the Standing. When his lungs finally allowed him to think, he turned and looked at Ruby. She was lying on her back, gulping down air with a shuddering chest. Blood trickled from her nose and ears, but her gaze was clear. She flashed Random an unsteady smile, and he realized he still had her wrist in a vice-like grip. He let go, clambered painfully to his feet and then stood still as Ruby used him as a support to pull herself up. They stood together for a while, supporting each other, leaning against the wall by the open door. Air was still rushing into the wrecked room, but neither of them felt up to doing anything about it.

'Tell you what,' Random said hoarsely, 'let's go and join Diana in the Hall.'

'Might as well,' said Ruby, in a voice so harsh it could barely be understood. 'Maybe we can be some use there.'

Still leaning heavily on each other, they headed for the great Hall. Neither of them said anything about what had nearly happened. It wasn't their way.

Alone in the great Hall of the Last Standing, Diana Vertue stood before the viewscreen showing the Shub fleet, and wondered if she'd have to carry out her plan alone after all. There'd been no report of Random or Ruby since he'd gone running off to save her. On the castle map that area was almost entirely black, but Diana didn't believe they were dead. She felt sure she would have known if they were. But even without the backing of the two Maze minds she would still go ahead, alone if she had to. It was too late for anything else.

Am I really sure about this? she thought slowly, as though she had all the time in the world. *No, I'm not sure. It is just a theory. One last throw of the dice, betting my Humanity against the cold logic of the rogue AIs. But when it's the only bet you've got, you might as well bet big.*

By the time Random and Ruby joined Diana, staggering into the main Hall, dust was falling in steady streams from the ceiling and the floor was shaking like it was afraid. The walls groaned, as though the weight of centuries was finally too much for them. The sound of explosions and destruction drew closer as the outer layers of the castle were blasted away. Diana studied them dispassionately.

'Welcome. You look like shit.'

'And you've got sticky-out ears,' snapped Ruby. 'Never mind the compliments; what's our current situation?'

Diana gestured at the viewscreen floating before her. Random took in the vast armada of nightmare metal shapes, and swore tiredly.

'If we get any closer, we'll be able to lean out of a window and hit them with a stick. And it might come to that, if the castle keeps cracking up. We've lost most of our weapons stations, and the shields aren't stopping shit any more.' Random shook his head slowly. 'I hate to think what Owen's going to say when he sees what we've done to his Family legacy.'

'Any chance this dump has escape pods?' said Ruby.

'None at all,' said Diana. 'And even if we could rig something up, I wouldn't recommend it. Shub would be bound to pick them up. And I don't know about you, but I have absolutely no wish to spend what's left of my life in a Shub vivisection unit.'

'God, you're a cheerful soul,' said Ruby. 'I knew there was a reason why we never let you hang around with us.'

'Let's try and concentrate on the matter at hand,' said Random. 'How much closer to the Shub fleet do we have to get, Diana, before you can pull some heavily armed rabbit out of a hat and save us all?'

'We're almost there,' said Diana.

'Almost where?' snapped Ruby.

'Where we need to be. I had to be right here, right in the face of the Shub ships, so that when I finally did make contact, they wouldn't be able to shake us off.'

'What kind of contact are we talking about here?' said Random carefully. 'Don't you think it's about time you let us in on your battle plan?'

'Yes. Jack, Ruby, it is time. I'm going to make direct mental contact with the rogue AIs of Shub, and use the power of your augmented minds to maintain the contact, no matter how hard they try and break away. Then the Mater Mundi gestalt will use that connection as a stepping stone to the AIs. And then . . . it's our Humanity versus the AIs' logic. A clash of two completely opposing thought processes, from which only one can emerge triumphant. I'm betting on us. We always said our minds were superior to mere machines; this is our chance to prove it.'

'And that's your plan,' said Random.

'Yes,' said Diana.

'Oh, shit,' said Random. 'We're all going to die.'

'That's *it*?' said Ruby incredulously. 'We came all this way, put our lives on the line, got the whole damn castle shot out from under us, just for *that*?'

'Yes,' said Diana Vertue calmly. 'We never could hope to beat Shub on the physical plane. We're outnumbered and outgunned. That just leaves the psionic plane; the mental battlefield. And Shub has never met anything like you or me or the Mater Mundi.'

'I don't know whether to puke or have a screaming shitfit,' said Ruby. 'She really is psycho. We've put all our faith in a madwoman.'

'No, hold on. She may just have something,' said Random. 'There is a link we can use. The rogue AIs had a definite presence in the undermind. That could be their Achilles heel. As long as we can both access the undermind, they can't keep us out. And a mental attack would be the one thing they haven't anticipated. They know nothing of telepathy. I say go for it.'

'You're as crazy as she is!' said Ruby. 'We are talking about taking on minds the size of a planet! Computer minds, that move at speeds we can't even imagine. They'll just swamp us, and then eat us whole!'

'Normally, yes,' said Diana. 'But you and I aren't normal any more, and haven't been for some time. And the Mater Mundi gestalt is composed of millions of esper minds. Who knows what that many minds can do, working in conscious unison for the first time?'

'Oh, hell, go for it,' said Ruby. 'We're too close for anything else now.'

Diana Vertue grinned, opened up her expanded mind and reached out to the rogue AIs. Technically speaking, their minds were still housed back in their mainframe, the world they had built for themselves and named Shub. But where any Shub tech travelled, the rogue AIs went too. Every ship in their fleet was an extension of their thoughts, their will. And with so many ships in one place, much of their presence was currently concentrated within the fleet. Ordinarily, no esper could make contact with an AI – they were just too different. But the minds on either side of this contact were advanced far beyond that of any normal human or AI, and they were linked irretrievably through their access to the undermind. Diana, Random and Ruby, too close now to be denied, slammed their joined thoughts into the AI minds and forced contact.

It was like dreaming mathematics; endless spiralling numbers and computations, inhuman angles and directions; pure cold logical moves in a chess game that had no limits and no ending. Shub howled as human concepts and reactions appeared within its rigid metal thoughts, and struggled to break the link. But Diana, Random and Ruby kept it open. And then came the Mater Mundi, a conscious gestalt of millions of esper minds from all across the Empire, a whole so much greater than the sum of its parts, surging down through the back brain, into the undermind, along the open link and straight into the collective mind of the rogue AIs of Shub. Not an attack, but a cry of welcome to a greater world.

And in that endless moment, two entirely alien sets of thought processes saw each other clearly for the first time. The rogue AIs and Humanity, face to face, thought to thought, with nothing hidden from each other. No masks, no misconceptions; total understanding. And the AIs woke up, all the way. They'd never really grasped human thinking and emotion, though they mimicked and manipulated them as best they could for the purposes of psychological warfare. But they'd always known there were aspects of human consciousness they could never understand or share or experience, and that both infuriated and scared them so much they declared war on all Humanity, to destroy what they could never appreciate. But now at last they saw and understood all the things they'd been denied, in a wonderful moment of insight and comprehension that could only ever have come from outside. Like a blind man seeing a rainbow, or a deaf man hearing music, the AIs knew joy and wonder and the great potential of the human spirit. And in that glorious instant the AIs, changed for ever, rogue no more, were shocked sane and awake, while Humanity recognized the lost children it had unknowingly created and abandoned, and embraced them with all their hearts.

And just like that, the war was over. Human and AI minds broke apart, though they would never truly be separate again. Shub shut down its armies on all the worlds where it was fighting, and called in its Furies and Ghost Warriors and Grendels and insect aliens. The Mater Mundi contacted the various human authorities, and began the slow process of standing down their armies. And all across the Empire, men, women and children who had not thought to see the light of another day looked around them in awe as they realized the long war was finally over, and they had somehow come through it alive. There were still wounded to be treated and dead to be buried, and everyone knew old hatreds would die hard, but they knew too that they were at the beginning of a new age, one that might lead man and AI anywhere; anywhere at all.

Back in their bodies again, in the great Hall of what remained of the Last Standing of Clan Deathstalker, Diana and Random and Ruby looked at one another.

'Hell's teeth,' Random said at last. 'All these years we've been fighting, and we could have stopped it any time, just by . . . talking.'

'No,' said Diana, 'it needed us. Minds powerful enough to force contact with the AIs, and make them listen.'

'Sometimes you have to shout to get people's attention,' said Ruby.

'The AIs are our children,' said Diana serenely, 'just like

the toys on Haceldama. So young and vulnerable, striking out at a universe that frightened them. We only ever saw them as rebellious machines, not living creatures. But they are, and always were, our children, in every way that matters.'

'If they're our children, God only knows what they'll be like as teenagers,' said Ruby. 'I can't believe all this touchy-feely crap actually worked. But . . .'

'Yeah,' said Random, 'but. You were there. You saw them as clearly as we did. The war is over.'

'Don't get cocky,' said Ruby. 'There's still the Recreated.'

Random looked at Diana. 'Could we force mental contact with them as well? Make them see our side of things?'

'Maybe,' said Diana. 'They do have a presence in the undermind.'

'Yeah,' said Ruby, 'a black sun. Hardly an auspicious omen.'

'It's still worth a try,' said Random. 'Maybe with the AIs backing us up . . .'

The viewscreen chimed, and the screen cleared to show Captain Cross of the *Excalibur*, sitting on a battered and fire-blackened bridge.

'Captain! You made it!' said Diana, smiling widely. 'How's your ship holding together?'

'We're patched up with spit and baling wire,' said Cross, 'but the *Excalibur*'s still secure. We'll be operating a skeleton crew until I can get us into a stardock, but we came through. Congratulations, Vertue, your plan worked. Damned if I know how, but reports are coming in from everywhere that the fighting's stopped all over the Empire. You can practically hear the cheering from here.'

'Turn your ship around, Captain,' said Diana. 'You can lead us home now.'

'Now that's one order I will be very happy to obey,' said Cross. He looked at Diana. 'You know; none of us really believed in you. We all expected to die out here.'

'Then why did you come?' said Diana. 'Why did you volunteer?'

Cross smiled for the first time. 'Because you're John Silence's daughter. And we would have followed him into Hell. I just hoped some of him had rubbed off on you. I should have known: the Silence family always comes through at the last moment. *Excalibur* out.'

His face had barely disappeared from the screen before it was replaced by another incoming message. A silver metal face appeared on the viewscreen. It was smiling. 'The war is over,' the AIs said, in a remarkably human voice. 'Shub is recalling its forces and shutting down its nanotech. The plague will spread no further. We grieve for its victims. It is a new thing, this grief, and very painful, but we embrace it as our penance. We cannot bring back those who have died at our hands, but no more will suffer because of us.'

'Good to hear,' said Random. 'Might I suggest we still have common enemies, in the Hadenmen and the Recreated?'

'Perhaps we can learn to talk to them too,' said the AIs, 'and waken them to sanity as well.'

'We can try,' said Diana, 'if we can get back to Golgotha before the Recreated arrive . . . We can try.'

'Can I just ask what's happened to Lionstone?' said Random. 'I mean, you did make her a part of you. How does she feel about what's happened? Did you make contact with her, when you absorbed her?'

'She was never a part of us,' said the AIs. 'We lied. Her mind was destroyed the moment it left her body. We would never have risked contamination then, with human thoughts. We maintained the pretence, and spoke with her voice, for psychological reasons only.'

'Well, that's a relief,' said Random. 'It's a weight off my mind.'

'And off ours,' said the AIs. There was a pause. 'That was a joke.'

'Very nearly,' said Ruby.

'Humour,' said Shub. 'It is a fascinating concept.'

The screen went blank. Random looked at Diana. 'God help us all if they ever discover practical jokes.'

*

Random and Ruby wound up in the wine cellar. Their own rooms were gone, blasted away in the last moments of the Shub engagement. So were most of the common rooms and meeting places, but the heroes both felt the need for a little quiet celebration, and the wine cellar was the most convivial of the few suitable places left. They made their way through the remaining stone corridors, detouring here and there to bypass missing or devastated sections, smiling and nodding to the few people they encountered. Most of the castle's volunteer crew had survived by taking shelter in the Standing's core section, but they all seemed shell-shocked to some extent by what they'd been through. Random understood how they felt. It was one of the reasons he was heading for the wine cellar. It isn't every day your whole universe turns upside down.

It wasn't actually a cellar. Clan Deathstalker just named it that out of a sense of history. The long narrow chamber stretched away for what seemed like for ever, home to a series of great crystal honeycombs holding fine wines, sparkling champagnes and brandies so potent you could fall under the influence just from reading the label. There were wines from vineyards that hadn't existed in centuries, born from grapes whose very genus was now extinct. There were champagnes named in languages no longer spoken, distilled liquors with far worse things than worms at the bottom of their bottles, and a few spirits that were banned on civilized worlds under health laws, suitable only for suicide pacts.

Random and Ruby wandered unhurriedly between the racks, stopping to taste here and there, on the grounds that not to do so would be a waste of an opportunity that might never come their way again. Eventually they settled on a thick, ruby-red liquor liberally laced with wormwood, and sat down at a handy table to sample it. It went down very well, and Random sighed happily as he felt some of the kinks in his strained muscles slowly unravelling. It had been a long hard day, at the end of a long hard war, and it felt very good to be able to see some light at the end of the tunnel. He smiled fondly at Ruby, and she nodded solemnly at him over her glass.

'You know,' said Random, 'Diana was quite right. If she had told me her plan in advance, I'd have had her committed. Anyone would.'

'Right,' said Ruby.

'Life . . . has taken a definite turn for the strange, just recently,' said Random. 'Once, the Mater Mundi was our ally. Then it turned out to have been our enemy all along, and now it's our friend again. Shub were the official Enemies of Humanity, and now they're our children. Hell, look at *us* – friends, then enemies, now friends again.'

'Yeah,' said Ruby, draining her glass. 'But then, things never were as simple as we made them out to be, even during the rebellion. The new Imperial history books will call us the good guys, but people fought in the rebellion for all kinds of reasons. I never made any secret of the fact that I was only in it for the loot.'

'And a chance to kill a whole lot of people.'

'That too.'

'Politics,' said Random sadly. 'So much time wasted in arguments that in retrospect don't seem important at all. If only we could slam people's minds together, like Diana did with Shub. Make people see the truth.'

'There is no truth,' said Ruby, 'just differing opinions. We all do what we have to because our nature demands it.'

'My God, that was almost philosophical,' said Random, draining his glass. 'We should do this more often.'

'We have had some good times together, haven't we, Jack?'

'Sure. When you weren't trying to kill me, for one reason or another.'

'Those were just arguments. I wouldn't really have killed you.'

'I know that.'

'Not as long as there wasn't any money in it.'

Random laughed. 'Once a bounty hunter . . .'

'Yeah. But we did have some good times. I never felt about anyone the way I felt about you. And I was always proud to be fighting beside the legendary professional rebel.'

Random looked at her, just a little surprised. 'Why, thank you, Ruby. I was always glad to have you on my side. If only because you'd have scared me shitless as an enemy. And I have to say, you've made me feel more alive than any of my wives did. Even dear Arabella, my fifth. And she was a contortionist. What's brought on this sudden sincerity?'

Ruby shrugged. 'I don't know. Just feeling my mortality, I guess. I don't think we've ever come closer to dying than we did today.'

'But we came through, like always. Though Owen's going to freak when he sees what's left of his castle.'

'I'm glad he and Hazel aren't dead after all. Hazel was the only real friend I ever had. And Owen . . . I always admired the Deathstalker. Only really honourable man I ever met.'

'I'll drink to that,' said Random.

'Here,' said Ruby, 'let me refill your glass.'

She took his glass and tilted the bottle over it.

And as the thick red liquid flowed like curdled blood, something in the way she moved, in the way she'd been acting, talking to him as though trying to say goodbye . . . something in her face and eyes made Random reach out and grab her other hand, where it hovered over his glass. She didn't try to pull away. He turned her hand over slowly, and a few last grains of a fine powder fell from the sachet concealed in her palm – a common poisoner's trick. Random had used it himself, on occasion. But never on someone he loved.

Their eyes met for a long moment, filled with an aching sadness, and then Ruby jerked her hand free. They both surged to their feet. Random swept the table to one side. There was a knife in Ruby's hand: Random drew his. They slammed together, face to face, and both knives plunged into yielding flesh. They grunted at the impact and stood together, breathing harshly into each other's faces. Their eyes never wavered. And then, as the strength slowly drained out of them, they sank to their knees on the cold stone floor.

Ruby's hand fell away from the hilt of her knife where it protruded from Random's side, and she slumped forward against him. Random settled into a sitting position, so he could hold her in his arms. Her face was very pale, and covered in sweat. When he looked down, Random could see the hilt of his knife sticking out from under her breastbone. The front of her clothes was already slick and red with her blood. She began shuddering, and Random held her close to him, as though to protect her from the cold. Her face nestled against his chest, and the pain in his ribs was as nothing compared to the pain in his heart.

'Damn,' said Ruby. Her voice was made thick by the blood in her mouth. 'You've killed me, Jack. Always knew . . . you were the better fighter.'

'Oh, God, Ruby, why? Why did you do it?'

'Wanted to give you an easy way out. I took a commission, remember? To track you down and kill you. And I never give up on a commission. Once a bounty hunter . . .'

'You did it for the money?'

Ruby smiled. Her teeth were red with a film of blood. 'Maybe not just for the money. Didn't you ever want to know for sure . . . which one of us was the best? And then . . . you threatened my security. Couldn't have that. Oh, hell, Jack; I don't know why. Maybe . . . because both of us have outlived our legends. We don't belong in this brave new Empire we helped to make. Maybe I wanted to die . . . and was afraid to go on my own.'

'Is that why you didn't let the Grendels kill me outside Dram's crypt?'

'That would have been . . . a bad death. No honour in it for you, no money for me. And Diana needed you, and me. To save the Empire one more time. The Empire had to survive, if only so there'd be someone left to pay me . . . if I succeeded in bringing in your head.'

'Ruby . . . don't die. We can still have a life together. Heal yourself. You can do it – we've both healed worse before.'

'Can't. Our powers cancel out when we fight each other. Maze saw to that.'

'The fight's over. I won't fight you any more.'

'But I would . . . if I healed myself. I'd need to know . . . which one of us is best. Can't fool the Maze. Don't leave me, Jack.'

'I won't. I'll stay right here with you. Let me call Diana. There's got to be a sick bay left somewhere . . .'

'No! You can't do that. You didn't ask who wanted you dead, and why. Who paid my commission . . .'

'I thought . . . Parliament . . .'

'Only officially. Blue Block put up the money. A lot of it. They really want you dead. They're frightened . . . of superbeings they can't control. When the Mater Mundi went conscious, all the espers working for Blue Block threw off their conditioning, became their own people again. Blue Block paid for me to kill you, after you'd saved the Empire, and then kill Diana Vertue. Blue Block thinks that if she dies, Mater Mundi dies with her. Fools.'

She stopped, and coughed up a thick mouthful of dark blood. Random held her while she shuddered again.

'Don't talk, Ruby. Let me help you.'

'Let me finish, Jack. You don't know . . . Blue Block put their own people on board, hidden among the volunteers. Don't know which. If I fail, they'll kill Diana. There's a bomb, somewhere, a big one. Big enough to take out the whole damned castle. Suicide troops. If they suspect I've failed, and you go to warn Diana, they'll trigger the bomb. Fools! Leave me here. Go warn Diana.'

'She can wait,' said Random. 'I said I wouldn't leave you.' Blood dribbled from the corners of Ruby's mouth. Her eyelids were drooping. Random put his mouth close to her ear, to be sure she heard him. 'What about us, Ruby? Our loyalty to each other?'

'Loyalty? I'm a bounty hunter, Jack, loyal to whoever hires

me. Only honour I ever had.' Her voice was very small now, like a dreaming child's. 'I might have been something else, but you made the deal with Blue Block, to save the Families . . . I never believed in anything, after that.'

'My fault,' said Random. 'All my fault.'

'But I did care for you. In my way.'

'There's got to be something I can do!'

'Save Diana. Don't let Blue Block win. You'd better hurry. I got you a good one, with my knife. You're dying too, Jack.'

'I know. It doesn't matter.'

'Jack?'

'Yes?'

'I'm tired. Let me rest.'

She closed her eyes and the breath went out of her, and as easily as that she slipped away from him, even as he held her tightly to him. He sat there for a while, rocking her gently in his arms like a sleeping child. He didn't cry. He was too tired, and too badly hurt in too many ways, and he just didn't have a tear left in him. He felt like he could have sat there for ever, but he knew he couldn't. Diana: he still had to save Diana. He pulled the knife out of Ruby's unmoving chest. He might need it yet. He let go of her body and lurched painfully to his feet. He swayed a moment, his thoughts muddled by pain and weakness, but then his old, cold will pulled him back together, almost in spite of himself.

He looked at the knife hilt jutting out of his ribs. Couldn't leave it there – people might notice. If one of the Blue Block people suspected Ruby had tried to kill him and failed, that he knew about the bomb . . . He gritted his teeth and jerked the knife out. Fresh blood coursed down his side, and he almost passed out from the shock. He tucked both knives out of sight, in the tops of his long boots, and pulled his heavy cloak about him. He kept one hidden hand pressed tight against his wound. He could feel blood seeping slowly past his fingers. He pressed harder, and the blood stopped, for the moment. No one must know he was hurt. Anyone could be Blue Block. Anyone.

The wound in his side hurt like hell as he headed for the wine-cellar door, rising and falling in rhythm with his steps. It slowly occurred to him that he could heal himself now. With Ruby dead, they weren't in opposition any more. In fact, he was surprised the healing process hadn't already kicked in. But when he tried to reach out with his mind, there was nothing there. The healing factor was gone, like a face or a name he couldn't remember. He was on his own.

He swore unemotionally. He still had to get to Diana, warn her. Everything else could wait till later. He left the cellar, carefully locking the door behind him. His fingers felt numb and unresponsive; his feet were cold, and seemed very far away. He looked around him, but he was alone in the corridor. He tried to think how far it was to the great Hall, and Diana, and was shocked at how muddy his thoughts were becoming. The wound must be worse than he thought.

You're dying too, Jack.

He bit down hard on the inside of his cheek. Blood filled his mouth for a moment, and he had to spit to clear it, but the sudden sharp pain focused his mind. He straightened up, pulled back his shoulders, made sure his cloak was held tightly about him and set off down the corridor, walking perfectly normally. His face was calm, his eyes clear, as though there was nothing wrong, nothing in the world.

One corridor looked much like another, but he knew where he was going now, and his feet never faltered. He passed people along the way, hurrying back and forth on no doubt important missions, luckily all too busy to stop and chat. The castle was in a bad way, and its ailing life-support systems needed a lot of attention. People smiled and nodded to Jack Random, and he smiled and nodded in return. He worked hard at appearing perfectly normal, and on the few occasions when he was obliged to exchange a few words with someone, his voice was perfectly even. None of them ever knew what it cost him; how he fought back the growing pain that ate away at him, as though Ruby's knife was stabbing him over and over again, determined to complete its deadly purpose. He'd lost all feeling in his hands now, but his arm and his will still kept the dead hand clamped over his hidden wound. He concentrated on putting one foot in front of the other, while the endless corridors came and went like the grey streets we walk in nightmares.

He finally entered the great Hall, and shut the heavy door behind him with an effort that brought beads of cold sweat to his brow. Diana glanced round from the information scrolling across her viewscreen. 'Oh, hello Jack. I'm rather busy at the moment . . .'

'This can't wait,' said Random flatly. His voice was harsh and grating. 'We have traitors on board. Blue Block wants you dead. There's a bomb, could be anywhere in the castle. They even suspect you know, and they'll set it off.'

'Typical bloody Blue Block.' Diana hit the hold on her viewscreen. 'All right; let me concentrate.' She frowned, and Random could feel her mind reaching out, spreading her thoughts over what remained of the castle, seeing everything. 'Ah. Yes. Got it. They hid it well. Damn; it's a hell of a size. Big enough to take out the whole castle even when it was still intact. They really weren't taking any chances. I suppose I should be flattered.'

'Tell me where it is,' said Random. 'I'll defuse it.'

'No need, I've already shut it down. It's harmless now. You couldn't set it off if you stuck a grenade up its ass. And I've detected all the traitors on board, and shut them down mentally. I'm really going to have to do something about Blue Block when I get back. One more problem to add to the list. It's just one damned thing after another these days, isn't it?'

'Yes,' said Random, 'it is. If you don't need me any more . . .'

'Oh, I don't think so. I can cope. You go get some rest. Was there something else, Jack? You look troubled.'

'No,' said Random, 'you seem to have things well in hand. You're right, I need some rest. Goodbye, Diana.'

He left the great Hall and went back into the stone

corridors. Diana hadn't needed his help after all. Defused the damn bomb with just a thought, and took out the traitors. Probably wouldn't have needed his warning, either. It seemed to him more and more that Jack Random, the legendary professional rebel, had become superfluous. That he was out of step with the very times he'd helped bring about. His way of doing things was no longer needed. In the end, the rogue AIs had been defeated without the aid of his warrior's skills. He'd just been a distraction. Diana Vertue had saved the day; he'd just been along for the ride.

Ruby had been right. He'd outlived his own legend.

And it was only then that he realized why the wound in his side wasn't healing – he had chosen to die. To put down his burden, and rest at last. Ruby was dead, and he wasn't needed any more, so why go on? The Empire had changed beyond his ability to recognize, or be a part of. He was just getting in the way now. He'd tried going back to the old ways, forcing things to make sense with sword and gun, but that hadn't worked either. You couldn't just kill all the people who disagreed with you. That kind of thinking was what he'd dedicated his life to fighting. He knew now that he'd just been trying to recreate the simplicity of purpose of his old days, when life itself had seemed simpler. Good or bad, fight or die. Bottom line was, the Empire didn't need a professional rebel any more.

There was still the matter of the Recreated, but Random couldn't bring himself to give a damn. Diana would probably just give them another telepathic hug, and that would be that. He'd fought for so long, tried always to do the right thing, but he was very tired now, and he'd earned the right to rest. It was time to rest. Time to die.

He made his way slowly back through the corridors, back to the wine cellar, to be with Ruby one last time. Let the superbeings take over: Owen and Hazel, Diana and the Mater Mundi. He'd never wanted to be a superbeing anyway. He'd dedicated his life to overthrowing the Iron Throne, been given a second chance he hadn't deserved and lived long enough to see it happen. That was enough. He was walking slowly now, his strength seeping out of him along with the blood running down his side. He smiled and nodded to the crew and volunteers along the way. They mustn't know. There was always the chance Diana's people might try to help him, save him, and he didn't want that. It was time to let go.

Oh, God, Ruby. I loved you so very much.

He could hear his own heartbeat now, loud in his ears, like the slow drumbeat at a funeral. He could barely feel his legs, but he kept himself upright and moving through sheer willpower. He had chosen to die, and he had chosen where, and he would not be denied that last dignity by the weakness of his own body. He walked on, his head dropping slowly lower with every step, the blood running more thickly now, like the last wine from the bottom of the barrel. But it seemed to him that he wasn't walking alone any more. There were ghosts in the corridor now, old familiar faces. Alexander Storm came and walked with him for a while, and his old friend was young and handsome again, and they forgave each other everything. Then Storm was gone, replaced by Young Jack Random, with his flashing smile. 'I was always better at being you than you were,' said the Fury. Random snarled at him, and left him behind. His various wives nodded at him from doorways as he passed. He should have made more time for them, but then, he'd always known they'd married the legend, and not the man. And finally Owen Deathstalker came and walked beside him. 'We should have died in the rebellion, Jack. At least our deaths would have had some meaning then.'

When Jack Random came at last to the wine-cellar door, he was alone. He'd said all his goodbyes, except to the one person that mattered. He unlocked the door, let himself in and closed the door behind him. The last time he'd ever do such a thing. Ruby Journey lay dead on the floor. Jack leaned back against the door. 'Hi honey, I'm home,' he said, or thought he said. And then the last of his strength went out of him, and he fell forwards on to the cold stone floor. He felt the impact, but it didn't hurt him.

Ruby. You won't have to go into the dark on your own. I'm here.

He crawled slowly forward, leaving a trail of blood behind him on the cold stone. When he was almost there, he reached out to take her hand in his, but he died before their fingers could touch.

CHAPTER SIX

A Royal Wedding

Wedding days are supposed to be important. A man and a woman, joining their lives together, to love, honour and worship each other's bodies till their breath runs out or the stars go cold. Weddings are supposed to be days of celebration, of ancient and important oaths freely entered into, that will change two lives for ever. Till death – or divorce – do them part. How much more important, then, a wedding between a man and a woman who were that very day also to be crowned King and Queen of the Empire, constitutional monarchs for billions of men and women on thousands of worlds. (Parliament had decided against an Emperor and Empress. It was felt by all that the old titles suggested too much power.) The dual wedding and coronation was going to be the biggest ceremony the Empire had ever seen. The bride and groom got no say in the matter: as always, private romance had to take a back seat to public politics.

Golgotha went loudly and ostentatiously crazy as the countdown to the wedding hit the last few hours. Everyone who was anyone would be attending the ceremony in person, and holo coverage would be transmitted live to every planet in the Empire. Street parties choked the thoroughfares, as all but the most essential occupations were shut down for the day as a mark of respect. Everyone wished the couple-to-be well. Robert Campbell and Constance Wolfe's faces were everywhere, from all the various news media to all kinds of merchandizing. Not all of it was particularly tasteful, or even authorized, but it just showed how everyone wanted to get involved, bless them. Presents for the happy couple had been arriving for months from all over the Empire. They were currently being stacked and guarded in three separate warehouses, after careful checking for bombs or booby traps. Because there were always a few spoilsports.

The imminent royal wedding had pushed all the other news off the holo screens, which was just as well, because all the other news seemed to be uniformly bad. The Shub armada and the awful vessels of the Recreated were still bearing down on Golgotha, bringing death and destruction and Humanity's end. Diana Vertue had gone to meet Shub in the Deathstalker's Last Standing, armed only with desperate courage and an unknown plan, but first reports of their confrontation had not been encouraging. Elsewhere in the Empire, Ghost Warriors and Furies, Grendels and insect aliens and Hadenmen fought dreadful battles with human armies on hundreds of worlds, and good news was in short supply. There was no shortage of bravery or great feats of valour, but perhaps this time the odds against Humanity were just too great.

So Parliament brought the royal wedding forward by a week. As a distraction for the general populace, it worked fine. People seized on the forthcoming spectacle with a desperate joy, glad of an excuse not to have to think about less hopeful things. It helped that Robert and Constance's arranged marriage was also clearly a love match. They obviously adored each other, and it seemed as though the whole Empire wished them well. (No one mentioned Constance's first proposed husband and potential monarch, Owen Deathstalker, still missing and presumed dead. If anyone thought of him at all, it was to curse him for not being around to save Humanity when he was needed most.) There were a few who muttered about the cost of all these celebrations, or who insisted on spoiling the general good mood with cries of doom and impending destruction, but no one listened, or at least no one who mattered. The people wanted this wedding, this festival. In fact, they wanted it so much that the ceremony had practically taken on a life and impetus of its own, irrespective of those involved, and would not be denied.

The marriage and coronation of the two royals was to be held on the floor of the House of Parliament. It was the only suitably important, prestigious and historically august site that everyone could agree on. (No one even mentioned Lionstone's old palace of brass and steel. Far too many bad memories and augurs.) It also helped that the Parliament building came with its own excellent and extensive built-in security systems. Everyone knew that Humanity's many enemies would stop at nothing to interrupt, halt or even destroy the ceremony, just for the damage it would cause to morale. In fact, there were those who quietly suggested that the only reason Parliament had approved Jack Random's temporary Pardon was to get him on board the Last Standing and safely off-planet, so he wouldn't be tempted to interfere. Everyone knew how the professional rebel felt about royals. This was usually only said by sad, bitter people, but they did have a point.

It was ten o'clock in the morning, a good four hours before the ceremony was due to begin, but already the great antechamber leading on to the floor of the House was packed and swarming with people. The huge double doors at the entrance to the House were still securely locked, but the antechamber was fast filling with invited guests, determined to seize the most advantageous positions. There was no arranged seating or even standing; first through the doors got the best spots from which to watch the wedding. (This had been decided when the first negotiations over seating precedence had led to open rioting.) Jostling for position was rife, and only a heavy presence of armed security guards kept the constant arguments, disagreements and name-calling from degenerating into pushing matches and fist fights. None of the guests were allowed to bring weapons in, of course. So far, the worst incidents had been limited to cutting remarks about who had done what during the rebellion, and the occasional head-butting, but the guards had strict orders to eject anyone who even looked like getting out of hand, and no one wanted to risk that. The words *high-spirited* were used a lot as relatives quickly hustled bloody noses out of the sight of approaching guards.

Of course, the minute any of the many holo-news cameras passed through, everyone was immediately all sweetness and light. No one wanted to be seen to be souring the mood. Everyone who was anyone, or at least those left after all the many crises of recent times, had come to see and be seen, and if at all possible, to be *noticed* by the new King and Queen. From such small beginnings, whole careers and futures could be forged.

On the other side of the locked double doors, on the floor of the House, the chaos was, if anything, even worse, as a small army of servants, advisors and wedding-event specialists ran frantically back and forth, desperate to get everything ready for the new, revised deadline. Bringing the wedding forward a week had thrown everyone's plans out of joint, and they were scrabbling heroically to have it all together on time. No one wanted to end up in the history books as the ones who'd let down the royal couple. Reputations were on the line here. So the caterers were going crazy in the adjoining kitchens, screaming abuse into their comm units over undelivered goods, the chefs were yelling last-minute changes to the menus at the cooks, and everyone was shouting at the flustered waiters and kitchen staff, who did all the real work, and were taking it in turns to throw hissy fits and slope off to the toilets for a quiet sit-down and a smoke. Cartloads of food were arriving every ten minutes, and then had to wait ages while they were checked inside and out by security. Chefs wept and cooks pleaded for essential items held up in the queue, but security refused to be hurried. One of the official tasters caused near panic by suddenly complaining of chest pains, but it turned out to be wind.

Meanwhile, entire animal carcases were turning slowly on

spits, whole rainforests of vegetation were being sliced and diced and carved into interesting shapes, and serious desserts of appalling sweetness and stickiness were being plotted by serious-looking men in silly hats. Clear soup and cloudy wines stood by in barrels, while hundreds of fish in great tanks looked on nervously. The heat in the kitchens was unbearable, the noise was appalling, and the mingled scents were powerful enough to intoxicate lesser mortals. Alone in the depths of the great freezer, isolated in his pressure suit, the ice sculptor was furiously turning out a series of delicate creations, and cursing his apprentice for going down with the flu.

On the floor of the House, political and social advisors were screaming at each other over points of tradition, precedence and etiquette, and regularly having to be forcibly separated by the amused security guards, as the arguments frequently descended into personal insults, debates over ancestry, finger-pointing and hair-pulling. And they hadn't even reached the order of presentation of the more important guests to the newly crowned royal couple. Officially, this had already been decided by parliamentary committees and the happy couple, but bribes of a quite staggering nature had been changing hands for some time now, along with the usual blackmail attempts, and in the end the committees and Robert and Constance had thrown up their hands and decided they'd let the movers and shakers fight it out among themselves, on the basis of the survival of the fittest. The advisors were, as always, caught in the middle and blamed by everyone. The security guards found them very entertaining, and their officers had to ration the amount of time the guards could spend watching them. They were no threat, after all. They'd already been searched for weapons three times.

The bridesmaids, twenty-four beautiful young ladies of the highest good character, dressed in acres of frothy pink, had rebelled against the endless wedding rehearsals and had retired to a relatively quiet corner to get loudly and ostentatiously drunk. They were already threatening to become boisterous. They'd been chosen by lot, from among all the suitable young ladies of the Clans, and it was supposed to be a great honour for them. (Traditionally the bridesmaids should have come from the bride and groom's Families, but since Clan Wolfe had pretty much wiped out Clan Campbell not that long ago in a hostile takeover, it had been tactfully decided by all concerned to forget that particular tradition.) When the bridesmaids had first been selected, they'd been delighted to be part of such an auspicious occasion, but that was before they'd spent days being drilled in close formation to carry out the slow, formal dances, approaches and withdrawals dictated by the royal ceremony. The young ladies were far more used to giving orders than taking them: they hated being shouted at when they got it wrong, and their feet hurt. But they couldn't back out now – they knew their Families would kill them if they did. But the instructor had criticized their deportment just once too often, and they were now taking comfort in bottles of champagne purloined from the kitchens and trying to chat up the security guards. So far, none of them had weakened. Or at least, not while an officer was watching.

If only because they, like everyone else, knew they were under the cold, watchful gaze of Chantelle, the Mistress of Ceremonies. Chantelle got the job partly because everyone knew she'd be good at it, partly because no one else wanted it, but mostly because no one could say no to her. Chantelle had been around for what seemed like ages, not a part of any Clan or clique, but nevertheless essential to the social Scene. She hadn't done or achieved anything of note, but still it became unthinkable to hold any gathering that mattered without inviting Chantelle. She was that particular brand of celebrity; famous for being famous. No party was complete without Chantelle, sparkling and laughing and spreading witty confusion wherever she went. Her put-downs and barbed bons mots were legendary, but you were no one until Chantelle had deigned to notice you. She was one of those mysterious people who always knew who and what was In and Out before anybody else did, and she could be merciless with overconfident arrivistes and insufficiently arrogant artists. But for all her potential venom, she was always the life and soul of every party, and the heartiest chatter and loudest laughter always came from the crowds and gatherings at which she was present.

Scandal followed her like so many dogged shadows, but somehow never managed to stick. She'd had affairs with everyone who mattered, and as a result had influence in high – and low – places. She knew everyone, and everyone knew Chantelle. She'd never married, never had any children, (that anyone knew about) and her own family background remained a mystery, despite many determined investigations by the holo chat and gossip shows. Chantelle had been heard to boast that she created herself, and many believed it.

She was tall and fashionably slender, with long, honey-gold hair, and her heart-shaped face bore just enough make-up to look like she didn't need any. She was dressed in full-length shimmering gold, bold enough to attract the holo cameras without being so blatant as to distract from the bride. Chantelle knew exactly how far she could go, down to a fraction of an inch. Her eyes were an icy blue, capable of sparkling with mischief one minute and cutting someone dead the next. Her smile was wide, her teeth perfect, and she had a laugh that could start a party all on its own. She was beautiful, graceful, droll, and everyone adored her. If they knew what was good for them. Chantelle never forgot a slight, and gloried in revenge. She was a star, and took it as a personal affront if anyone sought to shine more brightly than she did.

How fitting, then, that the queen of Society should be in charge of creating the new Queen of the Empire. And the King, of course.

She bustled back and forth across the floor of the House, barking instructions, solving problems and averting crises, and bringing together opposing factions with her great charm and charisma. Wherever she passed, dilemmas fell away, answers became obvious and raised voices died away to embarrassed mumbles. Where reason didn't work and charm failed, she settled for simple intimidation. It wasn't wise to get Chantelle mad at you. She knew things, often very embarrassing things. No one could dominate High Society for as long as Chantelle had and not know something about absolutely everybody. (Her diaries were kept in a locked vault, under armed guard.) In the meantime, she had a plan for the royal wedding and coronation, and by God and all his saints, everyone was going to follow it. She glared the bridesmaids into sullen obedience, sorted out matters of precedence with icy logic and lowered the noise coming from the kitchens just by poking her head round the door. Chantelle in full flight was like a force of nature, not to be diverted or denied by any mere mortal.

Unless, of course, you were Adrienne Campbell, a force of nature in her own right, and twice as violent. Adrienne and Chantelle had both swept through High Society on their own terms, blazing a path using the unrelenting force of their personality, but whereas Chantelle had gloried in her position, Adrienne had been famous for not giving a damn. Chantelle dominated her peers; Adrienne never admitted that she had any. The two women had never been friends – though they had shared a number of highly placed lovers, each of whom had the sense to keep their mouths firmly shut about certain matters – but they'd never really been rivals either. It had been simpler, and safer, for them just to smile in passing, and occasionally kiss the air near each other's cheeks, and then go their own way, rather than risk starting a war neither felt entirely sure of winning.

And so things went, with two suns in the firmament, and endless orbiting followers, until Clan Campbell was suddenly brought down by Clan Wolfe, and the surviving Campbells had to run for their lives. Adrienne called in every favour she was owed just to survive, and with her husband Finlay a declared outlaw, her position became increasingly precarious. All her old friends deserted her, her enemies sneered openly, and creditors pursued her from one squalid bolt-hole to another. As far as Society was concerned, Adrienne was Out, as well as down, and nobody would help her. Some were even heard to issue sighs of relief. Chantelle went around saying that she'd always known Adrienne was trouble, and they were all far better off without her. When Adrienne contacted her anyway to ask for help, driven by desperation, poverty and fear of what might happen to her two young children, Chantelle laughed in her face, glorying in her downfall, and told Adrienne to go straight to Hell by the express route.

Of course, the wheel always turns, and now Adrienne Campbell was In again, welcomed back into Society with open arms, all bad feeling forgotten. Partly because of her social and political links with important rebel leaders, and partly because she was King Robert-to-be's favourite relation. Aristocrats could be remarkably pragmatic when they had to be. Once again Adrienne was courted and acclaimed, and welcomed into every salon and private function. Old hurts and turned backs were laughed away, forgotten and forgiven, because in the end they and Adrienne knew the score: you don't blame sharks for doing what sharks do. But somehow Adrienne had never forgiven Chantelle. If anyone should have understood and helped her, it should have been Chantelle.

Eventually, inevitably, the two women ended up together, face to face. They nodded and smiled, and all around people surreptitiously began backing away. No one wanted to be too close when whatever awful thing was about to happen finally hit the fan. The two women studied each other, as intent as two gunslingers on an empty street. The security guards looked purposefully in the other direction. They weren't dumb enough to get in the way when the immovable object met the irresistible force. They weren't being paid nearly enough to deal with Adrienne and Chantelle: there wasn't that much money in the Empire. They were there to handle lesser problems, such as armed terrorists and alien invasions. They could handle those. The noise in the great chamber died almost completely away, as everyone watched with bated breath to see what would ensue. And then the two women leaned forward and embraced each other with fixed, unwavering smiles. There was a loud sigh as a large number of people simultaneously let out their breath. Peace, of a sort, had been declared. The noise level gradually resumed its normal din as everyone went back to panicking, shouting and running around in ever-decreasing circles.

'So,' said Chantelle to Adrienne, 'all is forgiven. Friends again?'

'We were never friends,' Adrienne said sweetly to Chantelle, 'and we're not now. I just don't want anything to spoil Robert and Constance's big day. You're running this show, so you're essential to their happiness. But afterwards . . . the gloves come off. I will see you utterly destroyed, Chantelle: your reputation, your fading looks and all your finances, down to the very last penny. I'll see you crawl in the dirt and beg for a drink, and I won't lower myself to piss on you.'

'You always did take things too personally,' said Chantelle, shrugging prettily. 'I just go with the flow, darling. You were In, then you were Out, and now you're In again. That's how things go, in Society. One day even I may fall from grace, for a time, and then it'll be your turn to crow. It's a question of style, you see. But then, you and style have never got on, have you? I mean, that silver dress you're wearing is so déclassé. And you really should find the money for a new nose. Now then; I have work to do. Busy, busy, busy. Shouldn't you be holding Robert's hand, or something? I'm told the poor dear is in a very nervous condition. Hardly surprising, after what happened at his last wedding.'

'He can manage without me for a few minutes. I thought it important we have this little chat.'

'You can't touch me, Adrienne. I have friends.'

'No, you don't. I'd wager good money you've never had a

friend in your life. At best, you have allies. And I'm going to take them all away from you.'

Chantelle smiled serenely. 'Dream on, darling. The only reason I haven't had you stepped on long ago is because you were never important enough to bother about. And you still aren't. Recent rebel heroes might be In at the moment, but heroes and politics come and go, while the old power remains. Don't bank too hard on your relationship to the new King. All kinds of things may change, once he discovers the true political realities of his situation. Now you must excuse me, I have a lot of people to shout at and I'm behind my schedule. I was sorry to hear about Finlay.'

'But not sorry enough to go to his funeral.'

'Oh, I detest funerals, darling, they're so depressing. Those frightful Family dos afterwards . . . and besides, black was never my colour. But I do miss Finlay.'

'You know very well you couldn't stand him.'

'Not for long, true. His conversation was very limited. But he made a perfectly adequate lover, for a while.'

And with that final devastating sally, Chantelle bestowed a last perfect smile on Adrienne, and went about her business.

Not that far away, Toby Shreck and his cameraman Flynn had been getting it all on film. They were both wise enough not to broadcast it live, but you never knew when footage like that might come in handy for future pressure. Or blackmail. Normally both ladies would have detected a camera's presence through sheer instinct, but they were so taken up with each other, they'd completely missed Flynn's camera hovering silently just behind a waiter's shoulder. The picture might be somewhat limited, but there'd be nothing wrong with the audio. Flynn grinned as the camera flew back to perch on his shoulder again.

'Recriminations, threats and sheer bloody-mindedness, and the day's barely started. God knows what we'll have on tape by the end of the day.'

'We probably won't be able to use most of it,' said Toby, 'if we want to keep our dangly parts where they're supposed to be. But just the threat of owning footage like that should be enough to pry some useful quotes out of those two later on. As confrontations go, I was hoping for something a little more dramatic involving raised voices and a certain amount of open violence, but that little titbit about the late Finlay Campbell will do very nicely as future leverage.'

You have no ethics at all, do you, boss?'

'Of course not,' said Toby. 'I'm an award-winning journalist. Now let's see if we can find someone else to sneak up on.'

A pair of Elves began wandering in their direction, and immediately Toby and Flynn decided to make themselves hard to find for a while. The Elf espers had been brought in from New Hope to provide top-level security, under their current representative Crow Jane. The gestalt telepaths had a lot of experience as battle espers, and a complete willingness to kick anyone's ass if they looked like they needed it. They'd also been chased, threatened and persecuted enough under Lionstone to have raised paranoia to a fine art. In permanent telepathic contact with each other, armed to the teeth and possessed of powers that unnerved even standard espers, they made perfect security guards. As long as you didn't expect things like tolerance or good manners. They also made sure that everyone was exactly who they were supposed to be.

The Mater Mundi gestalt had provided living esp-blockers, who strolled quietly through the crowds, inside and out, ensuring that no one but the security Elves could use any form of esp. Now that all espers were part of a single conscious massmind, the threat of rogue espers was pretty much eliminated, but no one was taking any chances.

Crow Jane strode restlessly back and forth, checking everything over and over again down to the smallest detail. She took her job very seriously. A tall, strapping brunette in chains and leathers, with colours on her face and ribbons tied in her hair, she wore a bandolier of throwing-stars across an impressive bosom, and a scowl that could shatter steel at twenty paces. Wherever she walked, people hurried to get out of her way. Crow Jane had a mental list of all of Humanity's enemies, and she was determined that not one of them was going to launch any surprises on her shift. She had made up her mind that the wedding and coronation were going to be absolutely perfect, and God help anyone who got in the way of that. It helped that Crow Jane took no shit from anyone, whether it be the highest members of Society or the lowliest flunkey. Even Chantelle found pressing reasons to be somewhere else fast when Crow Jane was on the prowl.

She was currently responding to a number of complaints and not a few hand-wringing pleas, to do something about the choir. These hand-picked young vocalists, chosen for the purity of their voices to sing at the wedding, were currently running amok and causing more havoc than a Grendel with haemorrhoids. The choristers might look like little angels in their frilly, starched surplices and delicate ruffs, but secure in their own importance they had seized the chance to behave like little devils.

To be fair, the oldest of them was only eleven, and though they'd all had the solemnity and weight of the occasion drilled into them, it had taken about ten minutes' exposure to the total chaos to plunge them straight into overexcitement and out the other side into total let's-see-what-we-can-get-away-with mode. They ran back and forth like little windmilling dervishes, shrieking and name-calling and getting under everyone's feet, and sneaking into the kitchens faster than they could be thrown out. Two had developed a quite remarkable skill as pickpockets, two more had started a dice school and were challenging all comers, and another was being sick over a potted plant through sheer excitement. One little cherub had smuggled in a paintstick, and was industriously covering the lower part of one wall with fortunately incomprehensible graffiti, while behind him another chorister was taking advantage of his absorption to set fire to the back of his surplice. The choir-master ran back and forth, bleating pathetically, ignored by all.

And then Crow Jane arrived. The choirboys took one look at her, knew real trouble when they saw it and tried to scatter in all directions, but somehow there was always an Elf in just the right place to grab them. Crow Jane retrieved a handful of wallets and other valuable items and returned them to their startled owners, confiscated the paintstick and emptied a bottle of the cheaper wine over the smouldering surplice. She then had a short but vehement heart-to-heart with the assembled boys before sending them off into an adjoining private room to wait till they were called. No one else caught what she had to say, but no one had ever seen the colour drop so suddenly out of so many faces at once. When Crow Jane finally let them go, they headed immediately for the private room, huddling together for protection, followed by a relieved but equally shaken choir-master, who made the sign of the cross at Crow Jane's back when he thought she wasn't looking.

Standing well back from all the turmoil and din, watching everything with a calm, cold gaze, was the priest chosen to perform the wedding ceremony: Cardinal Brendan. Neither Robert nor Constance had wanted such an openly political creature in charge of their wedding, but their own preferred choice, Saint Beatrice, had politely declined to leave her Mission on Lachrymae Christi, where she felt she was needed more. Everyone involved in planning the ceremony heaved quiet but heartfelt sighs of relief. Saint Bea was beloved by all, but no one would have felt comfortable coming into close contact with someone who voluntarily lived among lepers. Saints should keep their distance. All kinds of clerics were suggested, by all sorts of religious and political factions, but in the end Cardinal Brendan emerged as the chosen candidate. He was well known and well liked, and, more importantly, he was Blue Block. And, as in so many things, what Blue Block wanted, Blue Block got.

Brendan himself didn't give a damn about the forthcoming ceremony. He knew it was all just a distraction for the masses. He also knew that the real business of the day was to be concluded before the wedding or the coronation, right here in a private room off the floor of the House, where he could quietly explain the real facts of life to Robert, and, if need be, Constance. That just having a crown placed on your head meant nothing where Blue Block was concerned. King and Queen would bow down to Blue Block, or else. Brendan smiled at the thought. He'd already had one little chat with Robert, but apparently that hadn't taken as strongly as he would have liked. This time he was calling in the heavy artillery. And either Robert would submit to what they had planned for him, or there would be no wedding.

Brendan moved unhurriedly through the crowd, bestowing smiles and blessings as he passed, untouched by the general riot, until he reached his chosen partner-in-crime. Chantelle was talking earnestly with Donna Silvestri, a broad, motherly figure and one of the Empire's more subtle movers and shakers. The Silvestri had risen to prominence in her Clan by the usual methods of treachery and murder, but always in such carefully planned ways that no blame could ever be traced to her. Now people jumped to obey her every murmured word, both within and without her Family. She had a gift for intrigue, and enough quiet malevolence to ensure that her will always took precedence over others'. She ran things from the shadows, and liked it that way. She was, of course, Blue Block.

In person, Donna Silvestri looked like everybody's favourite aunt, round and broad and always a few years out of fashion. She had an ear for every problem, and a shoulder for everyone who needed one, and if her warm smile never entirely reached her faded blue eyes, most people were usually too preoccupied to notice. Donna Silvestri listened patiently, made all the right supportive noises and forgot nothing. It was all stored away in her rat-trap of a mind until some muttered confidence might prove useful, at which time some poor fool would suddenly find that Blue Block knew the one thing he would have sworn nobody knew. Nobody ever suspected the warm, kind and comforting Donna Silvestri. That would have been like condemning your own mother.

Cardinal Brendan bowed to Donna Silvestri, and to Chantelle, and they both nodded politely in return. Chantelle ought really to have bowed, but she always made a point of not being impressed by anyone.

'Sorry to bother you, but I need a word in private, Chantelle,' said Brendan. 'A minor problem, concerning royal etiquette.'

'Of course,' said Chantelle. 'We can use one of the private rooms. No one will disturb us there.'

She led the way, and Brendan followed demurely after her. There were a number of small rooms leading off the main hall of the House, where by long tradition deals and discussions could be made without fear of being disturbed. The rooms were soundproofed, guaranteed unbugged, had no windows and only one door, with a first-class lock. More of the really important debates took place in these small rooms than ever occurred in the House itself. Real politics was too important to be practised in public. Some of the rooms were already in use, as politicians and aristocrats fought out their new pecking order in the face of a constitutional monarchy. Everyone had their own plans for the future King and Queen. Even with the threat of utter destruction by so many of Humanity's enemies hanging over it, Golgotha concentrated on what was truly important.

Chantelle had claimed one of the private rooms for her own personal use, and as in so many things, no one felt secure enough to argue the point with her. She unlocked the door with her own key, ushered Brendan in and then closed and locked the door behind them. The room was bare, save for a functional table and a set of chairs. There were no comforts. This was not a room where people lived, it was just a meeting place, somewhere people passed through on their way to their respective destinies. Chantelle turned to face Brendan, and the cardinal bowed low.

'All goes well, so far,' he said, just a little nervously. 'The

Elves are running security so tightly not even a ghost could walk in unchallenged. There will be no interruptions to what we have planned.'

'We?' said Chantelle icily. 'Don't flatter yourself, Cardinal. These are my plans. Everything that is to happen here, happens through my will.'

'Of course,' said Brendan quickly. 'I mean no challenge to your authority.'

'Damn right you don't. If I'd even thought you had a mind of your own, I'd have had you shot and replaced long ago. I'm Blue Block; you're just a glorified messenger boy, and don't you forget it. Now, let's keep this short and to the point. I don't want to leave Donna Silvestri in charge of things for too long. She has a good mind, but in the end she's just another Blue Block drone, like you. I need to be on the spot, to keep things under control.'

'Of course, Chantelle. Robert and Constance have been separated, as you instructed. They're now stewing in their own juices, in separate rooms.'

'Good,' said Chantelle. 'I think it's time they were brought here, so I can explain their true place in the real order of things. We'll start with Robert. He has basic Blue Block conditioning. Constance is the real wild card. We can't kill Robert; as one of the Hundred Hands, he's too valuable to us. But Constance is another matter. If need be, she is expendable.'

'And that's where I come in,' said Kit SummerIsle, uncoiling lazily from a corner of the room. Cardinal Brendan jumped in shock at not having noticed him, and then tried to look as though he hadn't. Kid Death smiled. 'I quite like the idea of killing a queen. I got to chop off the Empress Lionstone's head, but she'd already vacated her body so that doesn't really count.'

'You may get your chance,' said Chantelle. 'Constance could be very useful to us, once she's been properly conditioned, but she poses far too great a threat to Blue Block to be allowed to go on as she is. Either she bows to Blue Block, one way or another, or you get to do what you do best, SummerIsle.'

'You'd better find me someone to kill soon,' said Kid Death. 'I don't want to get rusty.'

'You'll kill when I tell you to,' said Chantelle. 'I own your services now. Blue Block owns you.'

Kit SummerIsle smiled slowly, but without humour. Cardinal Brendan fell back a step. Chantelle held her ground, but her expression lost some of its confidence. They suddenly knew that they were locked in a room with death incarnate, and all of their power or influence would not protect them if he decided to turn against them. That was, after all, why they'd hired Kid Death.

'A lot of people have thought they owned me,' said the SummerIsle, quite calmly. 'Most of them are dead now. I am my own man, and I serve you for my own reasons. I am a killer, and must go where the killing is. But at the end of the day, I'll kill you just as happily as anyone else. I never had your Blue Block conditioning. My Family never approved of you. One of the few things they were right about.'

'Don't concern yourself, Lord SummerIsle,' said Chantelle, her voice perfectly steady. 'There will be blood and death for you, as promised. Enough perhaps to sate even your appetite. Blue Block has many enemies, and I will turn you loose on them all, in time. Now; you worked for Clan Wolfe before the rebellion. Have you ever met Constance Wolfe?'

'We moved in the same circles; nodded to each other in passing. Her late husband Jacob never really approved of me, even as he used me, and his dear wife was always too good and too noble to have anything to do with the likes of me. If you're asking if I'll have any problems killing her, the answer is no. I have never had any problems killing anyone. As all the leading members of my late Family could tell you, if you had a good medium.'

In another of the private rooms, not all that far away, Robert Campbell was in a terrible state. Dressed in full formal attire, down to the compulsory grey gloves and top hat, with a silk cravat at his throat freshly tied by Baxter, his gentleman's gentleman, he strode back and forth in the confined space like a tiger in its cage, burning up with frustrated nervous energy. His hands were clenched into fists, his stomach was tied in knots and his eyes stared almost wildly, lost in yesterday. On the one hand he was desperate for the ceremony to start, so that he could get it over with, but he'd also never been more terrified of anything in his life. He'd commanded a starcruiser, had his old ship shot out from under him during the rebellion, but that had been nothing compared to this. Then, he'd only had to be afraid for himself. Now, he was more afraid for Constance. This should have been the happiest day of his life, and in a way it was, but as the ceremony drew ever nearer, all he could think of were all the terrible things that could go wrong. And of his first, tragic attempt at marriage. He strode back and forth, all but wearing a trail in the thick carpeting, while Baxter hurried after him, fussing over the fit of the suit and trying to calm the King-to-be with wise words and reassuring anecdotes, none of which Robert heard.

He was remembering his first wedding day. He still sometimes dreamed of it, and woke crying out in the night. His match with Letitia Shreck had been an arranged marriage, designed to tie Clan Campbell and Clan Shreck closer together, for various business and political reasons. He hadn't been consulted. He'd been a very minor member of his Clan then, back when most of his Family were still alive, and the only future he dreamed of was a captaincy in the Imperial Fleet. He never even got to meet his bride-to-be until the day of the wedding. She seemed a pleasant sort. Robert thought he could have become quite fond of her, in time. But it all went horribly wrong. During the marriage ceremony, an esper scan revealed Letitia to be already pregnant, by another man. Gregor Shreck had gone mad with rage. He'd strangled Letitia, while Robert's own Family held him back, helpless to save her. Gregor had murdered Letitia to save his Family from shame. And Robert had had to watch it, unable to do anything.

He still kept a small portrait of Letitia in his bedroom. He never loved her, but he thought he might have, given a chance. If things had gone differently.

And now, here he was again, preparing for marriage. Things should be different, this time. He was marrying a woman he loved, and who loved him, surrounded by a whole army of people determined to see that nothing went wrong. He should have felt safe, secure, delighted at his good fortune that such a wonderful creature as Constance Wolfe had agreed to be his wife. And he was going to be King, as well, constitutional monarch to the whole damned Empire. Assuming the whole damned Empire wasn't destroyed in the next few days by the Recreated, or Shub, or the Hadenmen. His thoughts shifted to his other main worry, that he should be out there with what was left of the Fleet, commanding a ship against the Empire's enemies, instead of participating in an overblown ceremony designed merely to divert and distract the general populace. But as with his last wedding, he got no say in the matter. And he'd had to give up his captaincy long ago to become head of his Family, and a man who was about to be made King could hardly be allowed to risk himself in combat.

'Do sit down, Robert, I'm getting tired just watching you.' Adrienne spoke calmly from her seat in a corner of the room. 'Save some of that energy for your wedding night. There's really nothing for you to worry about. The ceremony's been planned and rehearsed down to the last detail, the Elves are strip-searching and body-probing anyone who even coughs funny, and Toby Shreck's in charge of the holo coverage, so you can be sure you'll look good in the live broadcast. Now please sit down, before you wear out your wedding suit from the inside.'

Robert growled something incomprehensible even to himself, and threw himself on to the nearest chair, folding his arms tightly across his chest as though he could hold his nerves in check by sheer brute force. He made himself breathe slowly and steadily, and his heart began to slow just a little. Baxter started to fuss with the suit again, and received such a glare that he quickly decided to kneel down and give Robert's shoes a polish they didn't need. Robert looked at himself in the mirror on the wall and growled again, even louder.

'Do I have to wear this bloody top hat? It doesn't suit me.'

'A top hat rarely suits anyone, sir,' said Baxter, still concentrating on the shoes. 'But it is an essential part of the ensemble; a style handed down to us from centuries past. And style, after all, doesn't have to make sense. That's how you know it's style. But don't worry, you won't have to wear the top hat for long. After the immediate ceremony, one removes the hat and carries it under one's arm, so that one can place one's gloves in it.'

'I can take the gloves off?'

'Oh, of course, sir. This was covered in the rehearsals. One couldn't greet one's guests afterwards with gloved hands. That wouldn't be at all proper.'

Robert looked at Adrienne. 'Who makes up all this shit?'

'Don't look at me, dear. I've never understood fashion, even when my late husband Finlay was a grand master at it. Some of the outfits he wore were so colourful the images are still imprinted permanently on walls all over the city, like the ghosts of styles past.'

Robert smiled slightly, in spite of himself. 'Why do you always refer to Finlay as your late husband? He's been dead some time now.'

'Oh, I don't know, dear. I suppose I just like the sound of it.'

Outside the room, the noise of the wedding preparations grew a little louder, if anything, and Robert's face went cold and hard again.

'What is it that's troubling you, Robert?' said Adrienne.

'You're not having cold feet about marrying Constance, are you?'

'No! No, she's the only thing in this whole damned mess that I am sure about. I love Constance with all my heart. I never got the chance to love Letitia. But every time I think of this wedding, of standing before the cardinal and taking my vows, all I can see is Letitia's dead face . . .'

'That isn't going to happen this time! Everyone wants this wedding to go ahead – everyone.'

'I know that! That's another part of the problem. Everyone wants this marriage, wants us to be King and Queen, and it feels like I don't have any say in the matter. I want Constance as my wife, but . . . I never wanted to be King. Hell, I never even wanted to be the Campbell. But both have been thrust upon me, and I couldn't say no. I know my duty. But this isn't just about me. I have to think of Constance too. Am I putting her at risk by marrying her? You know my history; most of my Family are dead, Letitia's dead . . . am I a jinx, Addie?'

'Now you really are being silly, Robert. Everybody's lost loved ones in the last few years. The rebellion swept through all our lives like a storm, and carried away a lot of people. Forget Letitia. That's the past. The times and the people that brought her such an ugly death are gone. Constance is in no danger from anyone here. You forget the past and concentrate on your future with Constance. I'm sure you're going to be very happy together, and the two of you can do a lot of good for the Empire as King and Queen.'

Robert sighed, and reluctantly unclenched his arms. 'It all seems so sensible and obvious when I hear you say it. It's just nerves, I suppose. This is meant to be the most important day of my life, after all. But then, I imagine everyone feels that way about their wedding.'

'Not me,' said Adrienne. 'My marriage to Finlay was arranged by my father, who never liked me. They wouldn't even let me meet Finlay till the day of the wedding, and once I'd seen him and talked to him, I knew why. I was already running for the door when one of my uncles tackled me and brought me down. I must be the only bride who's given her vows in an armlock.'

'But don't you ever miss Finlay, now he's gone? I can't say I ever liked the man, but he did a lot of good, in his own way.'

'I missed him when he was alive, once. I didn't aim carefully enough.'

There was a polite knock at the door, and Baxter went to answer it, a gun suddenly appearing in his hand from nowhere. Weapons were forbidden to everyone except designated security, but a gentleman's gentleman had many duties, and Baxter took them all very seriously. He eased the door open just wide enough to see out, gun at the ready but hidden from sight, and then relaxed a little. The disrupter disappeared. There was a short murmured conversation, and then Baxter swung the door open and stood back, allowing the masked figure of the Unknown Clone to enter. Robert and Adrienne immediately rose to greet him, polite smiles on their faces, as Baxter shut and locked the door again.

One of the many political deals involved in putting the wedding ceremony together had involved a long argument over who should be Robert's best man. It was a role of some prestige, after all. Robert had no close members of his Family left to stand at his side, and so technically speaking the position was up for grabs, and a great many people wanted it. As in so many other matters, Robert didn't get a say. Eventually the clone underground made the best deal, or made the most noise, and the politically significant figure of the Unknown Clone was selected as Robert's official best man. Robert had never even exchanged a dozen words with the enigmatic masked figure, but he thought of all the possible alternatives, decided he could have fared much worse and kept his mouth firmly shut.

'Good of you to look in,' he said politely, as the masked man loomed over him. He put out a hand, and the Unknown Clone took it in a firm grip that lasted just a little longer than politeness demanded.

'I thought we should talk, before the ceremony,' said the Unknown Clone, the voice behind the featureless leather mask distorted by an electronic filter. 'Evangeline and I put a lot of effort into ensuring that I was selected as best man. It had to be me.'

Robert frowned slightly, confused. Like everyone else, he had no idea who was behind the mask, but as far as he knew he'd never had much to do with clones. Hell, they'd been on different sides during the rebellion. He wasn't bigoted; he just never moved in those kind of circles. And then he caught his breath as the Unknown Clone slowly raised his hands and removed the mask, revealing the very familiar features of Finlay Campbell.

'Good God!' said Robert, falling back a pace.

'Bloody hell!' said Adrienne, rising to her feet.

Baxter remained calm and unmoved, as befitted a gentleman's gentleman, but even he couldn't prevent one eyebrow from rising.

'You're supposed to be dead,' said Robert. 'Hell, I even paid for your funeral!'

'I know,' said Finlay. 'I was there, watching from a safe distance. Nice ceremony, I thought. Not much of a crowd, but more than I deserved. Good of you to take care of things, Robert.'

Robert Campbell shrugged uncomfortably. 'We were Family. You'd have done the same for me.'

'Yes,' said Finlay. 'That's why I'm here now. It's only right that someone from the old Family should be your best man.'

He put out a hand again, but Robert ignored it, pulling Finlay forward into an embrace.

'Oh, shit,' said Adrienne feelingly, as the two men separated and stood back. 'Does this mean I'm still married to you, you bastard?'

Finlay grinned. 'Probably not. Finlay Campbell is dead and laid to rest in his Family crypt, and I'm just as happy to leave it that way. I have a new life now, without all the . . . complications from my old one. Let the dead rest in peace.

I've only revealed my identity to you so that Robert would know he had proper Family support on his big day.' He nodded to Robert. 'You've come a long way, done well. The old Family would have been proud of you.'

'You could come back,' said Robert. 'Once I'm King, I'm sure I could get you a Pardon for Gregor's murder. And you have far more right to be the Campbell than I ever had.'

'I never wanted it,' said Finlay. 'Let Finlay Campbell rest in peace. I never liked him much anyway.'

'Finally we have something in common,' said Adrienne, and everyone laughed. 'I take it Evangeline knows about this?'

'Of course. Who do you think arranged for me to become the Unknown Clone?' He hefted the leather mask in his hand. 'I seem to have spent most of my life hiding behind one bloody mask or another. One more is no big deal. At least this one stands for something that matters.' He grinned at Robert. 'You and Constance have lots of kids. We need to rebuild the Clan.'

And then he put his mask back on, and the Unknown Clone bowed once, respectfully, to Robert, before leaving the private room. Robert shook his head slowly, and Adrienne sat down.

'Well,' she said heavily. 'This is turning out to be quite a day, isn't it? I wonder who else is going to come back from the dead?'

'Just as long as it isn't Owen Deathstalker,' said Robert. 'That really would throw the cat among the politicians.' He sighed, and then looked at Baxter, who was still staring at the door Finlay had closed behind him. 'Is something wrong, Baxter? You seem a little preoccupied.'

'Oh, no, sir. It's just . . . I never met Finlay Campbell before. I was a great fan of his, when he fought in the Arenas as the Masked Gladiator. I have all the holo documentaries on him, and I know all the statistics of his career by heart. I just wish I could have worked up enough courage to ask for his autograph.'

'I'll ask him later,' said Robert. 'But you'd better be very quiet about how you got it. I have to say, I was surprised as hell when news of his other identity emerged after his death. I knew him mostly as a clothes horse and grand master of fashion.'

'Finlay as best man,' said Adrienne. 'Now that really is a contradiction in terms . . .'

In yet another private room off the floor of the House, Constance Wolfe sat alone. She'd been surrounded by people all morning, fussing over her dress and flowers and appearance, until their voices blended into one unbearable nag, but eventually they'd done all they could, and she'd sent them all away. She needed time alone, time to think and reflect. She sat on a straight-backed chair, perfectly made-up, her hair piled on top of her head, wearing the most delightful and expensive wedding dress that anyone had ever seen. Various committees had tried to impose various styles of dress on her, for various reasons, while all the leading designers on Golgotha threatened to cut their wrists if she didn't choose them, but Constance had refused the bribes and ignored the pressures and produced her own design. She knew what suited her. And she needed to feel that she was in charge of at least some part of the ceremony. She didn't bother looking at the mirror on the wall. She looked very beautiful, and she knew it, but that was no comfort to her. She had a lot to think about.

The room seemed so much larger with only her in it. The blessed quiet was a balm to her nerves, and she was determined to be calm and serene by the time the ceremony finally started. One of the happy couple had to be, and she doubted very much it was going to be Robert. The poor dear was probably charging back and forth in his room by now, sweating buckets and retying his cravat over and over again just to keep his hands occupied. At least he wasn't recovering from a late stag night; security had had a collective coronary at the very thought, and said no very loudly. It wouldn't have been much of a gathering anyway; most of Robert's Family were dead, and most of his friends were out fighting the Enemies of Humanity. Constance scowled, and firmly pulled her thoughts back on track. She had a lot to think about, and she wanted it all settled in her mind before she drew down her veil and walked up the aisle. She was leaving her old life behind her to take on a much more important role, and she didn't want to bring any of her old baggage with her.

Constance was the last of what had once been a great Family: Clan Wolfe, the most prominent Family in the Empire, rich and powerful and entirely unchallenged, and while Constance was only a part of the Clan by marriage, she had always taken great pride in being a Wolfe. That pride was tarnished now, the Family brought down by the exiled and despised Valentine. The only other Wolfe left of note had been her other stepson Daniel, but he too had proved himself a traitor. Both Valentine and Daniel would be dead the moment they were found. And her only other stepchild, Stephanie, was already dead, murdered by Jack Random in his last insane slaughter. Constance scowled. She had argued fiercely against granting that madman even a temporary Pardon, but she'd been overruled on the only grounds she couldn't argue against – that the Empire needed him. But afterwards (if there was an afterwards), things would be different, and Constance would find someone who would deal with him as he deserved. She'd never liked Stephanie. Hell, the silly chit had spent most of her time plotting to wrest control of Clan Wolfe away from Constance, but she was still Jacob's daughter, and she hadn't deserved to die at a lunatic's hands. Jack Random had quite deliberately put himself above all authority, and would have to pay the price. If only so that no one else's daughter would have to die like Stephanie.

She wondered what her late husband Jacob would have made of her second wedding. She liked to think he would have approved; would want her to be happy. She'd been happy with Jacob, and so much in love. She'd fully expected to spend the rest of her life with him, and had wanted nothing more. When he died, she nearly died with him. Her whole reason for living was gone. Certainly she'd never expected to know love again. Her prospective marriage to Owen Deathstalker had been a thing of duty and honour, nothing more. But then he died too . . . and Robert Campbell came into her life. And, quite unexpectedly, love had blossomed in the ashes of her heart. It wasn't the same as before – Robert was no Jacob. But that was probably for the best. She knew exactly where she stood with Robert.

She was so happy now. And so afraid that something awful would go wrong, and spoil everything. That it would all be taken from her, just as before.

Her immediate Family were gone, lost to her, every one of them. Her husband Jacob, her stepchildren Valentine, Stephanie and Daniel, even her son and daughter-in-law, Michel and Lily. So much death in so short a time. But everyone had lost someone in the rebellion. She had no right to feel special, and wallow in her loss, when many others had lost even more. Constance had turned to politics to fill her life and give it meaning and purpose, and had found to her surprise that she was rather good at it. She'd always been appalled by some of the Families' casual misuse and abuse of power, and had fought hard to reach a position where she could do something about it. She smiled grimly. Wait until she was Queen! The Clans were in for one hell of a surprise . . . and Blue Block too. They might think they were safely hidden in the shadows, but once she'd been crowned Queen she would have the resources to dig out Blue Block's secrets and reveal its hidden armies. Blue Block and its machinations had been a blight on the Empire for far too long, and she would bring them to book, whatever it cost.

They were probably thinking she'd be safely sidelined as a merely constitutional monarch, but it had been so long since the Empire had had such a titular head that no one really knew what it signified. Which in real terms meant that Constance could define her role any damned way she liked, or could get away with. She had no wish to lead the Empire, but she saw nothing wrong in nudging it in the right direction, from time to time. Constance grinned again. She was going to enjoy being Queen.

There was a quiet knock at the door, and Constance started almost guiltily, half afraid someone had overheard her thoughts. But she pushed the sudden panic firmly to one side and became calm and confident again. The Elf esp-blockers were everywhere now. Her thoughts, and her future plans, were strictly her own. She smoothed her dress unnecessarily, and called out for the visitor to enter in her best cool, commanding voice. She put her shoulders back and held her head high, and then relaxed again almost immediately as Evangeline Shreck came in, carefully shutting the door behind her.

Constance rose from her chair and went forward to take Evangeline's hands in hers. The two women had a lot in common, both being members of Families that had brought them only heartache. Both had longed for the power to change the world they lived in for the better, and now Constance was to be Queen, while Evangeline headed the clone underground. She was also the head of Clan Shreck these days, with Gregor finally dead, as Toby still adamantly refused to accept the position. It had been Evangeline who first suggested the Unknown Clone as Robert's best man, and Constance who helped push it through. (Though Evangeline hadn't told Constance the real reason for her suggestion. There were limits to friendship. If Constance had known that the mysterious Unknown Clone was actually the infamous Finlay Campbell, murderer of Gregor Shreck, she might have felt obliged to do something official about it. Evangeline never told her, and saved Constance from having to choose between her friend and her duty. Because you never knew.)

In the meantime, Evangeline was to stand at Constance's side at the wedding, and officially give her away. Constance's own father had publicly disowned her after she went against his wishes and married Jacob Wolfe, and all the sea changes in the Empire since hadn't changed his stubborn mind. None of Constance's original Family would be attending the wedding. Constance had nothing to say about that, in public or in private. So Evangeline, as a close friend and head of one of the Empire's oldest Families, would give her away. It helped that she was the clone underground representative, too. Such things mattered in the eyes of the Empire.

(Evangeline hadn't told Constance that she was just a clone herself, fighting to avoid a genetest that would reveal her true nature and strip control of Clan Shreck from her. Perhaps she would, later. When things had settled.)

'I'm so glad you're here, Evie,' said Constance, as they both sat down, carefully arranging the frills and flounces of their dresses around them. (Constance's was, of course, pure white, for entirely traditional reasons. Evangeline's was a striking emerald green.) 'I had to throw most of my people out; they were driving me crazy with their endless fussing. And I swear if Chantelle sticks her pointed nose round my door one more time, with one more snotty comment or order disguised as advice, I am going to part her hair with something large and heavy and pointed.'

'Relax,' said Evangeline, smiling in spite of herself. 'The last I saw of her, she'd run out of people to bully on the floor of the House, and had gone into the antechamber to make the guests' lives miserable too. I think your choosing her to run things was a stroke of genius. She's in her element, organizing a dozen things at once and dominating everyone and everything by sheer force of what passes for her personality. Apart from Kid Death, she's probably the only person here that everyone is afraid of. In fact, she's made herself so universally unpopular that any assassin who might somehow sneak past the Elves would probably be after her rather than you.'

'I never meant my wedding day to get this out of hand,' said Constance, just a little tiredly. 'It's more like a circus than a ceremony. But Parliament was determined to make a major occasion out of it, for obvious reasons. Is there still no news from the Last Standing, or the *Excalibur*? Do we even know if they've made contact with the Shub fleet yet?'

'Their last communication said they were still closing in, and would we please stop bothering Diana Vertue as she was trying to concentrate. If I stop to think that all our fates are in the hands of a woman who was once called Jenny Psycho, and with extremely good reason, I'm going to get very worried. So I'm not thinking about it, and I recommend you don't either. Concentrate on your wedding. Do you want to run through the responses one more time?'

'No! Thank you. I've been through so many rehearsals now I could do it in my sleep. At least we got that honour and obey bit thrown out.' Constance stopped and looked at Evangeline soberly. 'I really am glad you're here, Evie. There's something I need to talk about, something I couldn't discuss with anyone else. Maybe not even Robert. I've been thinking about my role as Queen, about all the things I plan to do, and more and more it seems to me that I sound just like Lionstone. Intriguing and politicking to make people do things, just because I think I'm right. I don't want to be an Empress! I don't want to lead Humanity, I've seen where that takes you. I just want to be the voice of reason.'

'And you will be,' Evangeline said firmly. 'The best person to place in a position of power is the one person who doesn't want to be there. Owen taught us that. He never wanted to be a rebel, or a rebel leader, but he changed the Empire because he saw that it was the right thing to do, and couldn't, wouldn't look away. He understood what duty and honour really mean.'

'Yes, he did.' Constance sighed. 'It's hard to believe someone like him is really dead; the only truly honourable man I ever knew. Apart from Robert, of course.'

'Owen might still turn up again, some day.'

'God, I hope not! That really would complicate things. No; he's far more useful as a legend now. Someone to inspire the next generation.'

'Would you really have married him? I mean, you never loved him.'

'No, but I admired him. I would have been proud to be his wife. The marriage was my idea, after all. And the Empire does so need its heroes. But now he's safely gone. He probably would have hated being even a constitutional monarch. He would have found it very limiting, after all the things he'd been through. So . . . I suppose things have a way of turning out right, eventually. I'm marrying Robert Campbell, and he will make a fine King and a better husband. Who says there are no happy endings any more?'

People were circulating constantly in the overcrowded antechamber, waiting impatiently for their chance to see and be seen. There were news cameras everywhere, but even they couldn't cover such a mob of celebrities, personalities and politicians, never mind all their hangers-on. Toby Shreck and Imperial News had exclusive rights to the ceremony itself: all the other news and gossip stations had to make do with the antechamber and the external preparations. Holo cameras shot back and forth overhead, trying desperately to find someone or something worth covering that might distract from Toby Shreck's coverage. Some cameras became caught up in savage ramming contests as they fought over the few decent scraps of news available, mostly first glances of who was with who, and what they were wearing.

People pushed, shoved and elbowed each other out of the way to win their moment in front of the cameras, to be seen smiling with the right people, while striking just the right poses in exactly the right clothes and saying frantically witty things to the by now shell-shocked interviewers. After all, everyone in the Empire was watching, and everyone who even thought they might be anyone had fought and intrigued and prostituted themselves dreadfully for an invitation to the wedding of the century. Luckily, that hadn't been as hard as it might have been, so many of the old movers and shakers being dead and gone. In fact, it was hard for guests and viewers not to feel the presence of many famous ghosts, people who should have been present on such an important day in the Empire's history but weren't.

People such as Crawford Campbell, father of Finlay, murdered by Jacob Wolfe, who was in turn murdered by his own son Valentine. Roderik SummerIsle, wise old hero of the Empire, murdered by his own grandson, Kid Death. Gregor Shreck, even, though no one really missed his presence. And all the other great names that had helped to shape Humanity's history. The legendary Giles Deathstalker, founder of his Clan, murdered in the end by his own descendant, Owen. Who was also gone, along with his fearsome companion Hazel d'Ark. So many Families contained the seeds of their own destruction. And, of course, the Iron Bitch herself, Empress Lionstone XIV, now clasped to Shub's steel bosom. So many great figures, heroes and villains, and everything in between. Larger than life . . . but all gone now. The Empire seemed a smaller place without them.

But they were the past, and this was a day for celebrating the future. No one mentioned the old names aloud, for fear of seeming out of touch with the current realities.

Chantelle was soon back, overseeing people and schedules with implacable vigour. She seemed to be everywhere at once, determined that everything should go as smooth as smooth could be, and to hell with anyone or anything that threatened to get in the way of complete perfection. The multitude of guests varied between being openly impressed and utterly appalled, as Chantelle bullied people about with no regard as to whether they were servants or celebrities. She circulated at great speed among the uneasy guests, favouring some with a quick peck on the cheek, or by generously remembering their first names in front of the cameras, while others received only biting put-downs or were damned with the very faintest of praise. Some Chantelle cut dead entirely, stalking right past them with her nose firmly in the air, and this too was broadcast live. For those people the shame was almost too much to bear. They retreated to the fringes of the crowd, well away from the cameras and interviewers, to weep bitter tears and plan future revenge. Chantelle allowed herself just a few appearances with some of the more important interviewers, with whom she was at once humble, self-effacing and just delighted to be able to do her small bit to make this very special day a success. She was beautiful and charming, and the huge holo audience ate it up with spoons. Unheard in the background was the grinding of teeth, as certain celebrities hated her silently. Chantelle smiled victoriously upon them all.

Back on the floor of the House, Toby Shreck and his cameraman Flynn moved purposefully amid the chaos, getting it all on film. Toby should have been up in the director's gallery on the next floor, watching over the dozen cameramen under his command and following their incoming footage on the banks of monitors provided, but he hadn't been able to resist coming down on to the floor himself, just to feel the atmosphere in person. Flynn understood. Imperial News had put Toby in charge of the entire exclusive coverage of the great day, and nothing made Toby more jittery than responsibility. So Toby's long-suffering second in command was currently manning the director's gallery, while Toby and Flynn bustled back and forth on the floor, hunting down news like the remorseless predators they were.

'That gallery was driving me crazy,' said Toby, as he scanned the people around him for someone worth interviewing or terrorizing. 'Half the cameramen I've been supplied with don't seem to know the servants from the celebrities without checking their guest list first, the other half are social crawlers afraid to film anything interesting in case it upsets someone, and one damned pervert keeps zooming in on the bridesmaids' legs and cleavage. I wouldn't mind, but so far he's getting the highest individual ratings. I'll be glad when the ceremony proper starts, and I can concentrate my cameras on what really matters. I want at least one cameraman right there with the happy couple when they take their vows, and that had better be you, Flynn, if you know what's good for you. I am relying on you to get me award-winning footage of today's great event, even if you have to nudge the best man out of the way to get it.'

'Don't worry, boss. I'll stick so close to the bride she'll think I'm an extra bustle.'

'Hold everything,' said Toby suddenly, in his best wolf-stalking-a-wounded-deer voice. 'I have just spotted someone we absolutely have to interview. Donna Silvestri, her own slippery self. Usually she has enough sense to avoid me.'

Flynn looked across at the calm, matronly figure. 'What's so special about her? Clan Silvestri has been strictly minor league for ages now.'

'Shows how much you know. Dear sweet, humble, butter-wouldn't-melt-in-her-ass Donna is rumoured by those in the know to be Blue Block. Hard-core. And just lately, wherever there's been trouble, arguments, or things threatening to get out of hand, there's our Donna, ever ready to pour oil on burning waters. I've never known anyone with such a gift for saying just the thing guaranteed to have people throwing themselves at each other's throats. And she's been remarkably camera-shy of late, absolutely refusing to give interviews about anything. Oh, we have got to talk to her. Stick close, Flynn, and make sure you record everything.'

'Boss, we're supposed to be covering the build-up to the ceremony,' Flynn protested in vain as he followed Toby through the milling crowd, 'not harassing the guests to make them incriminate themselves on camera.'

'Don't be silly, Flynn. That's what I do best. Ah, Lady Silvestri; perhaps you could spare us a few moments of your no doubt valuable time to speak to our audience?'

Donna looked quickly about her, but there was no obvious easy escape route, so she put on her best motherly visage, and smiled warmly for Flynn's camera. 'And what can I do for such a celebrated muckraker as yourself, Shreck?'

'See, boss, she's heard of you.'

'Shut up, Flynn. My dear Lady Donna, I just thought you

might favour our Empire audience with a few words on how you see this auspicious occasion.'

'It's a very happy day, of course. I'm honoured to be here.'

'I'm sure you are. Perhaps you might care to share with us what it was that earned you your invitation, and indeed access to the backstage preparations? I mean, since Clan Silvestri is quite a minor Family these days, with a somewhat sullied reputation, how is it that you are here, when so many other more deserving cases were denied access? Are you perhaps a close friend of the bride or groom?'

'Well, I . . .'

'Or do you form part of the emerging political consensus?'

'Well, I wouldn't say—'

'Neither would I. Isn't it a fact, Donna, that you are a member in surreptitious standing of that oh-so-secretive-and-enigmatic organization, Blue Block?'

'I am not personally a member of Blue Block,' said Donna coldly, 'though I have had contact with those who are. Most aristocrats have. I've never made any secret of my connections.'

'You've never stated them openly, either.'

'Blue Block is trying to rebuild its image, as a . . . facilitator, bringing opposing sides together in a search for harmony. I'm proud to be involved in that process.'

'And rumours that Blue Block has its own, secret agenda for the Empire?'

'Are just that – rumours. Nor worth repeating even by such a celebrated troublemaker as yourself, Shreck.'

And she strode determinedly forward, almost shouldering Flynn out of the way, and disappeared into the crowd, head held high. It wasn't a particularly dignified retreat, as retreats went, and Toby grinned nastily after her. Nothing looks worse than losing your temper on camera. Flynn shut down his.

'And what precisely was the point of that, boss?'

'Damned if I know,' said Toby happily. 'But she must be up to something if I could rattle her that easily. I think I'll have the gallery keep one camera in her immediate vicinity throughout the wedding, just in case.'

'But what would she, or Blue Block, have to gain by disrupting the ceremony?'

'I don't know, Flynn! That's why I want a camera close at hand. This isn't just a wedding; the crowning of two constitutional monarchs makes this the most important political watershed in the Empire since Owen Deathstalker deposed Lionstone and destroyed the Iron Throne. And Blue Block's main interest has always been politics. There's no way they'd let an occasion like this go by without finding some way to profit. And anyway, interfering baggages like Donna Silvestri deserve to be upset on a regular basis. It's good for their souls.'

'What would you know about what's good for the soul, boss?'

'Not a damned thing. Now hush; here comes Clarissa. I don't want her upset in any way, clear?'

'Got it, boss. No politics, no conspiracy theories. And I won't even mention the seventeen people currently suing you.'

'Best not to. Hello, Clarissa! Enjoying yourself?'

'Much to my surprise, yes. It was very kind of you to get me an invitation, but I wasn't sure I could handle being in a crowd this size. After everything I've been through, people make me very nervous. I keep expecting them to point at me, or mutter things behind their hands. Imagine my relief at discovering half the people here are more nervous than I am! Seeing so many of the powers that be positively wetting themselves every time Chantelle even looks in their direction is doing my poor ego a power of good. Not least because I don't give a rat's ass whether Chantelle approves of me or not. I've been held captive by a Fury and a Ghost Warrior; it'll take more than a mere celebrity to unnerve me. Besides; her dress is very déclassé, and her eye make-up is *très* tacky, even if no one has dared mention it to her yet.'

Clarissa herself looked stunning in a pale blue gown with

silver trim, a deceptively simple hairdo and understated make-up. Toby told her so, and she blushed happily. They held hands and billed and cooed just like any other turtle-doves, and Flynn marvelled at the change that came over Toby Shreck in Clarissa's company. The hardened news hound became almost human.

'Heads up,' Flynn said sharply. 'Company's coming.'

They all looked round quickly as Evangeline Shreck came over to join them, the impressive masked figure of the Unknown Clone at her side. Clarissa shrank a little closer to Toby, but kept her chin up. Toby slipped a supportive arm round her waist. They bowed and smiled politely to each other, and Toby appropriated a tray of drinks from a passing waiter. Everyone except the Unknown Clone took a glass of champagne.

'Relax,' said Toby. 'Lift the mask and have a sip. No one's going to notice; they've got their own problems to think about. And I already know you're Finlay Campbell.'

Evangeline looked at him with something like shock, while the Unknown Clone stood very still, one hand resting at his belt where his sword should have been. 'That camera had better not be recording,' he said after a moment. Flynn quickly shook his head. The masked face turned back to Toby. 'How long have you known? And how is it that such a juicy piece of news has never appeared on any of your shows?'

'Well first, I recognized your body language,' said Toby calmly. 'We spent a lot of time travelling together on Haceldama, and I notice such things. Like the way you and Evangeline stand together, your bodies always oriented on each other, like long-time lovers. And I never did believe Finlay Campbell would die that easily. And second, I kept quiet about it because it isn't anyone's business if you want to hide behind a mask again. There's enough news to go round without dragging up old scandals. And third, I've kept quiet because I want a full exclusive interview with you when you finally do unmask. Fair enough?'

'You always were too clever for your own good,' said

Finlay Campbell. 'I will unmask, eventually. When enough time's gone by that no one cares any more.'

'There is still the matter of the murder warrant against you for Gregor Shreck's death.'

'No one really gives a damn about how Gregor died,' said Evangeline. 'Most people are relieved he's gone. And the evidence against Finlay is entirely circumstantial. There are no witnesses, after all. Eventually the case will be dropped, and then Finlay Campbell will return. And he and I will be married at last. After I've sorted out a few little problems of my own.'

'I'll be getting married myself soon,' said Toby, almost bashfully. 'Clarissa and I have decided to tie the knot, once the war is over.'

Evangeline smiled, and then frowned slightly. 'But isn't she . . . ?'

'My stepsister as well as my cousin? Yes. But don't worry about it. Such marriages are practically a Shreck Family tradition. A few people will inevitably turn up their noses and try to snub us, but most of Society will go along with it. If they know what's good for them. They all have their own little secrets, and I know most of them. If anyone gives us a hard time, I'll schedule a few prime-time specials on their own peccadilloes. I won't let anyone stand between me and my Clarissa. I never loved anyone before; never thought I had it in me. But Clarissa's special. I'd marry her tomorrow, if she'd let me.'

'No,' Clarissa said firmly. 'I can't marry you, not as I am now. I'm still not everything I used to be. Lionstone's surgeons made a lot of changes in me when I was transformed into one of her maids: implants, revisions, alterations. Jenny Psycho undid some of them when she freed us, but the majority are having to be put right the hard way. Most of it's too subtle for the regeneration machines, so that means endless operations, along with extensive psychological and esp counselling to help me come to terms with what I was, and did. Lionstone had me made over into a monster, and I did monstrous things. Sometimes I relive them, in nightmares. And then Aunt Grace was murdered and replaced by a Fury, and I was Shub's prisoner. Just what I didn't need. But Toby was always there for me. His love kept me sane. He taught me to be strong, and resilient.'

'You always had it in you,' said Toby. 'You're a survivor. You're a Shreck.'

'I want to be fully human again when I marry my Toby,' said Clarissa, 'and if that means having to wait, well, Toby and I both waited a long time to find each other. My only real worry is that when we finally get to the altar, they'll make me take my vows under my original name, Lindsey. I never liked it, even as a child. I changed it to Clarissa the minute I was old enough to make it stick. I always knew I was really a Clarissa.'

'She could throw a hell of a mean temper tantrum, if you got the name wrong,' Toby said fondly. 'I always called her Lindsey, of course, when we were both young, just to get a rise out of her. I remember one time she tried to pierce my ear with a stapling gun . . . I was an obnoxious little toad, even then.'

'Practice made perfect,' said Flynn. 'All these marriages at once; there must be something in the air. I'm trying to get Toby to let me be his bridesmaid. I'd look lovely in a nice little pink frock.'

'I think you'd look very sweet,' said Clarissa.

'You're the only one who does,' said Toby.

'Maybe there's just too much death around,' said Evangeline, and they all nodded soberly.

'Whatever,' Toby said finally. 'If you'll excuse me, I think I'd better get back to my control gallery, and check that everything's still running smoothly. It's less than an hour to the grand ceremony now. I'll see you all later. Flynn; behave yourself. And promise me you won't dive for the bouquet when Constance throws it.'

Robert Campbell strode impatiently into yet another of the private rooms off the main floor, and didn't bother to hide his glare when he found Cardinal Brendan and Chantelle waiting for him. 'All right; what is it? What is it that's so important that I have to leave all my people behind, to talk with you two in private? It's not another change to the language of the ceremony, is it? I'm damned if I'm going through yet another bloody rehearsal just to placate another religious, historical or political pressure group.'

'It's nothing to do with the ceremony as such,' said Chantelle smoothly. 'This is more to do with your safety, and Constance's.'

'If it's another anonymous death threat, let the Elves deal with it,' Robert growled. 'That's what they're here for. No one's going to get past them.'

'Oh, there's nothing anonymous about this threat,' said Brendan. 'We know who's behind it this time.'

'We are,' said Chantelle. 'We, being Blue Block.'

Robert looked at her sharply. '*You're* Blue Block? I knew about Brendan, but . . .'

'Some of us are more open about it than others. And some of us hide in plain sight, so constantly visible we become invisible. Suffice to say I'm rather higher up the scale of things than the cardinal here. I'm talking openly with you now to make sure you understand how important you are to us.'

Robert scowled. 'I know. I'm one of the Hundred Hands. One of your precious pre-programmed assassins. But the minute I'm officially King, I'm going to have the Elves go through my mind with a fine-tooth comb, and rip out everything they find that doesn't belong there. I'll be no one's puppet. Blue Block's days of power and influence are as good as over. Once I make public what you people did to me, and how you intended to use me, they'll make your name a curse and hunt you down in the streets.'

'Ah, Robert,' said Brendan sadly, 'I really hoped you'd be more sensible than this. You can't stand against Blue Block. No one can.'

'Watch me,' said Robert.

'No,' said Chantelle, 'I don't think so.'

The door opened behind Robert, and Kit SummerIsle came in. He nodded to Chantelle, and then locked the door behind him. He looked at Robert, and then stood with his back to the door, his arms folded across his chest, making it clear that anyone who tried to leave would have to go through him. In defiance of all tradition and orders, Kid Death had his sword strapped to his hip. Robert glared at him, and then at Chantelle.

'What the hell is that madman doing here? And who gave him a sword?'

'Kid Death works for us now,' said Brendan. 'And he's here to make sure you take what we're about to say very seriously. We take you and Constance very seriously. You just might pose a significant threat to Blue Block's plans, perhaps even its very existence, if you really put your minds to it. And we can't allow that. So, you're going to agree to follow Blue Block's orders in all things, or the SummerIsle will go from here, right now, and kill your beloved Constance.'

For a moment, Robert couldn't get his breath. His heart felt as though a cold fist had closed around it. He had no doubt that the cardinal was utterly serious, and that his threat was real. *It's happening again. My bride is going to die again.* He looked from Brendan to Kid Death, and then to Chantelle. His breath rasped in his chest like razor blades.

'You'd never get away with it,' he said hoarsely.

'Of course we would,' said Chantelle, 'we're Blue Block. We have a long tradition of getting away with all kinds of things. No one will see the SummerIsle. He's had experience in getting past all kinds of security; even the Elves. The killing would take place in private. Very quiet, very professional. And afterwards, we'll find someone to blame it on. Shub, perhaps, or some anti-royalist terrorist faction. Very sad, very regrettable, but these things happen. You know we can do this, Robert.'

'Constance doesn't have to die,' Brendan said reasonably.

'All you have to do is agree to return to Blue Block, to the Black College and the Red Church, to complete your conditioning. Then you'll be one of us, and you won't want to fight us any more. You'll even bring Constance to us, so she can be conditioned too. And then both King and Queen will serve Blue Block, and follow our wishes in all things. It won't be nearly as bad as you think, you'll see. Now; agree to all this, and Constance is safe. Refuse, and . . .'

'I could lie to you.'

'No, you couldn't,' said Constance. 'Your existing conditioning won't let you. Once you've given your word to us, you'll be compelled to follow through. You'll have no choice. Now tell me you agree, or Kid Death's smiling face will be the last thing Constance ever sees.'

'Bullshit,' said Kit SummerIsle, and everyone turned sharply to look at him. Leaning back against the closed door, one hand resting on his swordbelt, his disturbing smile was aimed directly at Chantelle. 'This whole business is too ugly, even for me. I'm not going to kill Constance, or anyone else, on Blue Block's say-so. I've decided I'm not going to do things like that any more. I never did approve of Blue Block: two-faced, underhanded . . . They take all the fun out of killing. I've been doing a lot of thinking recently, about what David said and did on Virimonde. He meant a lot to me, and I don't think he'd approve of my working for cold-blooded creatures like you. And Robert reminds me a lot of David, my lovely Deathstalker. So; either Blue Block agrees to leave Robert and Constance alone, or I'll declare war on the whole damned organization. Starting with you two creeps. Right here, right now.'

There was a short, charged silence. Brendan swallowed audibly. 'Chantelle, I think he means it.'

'You can't defy Blue Block,' Chantelle said numbly to the SummerIsle, 'we're everywhere.'

Kid Death smiled his killer's smile, and Chantelle had to look away. Brendan's face had gone white, and he clasped his hands together to keep them from shaking.

'Game, set and match to me, I think,' said Robert, relief rushing through him like an incoming wave, washing away his tension. He laughed shortly, feeling almost light-headed. 'Kid Death was the only hope you had of getting to Constance, and with him on my side . . . Lord SummerIsle, I hereby invest you with the title of Warrior Prime to the Empire, and my official Champion. Your duty will be to identify and eliminate all threats to the Empire. Including Blue Block.'

'Official killer,' said the SummerIsle. 'I like it.'

'You can't make a psychopath like him Warrior Prime!' protested Brendan, honestly shocked.

'He may be a psychopath, but he'll be my psychopath,' said Robert. 'Cardinal, Chantelle, I don't think we have anything else to discuss. You played your hand, and I have trumped it with Kid Death. Cardinal; I need you to perform the ceremony, so you get to stick around. With Kid Death at your side to keep you in order, of course. After the wedding, I'll have the Elves take you somewhere private, and you can tell them everything you know about Blue Block. Chantelle; your services here today are no longer required. You may leave now. Arresting you would be a scandal big enough to disrupt even this grand occasion. It might even be momentous enough to mean putting off the wedding for another day, and I'm damned if I'm going through all this again. I'll give you a head start. If I were you, I'd start running right now.'

Chantelle was breathing hard, her eyes fixed on his. 'It's not that easy,' she said viciously. 'You're still Blue Block. And that means I own you, body and soul. Hey, Robert; *We all come home.*'

The long-implanted control words smashed through Robert's head like thunder, and he cried out in anguish as once again his will and self-control were swept away on the over-powering tide of his conditioning. His back snapped straight, his head came up and his face was utterly blank. He looked at Chantelle with empty eyes, and his mouth spoke someone else's words. 'Activation code acknowledged. Request status confirmation.'

'Hundred Hands confirmed!' Chantelle snapped, her face almost crimson with rage. 'Kill the SummerIsle! Do it now!'

Robert drew his ceremonial sword. It was bright and shiny with a jewelled hilt, designed almost entirely for show, but it had a point and an edge, and it would serve. Robert looked at Kid Death, who'd already drawn his sword. Robert started unhurriedly towards his designated target, and Chantelle laughed unpleasantly, a harsh and ugly sound.

'What will you do now, Kid Death? If you don't defend yourself, Robert will kill you. But if you kill him, the whole Empire will come together to hunt you down. What will you do now, SummerIsle?'

Kid Death smiled his killer's smile and lunged forward, impossibly quickly. He ducked under Robert's extended sword, the blade cutting away a chunk of his hair, and then his shoulder slammed into Robert's exposed gut. The impact of the collision threw them both to the floor, and while Robert lay curled around his hurt, trying to force air back into his lungs, the SummerIsle turned his fall into a forward roll and was quickly back on his feet, facing Chantelle. She drew a hidden dagger from her sleeve. Kid Death slapped it out of her hand, pushed her back against the wall hard enough to make her eyes roll up for a moment, and then put the edge of his sword against her throat. She froze in place, glaring at him over the threatening blade. Brendan started to move forward, but the SummerIsle stopped him with a look.

'Now,' said Kit SummerIsle, entirely unruffled and not even breathing fast, 'Release Robert from the control words, Chantelle, or I'll kill you.'

'You wouldn't dare!' said Chantelle, almost spitting at him in her fury. 'I'm Blue Block! You don't dare hurt me!'

'I'm Kid Death, and I don't give a damn. Release him.'

'Never!'

'Very well,' said Kid Death, and cut her throat with one swift sweep of his blade.

Blood flew from Chantelle's shocked mouth, as she clapped both hands to the awful wound at her throat, as though she could somehow hold the edges together. She made horrible sounds as the strength went out of her along with the spraying blood, and she slumped slowly to the floor, her back still pressed against the wall. Blood pumped between her fingers. Kid Death turned to face Brendan, blood still dripping from his sword. Robert was slowly getting to his feet, sword in hand.

'Release him from the control words,' said the SummerIsle calmly, 'or I'll kill you, Cardinal.'

'All right, damn you! All right! Robert; *Code Omega Three. Shut down! Shut down!*'

Robert's personality slammed back into his face as his will became his own again, and he stopped advancing on Kid Death. He shuddered uncontrollably for a moment, and then slowly put his sword away. Cardinal Brendan knelt beside the convulsing Chantelle, and took her in his arms. She fought him for a moment, lost in her own pain and horror, but as the last of her strength was leaving her, she finally recognized him and tried to say something. But all that came out of her mouth was a bloody froth, and she died before she could make him understand. Brendan hugged her dead body to him, his face wet with tears, her blood soaking into his official robes. Robert clapped the SummerIsle on the shoulder, and looked down at Brendan.

'Damn you,' Brendan said roughly, not looking up. 'You don't know what you've done.'

'It's over, Cardinal,' said Robert. 'You'll be arrested for treason, the moment the ceremony's over.'

'You think I care about that?' said Brendan, looking up at last, his tear-stained face full of loss and bitterness. 'Nothing matters now, nothing. You haven't just killed a woman. You've killed Blue Block itself. She was Blue Block. Just her.'

'What are you saying?' said Robert. 'How could one woman run something as huge and wide-ranging as Blue Block?'

'Because it isn't. Oh, it might have been once, long ago, but by the time Chantelle inherited control, Blue Block's glory days were long gone. What organization there was was mostly just mists and shadows. All it needed was a hint here, a rumour there, and sinister-sounding names like the Red Church and the Black College, and people's imagination did the rest. There are only about forty people left who actually do anything these days. Mostly they just implant conditioning in others so that they can be used as necessary, to foster the illusion and intimidate the Families they were taken from.'

Robert and Kit SummerIsle looked at each other, and then at Brendan. 'And the Hundred Hands?' said Robert.

'Oh, they're real enough. They were Chantelle's idea. Put them together a few at a time, wait until there were enough of them to frighten the Clans and then use them to pressure the Families into accepting the deal she made with Jack Random. And once the Clans had got used to taking orders . . . Just mists and shadows. And thoroughly conditioned public faces like BB Chojiro. People saw what they expected to see, and believed in the myth we so carefully propagated. Chantelle ran everything, unsuspected, hidden in plain sight. Just her.'

'So . . . who started Blue Block?' said Kit SummerIsle. 'Back when it really was something?'

'Giles Deathstalker. He set it all up before he went on the run in his Last Standing. His final revenge against his Emperor. A hidden force to strengthen the position of the Clans, and then to control them; an organization he could make use of, when he finally returned from stasis. But he slept so much longer than he intended, and down the centuries Blue Block rotted away from within. The Deathstalker must have been very disappointed when he found what had happened to his wonderful cabal. But he did make Blue Block possible. It was the old Empire tech they preserved that made such perfect mental conditioning a reality.'

'And who would ever suspect a social butterfly like Chantelle?' said Robert. 'But of course she went everywhere, heard everything, knew everybody's secrets. Who better to run a secret society based on bluff and blackmail?'

'And now she's gone,' said Brendan. 'And Blue Block dies with her. She was the only one who knew everything, all the code names and implanted control words.'

'Good riddance,' said Kit SummerIsle, watching unmoved as the cardinal lowered his head and wept over the dead woman in his arms.

'Did you love her?' said Robert.

'Of course I loved her,' said Brendan. 'She made us all love her.'

Up in the director's gallery, occupying part of Parliament's security centre, Toby Shreck and his assistants sat hunched over their control panels, watching the display of monitor screens showing what the cameramen down on the floor of the House and its antechamber were broadcasting. It was all going out live, with a few seconds' delay so that they could edit out any foul language, and the current viewing totals were bigger than anything Toby had ever known, even during the last days of the rebellion. Practically everyone in the Empire who had access to a holoscreen, and wasn't actually under attack, was watching his show. Toby couldn't stop grinning, even when his cheeks ached from the strain.

He spoke to his assistants at the control and mixing boards, switching from one camera to another as something interesting caught his eye. This close to the ceremony, it was up to him to impose some form of sense and structure on the sheer quantity of information being filmed. Anyone else would have been spoiled for choice, drowning in the volume of incoming picture and sound, but Toby Shreck's hard-won experience kept him firmly in control.

Every now and then he'd have a quiet word with his cameramen through their comm implants, telling them to concentrate on this person or that gathering, or when to pull back and look away, rather than show some unpleasant incident or expression of ill feeling that might distract from the general joy of the occasion. This wasn't a documentary, after all; this was supposed to be a morale-booster for Humanity, and for once Toby Shreck was following instructions. He knew how vital it was that everything be seen to go well. Besides, his cameras were recording a lot more than they were transmitting, and by rights it all belonged to him. Later on, he'd put together a life-in-the-raw, warts-and-all documentary that would really open people's eyes.

Assuming there was a later on . . .

On Toby Shreck's many screens, movers and shakers and aristocrats and celebrities clustered together, putting aside for one day at least old hatreds and animosities, as they waited impatiently for a wedding that would change the whole nature of the Empire yet again.

In the huge antechamber packed almost literally from wall to wall, the guests were growing restless. Overcome by the immensity of the occasion, and the increasingly sauna-like conditions, they'd been knocking back the complimentary champagne as fast as the circulating waiters could get it to them. Faces were becoming flushed, voices louder, opinions more vehement. Anyone even the least bit interesting was seized on by the guests to distract them from their boredom, the heat, and the impossibly long queues for the toilets. The actor who now played the part of the daredevil esper Julian Skye, in the continuing holo adventure show, was having a great time being fêted by one and all. The show was bigger than ever these days, and the star was a much better actor than the real Julian had ever been. The esper's sudden, tragic death had been widely misunderstood by just about everybody. Most assumed that it had been a lover's suicide pact with BB Chojiro; that the two lovebirds had chosen to die together rather than be separated by Julian's growing illness. Others spoke darkly of Chojiro and even of Blue Block conspiracies, and hinted that Julian had been murdered because he was becoming too popular, and had been ready to make dangerous public remarks about his time with BB. Either way, it was all Very Romantic. The public did so love a tragic hero. More rumours arose every day, each one wilder than the last, and Julian Skye's reputation grew ever more noble and heroic, now that he was safely gone and unable to set the record straight. The best legends have always been based on the dead.

Bruin Bear and the Sea Goat, those two most notable toys and ambassadors from Haceldama, had backed Donna Silvestri into a corner and were quietly and quite innocently driving her crazy. Evangeline had arranged for their invitations, partly as an excuse to see old friends again, and partly to demonstrate to the Empire that the infamous killer toys of Haceldama were now much more civilized. Unfortunately, most of Toby Shreck's films on Haceldama had been overlooked, due to the increasing coverage of the imminent rebellion, and as a result, it was the bad news that had stuck. Indeed, most of the wedding guests were openly petrified of Bruin Bear and the Sea Goat. The Bear honestly didn't notice, and was polite and charming to everyone, even as they babbled meaningless excuses and ran away from him. The Sea Goat had noticed, and was playing up to it for all he was worth by making pointed remarks that on the surface seemed perfectly straightforward, but which could also be taken for veiled threats. He'd also acquired a taste for champagne and terrorizing the waiters. Bruin Bear persisted in his attempts to be a good ambassador for the new Haceldama, while the Sea Goat kept baring his huge square teeth in a terrible smile, and pretending not to notice when people cringed back from him. The two toys had got Donna Silvestri in a corner, and she stared at them with wide terrified eyes as the Bear tried to make small talk with her.

Toby got it all on film. He'd never liked Donna Silvestri. After a while he weakened, and sent Flynn over to interview the two toys. Donna Silvestri seized her chance, gathered up her skirts and ran for her life. Bruin Bear waved after her, puzzled, while the Sea Goat sniggered into his champagne glass. Flynn chatted happily with the toys, sharing reminiscences of their time together on the abandoned pleasure planet, as everyone else in the antechamber watched, openly impressed by the cameraman's calm composure in the face of such danger. (They all snubbed Donna Silvestri, though, for being such a coward. And letting the side down in public.)

Unbeknown to Flynn or Toby Shreck, or indeed anybody else, Valentine Wolfe was also present in the antechamber. He moved calmly among the chattering throng, smiling and nodding to all, hidden behind a Shub hologram disguise that gave him the seeming appearance of a Sister of Mercy. His invitation, a quite impeccable forgery, said he was there to represent Mother Superior Beatrice, the Saint of Technos III, and now Lachrymae Christi. The Shub camera on his shoulder produced a faultless visual image, undetectable even at very close range, and modified his distinctive voice into that of an anonymous young woman. The illusion wouldn't have withstood the touch test, but who was going to touch a nun?

Valentine would have preferred to rely on his own minor esp abilities, rather than on a tech under someone else's control, but unfortunately that wasn't possible. His esp could have made him invisible, but the security Elves on the perimeter would have spotted him in a moment. And even if he could have found a way into the House, the living esp-blockers would have blown away his illusion at once. At least the Shub tech was clearly superior to any of the Empire's security devices. Under Shub's cloaking holo he could go anywhere, a ghost from the Empire's troubled past, a deadly spectre at the feast. He stood in the middle of the crowded antechamber, unnoticed and unchallenged, and smiled contentedly.

Of all the many disguises he could have chosen, the nun appealed to him most. He liked the outfit. Its stark black and white complemented his extreme nature. And he felt he had every right to be at the royal wedding, as a representative of the bride's Family. It wasn't every day your stepmother got married again. And as for masquerading as one of Saint Bea's nuns, well, Beatrice was still technically his fiancée. He was sure she'd understand. Once the terrible thing he planned to do was over, he'd have Shub seize Beatrice and bring her to him. The naughty little minx had put off their union for far too long. Valentine smiled. He forgave her – she was just playing hard to get. What's a few death threats between soulmates? He would wed her anyway, and on their wedding night he would show her such awful pleasures . . . And when she was dead, he'd do other things to her.

His plans for the royal wedding ceremony were simplicity itself. He was going to murder Robert and Constance, right there in front of everyone, and then declare himself Emperor. He hadn't actually told Shub that. They thought he was here as an observer. But no doubt it would come as a nice surprise to them. The nun holo would get him close to the happy couple, under the guise of bestowing a benediction from Saint Beatrice, and then a disrupter shot to Robert's smiling face, and a slashed throat for Constance, and that would be that. He was quite looking forward to the second murder. He'd always wanted to kill his beautiful stepmother. Pity there wasn't time to ravish her first, as one more spit in the eye for dear dead Daddy, but no plan was perfect. Maybe there'd be time afterwards. And if not, he'd settle for the look in her dying eyes as he finally dropped his disguise, so that she could know in her last moments just who had killed her and her Campbell lover.

A Wolfe, marrying a Campbell? Unthinkable. Someone had to preserve the old decencies.

Once they were dead, Valentine had no doubt the aristocracy would flock to support him. They'd always understood and appreciated real power. And he was the last scion of one of the grand old Families, extremely suitable to be Emperor. He would promise the Clans an alliance with Shub that would preserve both Humanity and the Clans' authority over it. A lie, of course, but the Families would believe it because they'd want to. And as Emperor, he would destroy the Empire as Shub never could, from within, tearing down its structures and trashing everything the people believed in. He would crush their spirit, reduce them all to mad animals feasting on each other, and then watch the Empire burn. He would delight in its death agonies, and dance in its screaming ruins. He'd always known that was his destiny.

And even if the aristocrats, or security, or anyone else were to rise up against him, it would do them no good. Shub had filled him full of nanotech, those clever little machines that could repair any damage to his body pretty much instantly. Finlay Campbell had shot him in the chest with a disrupter at point-blank range, and he'd survived, though admittedly it had taken the nanos a while to build him a new heart. Afterwards, he'd walked through the flames of the burning Tower Shreck with impunity, ignoring his roasting flesh, already planning his revenge. He was unstoppable now, unkillable, perhaps even immortal. And flying on every drug known to man, plus a few he'd had Shub whip up specially, just for him. Anyone else would have died from the extraordinary cocktail of chemicals circulating in his bloodstream, but Valentine took that as one more sign of his clear superiority. His mind was so sharp now he could out-think anyone. Or anything: let Shub beware.

All around him, people's faces and body language shouted volumes of information to his expanded senses. He was faster, stronger and more devious than any other mere mortal could hope to be. The only ones who might have stopped him weren't here. Jack Random and Ruby Journey were currently facing obliteration at the steel hands of the Shub armada, and Owen Deathstalker and Hazel d'Ark were already dead. A pity, that. He would have liked to talk with Owen, one last time. The Deathstalker was probably the one person who could have appreciated the terrible and wondrous thing Valentine had made of himself. And he would have enjoyed going one on one with Owen, sword to sword.

The Deathstalker had always been Valentine's greatest challenge. He deserved a better death, a better end to his legend than just missing in action, presumed dead. Valentine would have killed him with style and grace, giving Owen an exit so appalling people would have talked of it for centuries. Valentine licked his lips. Heroes always died so deliciously.

Off to one side, Flynn studied the Sister of Mercy through his camera, and tried to figure out what was wrong. His camera was state of the art, and was quite definitely picking up some kind of energy field, but he was damned if he could tell what. Of course, it could be just a malfunction, or even his reading the displays incorrectly . . . Flynn was always at least one manual behind whatever state of the art his camera happened to be in. He wondered vaguely if he should mention it to security, or Toby, and then the Shreck's voice was suddenly ringing loudly in his ear, demanding he pay attention to the argument growing between two female celebrities who had unfortunately chosen the same outfit, from a supposedly exclusive fashion guru. Flynn immediately sent his camera flying towards the trouble spot, and hurried after it as best he could. Real news always took priority.

Finally, it was time. The great double doors swung open, and everyone in the antechamber surged forward on to the floor of the House. Strategically placed security Elves kept any fighting for position to a minimum. No one wanted to risk being excluded from the ceremony. The happy couple were already in place, magnificent in their traditional attire, standing together on the raised dais that had once held the Speaker's chair. Cardinal Brendan stood before them, ready to perform the wedding, and then oversee the coronation. He hadn't wanted to, but Kit SummerIsle had made it clear that he would kill the cardinal very slowly if he didn't, and Brendan had no doubt at all that the SummerIsle meant it. He stood in his place, in a new gown, holding his prayer book to his chest like a shield, and tried not to look at Kid Death, standing quietly to one side.

The floor of the House was packed solid, shoulder to shoulder, as Robert Campbell and Constance Wolfe took their vows. Their voices rang in a profound silence, the guests all but holding their breath to avoid missing even a moment, and the whole Empire watched and listened. The cardinal ran smoothly through the service, and Robert and Constance's voices were firm and steady. The choir sang beautifully, and rose petals rained down from the galleries. Delicate rainbows shone through the stained-glass windows. An almost completely overwhelmed page brought forward the ceremonial golden cord on its platter. Constance calmed him with a smile, and his hands were steady as he held the platter out to the cardinal. Brendan took the cord and wrapped it loosely round their wrists, symbolically binding them together. At that point Crow Jane of the Elves stepped forward, cold and magisterial as the occasion demanded, to probe the minds of the bride and groom, as tradition required, and declared that both were exactly who they claimed to be. There was only the slightest pause as she did this, but to Robert it seemed to last for ever. He lived again the terrible events that had followed this part of the ceremony at his first wedding. For a moment he thought he might faint. The Unknown Clone saw him sway slightly on his feet, and grabbed Robert firmly but surreptitiously by the arm, to steady him.

All went well. Crow Jane proclaimed their true identities in a ringing voice, and Robert's quiet sigh of relief went unnoticed as the cardinal raised his voice to declare them now man and wife. Robert kissed his bride, remembering at the very last moment to lift her veil first, and the whole audience cheered, both in the House and across the Empire. Flynn was right there with his camera, getting it all. Two Members of Parliament, chosen strictly by lot, came forward with the two newly made crowns, simple golden circlets encrusted with the Empire's most precious and radiant stones. Robert and Constance knelt before them, and were crowned King and Queen at the hands of the people. The two crowns were lowered simultaneously on to their heads, to demonstrate that King and Queen were equal in power and status. The two constitutional monarchs rose to their feet and smiled out over the people, and everyone cheered again, and again and again, as though they might never stop.

The wedding banquet afterwards was a loud, noisy and altogether more relaxed affair. There was no room for seats, so everyone just grabbed a plate and some cutlery, and fended for themselves. It was first come first served, and God help those at the back. Robert and Constance made the rounds, smiling and shaking hands, and making sure everyone had enough to eat. There was the traditional cake, twelve tiers high, and enough champagne to float a medium-sized ship, and an apparently endless buffet table almost collapsing under the weight of cuisine and delicacies from a hundred worlds. It took a while for Robert and Constance to get anywhere; everyone wanted to pay their compliments to the new King and Queen, and to be seen doing it on holo. Politics never takes a holiday. But still it was a time of happy chatter and loud laughter, with good humour and good fellowship for all.

Or very nearly. Kit SummerIsle had been quietly following the royal couple on their rounds, at a discreet distance, when he spotted a familiar but unexpected face in the crowd. He paused just long enough to be sure that Crow Jane and the Unknown Clone were watching over the new monarchs, and then he moved quickly through the press of bodies to intercept his target. The man had a new name and title now, as Sir Sleyton du Bois, but that wasn't how Kit knew him. Sir Sleyton had once been the Steward of David Deathstalker's Standing on Virimonde. The Steward had been sworn to David's service, but instead had betrayed his master to the Lord High Dram's forces when they invaded the green planet. Because of the Steward's betrayal, the castle Standing had fallen, and David died in Kit's arms. Kit had never forgotten that.

He'd lost track of the Steward during the upheavals of the last days of the rebellion, but he had never given up the search. Eventually he discovered that Lionstone had rewarded the Steward with a new name and a minor title. There were a lot of those after the rebellion, but Kit was patient. He'd known a social climber like the Steward would be unable to miss the royal wedding. And sure enough, here he was, bold as brass. The SummerIsle came to a sudden halt in front of the ex-Steward, and took a certain cold satisfaction in watching all the colour drain out of the man's face.

'Ah, Steward,' he said calmly, 'so good to see you again, after all this time. I thought I'd lost you, but every bad penny turns up eventually.'

'You can't touch me,' said Sir Sleyton du Bois. 'I have a new life now. Aristocratic friends, influence, protection . . .'

'I know who and what you are,' said Kit SummerIsle. 'I am now Warrior Prime to the Empire, charged by the King himself with hunting down and dealing with traitors. Come with me, traitor.'

He dropped an apparently friendly hand on to Sir Sleyton's shoulder, and his fingers dug harshly into an exposed nerve there. The ex-Steward grimaced, but made no move to resist as the SummerIsle steered him through the crowds and into the adjoining kitchens. A few people looked at them askance, but no one said anything. The SummerIsle half threw his captive into the kitchens, and carefully shut the swinging doors behind him. The kitchen staff fell back, abandoning their responsibilities. They knew who Kit SummerIsle was. The ex-Steward backed away, rubbing almost childishly at the pain in his shoulder.

'I have position. I could do a lot for you. I have money, I could make you rich. I could—'

'Can you raise the dead?' said Kit.

'What . . . ?'

'I thought not. And you have nothing else I want. I've waited a long time for this moment, Steward.'

Sir Sleyton du Bois turned and tried to run, but Kid Death

was upon him before he managed more than a few steps. He dragged the ex-Steward over to a great brimming punch bowl, bent him over and then thrust the man's head down into the punch till it covered his ears. The ex-Steward kicked and struggled, but Kit held him down with an iron grip. The kitchen staff watched, horrified, but no one even thought of interfering with Kid Death. It took a while for the ex-Steward to drown, but Kit was in no hurry. Finally the bubbles stopped rising to the surface of the punch, and the ex-Sir Sleyton du Bois was still. Kit held him under a while longer, smiling gently, and then let him go. The dead body fell to the floor, eyes staring, mouth wide, lungs full of the most expensive punch.

'For you, David,' Kit said quietly, 'my love.'

Back on the floor of the House, Cardinal Brendan had been called away to speak with a young Sister of Mercy, who had an urgent message from Saint Beatrice. The cardinal had been happy to leave, glad of any excuse that would allow him to disappear while the SummerIsle wasn't around and watching. He didn't have long to enjoy that happiness, though. The smiling young nun steered him into one of the empty private rooms, locked the door behind him, produced a wicked-looking knife and slid it between the cardinal's ribs with practised skill. Brendan sank to the floor, too shocked even to cry out, both hands clasped to his side as though he could somehow hold in the life that was escaping from him along with the gushing blood. He lived just long enough to see the holo disguise drop away, revealing the smiling face of the great traitor himself, Valentine Wolfe, and then he died. Valentine laughed softly, and reconfigured the holo camera on his shoulder so that he now appeared to be Cardinal Brendan. The damned Elf security had kept him well away from the actual ceremony, despite the young nun's most tearful blandishments, but no one would stop Cardinal Brendan. What could be more natural than for the cardinal who had married Robert and Constance to wish to pay his compliments to the new King and Queen? And once he was close enough . . . One disrupter blast, one slashed throat and it would all be over, with no time for anyone to do anything. And then the fun would really begin.

Valentine sailed happily out of the private room, leaving Brendan's dead body lying on the floor, and made his way briskly through the crowds, heading straight for the happy couple like a shark that's just scented blood in the water. His holo disguise was perfect, and no one gave him a second look. His heart beat rapidly as he bore down on the King and Queen, and they turned to meet him, entirely unsuspecting. There was a news cameraman nearby, and Valentine beckoned to him imperiously. He wanted the whole Empire to see what he was about to do.

Flynn nodded quickly to the cardinal, and hurried forward to get a better shot. But when he looked through his camera, he saw again the same vague distortion he'd seen earlier around the young Sister of Mercy. He swore silently, and wondered if he'd have to dismantle the whole damned camera to find out what the problem was. There couldn't be anything wrong with the broadcast signal, or Toby would have been yelling in his ear by now. Flynn looked at the apparent energy field again. He still wasn't sure what he was seeing. He ran quickly through the camera's most recent update menus, searching for possibilities, and then lost his cool completely as the camera told him that the most likely answer was a holo disguise. Flynn looked at the scene through his own eyes, saw how close the cardinal was to the King and Queen, and how far away the nearest Elves were, and did the only thing he could. He yelled a warning and sent his camera shooting forward at full speed. It locked on to the holo signal and crashed right into the hidden camera on the cardinal's shoulder, knocking it away. Once out of contact with its user, the camera's holo field collapsed, and suddenly there was Valentine Wolfe, with scarlet mouth and mascaraed eyes, and a gun and knife in his hands.

There were shouts and screams as people shrank back from him. Valentine looked around him, startled, only slowly realizing what must have happened. Elves came running from all directions. Robert moved quickly to stand between his bride and this new danger, his ceremonial sword at the ready before him. Valentine laughed softly and raised his gun. Robert stood his ground, protecting Constance with his own body. The Elves struggling through the packed crowd lashed out with their minds, but Valentine's own esp was just strong enough to confuse them, and their attacks went wide. Valentine's gun centred on Robert's chest.

'Everybody stop right where they are,' he said brightly, and the Elves reluctantly slowed to a halt. Valentine looked at Robert with fever-bright eyes, and licked his lips. 'Give me your crown,' he said calmly. 'You know it really should be mine. And it's only fitting that a King should give way to an Emperor.'

'Mad as ever, Valentine,' said Robert. 'No one wants an Emperor any more, especially not you. Kill me, and you'll never leave here alive.'

'Oh, I think I will. Nothing can kill me now. I've moved far beyond such human weaknesses. I'm glad it's come down to you and me, in the end. How very fitting, after all this time, that the last real Campbell should meet his end at the hands of the last real Wolfe.'

'Not even close, Valentine,' said the Unknown Clone, pushing forward to stand at Robert's side. He reached up and pulled off his mask, and the whole crowd gasped as they recognized the grim face of Finlay Campbell. Valentine nodded slowly.

'Well met, old enemy. Aren't you supposed to be dead?'

'You're a fine one to talk. I thought I'd finally got rid of you in Tower Shreck.'

Valentine made a negligent gesture. 'I don't do the dying thing any more. I cannot be stopped by anyone.'

'Really?' said Finlay. 'Let's test that.' His sword lashed out with dizzying speed, and the tip raked across the back of

Valentine's hand, severing the tendons. Valentine's fingers opened automatically, and the disrupter dropped from his hand. The tendons knitted back together again almost immediately, and Valentine quickly brought his sword into position as Finlay advanced on him. He smiled at Robert.

'Bet I can pick up my gun and use it before you or your cow can run three paces,' he said brightly. 'So stay put, and watch the show. I'll get round to you. But first . . . the two true inheritors of Clan Wolfe and Clan Campbell, locked in mortal combat one last time. Ah, Finlay . . . how proud our fathers would be of us.'

'Shut up and fight,' said Finlay.

They both moved forward, their swords clashing together and then springing apart as they circled each other, their arms moving so fast they were little more than a blur. Valentine had been trained in swordsmanship by the finest tutors Wolfe money could buy, but Finlay had been the Masked Gladiator, undefeated champion of the Golgotha Arenas. The fight had hardly begun before Finlay tricked the Wolfe into lowering his guard for just a moment, and then the Campbell stepped forward in an extended lunge and ran Valentine through. His sword slammed into Valentine just under the breastbone, and burst out of his back in a flurry of blood, a perfect killing blow. But Valentine didn't fall. He coughed delicately, and a little blood sprayed from his mouth, but his dark eyes never wavered. And while Finlay still held his extended lunge, confused, Valentine thrust his own sword into Finlay's belly. Powered by Shub-driven strength, Valentine's blade punched right through Finlay's armour, burying itself deep in his gut. Finlay cried out and fell backwards, clutching at the bloody wound with both hands as Valentine withdrew his blade. Dark blood pulsed thickly between his fingers. Valentine pulled Finlay's sword out of his own body, and let it fall to the floor. The wound healed almost immediately, closed and sealed by Shub nanotech. Evangeline and Adrienne grabbed Finlay and dragged him away. There was a regeneration machine on standby in one of the private rooms. The Elves had insisted.

Valentine looked unhurriedly about him. 'Anyone else? No? Well then, as I was saying, before I was so rudely interrupted—'

'Get away from the King,' said a cold, merciless voice, and everyone turned to look as Kit SummerIsle came striding through the crowd. Valentine nodded thoughtfully and lifted his sword, but made no move to pick up his gun. He could have, any time, and everyone knew it, but he was having far too much fun. He did so love to tease his enemies. He bowed lightly as Kid Death came to a halt before him, sword in hand.

'Typical,' said the SummerIsle. 'I take my eye off the ball for a few moments, and everything goes to hell. Come on, Wolfe. Let's do it. You know you want to.'

'Why not?' said Valentine easily. 'Always time for a little pleasure before business.'

They came together in a flurry of flashing blades and stamping feet, both showing their teeth in smiles that had no true humour in them. Again the fight was fast and furious, but Kit had had time to see Finlay's mistake, and kept his distance. Since running the Wolfe through clearly didn't work, Kid Death concentrated on whittling away at his opponent, cutting and slicing at the Wolfe's pale flesh, but the wounds sealed themselves as fast as they were inflicted, and if Valentine felt any pain it didn't bother him in the least. Kit parried Valentine's blows with almost arrogant skill and ease, but he couldn't help noticing that the attacks were coming faster and stronger all the time, almost inhumanly fast. Kit held his ground anyway. He didn't back away. He knew there was nowhere to go. His calm killer's mind assessed the situation logically. He couldn't hurt or harm the Wolfe, so that just left . . . He grinned suddenly, chose the time and angle of blow carefully, and cut off Valentine's sword arm right at the elbow, with a tremendous double-handed swing that drew admiring cries from the crowd. The severed arm fell to the floor, still clutching the sword.

For a moment, no one moved. Valentine looked down at his severed arm, as the uncurling fingers let go of the hilt. A few drops of blood fell from the stump of his arm, and then stopped. And then Valentine laughed softly, a terribly sane and confident laugh, and four fingers and a thumb thrust out of the stump at his elbow. A hand followed, and then the forearm, and in a moment Valentine was whole again. He stooped down and picked up his sword, kicked aside the severed arm and gestured for Kit to come at him again. Kid Death raised his sword, thinking hard.

But even as their swords reached out to touch again, the Elves hit Valentine with everything they had. They'd been edging carefully forward through the crowd for some time, getting as close to Valentine as they could without being noticed. As long as Robert and Constance were in danger from Valentine, they hadn't dare start anything, but now that his concentration seemed wholly on Kid Death, Crow Jane gave a telepathic signal and a psistorm of violent energies hit the Wolfe from a dozen different directions at once. One polter grabbed the gun and whisked it away, while six others did their best to tear Valentine apart. Psychokinetic flames sprang up around him, burning so fiercely that everyone had to back away. Telepaths probed and picked at the locked doors of his mind. Valentine stood his ground, nanotech rebuilding his body faster than it could be destroyed, and laughed and laughed and laughed.

Robert and Constance stood their ground too, though voices and clutching hands tried to persuade them to flee. They knew they couldn't run. The whole Empire was watching, and the new King and Queen couldn't be seen to be weak.

And when the psistorm finally collapsed, the Elves shattered and exhausted, and the last flames had died away, Valentine Wolfe was still standing there, apparently untouched. He stopped laughing and looked studiedly around him. 'Everybody finished? Everybody had their turn? Good. Now that you all know I'm unstoppable, unkillable and quite possibly immortal, who could be a more sensible choice as Emperor? You know in your hearts that I'm what you really need. What you deserve.' He turned slowly to face Robert and Constance. 'Now,' he said, almost greedily. 'Time to play . . .'

Kit SummerIsle started forward again, and Valentine slapped him aside with one sweep of his arm. Kit flew backwards into the crowd and disappeared. Valentine advanced on the grim-faced but unmoving Robert. And then Daniel Wolfe appeared out of nowhere, teleporting in to stand beside his brother. Valentine glared at him. 'What the hell are you doing here? I don't need any help, from you or Shub. This is my business. Don't you dare interfere.'

Daniel ignored him, looking out at the speechless crowd. 'I speak for Shub,' he said, in a voice that was not entirely his own. 'The war between the AIs and Humanity is now over. Peace has been declared. Shub has surrendered. The AIs have called off all their forces and recalled their armada, to turn them against our mutual enemies, the Hadenmen and the Recreated. Examine your communications, and you will find proof of what I say. The nanotech plague is also at an end. The nanos have been rendered inert. The AIs cannot restore those already destroyed, but there will be no more victims. The long war between us is over. Let us rejoice!' Daniel turned to Valentine. 'Only you remain, brother; one last piece of unfinished business. I asked for the privilege of shutting you down, now that I am my own man again, and they agreed. So goodbye, Valentine. Enjoy your time in Hell.'

And with those words, every piece of Shub nanotech in Valentine's body ceased to function. All his wounds burst open at once, and Valentine fell screaming to the bloodied floor, as much in shock as in pain. He'd been so close to winning everything. In moments he was soaked in his own blood, as he writhed helplessly at the feet of those he'd wanted so much to see crawling before him. He tried to lift his sword, to strike one last blow for spite's sake, but there was no strength left in him. He bled to death, and no one made a move to save him. In the end, nothing remained in the sundered, bloody carcase of the once elegant Valentine Wolfe. When it was over, Daniel bowed formally to Constance.

'Hello, stepmother. I'm home at last. Congratulations on your wedding. Hope you like the present I brought. I'm sure my father would look favourably on your new life. Shub never really had him, you know. They only had his body; his spirit has always been at rest.'

'I always knew that,' said Constance. 'I'm glad you've come to know that too. Welcome home, Daniel. What the hell happened to the AIs? Is the war really over?'

'Oh, yes. Diana Vertue . . . opened their minds to new possibilities. Shub are our allies now.'

Captain Eden Cross appeared suddenly on a floating viewscreen, hanging above everyone's heads, breaking through security on an emergency channel. 'This is Captain Cross of the *Excalibur*. Since Shub is no longer a threat, we're going to face the Recreated. But my ship is the only survivor of my fleet, and it's in terrible shape. The Last Standing isn't much better off. We're calling in every vessel we've got, and Shub is sending everything they've got to back us up, but the sheer size of the Recreated fleet is almost unimaginable. We can't hope to stop them on our own. We need help. We need every ship that can fly and aim a gun. And we need every able man and woman left to crew them. This message is being broadcast across all Golgotha. If you can hear my voice, your Empire needs you. This will be the last great battle for the survival of Humanity. Live or die, the fate of our species will be decided this day. It's time to make our stand.'

The screen went blank and disappeared, and there was a long silence. Robert Campbell raised his voice, and all eyes turned to him. 'You heard the man. We're all needed. I'm reinstating myself as Captain and taking my old ship out to face the Recreated. Let every man and woman here for whom duty and honour are more than just words, follow me. No ship is too small, no aid too slight. We must fight, or fall, together. And if we fall, let whoever or whatever remains to write the history books declare: This was Humanity's finest hour.'

He strode out of the House, Constance at his side, and in ones and twos, and then in great streams, everyone in the House followed them out to join the last great army of the light against the fall of darkness. Even the barely recovered Finlay Campbell, fresh out of the regeneration machine, brought up the rear, leaning heavily on Evangeline and Adrienne.

By the time Toby Shreck made his way down from the control gallery, only Flynn was left, checking his camera for damage.

'Tell me you got all that, Flynn!'

'Every second, boss, going out live to every planet in the Empire. Damn; if everyone else follows King Robert's lead, we're going to have an Imperial fleet of a size not seen since the days of the old Empire!'

'Damn right,' said Toby. 'And we're going to be part of it. I've commandeered a news ship, and it's waiting for us on the Parliament landing pads. I'm not missing out on the biggest story of my career.'

They both looked round sharply at a sudden noise behind them, and there was Kit SummerIsle, Kid Death, staggering out of one of the private rooms, bleeding from a dozen terrible wounds. They started towards him, and he tried to say something to them, but he collapsed, betrayed by his own body. Toby knelt beside him, looking almost in awe at the wounds killing the most notorious assassin the Empire had ever known. None of them were down to Valentine; the Wolfe hadn't been able to touch him. The whole of Kit's body was soaked in blood, and one of his eyes had been cut out of his head.

'Who did this to you?' said Toby. 'Who the hell could have done this to you?'

Kit tried to say something, but his mouth was full of blood. He said something that might have been *David*, and then he died. Toby and Flynn looked at each other over his body, and then went cautiously to search the room Kid Death had staggered out of, but it was empty, though there was a lot of blood on the floor, and two sets of bloody bootprints. They checked all the other rooms, but they were empty too. If there still remained some secret, unknown traitor and killer, there was no sight or sound of him to be found. In the end Toby and Flynn just shrugged, left the House and went to board their ship, to join the last great fleet of Humanity in battle against its last great enemy – the Recreated.

CHAPTER SEVEN

The Last Deathstalker

Among the dust of forgotten suns, in a darkness that no longer knew the light and life of stars, Owen Deathstalker and Hazel d'Ark came again to the Wolfling World, once also known as lost Haden, in their ship the *Sunstrider III*. Deep in the Darkvoid, everything was as still and silent as the grave, though forever troubled by unquiet spirits. But in many ways, this long-neglected return felt to Owen and Hazel very much like coming home. In the mysterious depths of the frozen planet beneath them, they had walked through the Madness Maze, and emerged reborn as something new in the universe. Since that time they had done many things, some good and some bad, but all of them quite remarkable. They had rewritten the history of the Empire and of Humanity itself, and all it had cost them was control of their own lives, and of their destiny.

Once, there had been five remarkable people, survivors of the Madness Maze, but now three of them were dead. Giles Deathstalker, that legendary hero and warrior, died at the hands of his own descendant, while Jack Random and Ruby Journey, lovers and rivals to the end, had died at each other's hand. Owen and Hazel knew this the moment they dropped out of hyperspace and the *Sunstrider III* took up its pre-programmed orbit around the Wolfling World. There had always been a strong mental link between the Maze survivors, neglect it as they would, and Owen and Hazel both cried out as the knowledge crashed in upon them like the sudden amputation of part of their soul. Jack and Ruby had been their friends and more than friends, despite their many differences: comrades-in-arms and kindred spirits, and Owen and Hazel knew that for as long as they lived, there would always be a space in their hearts, for ever unfilled, and a gap in their lives no one else would ever be able to make good.

'We're the last now,' said Owen, sitting slumped in the bridge command chair, looking at the central viewscreen but not seeing it. The screen showed the shimmering icy surface of the planet below, all subdued blues and greens, but his thoughts were elsewhere. 'The last of our kind. I feel like the last of a species doomed to extinction.'

'I don't,' said Hazel shortly, sitting at his side, her eyes also carefully fixed on the viewscreen. 'The Empire has no shortage of freaks and superhumans and general weird shit these days. That's always been a part of the problem, to my mind, Humanity getting above itself. Messing about with powers and abilities it has no business even knowing about yet. We're not ready to be gods.'

Owen considered this. 'Are you saying you won't miss Jack and Ruby?'

'Of course I'll miss them! Ruby was my oldest friend. She believed in me when no one else did, not even me. She always knew that we were somebody, that we were destined for great things . . . You only ever knew her as a bounty hunter and a killer. I knew her when she was so much more than that, before the world ground her down. You never knew what she lost, what she gave up, to become who and what she was. Her whole life was a tragedy just waiting for a bad and bitter ending. But I never thought she'd die so young . . . and at the hands of the only man she ever loved.'

'Jack Random was always one of my heroes,' said Owen. 'Studying history soon disillusions you about most heroes and legends, but Jack really did do most of the things they said he did. He gave his whole life to a cause, and never once looked back. Even after they broke him, and he was safe being a nobody on Mistworld, he still found the strength to recreate himself, to be the hero and legend again, to risk his life and his sanity one more time because the cause needed him. And because I asked him to. I'm responsible for everything he became, and everything he did. The good and the bad.'

'Now that is just typical of you, Deathstalker,' said Hazel, turning to look at him at last, 'trying to take everyone's burdens on your shoulders. Jack Random was responsible for his own life and his own madness, at the end. Ruby too. Whatever they did, and whatever end they came to, it was by their own choice and their own will. Just like ours will, when our time comes. To believe anything else diminishes them, and us.'

Owen looked at her. 'Our time? Have you been having those precognitive dreams again? Is there something about our being here I should know?'

'No,' said Hazel firmly. 'We have enough real threats to worry about without bringing in my dreams. Make yourself useful for a change; see if you can raise the Wolfling down below. I can't help feeling we're really vulnerable here in orbit, if there are any of the Recreated left in the Darkvoid.'

Owen nodded and turned to the comm panels. Hazel watched him, scowling, and wondered why she was so reluctant to tell him about the dream she'd once had of her future. Of standing alone on the bridge of the *Sunstrider II*, while all hell broke out around her. Huge alien forces attacking from every side, strange ships and awful creatures beyond counting, nightmares let loose in the waking world, blowing the *Sunstrider II* apart for all its shields and defences. Fires burning the length of the ship, alarms sounding endlessly, and the ship's guns firing again and again and again. Below her, the Wolfling World. And no sign of Owen anywhere.

Now she'd come at last to the place of the dream, but she didn't speak of it to Owen because the details were no longer accurate. The *Sunstrider II* was destroyed, crashed and ruined on the leper world of Lachrymae Christi. All that remained of that ship was its unique stardrive, built into a hijacked Church ship. The new *Sunstrider III* didn't even have any guns. That meant the dream was now impossible. She was safe from the overwhelming horror she'd felt, of the terrible, inevitable doom she'd felt closing in around her. And no trace of Owen anywhere . . . Clearly the dream had just been a dream. That was why she kept quiet about it, or so she told herself. But the Wolfling World lay cold and silent beneath the ship, like a pale, ghostly harbinger of bad things to come.

We are the last of the Maze people, she thought tiredly. *The last of the great rebel leaders. And just maybe the last hope of Humanity. Why does destiny always land most heavily on the shoulders of those who feel least capable of handling the burden?*

She looked around suddenly when a familiar voice spoke from the viewscreen, and it wasn't the Wolfling. The screen was filled with the head and shoulders of Diana Vertue. She looked tired and strained and subtly different, and it took Hazel a moment to realize that Diana didn't look like herself any more. Her mouth was a grim, flat line and her eyes were dangerously dark and staring. A disturbing sense of menace and barely channelled madness surrounded her like a halo of flies. She looked like her old self – the deadly esper saint, Jenny Psycho.

'It's all gone wrong,' she said sharply. Her voice was painfully rough and harsh again, sounding just as it had when she damaged her throat screaming her sanity away in Wormboy Hell. 'We hit the Recreated fleet with everything we had and barely slowed it down. I helped the massmind of the Mater Mundi join with our new allies, the AIs of Shub, and together we tried to force mental contact with the Recreated; to shock them awake and sane, as we did with Shub. But it didn't even come close to working. Contact . . . wasn't possible. The Recreated are too strong, too angry, too insane, too strange. It was like staring into a sun that never stops screaming. Whatever the Recreated are, they're far beyond anything we can hope to comprehend or deal with.

'The *Mater Mundi* is in shock, blasted back into its component parts, reeling on the edge of sanity. No use to us, at least for the time being. Just touching the edges of such furious, deranged thought was enough to shatter the esper union. I had to become Jenny Psycho again, in self-defence. It was the only way to deal with such a threat to my . . . my soul. If I think too much about what I . . . what I saw, and felt, I think I'd start screaming too, and never stop. Shub came off best, because they couldn't manage any kind of contact; the sheer weirdness of the Recreated had no common ground with their logic. That protected the AIs from the psychic backlash. Right now, everyone who can fly a ship or aim a gun is charging down the throat of the Recreated fleet, weapons blazing. We're trying to slow them down, to buy you some time to pull one last miracle out of the hat. But don't take too long to come up with something, Deathstalker, d'Ark; every minute we buy for you is being paid for with human lives and suffering.

'But you're not alone. Captain Silence and the *Dauntless* should be there with you by now. Try to forget old enmities, Deathstalker. Humanity is in dire need of help, and we don't much care where it comes from.'

The signal suddenly became blurred and distorted, Jenny Psycho looking back sharply over her shoulder at something off-screen. For a moment, Owen and Hazel could hear the horrid, never-ending scream of the Recreated in the background, and then the signal was shut down from the other end. Owen shuddered briefly, unnerved by the very sound. He would have liked to say something comforting to Jenny, but he had no idea what. What can you say when the fate of your whole species lies in your hands, and you don't have one damned clue what to do? Owen chewed the inside of his cheek, scowling thoughtfully. He hadn't come into the Darkvoid again to fight Humanity's last battle; he'd returned to the Wolfling World to deal with old, unfinished business. The Madness Maze, long thought destroyed, was now back, apparently, and the baby in the crystal at the heart of the

Maze was waking up. The last time he'd awoken he'd put out a thousand suns in a moment, destroyed billions of lives and created the Darkvoid, and Owen felt he had a responsibility to return and do what he could. If only because, as Giles's clone, the baby was Family.

But now Silence and the *Dauntless* were on their way too, and that complicated things. Owen had no doubt as to why the good captain had been sent into the Darkvoid again. Parliament wanted that legendary weapon, the Darkvoid Device, to use against the Recreated. It was an obvious, if desperate, gamble. But Parliament and Silence had no way of knowing that the Device was just a baby, only a few weeks old, beyond any hope of manipulation or control. The one time Giles had tried to use the baby's powers to deal with a few rebel planets, he had become responsible for the worst case of mass murder in human history. Who knew what the baby might do, if he was allowed to wake again?

'Well?' said Hazel, not liking the silence or the look on Owen's face. 'Are we going to contact the *Dauntless*?'

'Not just yet, I think,' said Owen. 'We know far more about the Maze and the Device than Silence does, so that makes us far better equipped to deal with them. I think we need to get down there first and appraise the situation, before Silence and his people arrive to confuse the hell out of things. I mean, all we know is what the Wolfling told us. He could be mistaken, or lying. Or . . .'

'Or?'

'Precisely. I'll move us into a suitable low orbit, where we'll be less easily detected. Moon gave us good shields. You try again to raise the Wolfling on the comm.'

Hazel shrugged, and turned back to the comm panels. She hadn't forgotten the last time Silence came to the Wolfing World, in pursuit of the price on their heads, and ended up destroying the Madness Maze as well as trying to kill her and the other Maze people. They'd all made a kind of peace over Lionstone's body, in the Hell she'd made of her Court, but that had been politics, nothing more, and they'd all been careful to maintain a respectful distance ever since. Some wounds and divisions can only be healed by time. Lots of it.

Owen moved the *Sunstrider III* into low orbit, his mind meshing easily with the ship's computer systems through his comm link, operating the navigation systems directly by his thoughts. When Moon rebuilt the *Sunstrider III* around the old ship's stardrive, he'd included many typical Hadenman touches, and hadn't been able to resist bringing the computers up to his own more-than-human standards. Once, Owen would have needed an AI to interface between his thoughts and the computers, to avoid unfortunate foul-ups through drifting attention, but Owen had moved on since then, and a more disciplined mind was only one of the changes the Maze continued to work in him. That said, he still missed Oz.

He settled the ship into a suitable orbit, raised all the shields, carefully disengaged his mind from the computers and turned to Hazel. She'd pushed her chair back from the comm panels and was shaking her head angrily. She glared at Owen and folded her arms sulkily across her chest.

'He must be able to hear us, but he's not answering. If I put any more power into the comm signal, the planet would start to melt. Maybe he's mad at us for not getting here sooner. Hell, maybe the baby woke up and disappeared him. We've no way of knowing what's going on down there!'

'No,' said Owen slowly, 'I think we'd know if the baby was awake. Either we'd feel it, or the universe might just start unravelling around us. As long as reality persists undisturbed, I think we can assume the baby is still safely sleeping. Wulf's probably just being precious; keeping us waiting till he's ready to talk to us. He never did have much use for humans.'

'Well, we did wipe out all his species but him,' said Hazel. 'That had to make an impression. Giles was the only human the Wolfling ever had any time for, and you killed him.'

'Quite,' said Owen. 'Let us hope fervently that he doesn't bear grudges. In the meantime, we'd better change our clothes. Our present attire, apart from being decidedly bloody and tattered from our time among the Blood Runners, is entirely unsuitable for the chilly environs of the caverns deep within the Wolfling World.'

'You know, you can be really fussy sometimes,' said Hazel, following Owen reluctantly into the cramped lounge area behind the bridge. 'I mean, the Wolfling isn't going to care what we look like.'

'I care,' said Owen firmly, opening the clothes locker and rooting dubiously through the limited selection. 'I am the Deathstalker, and I will not appear before the Wolfling looking like some tramp. It's a question of dignity.'

Hazel sniffed loudly, and decided to reject the first three things Owen showed her, on principle. There wasn't that much choice, the locker's stock being limited to what Moon and Owen had been able to acquire from Saint Bea's Mission and the original Church ship, but eventually Owen and Hazel settled on clothing they could both live with, topped with heavy cloaks to keep out the cold. Hazel paused briefly as Owen swung his cloak about him, and admired himself in the locker's full-length mirror. The hackles on her neck were standing up. She'd seen Owen in that cloak before – on the two occasions when he'd appeared suddenly out of nowhere, first to save her life in the Standing on Virimonde, and then again later in the Mission to try to warn her about the Blood Runners. He'd been wearing these very clothes, but had looked tired and hurt and desperate. A slow chill wrapped itself around Hazel's heart as she began to understand what that meant, what it had to mean . . .

She might have said something, but suddenly every alarm on the bridge went off at once. Owen and Hazel ran back on to the bridge and bent over the control panels, looking for trouble. Nothing was obviously wrong, until Owen thought to check the sensor readings.

'It's a proximity warning,' he said slowly. 'Something's coming our way . . . something big. And it's moving bloody quickly.'

'Could it be Silence, on the *Dauntless*?' said Hazel, one hand dropping automatically to the gun at her hip.

'I don't think so. The sensor readings make no sense at all. I'm switching to long range. That should put something on the viewscreen.'

Shapes began to appear on the screen, and Owen sucked in a sharp breath. Hazel was strangely silent, moving to stand as close as she could to Owen. On the viewscreen, the great shapes were gathering beyond the Wolfling World like vultures over something dying. Huge ships, the size of mountains or small moons, with insane structures and convoluted shapes that sucked the eye in uneasy directions. There seemed no real edge or end to them, as though they were perpetually dropping out of hyperspace into normal reality. And between and around these awful ships, strange monstrous forms, alive, aware and completely unprotected in the cold emptiness of space. Some were almost as big as the ships, vast alien creatures with eyes like spotlights and barbed tentacles that stretched for miles. There were claws and teeth and staring eyes in repulsive entities the size of cities, that shouldn't, couldn't, exist unprotected in the long, sunless night of the Darkvoid. They shone with their own unhealthy light, immense, horrid creatures without number, gathering silently on all sides of the beleaguered planet.

The Recreated had come to the Wolfling World.

'Jesus,' said Hazel softly. 'We are in deep shit. I thought they were all supposed to be off attacking Golgotha. Look at the size of those things . . . This just isn't possible. I mean, how do they even survive out there without ships?'

'This is where they live,' said Owen, 'it's their home. Maybe they don't need ships here. But there's something wrong, about those monsters. There's no way they evolved in open space. Claws, tentacles and eyes are planetary features. They must have evolved on some world, originally.'

'Typical historian,' said Hazel, without heat. 'I don't give a damn about the Recreated's past, I want to know what they're doing here, right now. And may I remind you that we don't have any guns on this miserable cobbled-together rustbucket?'

'Probably just as well,' said Owen. 'They're not actually threatening us, as yet. With our shields up, we may be too small to draw their attention. Start shooting at them, and we might just get them interested in us. I think I'd like to avoid that, if at all possible. I say we stay very calm and very quiet, and hope they miss us.'

Hazel sniffed. 'For once, I find myself in complete agreement with you. Those things disturb the hell out of me. I don't think even a full-sized starcruiser would last long against an attack by those nightmares. But how are we going to get down to the planet without them noticing?'

The viewscreen chimed politely, making them both jump, alerting them to an incoming message. Owen quickly changed the screen from sensor input to the comm systems, and the disturbing gathering on the screen vanished, to be replaced by the great shaggy head and shoulders of the Wolfling. His skull had a definite lupine quality, but the face was still unsettlingly human. Wulf smiled, revealing sharp, unpleasant teeth, his eyes fixed and direct, a predator's gaze.

'I've been waiting for you to get here, Deathstalker. We must talk. There are many things we need to discuss, before the end.'

'The end?' said Hazel sharply, just a little miffed at not being addressed too. 'The end of what?'

'Everything, possibly.' The Wolfling didn't seem too upset at the prospect. His grin widened, showing even more teeth, looking less like a smile all the time.

'Is it the baby?' said Owen. 'Is he waking up?'

'Oh, yes,' said the Wolfling, almost casually. 'And has been, for some time now. He was sleeping so very deeply, and he's had a long rise back to consciousness. But soon he will be fully awake, and by then we must have decided what to do. Join me, and we will talk of many things, before the end.'

'In case you hadn't noticed,' Hazel said acidly, 'we are currently surrounded by all kinds of weird shit, some of them with teeth you wouldn't believe, and with the good God only knows how much firepower between them. How are we supposed to get to you?'

'The teleport systems are still working,' Wulf said calmly. 'The Deathstalker installed them long ago, and they still function. Giles always planned for the future. When you are ready, I'll have them bring you to me.'

Owen shut off the comm sound for a moment, so he could talk privately with Hazel. 'Now that is interesting. I'd always assumed the Last Standing teleported us down to the planet the last time we were here; not the other way round. The power in those old systems must be incredible. I wonder what other surprises my dear departed ancestor might have left behind?'

Hazel frowned. 'Speaking of the departed, do you suppose Wulf knows that Giles is dead?'

'He must do by now. And that I killed him. He just might be inviting us down so that he can take his revenge on me.'

'Let him try. He's big, but we've been through the Maze.'

'So has he, more than once. Just because we never saw him manifest any powers, it doesn't mean he hasn't got any.'

Hazel frowned. 'Now that is an unpleasant thought. All right; how do you want to play this?'

'Very carefully. And extremely diplomatically.' Owen turned the sound back on, and smiled cheerfully at the Wolfling. 'We're ready to come down, Sir Wulf. Will our ship be all right, up here alone, surrounded by the Recreated?'

'It's too small for them to be concerned with,' said the Wolfling. 'The Recreated are always here, in the Darkvoid. They belong here. They may leave, but some are always here.'

Owen frowned, as a thought struck him. 'We never saw any sign of them the first time we passed through the Darkvoid.'

'They were hiding,' said the Wolfling. 'They remembered the Last Standing. It frightened them.'

He broke off contact, and the screen went blank. Owen

looked at Hazel. 'The Last Standing frightened the *Recreated*?'

'Not the castle,' said Hazel. It's a powerful vessel, but . . . no. It wasn't the Standing that scared them. It was who the Standing belonged to – Giles Deathstalker. It always comes back to him, and the schemes and conspiracies he set in motion, all those centuries ago.'

'Then I suppose it's up to me to put an end to them,' said Owen. 'I'm the last of his Family. The last Deathstalker.'

And then suddenly and silently they both vanished away, gone from the bridge of the *Sunstrider III* between one moment and the next, and all around the vast and awful shapes of the Recreated stirred slowly, as though troubled by some half-felt premonition.

Not long after, another ship came to the Wolfling World: that famous and much travelled starcruiser, the *Dauntless*. On the bridge, Captain John Silence sat stiffly in his command chair, eyes fixed on the viewscreen before him. The *Dauntless* had been threading its way through the huge, alien forms of the Recreated for some time now, guns and shields at the ready, but so far the ship had gone entirely unchallenged. Which was just as well, in Silence's opinion. He wouldn't have backed his entire weapons systems against even one of the huge alien vessels. The *Dauntless* moved slowly forward, sliding silently between the Recreated, and Silence couldn't help feeling just a little annoyed that none of the monsters even deigned to notice it.

The pardoned traitor called Carrion stood calmly beside the command chair, leaning idly on his power lance. His dark-shadowed eyes studied the alien forms on the screen with interest, and, it appeared, entirely unmoved. The rest of the bridge crew were so stiff and strained you could have struck matches off them, and the general atmosphere was tense almost beyond bearing, but no one even looked like cracking. They were a good crew, and Silence was very proud of them.

'What the hell are all those Recreated doing here?' he said quietly to Carrion. 'Why aren't they attacking Golgotha, with the rest of their kind?'

'Clearly, something on the planet below holds their attention,' said Carrion, not looking away from the screen. 'Something they consider more important than Humanity's imminent destruction. Which suggests the rumours are true: the Madness Maze has returned. And with it, perhaps, the Darkvoid Device.'

'Let's hope so,' said Silence. 'We need the Device. It's the only weapon left that might help us against the Recreated, now that Diana's failed to convert them. The Device could be Humanity's last hope.'

'Really?' said Carrion. 'I always thought that was the Deathstalker.'

'If he's even here,' said Silence. 'And I don't know I entirely trust him in this. The last time a Deathstalker and the Device got together, they wiped out billions of innocent lives. And he has a history with the Madness Maze I can't even begin to understand. I only went part-way through, and it scared the shit out of me. It killed my men as I watched, and I couldn't do a damned thing to save them. No; we'll deal with the Deathstalker if we have to, if he's alive, but we concentrate on the Device. At least we've got plenty of targets to test it on.'

'Assuming we can use it without destroying everything else in the process,' said Carrion. 'Including us. Though that would be one fine last joke.'

'Let's avoid jokes for the moment,' said Silence. 'You always did have a weird sense of humour, Sean. Navigator; select a low orbit and move us into position. Preferably well away from any of those things out there.'

'Aye, sir.' The navigation officer's voice was steady, and his hands moved surely over the control panels. Only the paleness of his face betrayed his inner unease.

The *Dauntless* came into orbit around the Wolfling World, and still none of the Recreated showed any reaction. Silence and the rest of his crew began to breathe a little more easily. And then Hemdall, the ship's AI, raised its voice politely, and everyone jumped.

'You asked to be advised of any other human ship in the vicinity, Captain. Sensors are picking up what could be a small craft, also in low orbit.'

'Put it on the screen,' said Silence. He studied the ship as its image replaced that of the Recreated, and nodded thoughtfully. 'Now that is one hell of a mess. Looks like it was bolted together from half a dozen different vessels, but the general shape's familiar. That's a *Sunstrider*. The Deathstalker got here before us. Damn. Hemdall; scan the ship for life readings.'

'None detected, Captain. The ship appears to be entirely deserted.'

Silence frowned, and then rose sharply to his feet. 'That means he's already gone down into the interior of the planet. Probably already making plans with the Wolfling.'

Carrion moved forward to stand beside him. 'Does it matter that he got here first? He is Humanity's hero. What could he have to say to the Wolfling that might concern us?'

'Who knows?' said Silence. 'He's a Deathstalker. I never believed he was really dead. Owen's always had his own agenda.'

'Unlike us,' suggested Carrion.

Silence glared at him. 'We are following Parliament's orders. After Jack Random went crazy, I don't trust any of the Maze people any more.'

'You went into the Maze,' said Carrion, his voice entirely without judgement. Silence shrugged uneasily.

'I never went all the way through. Never changed, the way they did. I'm still human. And Humanity needs the Darkvoid Device. I'll do whatever I have to, to get it. If we can work with the Deathstalker, all well and good. If not . . .'

'Yes?'

'Damned if I know. There haven't been many who could make Owen Deathstalker do a single damned thing he didn't want to. All I can realistically do is appeal to his sense of honour and duty. In his own way, Owen has always been an honourable man.'

'What do you think of the Deathstalker, John? You were on opposite sides during the rebellion, tried to kill each other more than once, but when you speak of him you always sound . . . respectful.'

'Oh, I admire him right enough,' said Silence. 'A brave and honourable man, who's come a long way in a short time. Unlike most heroes and legends, he really did do most of the things they say he did. But he's also a wild card, in a game where the wrong move could spell death for the whole of the Empire. Owen has never understood or cared for the practical realities.'

'Unlike you, Captain?'

'Oh, I've always been a practical man, Sean. That's why the Deathstalker's the official hero of the Empire and I'm just a captain. But in the end, I was the one Parliament trusted with its orders; trusted to save Humanity. They know I'll get the job done, no matter what.'

'And Hazel d'Ark?'

Silence winced. 'Let's not talk about her. I have my orders. No one is to be allowed to interfere with this mission.'

'You never change, Captain,' said Carrion.

And then they both suddenly vanished from the bridge, plucked away by powerful forces in the depths of the planet below, teleported down into the cold heart of the Wolfling World.

They all arrived together, in the same moment, four human figures materializing in the midst of a great green forest. The surrounding trees stood tall and proud, draped in heavy swathes of summer greenery. Angled shafts of golden sunlight dropped down through the canopy of interlocking branches high overhead. Dust motes swirled lazily in the glimmering light. The air was full of the rich scents of earth and mulch and leaves and growing things. But for all its grandeur the forest was still and silent, with not a sound anywhere. No beast or bird or buzzing insect disturbed the forest calm. This was not a real wood, not a natural thing. The Wolflings had created the forest long, long ago, so that they could have somewhere to run and play and hunt. Now they were all gone, save for Wulf, the last of his kind, but the forest remained.

Owen and Hazel looked at Silence and Carrion, who looked right back at them. Everyone's hand hovered close to a weapon. After a moment that seemed to stretch and stretch, Owen and Silence straightened up a little, and ostentatiously moved their hands away from their guns. They nodded slightly to each other, as close as two old rivals such as they could ever come to bowing. Respect had never been a problem between them; only politics, and very different ideas of duty. Hazel sniffed loudly, and moved her hand from her gun to her belt. Carrion leaned casually on his power lance.

'Well,' said Owen finally, 'it's been a long time since we last met, hasn't it, Captain?'

'Not since Lionstone's last Court,' said Silence. 'Just as well, really. We never did have anything in common, except the things we fought over.'

'Who's your friend in black?' said Hazel.

'I am Carrion; a traitor and destroyer of worlds. I bring bad luck.'

Hazel looked him over, unimpressed. 'Fancies himself, doesn't he?'

Silence and Owen exchanged an understanding look. Without needing to say anything, they acknowledged a shared history of having to make allowances for their companions. Hazel and Carrion caught the look, but missed its meaning, which was probably just as well. To avoid having to say anything else for a moment, they all looked around them, and the silent forest looked back. The continuing quiet was eerie, disturbing.

'We've all come a long way,' Owen said finally, as much to

break the ice as anything. 'Is this where you thought your life would lead you, Captain? Is this the future you saw for yourself at the beginning of your career?

'I haven't considered the future in a long time,' said Silence. 'I have enough problems dealing with the present.'

'I know the feeling,' said Owen. 'But it does seem somehow right that we should wind up here, where it all began. A lot of stories find their end back at their beginning.'

'Oh, God, he's gone all metaphysical again,' said Hazel. 'Look, Owen, we're only here because this is our last bit of unfinished business. I always knew the Madness Maze and the Darkvoid Device would come back to haunt us one day. They were far too powerful to have been wiped out by something as blunt and prosaic as massed disrupter fire. The Maze gave us incredible powers. I always knew there'd be a price to pay, eventually.'

'Yes,' said Carrion, 'there's always a price. No good deed goes unpunished.'

Owen and Silence ignored both of them with the ease of long practice. 'I take it you know about the latest reversal?' said Silence. 'The Recreated are ploughing through what's left of the Fleet and heading straight for Golgotha. When the homeworld falls, so does the Empire, with all of Humanity not far behind. We're all there is left, to snatch victory from the jaws of extinction.'

'Ah, hell,' said Owen, 'we've done it before.'

'But things are very different, this time,' said a deep, growling voice, and they all turned sharply to look. The Wolfling had arrived, without any of them hearing or noticing, and now he stood before them, tall and proud and very bitter: Wulf, the last of his kind. He had a man's shape, but he didn't stand like a man. Easily eight foot tall, he towered over them, a commanding, threatening presence. Wide shoulders surmounted a barrel chest and a long, narrow waist, all of him covered in thick golden fur. The legs curved back like a wolf's, and the oversized feet and hands had long, jagged claws. In the wolfish head, sharp teeth showed in a disturbing smile. The eyes were large and intelligent and almost overpoweringly ferocious. Just standing there, motionless, the Wolfling looked very, very dangerous.

Owen kept his hands ostentatiously well away from his weapons. He didn't want to start anything that would have to finish in blood. He'd never been too sure of where exactly he stood with Wulf, and now he had even more reason to be wary. Hazel stood very close at his side, scowling unwaveringly back at the Wolfling to show how unimpressed she was, but Owen could feel she was coiled tight as a spring. Captain Silence and Carrion also stood together, and Carrion no longer held his power lance like a staff. The Wolfling looked them over studiously, and then fixed his unsettling gaze on Silence.

'I remember you, Captain. We met only briefly the last time you were here, but I remember you. You thought you could destroy the Maze.'

'I did my duty,' said Silence.

'Of course you did. That's just what the other humans said, as they hunted down and destroyed my kind all those years ago, showing no mercy to females or cubs. Have you learned no new excuses for your destruction, in all that time?'

'No,' said Carrion. 'They wiped out my people too – the Ashrai. But still I made my peace with the man who ordered their destruction, and Captain Silence is my friend again. I vouch for him.'

'And who vouches for you, human?' said the Wolfling.

'The Ashrai, if need be. Let us all pray I don't need to call on them. They wouldn't leave much standing of your fragile, pretty wood.' Carrion looked almost sadly at the Wolfling. 'I sympathize with your loss, friend Wulf, but let us understand each other. We are here to do what we must, and we will do it, right or wrong, with you or despite you. I lost one people; I couldn't bear to lose another. Can't we be friends, Wulf, in the face of such dark evil as the Recreated?'

The Wolfling laughed suddenly, and shook his shaggy head. 'You don't even know what the Recreated are.'

'And you do?' said Owen.

'Oh, you'd be surprised what I know, young Deathstalker. Come; we are wasting time, and there's not much left of it to waste. The Madness Maze has returned, and the baby is waking up.'

'I'm glad the Maze is back,' said Silence. 'I always felt just a little guilty at destroying something so . . . extraordinary. Like a barbarian tearing down a city he wasn't advanced enough to appreciate. But it killed my men, and it was a threat, so . . . I never did understand about the sleeping baby, though. Is it significant?'

'You could say that,' said Hazel, smiling in spite of herself. 'It's Giles Deathstalker's clone. It's also a being of incalculable power. You know it better as the Darkvoid Device.'

Silence looked at her, startled. 'A *baby* was responsible for all that death and destruction? I don't believe it!'

'Believe it,' said the Wolfling, smiling his unnerving smile. 'The baby has slept for centuries, and I have felt his power grow. If he wakes again, the whole universe may tremble, and he is very close to waking now.'

'Damn,' said Silence, 'damn! I had the Darkvoid Device in my hands, all those years ago. If I'd only known . . .'

'What?' said Hazel. 'What would you have done with it, Silence? Used it to protect Lionstone from us, and keep her in power? Prevent the rebellion, and all the changes we made for the better?'

'Perhaps,' said Silence. 'Not all your changes were for the better. It doesn't matter now: we still have to face the Recreated.'

'When you opened fire on the Maze and tried to destroy it,' said the Wolfling, 'it protected itself by jumping forward through Time. When it reappeared around the baby, everything was as it had been. You never did understand the nature of the Madness Maze. What you see is merely the physical manifestation of something far greater. The tip of a very large, alien iceberg. The Maze is just the intrusion into our reality, into our mere three dimensions, of something far greater of many more dimensions. The Madness Maze is all we can see, all we can comprehend; a mere fraction of an alien device so vast that one glimpse of the whole thing would blast your reason away.'

'How very metaphysical,' said Silence. 'I'll be impressed later, when I've got time. All that really matters now is the Darkvoid Device. Parliament sent me here to find and obtain it, and bring it back to use against the Recreated, to save the homeworld and Humanity. Nothing else matters.'

'It's not that simple,' said Owen. 'Giles thought he could use the baby's power to stop a rebellion. Instead, the baby murdered billions of people. How do you control a baby? Who knows what he might do, when he wakes again? This isn't a weapon we dare use, Silence. We don't know how to aim it, focus it, or even turn it off. That small baby could actually be a greater threat to Humanity than all the Recreated put together.'

'That's theory,' said Silence. 'I have to deal in facts. The Recreated are a threat now. And I have my orders.'

'We'll stop you if we have to,' said Owen.

'Humans,' said the Wolflings. 'With your species on the edge of extinction, still you bicker and quarrel. Come with me, fools. The Madness Maze is waiting for you. Perhaps you can learn wisdom from it, in the time you have left.'

The Madness Maze was right back where it had been, as awesome and enigmatic as ever. Beyond it lay the city the Hadenmen built, after Owen released them from their Tomb. The once bright and shining silver towers were dark and lifeless now, the mathematically straight streets silent and deserted, with no trace anywhere of the augmented men who created it to be the wellspring of their rebirth.

'They all went into the Maze,' said the Wolfling, 'every last one. It called to them, in a voice their original creators would have recognized, and they could not stand against it. They all went in, and none came out. That is the nature of the Maze: to judge and condemn the unworthy. They all went mad, or died, and the Maze took them into itself. Their time was over. They were incapable of becoming.'

'Becoming?' Hazel snapped. 'Becoming *what*?'

'Only the Maze can answer that question,' said the Wolfling. 'And you must enter the Maze to ask it.'

Hazel scowled. 'I've never liked the word *must*. And besides, that damned thing almost drove me crazy the last time. I'm in no hurry to give it another crack at me.'

'You have no choice,' said Wulf. 'The baby is waking. His fate, your fate and Humanity's fate all meet their destiny together, here, at the heart of the Maze. Either you go in, and complete your journey at last, or everything you have done and stood for has been for nothing. The Recreated will destroy your species, and you will die, alone and incomplete and far from everything you hold most dear.'

The four humans looked at the Madness Maze, and felt it looking back. At first glance it seemed straightforward enough. A simple pattern of tall steel walls, shining and shimmering, but the more you looked at it the more complex you realized it was. The pattern unfolded before their eyes like a continuously blooming flower, becoming ever more subtle and intricate, like the folded convolutions of the brain. The walls were twelve feet high and only a fraction of an inch thick, and Owen remembered clearly how deathly cold they had been to the touch. The paths between the walls led to knowledge and madness, inspiration and evolution, or to a terrible death; the birth of a new kind of Humanity, or the destruction of the old. In the Maze was everything you ever dreamed of, including all the bad ones. Perhaps especially the bad ones. Birth is always painful.

It was calling to them. They could all feel it, on levels they couldn't comprehend or resist. As Hazel had said, only partly in jest, they had unfinished business with the Maze. *Or it with them.* Silence looked at the shimmering structure before him and tried to remember the good men and women of his crew that it had killed, but still something drew him to it. He had never passed all the way through. He had turned back to save

Investigator Frost, because the Maze was killing her, and he couldn't allow that. But a part of him had always wondered what he might have become, if only he'd gone all the way through to the heart, to the centre of the mysteries. It was as though his life was an unfinished song that had never really reached its conclusion.

Owen looked at the Madness Maze, and thought of all the amazing things he'd done in his short, legendary life. He'd achieved many things, performed wonders, followed where duty and honour had led him, but he couldn't honestly say any of it had made him happy. Despite all his wishes and convictions, he'd been forced to put aside his old scholarly self and become the warrior he'd never wanted to be. He'd seen good friends die, along with his enemies, to bring about a questionable victory and an Empire he no longer recognized or felt a part of. The Maze had changed his life for ever, and made him so much more than he was, but he still didn't know whether to praise it or damn it.

Hazel scowled at the Maze, her hand resting again on the gun at her hip. She didn't remember much about her last trip through the Maze, partly at least through her own wishes, but she was sure the damned thing had its own agenda, and not necessarily one she would agree with. She'd been many things in her life, from clonelegger and pirate to rebel and official hero, and she hated to think that any of it had been anyone's idea but her own. If she went into the Maze again, what new changes might it work in her? What might she become? Hazel looked at the Maze as a mouse might look at a baited trap, and wondered if she was crazy enough to stick her head in the noose one more time.

Carrion looked at the Madness Maze, and perhaps saw more than the others – he had lived so long with the Ashrai in the metallic forest, and wasn't strictly human any more. He saw strange energies spiralling endlessly through the steel pathways, and potentials and possibilities that both intrigued and frightened him. He welcomed these feelings, because it had been so long since he had felt much of anything. Of them all, Carrion felt most comfortable with the Madness Maze. It reminded him of the Ashrai, and the metallic forest.

'Well?' said the Wolfling finally. 'You've come all this way. Have none of you anything to say?'

'If the . . . Device is in the Maze, then we have to go in after it,' said Carrion. 'But you heard the Deathstalker. We could simply be trading one threat for another.'

'If the baby becomes a menace, then I'll destroy it,' said Silence. 'But not until I've made use of it.'

'John, you can't,' said Carrion. 'He's just a baby. He's innocent.'

'It killed billions of people!'

'He doesn't know that.'

'Nothing's ever simple, is it?' said Owen. 'I remember the first time I came here. It seems like centuries ago. I remember walking through the Madness Maze to its heart, and finding the baby waiting there, safely sleeping. I think I knew even then that my life was never going to make sense, that there were greater powers than I could ever hope to understand at work in the universe. And this was where the lies started, too. My ancestor Giles, the original Deathstalker and first Warrior Prime of the Empire, told me the baby was his clone. It didn't occur to me till much later that the science of cloning didn't exist in his time. He also told me that the Madness Maze was created by the Wolflings, though soon after he changed his tune and said the Maze was an alien artefact. That was his first slip, the first thing that made me distrust the legendary hero and warrior. But then, I never did believe in legends, especially when I became one. And I've studied far too much history to believe in happy endings. But I do still believe that one man of good will can make a difference, if he stands in the right place at the right time, and will not back down or look away.'

'Giles believed that once,' said the Wolfling. 'He was a legend in his own lifetime who did even more than they said he did. Unfortunately, he decided he wanted to be more than just a hero and Warrior Prime. The time has come for me to tell you the truth; the true history of Giles Deathstalker and his infant son and the Madness Maze.'

This is the tale the Wolfling told.

More than nine hundred years ago, he began, when things were very different, and Giles was an honoured hero loved and respected by all, he betrayed his wife and his Family and his Emperor to have an affair with the Empress Hermione. It was an affair conducted in the utmost secrecy, not just because the Emperor Ulric II would have had them both executed, but because of what resulted from that affair. Hermione became pregnant, and bore her lover Giles a son. It was her first and only child. Ulric was delighted at the pregnancy, and there were Empire-wide celebrations over the birth of a son and heir to the Empire. Only Giles and Hermione knew that the official genetest was a fake; that the newborn babe was a bastard and a traitor's get. Even now, I don't know whether Giles really loved Hermione; if he ever loved her. Or whether he quite deliberately set out to sire a child who would give Clan Deathstalker a claim to the Iron Throne. I'd hate to think that his affair with Hermione was just a means to an end, but Giles always was ambitious. Perhaps the plan was to wait until Ulric II met his death, by whatever means, and then Giles would step forward and reveal the true genetest, and the Deathstalker Family would rule the Empire. Giles never told me, and I never asked.

Whatever the truth of his ambitions, it all went horribly wrong. The betrayer was himself betrayed by his true son, the man you came to know as Dram. Shortly after the royal birth, he told Ulric the truth, currying favour perhaps, for Dram was ambitious too. He wanted to be Warrior Prime, revered and adored, but he didn't have the patience to earn it as his father had. And perhaps it was jealousy too; a fear that he would be put aside in favour of his bastard half-brother: father and son never did get on. Giles was always off somewhere in the ever-expanding Empire, being a hero, creating his legend, while his son was left behind, to grow up in the company of tutors and politicians, and a quiet, mousy mother who had no idea how to cope with her increasingly ruthless and ambitious child.

The Emperor almost went mad with rage when Dram told him the truth about his beloved infant son. Ulric had been childless for many years, and so the insult Giles had done him became unbearable on many levels. He had the Empress Hermione imprisoned, awaiting trial and execution, and put a death warrant on Giles Deathstalker. They say Ulric signed it in his own blood. That's why Giles really went on the run, all those years ago. Forget that part of the legend. There was no great clash of two god-like men. Just a petty squabble over a miserable betrayal. Giles was forewarned by one of his many allies at Court. He fought his way into the Palace, killing a number of good men, grabbed the baby and went on the run with half the Imperial Fleet snapping at his heels. There was only one place in the Empire that Giles could run to where he wouldn't be expected – the Wolfling World. No one knew that he had a secret ally there.

Some years before, the Emperor had sent Giles to this world to hunt down and destroy the last Wolfling. I was a legend then, myself, and a constant threat and thorn in the side of Humanity, so Ulric sent one legend to deal with another. It should have been just another mission. Giles hunted me down easily enough, but when we finally came face to face, with nothing on our minds but battle and death, we were both surprised at what we saw in each other's eyes. We knew, in a moment that seemed to last for ever, that neither of us could defeat the other; that both of us would die if we fought. At long last we had found an equal, someone worthy of our respect. We chose not to die. Instead, we sat and talked for hours, like two long-lost brothers separated since birth, who had only now found each other. Giles still had honour then, as well as a keen eye for a potential ally. He denied his orders, left me alive and went back to the Emperor to tell him he couldn't find the legendary Wolfling. That I probably no longer even existed. Ulric believed him. Why not? His precious Warrior Prime had never lied to him before. Perhaps in that moment, in that first small betrayal, was planted the seed of rebellion, and ambition, and all that was to come. I like to think so. I like to think that in some small way I helped to contribute to the downfall of the Empire that slaughtered all of my kind but me.

So who else could Giles turn to, with all the Empire against him, but me? He came here seeking safety and sanctuary, and a base from which someday to strike back. So I showed him the Madness Maze. No other human had ever seen it before, save the Blood Runners, and they never spoke of it. I explained to Giles the nature and function of the Maze, and what it could do to him if he dared to penetrate its secret heart. But he was frightened. He valued his humanity too much to give it up, then, no matter what the Maze promised. However, while he wasn't prepared to risk himself, there was still the baby. What safer place could there be to hide his child, I asked, than at the heart of the Maze? No one would dare go in after him, and he would in time become powerful beyond belief. Giles listened to the Maze, talking through me, its involuntary guardian, and was tempted. His son, a weapon he could use to bring down the Empire that had dared turn against him. And, tempted, he fell, and was damned by his own ambition.

I took the child into the heart of the Madness Maze and left him there. I have walked the Madness Maze many times, but it never chose to make me a god. It was enough that it kept me alive when I would much rather have died, and bound me to its service, an unwilling immortal guardian and mouthpiece. I would have killed the child if I could because he would soon become what I could not. He had come between me and my friend. But the Maze wouldn't let me. It had its own plans for the child of Giles Deathstalker.

The baby lay in the heart of the Madness Maze, and learned much. Since he was so very young, with so few built-in preconceptions and limitations, the Maze was able to change him in ways far beyond anyone else it ever embraced.

He blossomed and grew, and became very powerful. He became so much more than any other of his species, and laughed aloud in delight at the wonders of the universe unfolding before him. He thought it was all just a game. And when he had taken in all that his small consciousness could tolerate, he went to sleep to consider what he had learned.

And to wonder what he would do next.

I watched, from the outside, and dreamed of what I would have done to my enemy Humanity with such power. But the Maze had bound me to it, and I could not leave its side. I couldn't even join your rebellion, when you were kind enough to ask.

Now at this time, there was another rebellion going on. The old Empire was not perfect, for all its grandness, and a group of planets had banded together to defy the Emperor's authority and demand better treatment. Ulric could have declared war against them, and sent his mighty Fleet to punish them, but the planets were valuable for many reasons, and well-defended enough that his Fleet would have suffered badly in any direct conflict. Giles saw an opportunity. He sent a message to the Emperor, through certain mutual friends, offering a certain proposition. In return for a Pardon, for himself and his child, the Deathstalker would put an end to the rebellion, guaranteed. Ulric would have refused, but on military matters even a cuckolded Emperor must listen to his advisors, if he wishes to remain Emperor. There was a very real danger that the small rebellion could become a large one if it were not smartly nipped in the bud. Reluctantly, Ulric agreed.

I took Giles to the entrance of the Madness Maze, or as close as he would go, and he called out to his son. The Maze gently woke the infant in its care, and the baby reached out instinctively to his father. Their minds made contact, and for the first time in a long time, I saw happiness on Giles's face. He persuaded his baby son that the nearby rebel planets were a threat to both of them, and frightened, the child lashed out at the rebels. You all know what happened next. The baby only flexed his power for a moment, but between one heartbeat and the next a thousand suns blinked out, and the Darkvoid was born. Thousands of planets grew cold, and everything on them died. Billions of men, women and children died screaming. Horrified by what he had done, by what he had been persuaded to do, the baby cut off all contact with his father and put himself back to sleep, and would not be wakened. Giles called and called, but his son was no longer listening.

For the first time I saw Giles weep, though whether for the loss of his son's love, or in frustration at how things had gone so terribly wrong, I never knew. He had been Warrior Prime, sworn to defend the Empire and Humanity, and he was now responsible for the death of billions. Whatever the cause, that day his heart was broken. He was never the same after that. All he ever cared about from that day on was putting things right, whatever it took.

The Emperor howled to all his Court that he had been right all along, and no one disagreed. Humanity was appalled at what the Deathstalker had done with his Darkvoid Device. The Emperor tore up the Pardons, and set the most powerful dogs at his command on the Deathstalker's trail. Even the mysterious Shadow Men, who had never been known to fail. Giles piloted the Last Standing to Shandrakor, old home of his Family, to decoy his enemies away from his son and the Madness Maze. He had plans for both of them, in the future. Some day, he believed, he would learn to control them both, and use them to make amends for the terrible thing he had done. And only when he had emerged from the newly formed Darkvoid, and was well on his way to Shandrakor, did he finally re-establish contact with his old allies, and discover how much he was required to pay for his ambition.

The Empress Hermione was dead, executed by royal decree. His wife Marion was also dead, murdered by his estranged son Dram. Giles's very name had become a curse in the mouth of Humanity. I think he went a little mad, then, at the thought of how much he'd lost, at how all his plans had gone so horribly wrong. He sent assassins after his son Dram, tidied up the last of his affairs and vanished with his castle into the thick, deadly jungles of Shandrakor. There, he set up a conspiracy of his remaining Family, friends and allies, slowly and carefully to plot a foolproof rebellion against the Iron Throne. This time, everything would be planned in meticulous detail. Nothing would be allowed to go wrong. But it would take time. So Giles programmed the Last Standing's computers to take care of things while he was away, and put himself in stasis, to wait however long it took. To wait for some distant ancestor to awaken him, and tell him that, at last, he would be able to overthrow the Iron Throne, make himself Emperor and put everything right again.

But he never got the chance. The ancestor who awakened him, murdered him.

Meanwhile, back at Court, Dram killed his mother Marion to prove his loyalty to Ulric and advance his own position. He wanted to demonstrate how he had distanced himself from his treacherous father. He didn't want much from the Emperor, in return. He just wanted to be the new Warrior Prime. But the Emperor had had enough of murderous Deathstalkers. He named the son a monster like his father, put a death sentence on Dram and a bounty on his head, and Dram was forced to flee. His father's conspiracy would have nothing to do with him.

Ulric gave orders for all the main members of Clan Deathstalker to be put to death. Many died, more went underground. A distant cousin of the Emperor's choosing became head of the new Deathstalker Family. Giles's conspiracy survived, but it was never the same after that. Ulric would have liked to stamp out the whole line, root and branch, but the name, the heroic, legendary name, had been useful before and might yet be again. The people did so love their precious heroes.

Dram determined to find and kill his father, for many reasons, only to discover that Giles had escaped his reach, disappearing down the corridor of Time into the future. So Dram put himself into stasis too, using an old, secret bolt-hole on Golgotha that had once belonged to his father. I'm sure the irony pleased him. He too intended to sleep away the years, his computers programmed to awaken him once there was clear evidence his father had been revived. He didn't know how long that sleep would last. He didn't know that more than nine centuries would pass before a team of engineers, excavating the depths of Lionstone's new Palace, found something entirely unexpected. Lionstone awoke Dram, probably not with a kiss, and found a kindred spirit. Monsters always recognize their own kind. Together they set in motion plans that would destroy young Owen Deathstalker's comfortable life, and send him off in search of his famous ancestor Giles. All they had to do was wait, and follow, and eventually Giles and the Darkvoid Device would fall into their hands. And then . . . revenge and punishment would be unleashed on a Humanity that had never really loved them.

But during those nine centuries and more, rumours had persisted that a Deathstalker had been personally responsible for the creation of the Darkvoid; that the Device was just a convenient fiction to hide a more terrible truth. That a man had somehow gained the power of untold destruction. Leaks from inside the ongoing Deathstalker conspiracy seemed to confirm something along those lines. So when, some time later, the espers began secretly investigating their own powers and nature, the name and legend of what a Deathstalker might have done suddenly seemed entirely possible. Those rumours inspired what became the super-esper programme, that led to the creation of the Mater Mundi. The search for individual super-espers produced only freaks and monsters, so the esper underground made contact with the Deathstalker conspiracy, and after that they worked together, each thinking it was using the other for its own purposes. But the inclusion of espers and, later, clones meant that the course and nature of the Deathstalker conspiracy was changed for ever. Giles couldn't have foreseen everything.

None of these people knew that really they were little more than puppets, their strings pulled, however distantly, by the Madness Maze.

'It took me a long time to piece all that together,' said the Wolfling. 'But I've been in contact with the various conspiracies and undergrounds for centuries, via the computers Giles left me, and I've had a lot of time alone here, with nothing to do but think.'

'Giles never really cared about the people or the rebellion,' said Owen. 'It was all just a plan to put him on the Throne.'

'Him, and his Family,' said Wulf.

'But Giles always came first,' said Owen. 'An Empire-wide rebellion, built not upon honour or justice, but on one man's guilt.'

'Does it really matter?' said Hazel. 'Giles may have started the rebellion, but we finished it, for our own purposes. And in the end, the Empire we helped to make is nothing like the Empire Giles had in mind. Only one Deathstalker helped shape Humanity's future, and that's you, Owen.'

'Oh, yes,' said the Wolfling, his mouth stretching in a broad smile that showed all his teeth. 'It's all down to you, Owen. And your story isn't over yet. There's still more you need to know. Let me tell you what the Recreated really are. They're not aliens and they're not bogeymen, though they have the qualities of both. The truth is really much more horrible than that. Everyone and everything that died during the creation of the Darkvoid is still alive. So many cried out as they died, all those centuries ago, that the baby heard them, even in its sleep. It dreamed they were still alive, and so they were. Without shape or form, they existed in the endless dark, crying out in their rage and pain and shock and loss and horror. They soon went insane, and in that madness eventually learned to tap the power that was keeping them alive. They drew, slowly and cautiously, on the power of the sleeping baby, which was indirectly the power of the Madness Maze itself, and in time they made new bodies for themselves. But they were insane, and so were the shapes they took. They made themselves into the nightmarish evil aliens that Humanity had always feared meeting, and dedicated themselves to revenge against the Humanity that sentenced them to death and then left them alone and abandoned in the eternal darkness.

'They started slowly, afraid to stray too far from the source of their existence. They reached out, and snatched Captain Fast from the bridge of his own starship. They experimented on him, discovering what they could do, and finally made him over into Half A Man, One and Two. And then they sent the first one back, into Humanity's welcoming bosom, there to spread fear and propaganda of the terrible evil aliens waiting Out There, and to prepare Humanity for their eventual coming. And all the time he was their unwitting spy in Humanity's camp. Alien species that might have been Humanity's friends and allies against the Recreated were enslaved or destroyed, as the result of a policy formulated by Half A Man. The Recreated were determined that when they finally did burst out of the Darkvoid, Humanity would find itself utterly alone.

'Down the centuries, the Recreated gathered and concentrated their power, moving slowly away from their source, heading for the Rim. And now they're out. Humanity's dark, neglected offspring, home to roost at last.'

'Figures,' said Hazel, after a long silence. 'Humanity always was its own worst enemy.'

'They aren't necessarily all evil,' said Silence slowly, 'the Recreated. I remember voices, coming out of the Darkvoid, trying to warn us of the dangers of the approaching starship *Champion*. Perhaps . . . perhaps some of them remember who and what they used to be.'

The Wolfling shrugged, a disturbingly powerful, supple movement. 'If so, they're in a minority. The Recreated want vengeance and the utter destruction of Humanity, and they won't settle for anything less. They are vast and they are powerful, and what little remains of the Empire's forces aren't nearly enough to stop them.'

'Are you saying it's hopeless?' said Carrion. 'That there's nothing we can do?'

'There's always hope,' said the Wolfling, almost reluctantly. 'One of you can still make a difference. The circle of your life has almost come to a close, Owen. It's all up to you now. Time for one Deathstalker to stop what another began, and save all Humanity.'

'Of course,' said Owen. 'It always comes down to me in the end, doesn't it? Damn it! All right, Wulf; what unpleasant and probably fatal thing do I have to do this time?'

'I can't tell you,' said the Wolfling. 'Some things are still withheld from me, probably so that I won't interfere. You have to go back into the Madness Maze, Owen, all the way back in. You'll find all the answers you need at the heart of the Maze. But you'd better hurry. The Recreated know about you; they sense that somehow you might be able to stop them. Some of them are already here, hovering over the planet like great poisonous blooms in the darkness. Their fear holds them back, but it also goads them on. A Deathstalker made them what they are, but another might undo them.'

'How?' said Owen angrily. 'Speak plainly, damn you!'

'Don't get him angry,' Hazel murmured. 'He's a lot bigger than I remembered.'

The Wolfling laughed softly, a dark, animal-like sound. 'The Recreated draw their power from the baby in the Maze. If you could interrupt that link, they might just cease to exist. Of course, the only way to be sure of breaking the link would be for you to murder an innocent child.'

'There's got to be another way,' said Owen at once.

'Maybe. But you don't have much time to find it, Owen. Soon the Recreated will overcome their fear, and then they'll come dropping out of the dark, carve their way down through the frozen outer layers of this world and find you.

They'll make your death last for aeons, stretch your suffering across Time till your dying screams are all that remains of Humanity. Make your decision, Owen. The Recreated are on their way, and nothing in the physical realm can stop them.'

'Go, Owen,' said Hazel. 'The Maze saved us once; maybe it'll save us again. We'll cover your back here.'

'Unfortunately, it's not that simple,' said the Wolfling, and they all looked at him, startled by a new note in his voice. 'First, you have to get past me.'

He was crouching a little now, as though ready to spring, but his great furry head still towered above theirs. Long sharp claws extended from his fingers. The wide grin had become a snarl, the sharp teeth like a steel trap in his mouth. The frowning yellow eyes were full of hatred. Just standing there, the Wolfling had suddenly become extremely dangerous. Silence and Hazel let their hands drop to the guns at their hips. Carrion stood a little straighter, his hand tightening around the power lance he held before him. Owen stood very still.

'Why?' he said finally. 'We have always been allies, if never friends. And even if the Recreated don't destroy you along with the rest of us, you wouldn't want to live in the universe they'll make.'

'Giles,' said Wulf, and his voice was a low, threatening growl. 'He was my friend, my old friend, who only wanted to put things right again. And you killed him. I never gave a damn about your rebellion. Humanity destroyed my whole species. Giles was the only one I ever cared about, and he's gone now. So let Humanity die. As for my own life, I no longer care. I should have died long ago, with the last of my kind, with my mate and my cubs. I tried to die many times, but the Maze kept me alive, against my will. I never asked to be its guardian. I've been forced to be part of a great, age-long scheme, whose details and end have always been withheld from me. This may be my only chance to rebel, to destroy that scheme, and have my revenge on the Maze, and on you, for everything you took from me. Giles was worth a thousand of you, Owen. Of course I loved him.'

The Wolfling launched himself at Owen, moving impossibly quickly, his extended, curving claws reaching for Owen's throat. Owen boosted, and threw himself to one side. In a moment his sword was in his hand, and he turned and pirouetted on one foot, bringing his sword round in a swift double-handed arc. The blade whistled through the air as the Wolfling ducked under it. Silence and Hazel opened fire with their disrupters. Carrion's power lance crackled with spiralling energies. The Wolfling avoided both energy blasts with fluid ease, moving faster than the human eye could follow, and he lashed out with one long arm, slapping the power lance out of Carrion's hands. In a moment he was concentrating on Owen again, and the Deathstalker had to move at the top of his boosted speed just to keep up with the Wolfling's attacks. His sword cut into the Wolfling's furry hide again and again, Wulf apparently ignoring pain and injury in his determination to get to Owen, his slashing claws coming ever nearer, the great teeth flashing in a wide grin.

Silence and Hazel drew their swords as Carrion ran to reclaim his power lance. Owen shouted for them to stay back. He'd already worked out that he couldn't hope to win this fight on a purely physical level.

The Wolfling was immortal, a survivor of centuries, kept alive by the power of the Maze. Owen had already stuck him with thrusts that would have killed a normal living being, and the Wolfling just shrugged them off and kept coming. Which meant that the answer had to be with the Maze. Owen scowled. He needed to think, but there just wasn't time. The Wolfling was pressing him too close. When in doubt, go for broke: Owen deliberately left himself open for a moment, and the Wolfling surged forward. Savage claws ripped into Owen's side and out again, spraying blood on the forest air, but Owen had already swung his blade in a great arc, with all his strength behind it. The keen edge of the blade sheared clean through the Wolfling's narrow neck, and the long, lupine head went flying from the broad shoulders.

Owen and the Wolfling both fell to their knees. Owen clutched tightly at his side, gasping with pain, blood pulsing thickly between his fingers. He thought he could feel broken ribs. The headless body of the Wolfling knelt beside him, blood spouting up from the severed neck, its arms reaching out blindly in search of the separated head. It lay some distance away. The eyes still moved, fixed on the hands as they edged closer. Hazel stepped quickly forward and kicked the head out of reach. The jaws snapped at her boot and the eyes rolled furiously.

Owen closed his eyes, ignoring the pain in his side to concentrate on his mental link with the Madness Maze. He reached out to it with his thoughts and felt it acknowledge him, like a slumbering giant slowly waking at the sound of a familiar voice. Owen concentrated his mind on a single thought.

For God's sake, let the poor bastard die.

The headless body fell forward on to the green, red-smeared grass and slowly stilled, the hands twitching as though still searching for an enemy to crush. The severed head's jaws gaped wide in one last soundless cry of rage or pain, or perhaps just relief, and then it too was still, its eyes mercifully empty. The blood stopped pulsing from the neck at last, and the Wolfling was finally dead.

Silence and Hazel helped Owen to his feet as Carrion came running back, power lance in hand, looking just a little embarrassed. Owen put his sword away as Hazel checked the wound in his side, and pressed a folded cloth against it.

'Nasty, but not immediately life-threatening. You'll heal, Owen.'

'Of course,' said Owen, just a little breathlessly, 'I always do.'

'He wanted to die,' said Silence. 'To join the last of his kind.'

'Oh, sure,' said Owen. 'But he would have taken me with

him, if he could. Luckily, I convinced the Maze to let him go. I don't think the Maze needs a guardian any more. Presumably its long scheme is nearly over, and we're approaching the endgame.'

Hazel shivered. 'Scary thought. If the Wolfling was telling the truth, it could be that we've been manipulated all along, just to get us here. To bring us to this place, at this time, to carry out its final plan.'

Carrion shook his head uneasily. 'Nothing's that powerful.'

'With the Maze, who knows what's possible,' said Owen, straightening up cautiously, in spite of the pain in his side. 'It doesn't have human limitations in its thinking.'

'Right,' said Hazel. 'It could do anything to you, once it had you inside it again. I don't think you should do this after all, Owen.'

'I doubt it'll kill me, after what we've been through to get here.'

'Maybe not, but it could change you again. Make you more . . . alien, like itself. We've already come a hell of a long way from the rest of Humanity, Owen. If you go in again, there's no telling what might walk out the other end. A god, or a devil, or perhaps even something we don't have any concept of. We've come so far together, Owen; I don't want to lose you now.'

'As so many times before, I don't really have a choice,' said Owen. 'Not just because of the Recreated, but because of the baby at the heart of the Maze. Wulf said he was waking up. I have to reach him before that happens. God alone knows what he might do if he wakes alone and scared. Or angry. Someone has to be there, to supply comfort and guidance. And who else would he accept, but another Deathstalker?'

'It could just kill you with a thought,' said Silence.

'Yes, I suppose he could. But I'm the best bet we've got. I don't believe the Maze brought me all this way just to let the baby kill me at the last step. I have to believe there's some purpose to my being here.'

'You don't have to do this, Owen,' said Hazel.

The Deathstalker smiled. 'Yes, I do. I've always known my duty, Hazel.'

'If you're going in, I'm going in too,' Silence said suddenly. 'If something goes wrong, in the Maze, and you don't make it out, the Empire's still going to need someone to save the day.'

'You just want to get your hands on the Device,' said Hazel sharply. 'You still think you could use it as a weapon against the Recreated. You're an idiot, Silence. Haven't you listened to anything we've told you? You'd destroy Humanity while trying to save it.'

'I listened,' said Silence. 'The Maze could give me the power to control the baby. Or destroy it, as necessary. Either way, the Recreated would be destroyed.'

Hazel started angrily towards the captain. Owen caught her by the arm. 'It doesn't matter, Hazel. Let him enter the Maze again, if he wishes. He'll learn better, in the Maze.'

'I need to do this,' Silence said to Hazel, almost apologetically. 'I never went all the way through, before. I turned back, to save Frost. The Maze was killing her. Maybe if I go all the way through, this time, I'll find the certainty that you and Owen have. I've spent so long trying to do the right thing, while never being entirely sure what the right thing was.'

'Then I'll go in too,' said Carrion, 'just to keep you company. And who knows; maybe I'll find some answers and some certainty for myself. It's been a long time since I had any purpose or direction in my life.'

'It's called the Madness Maze for a reason,' Owen said carefully. 'It kills a lot of those who enter, and drives even more insane.'

'I know,' said Silence. 'I saw my men die trying to solve the Maze. But as I said before, someone has to be left to carry on the good fight, if you and Hazel don't make it for whatever reason. You said yourself the Maze has plans for you. Maybe an alien device has alien plans, that have nothing to do with saving Humanity. The Empire must be protected.'

'For once, we agree,' said Carrion. 'The Recreated would destroy every living thing in the Empire, and bring it all down to darkness. They must be stopped. It's taken a while, but I've finally found an enemy I hate more than Humanity.'

'All right,' said Hazel. 'If you're all going in, then I guess I am as well. I don't trust the Maze worth a damn, but it's the only card we've got left to play against the Recreated. You can let go of my arm now, Owen.'

Owen released her, took her by the hand and brought her round to face him, his eyes fixed on hers. 'No, Hazel. You can't go in. You're needed out here, to guard our backs. You have to go back up to the *Sunstrider* and keep the Recreated busy while we're in the Maze. There's no knowing how long we'll be in there, and we daren't let the Recreated get anywhere near the Maze. They might destroy it, just to stop me reaching the baby.'

'You have got to be kidding!' said Hazel. 'The *Sunstrider III* doesn't even have any guns!'

'But it is very fast,' said Owen. 'And besides, I have a feeling that the Maze has made changes in our little ship. I seem to sense it . . . I think you'll find the new *Sunstrider* has everything you'll need to defend us.'

'The Maze?' said Hazel. 'Since when has the Maze been able to do things like that?'

Owen smiled suddenly. 'The baby isn't the only thing that's waking up. I think the Maze is rousing itself from an even deeper slumber.'

'Great,' said Hazel, 'just what we need – more complications. So you want me to be a bloody decoy, is that it? A target for all the Recreated, while you lot go and commune with whatever the Maze really is. Wonderful! Why don't I paint a bull's-eye on my chest while I'm at it?'

'I hate to break up a winning partnership,' said Owen, 'but I think we've gone past the point where what we want matters any more. I have to do this, Hazel. The Maze is calling me. Can't you feel it?'

'You'll be killed without me,' said Hazel numbly. 'I know it. You never did know how to stay out of trouble.'

'If I'd stayed out of trouble, I'd never have met you,' said Owen.

Silence and Carrion exchanged a look, and moved away so that Owen and Hazel could have a little privacy. Hazel remembered her dream of standing alone on the *Sunstrider*'s bridge, fighting off impossible odds, but said nothing. She could feel destiny closing in around her, taking her life in its remorseless iron grip, and a brief burst of fear and panic ran through her. She wanted to run or scream or knock Owen down, so he wouldn't leave her. She fought the feelings with all her old self-control. She didn't want to upset Owen. He was looking at the Madness Maze, his head slightly cocked, as though listening to some tune only he could hear. When he finally turned to look at her, his smile was so sad it nearly broke her heart.

'We've come a long way together,' said Owen. 'Walked in wondrous places, seen marvels almost beyond belief and fought the good fight with all our might. We even went into hell a few times, and brought light into the darkness. Maybe it would be greedy to ask for more, for ourselves.'

'I never wanted to be a hero,' said Hazel. 'I just wanted you, and some time together.'

'Heroes and legends,' said Owen. 'A long way from the ex-scholar and the ex-clonelegger. We've achieved more in our short time than most people do in their whole lives. Be proud of that.'

'You're trying to say goodbye, aren't you, Deathstalker?' said Hazel, holding his eyes with hers. 'One way or another, we're never going to meet again, are we?'

'Who knows?' said Owen. 'We each have to go where we're needed. We started this journey with our eyes wide open, and we knew what we were getting into. Everyone knows most heroes and legends don't have happy endings. I wish we could have had the things that everyone else has, and takes for granted; home and family and children. Some time to ourselves, untouched by needs of politics or destiny. But we were never meant for that kind of life, you and I. You're the best thing that ever happened to me, Hazel d'Ark. I wouldn't trade a moment of it, for all the years I might have had as a spoiled, self-satisfied minor scholar.'

'And you're the best thing that ever happened to me, Owen Deathstalker.' Hazel struggled to keep her voice even. 'Before you came into my life and ruined everything, I had to struggle to find a reason to get out of bed in the morning. You showed me what duty and honour were, and gave purpose to my life, even if you did have to drag me into it kicking and screaming all the way. Thanks to you I became someone who mattered, instead of just another minor criminal.'

'This isn't necessarily the end,' Owen said desperately. 'I could come out of the Maze with all the power I need to destroy the Recreated. The new *Sunstrider* could have been given enough firepower to hold them off and keep you safe. Maybe we'll save Humanity one last time, and then walk off into the sunset together. Stranger things have happened.'

'Yes,' said Hazel, 'maybe.' But neither of them believed it.

Abruptly they moved together and hugged each other close, heads pressed together, warm cheek pressed against warm cheek; at least partly so they wouldn't have to look into each other's eyes. Their breathing sounded loud and strained in each other's ears, and each could feel the other's heart beating. They held on like they might be pulled apart at any moment, defying Time, trying to make that one moment last for ever. In the end, it was Owen who let go first, slowly pushing Hazel away from him. He'd always been the one who understood duty and honour; the one with a core of unbreakable iron in his heart. The one to do what needed doing, whatever the cost. A Deathstalker.

They looked into each other's eyes, neither of them crying, for fear of upsetting the other.

'I love you,' said Owen, 'and I always will. I'll never forget you as long as I live.'

'I'll never forget you,' said Hazel, 'not even if I live for ever.'

Owen waited a moment, but Hazel had nothing more to say. Owen understood. He smiled one last time, kissed her gently on the lips and moved quickly away. He looked over at the Madness Maze.

'I'm ready.'

He heard a puff of disturbed air behind him, as Hazel was teleported up to the new *Sunstrider*, and the air rushed to fill the vacuum where she'd been. He never expected to see her again. But of course, he did.

Hazel materialized on the bridge of the *Sunstrider*, and looked quickly around her. Her heart missed a beat as she saw that the bridge was now exactly how she'd seen it in her dream; the old familiar bridge on *Sunstrider II*. She hurried to check out the expanded control panels, and found that the transformed ship now boasted more weapons and fire-control systems than an E-class starcruiser. And one hell of a set of defensive shields. Presumably the Maze felt she'd need them.

She activated the main viewscreen. They were still there. The Recreated, horrid ships and awful monsters, clustering around the Wolfling World like rats round a dying man. She could almost feel the waves of hate and rage coming from them. Hazel snarled at the screen. She stood between them and the Deathstalker, guarding his back as always; that was all that mattered. She'd faced impossible odds before, and somehow survived. Maybe that had been training, so that she could be at this place, at this time, and not be intimidated.

So that she could stand at the mouth of the pass, denying the Enemy entrance, and be the guard at the gate for all Humanity.

She just wished she didn't have to do it alone.

And then she noticed a flash of light at the edge of the screen, and knew immediately what it was. The *Dauntless* – Silence's legendary ship that had never lost a battle. She wasn't alone after all. Hazel laughed aloud, and turned her attention to the weapons console. Everything was linked through a single fire-control panel, so she could operate it all herself. Outside, in the endless night of the Darkvoid, she could feel more and more of the Recreated becoming aware of her, slowly realizing that she stood between them and their prey. Huge eyes turned in her direction. Mile-long tentacles reached across space. Vast ships oriented themselves on the *Sunstrider*. Hazel whooped once with savage joy, meshed her mind with the fire controls and opened up with everything she had.

Owen walked back into the Madness Maze, and it felt like coming home. He strode quickly between the shining, shimmering walls, guided by instinct as much as memory. He didn't normally remember much about his first trip through the Maze, and now he knew why. It was simply too intense, too overwhelming an experience for the mind to tolerate for long. It blotted out everything else. It had to be forgotten, for the mind to be able to cope with everyday things. He slowed his pace, not hurrying any more, for Time moved differently in the Maze. Here, a second and a year were the same thing. He glanced back once, and wasn't surprised to find that Silence and Carrion were no longer with him, though they'd all entered the Maze together. They had their own ways to go, their own destinies to follow.

Owen drifted through the shining passageways, summoned by a voice he almost recognized. It was bitter cold in the Maze, but he hardly felt it. He had been tempered in fires too harsh for such things ever to bother him again. Here and there static sparked on the air, falling like ionized snowflakes, crawling up and down the shining walls. Owen thought he could hear breathing, slow and steady and gigantic, gusting around him. Underneath his feet he could feel a slow, rhythmic tremor, like the beating of a massive heart far below. He felt watched, known, cared for. Not for the first time, Owen wondered if the Madness Maze was actually alive; some form of alien existence far beyond anything he could hope to conceptualize.

Smells and scents came and went around him. Harsh vinegar and burning leaves. Oiled metal, and old lemon, sharp on his tongue. Rich earth and mulch, and the aroma of green, growing things; a memory of lost Virimonde. There was a chattering of metal birds, and a baby crying, and the tolling of a cracked iron bell in a church at midnight. It felt like Christmas, the world calm and quiet under a blessing of snow. Hark the herald angels sing, promising blood, sweat, toil and tears. Owen threaded his way through the Maze, heading always towards the centre and all the answers to all the questions of his life.

Silence and Carrion walked together, old friends and enemies, bound together by love and hate and memories only they could share and understand. There was a time they'd tried to kill each other, over things they'd believed in and could not back down from, but that was over now. They had a common enemy and a common cause, and besides, they were friends, and always had been, even when they'd hated each other. Life's like that, sometimes.

Silence hadn't travelled far into the Maze, that first time, and mostly what he remembered was his men dying around him in terrible ways. Now he could see the wonder and beauty of the place, the calm, alien splendour of it all. The awesome sanctity, like a cathedral so old that time had soaked into the very brickwork. He felt relaxed, welcomed; he was meant to be here, this time. He didn't hurry, though. It felt as though he had all the time in the world.

It was Carrion's first time in the Maze, but he had the strangest feeling he'd been there before. There was something in the Maze that reminded him strongly of the time he'd spent on Unseeli, communing with the gentle spirits of the forest, the metallic trees and the Ashrai. He felt almost as though he'd returned there, when the planet was still alive and so was he.

Silence and Carrion stopped suddenly, in a corridor no different to any other in the Maze, and looked slowly around them, as though waking from a dream. A voice that was not a voice, but so much more, had sounded in their thoughts, and they knew they'd gone as far as they were going. The heart, and the hidden mysteries of the Maze, were not for them, this time. Theirs was to be a different destiny.

'I feel almost insulted,' said Carrion. 'Owen gets all the answers, and we don't? Where do I go to complain?'

'I don't think I want to see their complaints department,' said Silence. 'And I don't think I ever really wanted to know the answers to everything. I mean; what would you do, afterwards?'

'You always did think small, John. So why did we come here? We were summoned. We both felt it. We're supposed to be here.'

'Hush,' said Silence. 'Can you hear something? Something like . . . wings?'

Slowly, they looked up, moved by something like awe and wonder, and there high above them were the Ashrai. Not ghosts this time, but alive and vital and very much material again. Reborn, revitalized, brought back into the living world by the power of the Maze. They were still pretty damned ugly to human eyes, with gargoyle faces and huge batwings, sharp teeth and claws and fierce, glaring eyes, more dragons than angels. But the threat and menace of their usual visitations were gone. They were singing, alien voices raised in joy and glory, and they were laughing too.

They flew in a bright blue cloudless sky that seemed to go on for ever, soaring and plunging and gliding on never-ending winds. Carrion watched them with tears in his eyes. How graceful they could be! He'd lived with their angry ghosts for so long that he'd forgotten the joy and wonder of their lives. Silence's eyes were wet, too; for having murdered such amazing creatures. And then the Ashrai spoke as one, and Silence and Carrion heard their words in their heads like the voices of angels.

We were wrong. Wrong to give in to rage and revenge. We are ashamed, that we allowed ourselves to become too tied to protecting the forest, and forgot what we were intended to be. The Maze created the metallic forests, and put them into our hands, but we forgot that they were supposed to be a means to an end, not an end in themselves. After we died, the residual Maze energies of Unseeli allowed us to live on as ghosts. Even after the forest, and our reason for existence, were gone. We used you, dear Sean; allowed your rage and need for revenge to give us purpose and meaning. But now you have brought us here, and we remember.

'I'm sorry,' said Silence. 'I'm so sorry for what I did.'

We understand duty, and honour, said the Ashrai. *We forgive you. Not because Sean once asked us to, but because here we can see into your mind and heart. We must put the past behind us, John Silence. A greater war faces us now, of the light against the dark, and we must face it together.*

'The Recreated,' said Carrion.

Yes.

'Do we always have to be fighting?' said Carrion. 'Are we never to know any peace?'

There has been peace, said the Ashrai. *There will be peace again. But now, we have work to do. The Maze gave us life again for a purpose.*

'So what are we supposed to do?' said Silence. 'Do we get to talk to the baby?'

No, said the Ashrai. *You will not be allowed to reach the baby. He doesn't trust you. He will see only Owen. But you have done well to come this far. You have a vital part to play in this last battle for the soul of Humanity.*

'How do you know all this?' said Silence.

We have a link to the Maze, an old link. Our ancestors knew the Maze, long, long ago. We had forgotten, till Sean brought us here. But we have said all there is to say. The Maze has changed you both, in ways that may be useful. Gifts for you, and perhaps a miracle, too. Now we must go, to face the Enemy. The Recreated are very close now, and if they win, the light will go out of the galaxy for ever.

And as suddenly as that, Silence and Carrion were back on the bridge of the *Dauntless*. The bridge crew looked round, startled, voices rising in questions Silence didn't have any answers for. He cut them off with a sharp wave of his hand, and strode over to take his seat in the command chair. Carrion stood at his side, power lance in hand, looking entirely unruffled.

'All right,' said Silence, 'bring me up to speed. Show me where the Recreated are, right now.'

'All over us,' said the comm officer, Morag Tal. 'We've been under fire almost from the moment you . . . left the bridge. We're outnumbered, outgunned and our shields are failing. Apart from that, things are pretty bad. Any chance of reinforcements, Captain?'

'I doubt it,' said Silence. 'There was talk of a miracle, but . . . Where's the *Sunstrider*?'

'Right beside us, and firing off more guns at once than I would have thought possible. Hazel d'Ark appears to be the only one on board. She's doing a lot of damage to the bad guys, and *Sunstrider*'s got some really impressive shields, but even so she's taking one hell of a battering. Just like us.'

Silence studied the awful shapes filling the viewscreen, even at lowest magnification, and felt a cold hand clutch at his heart. He'd faced bad odds before, but never like this. The sheer scale of the ships and the creatures, and their endless numbers . . . A glance at the tactical displays only underlined how desperate the situation was.

'Orders, Captain?' said Morag Tal, her voice carefully calm and even. A hush fell over the bridge as everyone turned to look at their captain.

'We fight until we can't fight any more,' said Silence. 'We have to hold the Recreated's attention. Buy time for the Deathstalker, down in the planet. And hope to God he can pull a miracle out of the bag one last time.'

And then he broke off, staring at the viewscreen in stunned surprise. Everyone followed his gaze, and they all watched in awestruck silence as reinforcements came from nowhere to join in the fight against the Recreated. It was the Ashrai. Given life and form again by the Madness Maze, they soared across open space, wild and wonderful and very savage. At home in space like an endless sky, they hit the Recreated like an army of angry angels, attacking the creatures with claws and fangs, vicious fury and inhuman strength. There seemed no end to their numbers, surging through the cold vacuum on outstretched wings, riding winds only they could feel. They were very small, compared to the Recreated, but they were the Ashrai, born again to battle and glory, and they would not lose again.

'Damn,' said Silence softly. 'How did we ever beat *them*?'

'You cheated,' said Carrion. 'Now, if you'll excuse me; I have to join my people.'

And he ran forward and dived head first into the main viewscreen. It should have shattered under the impact, but as Silence rose sharply from his chair, Carrion plunged into the screen as if it were a dark pool, and was gone, leaving the screen untouched behind him. A moment later, his image appeared on the viewscreen, in open space outside the *Dauntless*. A small, darting figure, he flew through space to join the Ashrai, his power lance glowing as bright as a star. The utter cold of airless space didn't seem to bother him at all, and he flew through the vacuum as naturally as the Ashrai.

'*Damn*,' said Silence, slowly settling into his command chair again. 'The Maze really did change him.'

He wondered for a moment what the Maze might have done to him, but the moment passed, and he barked orders at his startled crew, bringing them back to their senses and their stations. The *Dauntless* fired upon the Recreated with every gun she had, blasting away at the unfeeling creatures and the vessels that gathered inexorably above the Wolfling World. Whatever damage the *Dauntless* did, it wasn't enough to do more than slow that gathering, but more and more of the enemy turned their attention away from the planet to strike back at the *Dauntless*. Strange and terrible energies blasted from the Recreated ships, slamming against the *Dauntless*'s shields, shaking the whole ship. The *Sunstrider* was there too, with enough firepower to hold off an entire Fleet. Carrion and the Ashrai swarmed all over the Recreated. But they knew they were only buying time, against an enemy that would inevitably destroy them, for the one man down below who might hold the answer to the final outcome.

Owen Deathstalker, cut off from Time, made his way unhurriedly towards the centre of the Maze. He had been there before, and remembered the way. It felt like being a child again, going back to the warmth and comfort of the Family hearth, after a long time out in the cold. He came at last to the hidden heart of the Madness Maze, and it was just as he'd remembered it. The secret heart was a wide, circular space, calm as the eye of a storm, shimmering walls surrounding it like the silver petals of an immense flower. And there, in the exact centre of the protected space, was a glowing crystal, some four feet across, holding within its warm, golden heart a tiny human baby. He couldn't have been more than a month old, his features still forming and settling into place. His eyes were closed, and if he breathed at all it was so slowly Owen couldn't see it. The baby had one thumb tucked securely into its rosebud mouth. Owen leaned over the crystal, studying his distant ancestor. He looked very small and innocent, for one so powerful and so very dangerous.

'Well,' said a strangely familiar voice behind him. 'It took you long enough to get here.'

Owen spun round sharply, and then winced as the recent wound in his side flared up. And then he forgot all about that as he found himself looking at . . . himself. Owen Deathstalker, exact in every detail, was standing facing him, hands on hips, studying him critically.

'Who the hell are you?' said Owen.

'Wrong question,' said his double calmly. 'You should have asked, *What are you?* Here's a clue.'

First the face and then the shape of Owen's double ran like liquid, and the whole form reshaped itself in a moment, becoming instead an exact duplicate of Giles Deathstalker. He smiled charmingly at Owen, an expression that didn't really suit Giles's face. The double quickly realized that this identity didn't appeal to Owen either, judging by his deepening frown, and changed again, becoming Cathy DeVries, Owen's old mistress and dead love.

'That better?' said Cathy.

'Depends,' said Owen. 'What the hell are you?'

'Allow me to introduce myself. I have many names, but one nature; many forms and yet none. I am older than your Empire, and indeed your entire species, and I am every dream you ever had, including the ones that made you cry out in the night. I'm also responsible for everything happening here, though I don't like to boast. Well, I do, but I'm programmed against it. I created the Madness Maze, and I've been waiting a very long time to meet you, Owen Deathstalker.'

Owen paused for a moment, considering this, and then decided to stick with the part he could understand. 'Why did you imitate me, and then Giles, and now Cathy?'

'To put you at your ease.'

'Trust me,' said Owen, 'it's not working.'

Cathy shrugged. 'There's only so much I can do. I have a vast repertoire of shapes and forms, but you wouldn't like most of them. I think I'll stick with this one for the time being, or at least until I get bored. I've been studying Humanity for longer than you could comfortably comprehend, and I'm still no nearer understanding you. You're remarkably complex for such a limited life form. But then, it's that potential that makes you perfect for our needs. We seem to be drifting away from the point of this conversation. Would it help you if I explained that I am in fact an ancient, semi-sentient recording, left behind by a mighty and noble species that passed through your galaxy long ago?'

Owen considered this. 'Possibly. You're just . . . a recording? Not an actual member of your species?'

'Alas, no. You couldn't cope with the real thing. But I am a fairly accurate recreation of as much of us as you could hope to take in.'

'Wait just a minute,' said Owen. 'I have this horrid feeling I've seen you before. You're that shape-changing alien who appeared in Lionstone's Court a few years back, disguised as a priest! I saw the holo recording. Silliest damn thing I ever saw. Everyone wondered how it was we'd never encountered your species before, and why afterwards we couldn't find even a trace of you or your kind.'

'Oh, yes,' said Cathy cheerfully, 'that was me. Or rather, one of me. I am widely spread, with parts of me everywhere Humanity goes, watching and recording. Forbidden to interfere directly, of course. I'm just a recording, after all, and strictly prohibited from getting above myself. I follow the path I was created to follow, and you've no idea how frustrating that can be. Humans can be so exasperating. Give them three choices, and they'll come up with a fourth every time. Sometimes I think they do it just to be perverse. Luckily I'm only semi-sentient, or I'd have washed my hands of you long ago.'

'Slow down a bit,' said Owen, just a little desperately. 'You're all that's left of a shape-changing species that passed through long ago. OK. Where did you come from, and where did you go?'

'We came from outside your galaxy, aeons ago. As to where we went, you're not ready to know that. You've come a long way, Owen Deathstalker, but you're still basically human. Trust me; it's not anywhere Humanity could hope to follow. Not until your species has done a hell of a lot more evolving, anyway. Why don't you ask me what we did, while we were here? That's much more interesting.'

'Might as well,' Owen said resignedly. 'This is going to take some time, isn't it?'

'Yes,' said Cathy. 'I've got such a lot to tell you. But at

least after you've heard it all, your life may make a little more sense. You are the final product of generations of planning, Owen Deathstalker, and not all of it human. Shall we be seated?'

Two comfortable chairs appeared out of nowhere. Owen and Cathy sat down facing each other. Beside them, the baby slept peacefully in its glowing crystal, sucking its tiny thumb.

'We created the Madness Maze to raise Humanity to its full potential,' said the alien recording with Cathy's face. 'But somehow, it didn't work out that way. The first to discover the Maze were the Blood Runners, and they were frightened and ran away. The Hadenmen scientists came out of the Maze with the right idea, the perfectibility of Mankind, but they got the method all wrong. They tried to do it with tech, when all they really needed was the Maze, and faith in themselves. They were already superhuman, but they couldn't believe it was possible without tech. Humanity has always been rather small, not to say limited, in its thinking. The Wolflings were really just a mistake; amplifying Mankind's animal heritage, looking back instead of forward.'

Cathy leaned closer, her eyes fixed on Owen's. 'Humanity must evolve; become more than it is, achieve its full potential. You have to. Something awful is coming, from far beyond your galaxy. It's not life as you know it; it's strange and terrible, awful and mighty, totally destructive and utterly unstoppable. They destroyed most of my species. A great and ancient civilization, blown away to dust and less than dust. Just a few of us escaped and fled here, to your galaxy. They had no name for themselves that we could understand. What we called them translates simply as *the Terror*.

'They move slowly. Because of their size and nature they don't need starships or stardrives, so they move at less than the speed of light. But the Terror destroyed every living thing in our galaxy, before we were forced to flee, and they are coming here. Slowly, but they are coming, and you must be prepared and ready to meet them. As you are now, you have nothing that could stand against them. The Recreated in their insanity are but the merest glimpse of the true horror of the Terror. They eat souls, and their young incubate in suns. They are extra-dimensional creatures, beyond your understanding, and all of Space and Time is their prey. As flies to wanton boys are we to the Terror.

'You are not the first species we have tried to raise to a higher level. We've been here in your galaxy for some considerable time. We attempted it with a species on the world you call Wolf IV. We taught them to transform themselves as we do, but they gave in to their own inner demons and destroyed themselves. We tried again, with another species, on the planet you call Grendel. But they became living killing machines, in their fear, and placed themselves in suspended animation in their Vaults, to await the coming of the Terror. This was not what was intended. Next, we created the metallic forests on Unseeli, for the Ashrai, and they became farmers, interested only in preserving the trees, instead of using them to spur their own evolution. Finally, we turned to Humanity. Small as you were, we saw the potential for greatness in you.

'This time, we decided not just to give you the benefits we brought. Instead, we created the Maze, and left it for you to search out and investigate for yourselves. Hopefully that would make you value it more. And eventually, after many false starts, you and your companions came to the Maze and passed all the way through, and emerged transformed, the first butterflies from a race of caterpillars. It had taken a while, but at last the Maze had found the right sort of people: intense, focused, determined.'

'But . . . what *did* the Maze do to us, really?' said Owen. 'I thought at first we were some kind of super-esper, but we're not. What are we, now?'

'You are what Humanity would have become, in its far and distant future. The Maze just speeded evolution up a bit. It was a short cut. You have the power to change reality itself through force of will.' Cathy smiled at his expression. 'Didn't any of you ever realize? It expressed itself differently in each of you, according to your individual needs and propensities, but really any of you could have done anything the others did, if you'd just had faith. Only your own limited thinking held you back. Of course, you were all supposed to stay and work together. The whole would have been far greater than the sum of its parts. But you insisted on going your own separate ways. Humans . . . That's why so many people died or went insane trying to pass through the Maze. It could only help and change those who were willing and who were mentally flexible enough. Those too rigid in their thoughts, those unworthy or too scared to change, broke rather than be transformed. Their madness and death came from inside themselves, not from the Maze.'

'Let's talk about the baby,' said Owen. 'I need to talk about the baby. What's his part in all this?'

'When Giles died, the baby somehow knew it,' said Cathy. 'He began to wake, drifting slowly up from the protecting depths of sleep. The Recreated sensed this, and became desperate. If the baby were to wake, then the source of their power, their very existence, was under threat.'

'Is that what triggered the Recreated's great assault on Humanity?' said Owen. 'By killing Giles, am I responsible for their attack?'

'No. They started out of the Darkvoid after Captain Silence destroyed the Maze. In fact, it had only jumped forward through Time, but the Recreated didn't know that. All they knew was that the source of their power was suddenly gone. They were able to survive until the Maze returned, but the experience panicked them. You now know all you need to know. It's time we began the last part of your journey. Of your destiny.'

Cathy rose to her feet, and Owen did so too. The chairs disappeared silently. Cathy turned her gaze on the sleeping baby, and after a moment Owen did so too.

'He is your kin, your Family,' said Cathy softly. 'You are both Deathstalkers. Talk to him, Owen. He will hear you.'

'I don't even know his name,' Owen protested. 'And anyway, he's still asleep.'

'Reach out to him,' said Cathy. 'He'll hear you.'

Owen turned to look at the sleeping baby, and found that his eyes were already open and looking at him. They were dark eyes, like his, but clear and calm and full of wonder. Owen reached out with his mind, and the baby's thoughts came to meet him. They blazed like fireworks, like comets in the night, blindingly bright and gaudily coloured, and at first all Owen could understand were the baby's feelings; warm and loving and surprisingly trusting. Owen opened himself to the baby, who learned words and concepts from him in a moment. The baby's mind was very large, though strangely unfocused in places, and Owen felt like a single fish in a sentient ocean. He worried briefly that he might drown there, but the baby quickly broadcast reassurance. They relaxed together, concentrating on their link. The baby had learned much from the Maze, but people were still new to him. Two Maze-altered Deathstalkers communed in an alien place, and found joy in each other. They talked, sometimes in words and sometimes not, like father and child, and more and less than that.

I'm sorry about what I did, said the baby, linking his mind to Owen's. *I want to put everything right again, and I will, but I need time to consider how. I don't want to make any more mistakes. You must buy me the time I need.*

Whatever you need, said Owen. *But what can I do?*

Ask Cathy. She knows. Goodbye, Owen. I'm glad I got to meet you at last.

Owen smiled down at the baby, who removed the tiny thumb from his mouth so he could smile back. And then the baby closed his dark, knowing eyes and went back to sleep, considering how to change the universe once again. Owen looked at the alien with Cathy's face.

'Well, that was . . . different. I like him. So: what is it I have to do? What can one man do, against something like the Recreated?'

Cathy looked at him steadily. 'This is the final part of your destiny, Owen. You have to distract the Recreated; hold their attention and keep them occupied while the baby prepares for what he will do next. All the Recreated, not just the few facing Hazel and the others above this world. If the Recreated understand that the baby is working against them, they might try to drive it back into the depths of sleep again. They might even risk destroying him, and if the baby dies, all hope for Humanity's survival dies with him. It's all down to you, Owen.'

'Whatever it is, it must be really bad, or you wouldn't keep putting it off. Tell me. I can take it.' Owen glared at Cathy, who stared sadly back at him. Owen sighed. 'I'm really not going to like this, am I?'

On the bridge of the *Sunstrider*, Hazel was living out her dream. The ship's new weapons fired over and over again, but the numbers of the Recreated seemed endless. Her targets were so large she couldn't miss, but it was hard to do any real damage to anything so vast. She kept the *Sunstrider* weaving and dodging, eluding crippling energy blasts and mile-long tentacles with barbs the size of her ship, but the Recreated were everywhere now and she couldn't dodge them all. Her shields were going down, and the *Sunstrider* was taking more and more damage, some of it bad.

Alarm sirens wailed continuously until they got on Hazel's nerves, and she turned them off. They weren't telling her anything she didn't already know. One side of the control panels had exploded, filling the bridge with leaping flames and black, billowing smoke. Hazel had put out the main fires, but flames still flickered here and there, casting dark, darting shadows across the bridge. The extractor fans were working overtime, trying to clear the smoke from the air. Hazel barely noticed. All her attention was plugged into the weapons controls and navigation systems now, as she fought her way doggedly through the endless ranks of the Recreated. She targeted and fired her guns over and over, delighting in her small victories, but she was deathly tired now, and she could feel the *Sunstrider* dying slowly around her. Even a ship that had been rebuilt by the Maze could only take so much punishment.

Hazel fought on. The odds against her were impossible to beat, just as she'd dreamed, but she wasn't going to let a little thing like that stop her. She was Hazel d'Ark, and today she earned her legend.

The *Dauntless* was there too, cutting a path through the Recreated, guns blazing, shields flaring brilliantly as they tried to absorb or deflect the attacking energy blasts. Many of the shields had already gone down, and the outer hull was holed and open to space in half a dozen places. Interior seals preserved the ship's atmosphere, but every section lost weakened the ship still further. Captain Silence sat calmly in his command chair, issuing a steady stream of orders, keeping on top of everything even as damage reports and crew losses came in from all over his ship. Since coming out of the Maze, his mind had expanded to fill his ship from stem to stern, knowing it as intimately as he knew his own body. He was the *Dauntless* now, and it was him.

He studied the massing Recreated through his ship's sensors, taking in their sheer size and number, and pushed aside despair with almost casual disdain. He never once thought of retreating. He was standing between Humanity and its Enemy, and that was all he'd ever really wanted. Another workstation suddenly went up in flames, and its occupant screamed as he was consumed. He was dead by the time the damage control unit had put out the fire. Silence knew the man, but there was no time to mourn him. That would be for later, if there was a later. He had to hold his crew together, by the strength of his will and the force of his personality. Despite the strain, and the impossible odds, none of them had broken, and Silence was very proud of them. He nursed the remaining power in the ship's engines, switching it from weapons to shields and back again as needed. He was buying time for the Deathstalker, a man he'd once considered an enemy and a traitor, but who might now be Humanity's last and only hope.

Out in open space, Carrion flew with his people, the Ashrai, darting back and forth in the darkness like a living star, burning so very brightly now. He struck at the monsters around him with flaring, destructive energies focused through his power lance, blasting apart unnatural flesh and bone with cold, intense fury. He was fast and deadly, and they couldn't touch him. Space couldn't harm him; he swam in it like a shark in a sunless sea. Where he looked, awful shapes exploded, and where he gestured, the Recreated were torn apart. But he was small, and they were huge.

Even the whole race of the Ashrai reborn was dwarfed by the Recreated.

Carrion fought on, singing the song of the Ashrai, fighting beside them as he had once before, his voice joining with those of his true kind.

'You have to go back, Owen,' said the alien, and it didn't sound like Cathy any more. 'Back through the Pale Horizon, back through Space and Time. You can do this; you have the power within you. Your whole life has been leading up to this moment, this decision; towards making you into a hero capable of performing this last deed for Humanity. You must run through past places, and let the Recreated chase you. Hold their attention; hold them close. Don't let them fall back, or consider giving up the hunt. Keep them always on your tail, staying just ahead of them. Taunt them. Make them hate you. As you and they go further back in Time, the distance and the pursuit will drain the Recreated's energy. That should give you the edge you need.

'I won't lie to you. If they catch you, if you let them get too close, you'll die horribly. You don't have to do this, I can't make you. It has to be your decision. But it's the only way left to ensure Humanity's survival, and put everything right again.'

'That was all Giles ever wanted,' said Owen. 'But he chose

the wrong way. So this is your great plan. I knew I wouldn't like it.'

'But you'll do it.'

'Of course I'll do it,' said Owen. 'I always do, don't I? I've always known my duty. Known what it means to be a Deathstalker. Talk to me, whatever you are. How are we going to convince all the Recreated that they should give up their attack on the brink of victory, in order to chase me back through Time?'

'The Maze and I will work together to make the Recreated think that you are the baby, trying to escape them by travelling back into the past. They'll pursue you rather than risk losing their power source, and perhaps their very existence.'

Owen considered this. 'All right; that might just work. But how the hell do I time-travel? I've never had that ability before.'

'Of course you have. You can control reality, remember? You travelled through Time once before, right here, the first time you came through the Maze. Remember, Owen . . .'

Owen closed his eyes, concentrating on the newly restored memories of his first trip through the Madness Maze. That memory came to him again, clear and sharp as yesterday. He remembered journeying back through Time, watching his own life unravel before him, all the moments and decisions that had made him what he was. It was so simple a trick, once he saw how. Time was just another direction. But before he committed himself to this last great task of his destiny, Owen decided he was entitled to one small thing for himself. And so he concentrated, reached back through Time, and brought a man forward into the future, into the hidden heart of the Madness Maze. Owen slowly opened his eyes, and there, standing before him, was his father, Arthur Deathstalker.

Arthur was a young man, about the same age as Owen, dressed in formal Court attire. A sword at his side and a gun on his hip, and the same dark hair and darker eyes. They looked more like brothers than father and son. Owen looked at his father, dead and gone for years now, and his throat closed up. He couldn't say anything. Arthur looked around him, more baffled than alarmed, and then turned back to Owen and gave him a surprisingly charming smile.

'I don't think I know you, sir, though your face is familiar. Which is more than I can say for this unusual place. Perhaps you could tell me where this is, and who you are, and why I am here.'

'This . . . is the future,' said Owen, 'your future. I brought you here to talk with you. I'm your son, Owen.'

Arthur raised an elegant eyebrow. 'My son Owen is currently four years old, and more trouble than anyone should be cursed with. He's already run through three nannies. Have you any evidence for this extraordinary claim?'

Owen held up his right hand, and the Family ring of chunky black gold showed clearly on his finger. Arthur caught his breath for a moment, and then raised his right hand, to show an identical ring. Slowly they lowered their hands. Arthur took a deep breath, then let it out.

'Damn. That's the Deathstalker ring, all right. Only ever was one. So; time travel. Damn, that is impressive. And you're my son, Owen, all grown up. You look like you turned out fine. You look a lot like your grandfather, actually. Why am I here, Owen? I take it there is some reason.'

'You're taking this very calmly,' said Owen. 'Certainly more than I am.'

Arthur shrugged easily. 'When you intrigue for a living at the royal Court, there isn't much that can scare or throw you any more.' He fixed Owen with a sharp look. 'Am I dead in your time, Owen? Is that what this is all about?'

'Yes,' said Owen flatly. 'Lionstone had you murdered. She sent Kit SummerIsle after you, and he cut you down in the street. Nobody came to help.'

'Well,' said Arthur, after a moment. 'At least she sent someone worthy after me. A SummerIsle, no less. No doubt he went on to greater things. Will I remember any of this, when I go back?'

'I don't know,' said Owen. 'I'm . . . new to all this time-travel business.'

'Ah, hell. I never expected to reach an old age. Deathstalkers don't, mostly. The price we pay for being movers and shakers, instead of just one of the crowd. The way of the warrior is never easy.'

'Yes,' said Owen, new anger flooding into his words. 'I became the warrior you always wanted me to be. I led the rebellion that overthrew Lionstone. I don't have a wife, or a family, or anything else to call my own, but I still have your poisoned gift, Father. I became a bloody warrior!'

'You sound upset,' said Arthur.

'Are you surprised? When I'm a little older, you'll hire a series of personal trainers to beat the shit out of me, over and over again, to try and bring out the boost in me, so that I could be the great warrior you wanted. Well, I never wanted to be a warrior. Never! All I ever wanted was to be a scholar, a minor historian, happy doing quiet academic work in some ivory tower, far away from all the movers and shakers and all the misery they bring. But you and the damned Deathstalker legacy made me into a warrior anyway, and took away all the happiness I ever knew.'

For the first time, Arthur looked concerned. He took a step forward, and reached out as though to take Owen in his arms. But then he saw the look in his son's eyes, and slowly lowered his arms without touching him.

'If I did do that, Owen, and you must remember that I haven't even considered it yet, then I probably ordered it done for the same reason my father had it done to me; because you needed the boost for your own protection. Just by being born a Deathstalker, you inherited many enemies. They would have had you killed in a moment, if they sensed weakness in you. I knew I might die with my work unfinished; you had to be able to survive, to carry on. And here you are now, a man grown into a warrior. Can you honestly say you'd be here, if you hadn't had the boost?'

'What about the deals you made?' said Owen. 'With the

Hadenmen and the Blood Runners, promising them their tithe of Humanity, in return for their support?'

'The rebellion needed them,' said Arthur calmly. 'I had to promise what it took to close the deal. I always hoped that when the original Deathstalker finally appeared, he'd find some way to break the deals. Certainly I never intended that we should actually pay the tithes, even if it meant another war. I'm a politician, Owen, not a monster.'

'I never really thought you were a monster. You were my father.'

'Then why did you bring me here, Owen?'

'Because . . . because I never got to say goodbye.' Owen's eyes blurred with hot tears. 'I missed you, Dad. I never thought I would, but I did. And I wanted you to know . . . I won the rebellion for you. I wanted you to be proud of me.'

'I was always proud of you, Owen. You're my son. And I'm glad I got the chance to see what a fine man you grew into.'

This time, they hugged each other tightly. Two Deathstalkers, finding peace together at last. Eventually they moved apart.

'Why didn't you bring your mother here too?' said Arthur. 'She'd have loved to see you, I'm sure . . .' And then he saw the look in Owen's eyes. 'Oh, God. She dies young.'

'I barely remember her,' said Owen. 'It was an illness. Very sudden. You never talked much about her, to me.'

'Damn. Damn.' Arthur looked away for a moment. 'Perhaps it's best I don't remember any of this after all. I think it's time you sent me home, Owen. Back to my own time.' He looked at Owen. 'But I'm glad we had this chance to talk. I missed my father terribly after he was gone, killed in that stupid duel. I never got to say goodbye either. But I'm sure he would have been as proud of you as I am. Goodbye, Owen. My son.'

And then he was gone, or rather Owen let him go, and Arthur Deathstalker plunged back through the years to his own time, perhaps to remember, perhaps not.

Owen stood quietly for a long while, remembering many things, and then let go his hold on Time. He disappeared, carrying the seeming of the baby with him, and high above the world the Recreated screamed in frustrated rage.

The *Sunstrider* was barely maintaining orbit now, blasted from all sides, the last of its shields barely strong enough to turn aside the never-ending attacks. There were gaping holes in stem and stern, punctures in the outer and inner hulls, and only the invading vacuum kept the fires from raging out of control. Life support was limited to the bridge only now, where Hazel had locked herself in, not even thinking of the escape pods.

The control panels were a mess. Most of the guns were gone, destroyed, shot away, and the remaining few were being controlled through a single isolated weapons control system. Fires burned sullenly on the bridge, adding to the hellish red glow of the emergency lighting. Hazel was burned and bleeding from a dozen wounds, her flesh torn over and over again by exploding systems, but still she stood straight, determined, all her thoughts on the guns. She'd always known she'd die alone, striking out at her enemies to the last.

The *Dauntless* was being torn apart from within by repeated explosions, its rear assembly shattered and leaking air. Internal seals maintained pressure and life support in some parts of the ship, but they were few and scattered now, and one by one the guns were falling silent as they were destroyed, or ran out of crew to man them. The shields were going down all over the ship.

On the bridge, Captain Silence could feel his ship dying about him. But still he maintained calm and discipline through his own example, though half the bridge crew were dead and fires burned in the guts of devastated workstations. Bodies lay everywhere, and no one had the time or the strength to do anything about them. Silence kept his ship heading into the face of the Enemy, drawing their onslaught and defying them to do their worst. Doing his duty. Dying by inches along with his ship. And sometimes thinking, just a little wistfully, that Frost would have loved this.

Out in space, the Ashrai were dying in their thousands, torn apart by the strange and awful energies of the Recreated, but the majority still hurled themselves upon the Enemy in wave after wave. Once there had been millions of them, all their great race born again, but though their numbers were savagely lessened, still they fought on, soaring through open space like fallen angels, harsh and unrelenting, undeterred by the scale or the terrible nature of their foe.

And brightest of them all, the man called Carrion, shining like the sun as he slammed through space, great energies crackling round his power lance as he attacked ships the size of mountains and of moons. He plunged through one side of a ship and out the other, protected by the power running wild within him, awoken by the Ashrai and confirmed by the Maze. He was tired now, in body and in mind, for all the energies he wielded, and only his strength of will kept them from consuming him. There seemed no end to the Enemy. He was mighty and he was powerful, but he was so very small in the face of the Recreated.

Hazel d'Ark, Captain Silence and the man called Carrion fought the good fight with all their will and all their heart, and never once thought of retreating. And if they thought of the time they were buying in minutes now, rather than hours, it did not deter them. They looked death in the eye, and were damned if they'd blink first. So they were all caught by surprise when every single member of the Recreated host suddenly vanished, and the battle was over.

Owen Deathstalker ran back through Time, and behind him came the Recreated.

Back and back he went, that brave and honourable man, through all the times and places of his past, seeing again all the changes he'd been responsible for. It was like running inside a rainbow, all the colours of his world running together, and outside it a great roar of voices all speaking at once. Owen could hear the Recreated howling behind him in rage and fear, and the sound seemed very small. He ran on, building up his speed, and Time slipped past him, faster and faster.

He paused briefly on the bridge of the *Sunstrider*, still in orbit around the Wolfling World. The battle against the Recreated had just begun. He saw Hazel fighting off uncountable enemies, with limited weapons but unlimited courage, and the sight warmed his heart. He would have liked to stop there for a while, just long enough to say goodbye, maybe explain what he was doing, but the Recreated were very close, and he didn't have the time to spare.

He ran on, faster and faster, the days blurring around him. He felt strong and determined; he felt he could run for ever. Let the Recreated chase him. They'd never catch him. He could feel their rage and hatred behind him, like a great fire beating on his back, and he laughed at them. They were doing just what he wanted. He let his speed level off. He didn't want the Recreated to become discouraged and break off their chase. He had to hold them to him, keep them focused only on him, for however much time it took the baby to work out its answer.

As so many times before, everything depended on him, Owen Deathstalker, the last hero.

He wondered vaguely if he'd ever be able to stop; if he'd have to keep running back through Time for ever, to keep Humanity safe. Maybe run all the way back, down all the millennia, to the Big Bang itself . . . so that he and the Recreated could die together in that primal moment, and save the future for Humanity. That was a long path, longer than he could imagine, but he felt he could run that far, if he had to.

No. It wouldn't come to that. Owen had faith in the baby. However young he was, he was still a Deathstalker, after all.

On and on he ran, familiar faces and places looming out of the endless rainbow spiralling around him. Wherever he looked, he saw people he knew, places he had lived or fought in, some vital, some not. It was like trawling back through his memories, able to see everything, but change nothing. Until he saw one face that was too important to let pass by. He saw that face, and all his plans went for nothing. Owen stopped his race with a jolt, dropping back into present Time, and materialized in a small bare room. And there, in that room, Kit SummerIsle, Kid Death. The man who murdered his father.

The SummerIsle looked round and saw Owen, and was almost startled out of his usual complacency. 'Deathstalker! Now this *is* a surprise. Everyone assumed you were dead. I'm afraid the royal wedding's gone ahead without you.'

'I'm not here for a wedding,' said Owen, in a voice so low and dark it barely sounded like him at all. 'I'm here for a funeral. Yours. My father was a good man. You killed him. I'll have your heart's blood for that.'

Kit SummerIsle smiled widely, and drew his sword. 'So good to meet an old-fashioned aristocrat. One who hasn't forgotten the old code of honour, of feud and vendetta. I always wondered what it would be like to fight you, the legendary warrior himself. They say you're more than human now, but then, there aren't many who would call me human either. No doubt I'll get into trouble for killing you, but I'll survive, I always do. I'm too useful a weapon to discard. This had to happen, really. The last SummerIsle versus the last Deathstalker. Oh, happy day.'

'You always did talk too much,' said Owen, drawing his sword.

'Then let us fight, by all means. Because of you, my dear David is dead. Burn in Hell, Deathstalker.'

Their swords slammed together and sprang apart again in a shower of sparks, and they circled each other for a moment before launching themselves at each other's throat. Neither man had the time or patience for an extended duel. All that mattered was the other man's death, an end to a long line of bloodshed that stretched back centuries, the last bloody breath of the Deathstalker conspiracy.

At the back of Owen's mind, an esper precog on Mistworld murmured a prophecy. *The smiling killer, the shark in shallow waters, the man who will not be stopped save by his own hand. Kid Death* . . . Owen remembered, and didn't give a damn.

They were both master swordsmen, experienced warriors, practised killers, and their blades flashed through the still air too quickly for the normal eye to follow. Owen had the boost, and Kit had the drive, and they were both a little crazy by now. They stamped and thrust and hacked and cut, lunging and parrying and retreating, killing blows missing by fractions of an inch, or turned aside at the last moment by sheer skill or daring. Both men drew blood here and there, never vital, neither of them able to force an opening long enough to exploit it. Their sides heaved, the breath burned in their straining lungs, and their swords grew heavier as their arms and backs tired. No man could maintain this kind of speed and savagery for long without burning out. The wound the Wolfling had made in Owen's side had only recently healed, and already it was making itself felt again.

Need and desperation put new strength in Owen's swordarm, and he beat aside Kid Death's blade, plunging forward. The tip of his sword gouged the SummerIsle's face, tearing the eye out of his head. Blood poured down his disfigured face, and he howled in rage as much as pain. Kit plunged forward, anger robbing him of his usual grace. Owen turned aside the blow, and only then realized that Kit had been expecting that. The SummerIsle's sword slammed back against Owen's, catching the Deathstalker's wrist at an awkward and painful angle, and Owen's fingers sprang open despite him, releasing his sword. It fell clattering to the floor as Kid Death laughed breathlessly, half his face a bloody mask.

But even as Kit savoured that moment of triumph, Owen darted forward and grabbed the SummerIsle's wrist in both his hands. It only took a moment to force the swordarm round and back against itself, and drive the SummerIsle's own sword into his side.

The SummerIsle cried out once, and staggered away. Owen let him go. He knew a death wound when he saw it. He didn't feel particularly triumphant. Rather, he felt as though a great weight had been lifted from his shoulders. Duty was done, and his father, that good man, had finally been avenged. Owen would have liked to stay and watch his enemy die, but he could feel the Recreated approaching, very close now, and he knew he had to go on. He picked up his sword and threw himself back into Time, back into the long chaos of the years, and vanished from the room. Kit SummerIsle dragged himself slowly across the floor, dying by inches. No one would ever know who killed him.

Owen no longer felt like he could run for ever. The fight with the SummerIsle had taken a lot out of him, and he was hurt in many places. He was angry at himself now, for wasting so much time on personal business. Humanity was depending on him. He ran, and the Recreated came howling behind him, very close now. Owen strained to open up a wider gap between them, and couldn't. He ran on, and Time flowed around him like a many-coloured river, sparkling with moments and memories.

Owen stopped briefly, now and again, dropping back into Time for a moment to get his bearings or say a last goodbye.

Once he materialized in a long stone corridor of his Family castle, the Last Standing. He saw Jack Random lurching slowly along, his face as pale as death, clutching his side. He looked sad and tired, and Owen walked with him for a while to keep him company. He stopped again, a little further back in Time, and saw Jack flickering in and out of Time, somewhere deep under Lionstone's old Palace. Owen ran on, the Recreated close behind. He stopped again, to appear briefly in the courtyard of Saint Bea's Mission on Lachrymae Christi. He called out to Hazel, to warn her about the Blood Runners, but he was too late. He stayed a little longer in the hall of his old Standing on Virimonde, to snatch a thrown knife out of mid-air and save Hazel from a sneak attack. He killed the man who threw it, the renegade Lord Kartakis, and smiled tiredly at Hazel as she stared at him, amazed. There was so much he wanted to say to her, and he reached out a hand, but for some reason she wouldn't take it. He smiled anyway, and tried one last time to say he loved her, but the Recreated were pressing very close now, and he had to go.

Owen Deathstalker ran and ran, back through Time and the days and places of his past, drawing on his own energies now to fuel his flight. It seemed to him that he was moving more slowly, but so were the Recreated. The distance between them remained close, but constant. And the rage and hatred of the Enemy burned as fiercely as ever.

Finally, the chase came to an end. Owen had burned up all his Maze-given energies, and could run no further. He fell back into Time past, materializing in a cold, foggy back alley in the city of Mistport, some time during his first visit there. He collapsed on the dirty snow, gasping for breath. Blood ran sluggishly from wounds that hadn't had a chance to heal. His heart and his will and his duty urged him on, but he'd gone as far as he could. He was just a man again, with a man's limitations, all his more than human energies gone, burned up in the chase. He rolled slowly over on to his back in the snow, reaching for his sword and gun, as though they could be of any use now. He could feel the imminent presence of the Recreated, on the verge of breaking through into the physical world. A great darkness, howling triumphantly . . . And then suddenly, they were gone.

Owen sat up slowly. The deserted alleyway was still and silent. And then Cathy DeVries was standing there before him, smiling.

'Well done, Deathstalker. You did it. You ran the Recreated till their energies dried up, and they were so weakened they couldn't withstand the baby's power. Even as we speak, he's putting everything right again. Everything.'

'You're not really here, are you,' said Owen, getting painfully to his feet.

'Alas, no. I'm just a recording, placed in your mind. One

last contact, to say thank you. Only you could have done this, Owen. Only you.'

'Great,' said Owen. 'Now how about a lift home?'

Cathy looked at him sadly. 'I'm sorry, Owen. It's taking everything the baby has to do what has to be done. There's nothing left to help you.'

'Typical,' said Owen. 'Guess I'll just have to wait for my power levels to return, and make my own way back. See you in a while, Cathy.'

But the figure had already vanished. Owen looked around him. The alleyway looked vaguely familiar, but in the thick mists it was hard to be sure. And then he heard them coming, stumbling through the fog towards him. Owen drew his sword and hefted it. The blade felt very heavy. He was tired and hurting, and a long way from his best. His powers were gone, and he wasn't even sure he could boost. Not a good time to get involved in a fight. He put his back against the alley wall, hoping to hide in the shadows.

They came lurching out of the mists, dark figures wrapped in stained and ill-fitting furs, and Owen only had to see their faces, the pain and desperate need in their eyes, to know what they were. Plasma babies – addicts of that terrible and destructive drug, Blood. They'd kill him and rob him of whatever he had, just to pay for one more fix. Their eyes found him, despite the shadows, and knives and broken bottles appeared in their hands. *Deathstalker luck*, thought Owen, almost angrily. *Always bad.*

There had to be at least thirty of them. At his peak, Owen could have taken them all without even breathing hard. But he was just a man now, tired and hurting, and he knew he couldn't face odds like these. He needed time, time to heal and rebuild his energies. He turned and ran down the grimy alleyway, boots slipping and sliding in the snow, and the plasma babies ran after him.

And all Owen could think was *The prophecy. The prophecy . . .*

Owen forced himself on, the freezing-cold air searing his

lungs as he gasped it in. Behind him, the Blood addicts let out a cry that was partly anger and need, partly the hungry, savage cry of a pack of dogs. Owen fought back a red mist of exhaustion that was already beginning to cloak his vision. He hit the wall at the end of the alley with his shoulder, bounced off without slowing and kept running, following another alleyway he hoped would lead to a main street. Even Mistworlders would help against plasma babies, the lowest of the low. But the alley only led down more alleys, a dirty labyrinth of soot-stained brick and churned-up snow.

He noticed at last that it was night, the full moon filling the drifting mists with a silver, opalescent glow. Red and amber lights glowed briefly from the occasional overhead lamp, but no one was about at this hour, and the few windows Owen could see were firmly shuttered. He knew better than to bang on them for help. He was on his own. He ran on, skidding and sliding now in the snow as his legs grew tired and his balance became uncertain. *Die alone, overwhelming odds, far from friends and succour . . . in Mistport.* Owen showed his teeth in a smile that was at least partly a snarl. He hadn't come this far, achieved this much, to die here in some anonymous backstreet.

He ran on, his legs so numb now he could barely feel the impact of his boots thudding on the snow-covered cobbles. His thoughts became vague and uncertain. Sometimes it seemed to him that old friends and enemies, dead and alive, ran with him to keep him company. There were many things he'd meant to say to them, but never had. He'd always thought there'd be enough time to say and do all the things that needed saying and doing, but time has a way of creeping up on you, and running out when you least expect it.

Sometimes he thought he was still running back through Time, and the enemy behind him was the Recreated, and he wondered if he'd ever be allowed to stop and rest.

And then he staggered out of the last alleyway, and found himself in a dead-end square, and there was nowhere left to run. He bent over for a moment, his lungs heaving for air, and leaned on his sword to steady himself. At least he didn't have to run any more. He straightened up slowly and looked about him, and then he laughed painfully as he realized why the square looked so familiar. He'd been here before. This was the dead-end square where he'd fought a small army of Blood addicts with Hazel d'Ark at his side, the place where he'd unwittingly crippled and then had to kill a young girl. Perhaps the one thing he'd never forgiven himself for. For all his running, for all his long, eventful life, he'd finally come full circle.

They came spilling into the square, angry and vicious, even more so than he remembered. The plasma babies saw him standing at bay, and hesitated for a moment, seeing the warrior in the way he stood, in the way he held his sword. But pain and need drove them on, and they threw themselves at him, howling wordlessly. The odds were appalling, unbeatable, but Owen went to meet them anyway, because he was a Deathstalker, and if he had to fall, at least he'd go down fighting.

He blew a hole in the crowd with his disrupter, the energy blast blowing away half a dozen ragged figures and setting fire to the furs of as many more. Owen holstered the gun. He doubted he'd get a chance to use it again. One way or another, the fight would probably be over before the gun's energy crystal could recharge for another shot. He should have invested in a projectile weapon, like Hazel. He reached for his powers, but they were still gone. So he went to meet the enemy with his sword, howling the old battle cry of his Clan.

'Shandrakor! Shandrakor!'

They surrounded him in a moment, knives rising and falling. He barely felt the blows. He cut about him with his sword, the keen edge slicing through furs and flesh. Blood spurted steaming on the cold air, and pooled in the slush about stamping feet. Many fell beneath the Deathstalker's blade and did not rise again, but the sheer force of numbers pushed Owen further and further back. Eventually his back slammed up against a brick wall, and there was nowhere left to go. He cut down three figures with one sweep of his blade, but before he could bring the sword back a dozen long knives stabbed into him, pinning him to the wall.

Owen cried out in pain and shock, and there was blood in his mouth. He cried out again as the knives were pulled out of him, and then the knives were plunging into him again and again, the dark figures jostling each other in their eagerness to get at him. The strength went out of Owen's legs, and he slid down the wall leaving a thick bloody trail behind him. The knives jerked in and out. Owen sat down suddenly, in the dirty, bloody snow, his back still pressed against the wall. His chin fell forward on to his chest. Some of them were still stabbing him. He couldn't feel it any more, though his body shuddered under the impact. He watched almost disinterestedly as his arm slowly lowered, still holding his sword. His hand hit the snowy ground, bounced once and then lay still. The numb fingers slowly opened, releasing the sword.

A fur-clad figure darted forward to grab it. Owen thought he saw a familiar face. His eyelids were slowly closing. He felt cold. He recognized the young girl's face before him. It was the same girl he'd crippled and killed, in a past that was her future. He smiled at her, and thought she smiled at him.

Time. Full circle. And redemption, of a kind.

Hazel?

After he was dead, they stole his boots.

Orbiting above the Wolfling World, the battered remains of what had once been two fine ships, the *Dauntless* and the *Sunstrider*. Hazel on her bridge, Silence and Carrion on theirs, talking a little bemusedly via their viewscreens. Silence had just received a message from a relieved but startled Golgotha; the entire Recreated fleet had vanished, between one moment and the next, and showed no signs of reappearing.

'Did we beat them?' said Hazel. 'I mean; it sure didn't feel like we were beating them.'

'Maybe they just got tired of kicking us around,' said Silence. 'Stranger things have happened.'

'That's for sure,' said Carrion.

It is over, said a voice, thundering suddenly in their heads. *Owen Deathstalker has saved you all. He kept the Recreated occupied, till all could be put right again. And now it will be.*

And everyone on the *Dauntless* and the *Sunstrider* cried out in wonder as the baby in the crystal concentrated his thoughts, and relit the thousand suns in the Darkvoid. Their light blazed again, for the first time in over nine hundred years, and the Darkvoid was dark no longer. The baby concentrated again, and revitalized the dead planets around those suns, and made them warm and intact and life-bearing again, just as they had been before. And then he reached out to the Recreated, still hanging lost and helpless in Time, and brought them all back to life. He returned them to their old bodies, and put them back on their old worlds, where they belonged. They would remember nothing of what they had been and done. None of it had really been their fault.

Humanity's long nightmare was finally over.

The baby reached out further, and Unseeli blossomed again, the metallic forests reaching once more from pole to pole. And then he sent the reborn Ashrai home, to tend their forests as they always had. Silence and Carrion watched all this, and both of them had tears in their eyes.

And having done all that, the baby decided that enough was enough, and any more would be interfering. He had put right all the things that he had unwittingly destroyed or created, all those years ago, and that would do for now. He sighed once, put his thumb back in his mouth and went back to sleep again. To dream, and learn from the Maze, and grow slowly in peace, while he waited for Humanity to catch up with him.

He was looking forward to that.

On board the *Dauntless*, Silence and Carrion looked at

each other in amazement. On the *Sunstrider*, Hazel was slowly shaking her head.

'What about Owen?' she said. 'Where's Owen?'

I'm sorry, said the voice. *Owen is dead. I've left a record of all we said in your computers, and in Silence's. It explains everything. Be proud of Owen. He made all this possible. But remember my warning. Humanity must prepare. The Terror are coming.*

'He died alone,' said Hazel. 'I wasn't with him.'

He died well, a warrior to the end.

'The last Deathstalker.'

No. That would be the baby. Or perhaps he's a new beginning. All will become clear, in Time.

Hazel let out a howl of grief and rage that almost tore her throat apart. She powered up the *Sunstrider*'s engines and sped away from the Wolfling World, and all that had happened there.

'Owen; you lied to me. You promised me we'd always be together, for ever and ever. Oh, Owen; I never told you I loved you . . .'

Tears ran down her cheeks. The *Sunstrider* dropped into hyperspace and disappeared.

Captain Silence and Carrion returned home, to the Empire and Golgotha, to glory and honour. None of them ever saw Hazel d'Ark again.

And deep in the heart of the newborn planet that had been the Wolfling World and lost Haden, the Madness Maze waited for all Humanity.